Taking a sip of her drink, Baines mustered up her courage. "There's somethin' you need to know about that quilt, Gray."

"Don't trouble yourself, my dear," Gray whispered.

His husky words carried on the soft breeze and wrapped around her, settling into the core of her. When he began to toy with her hair, she leaned her head into his hand. He seemed to move his fingers to the rhythm of the soft music floating around them. Each place he touched invited more. But they were on a bench in the darkness at his relatives' home with a world of differences and the location of a prized quilt between them. This could lead to nothing but disaster.

Patterns of Love

CHRISTINE HOLDEN

JOVE BOOKS, NEW YORK

A QUILTING ROMANCE is a trademark of Berkley Publishing Group.

PATTERNS OF LOVE

A Jove Book / published by arrangement with
the author

PRINTING HISTORY
Jove edition / April 1999

The Penguin Putnam Inc. World Wide Web site address is
http://www.penguinputnam.com

ISBN: 0-515-12481-8

A JOVE BOOK®
Jove Books are published by The Berkley Publishing Group,
a member of Penguin Putnam Inc.,
375 Hudson Street, New York, New York 10014.
JOVE and the "J" design
are trademarks belonging to Jove Publications, Inc.

PRINTED IN THE UNITED STATES OF AMERICA

10 9 8 7 6 5 4 3 2 1

To Mabel Polk, Mother and Grandmother, for her encouragement and support.

To Eloise Baptiste, my best friend and adopted sister.

To Deborah Boettner, a true friend and loyal supporter.

To Aunt Julia for her prayers.

To my sisters, Betty Salcedo and Diane Williams, for always being there.

To Theresa Peters my childhood friend.

To my sisters-in-law—Joyce, Elaine, Janice, Wanda, and Vanessa—who all add style and verve to the family.

And last but certainly not least, to Norbert A. Simmons, a true Champion of Causes. Thanks for the recognition.

1

MARY'S FORTUNE! MARY'S BLOODY *Fortune!*

Because of Mary's Fortune, Lord Grayling Dunston felt like a bloody idiot. Because of Mary's Fortune and *duty.*

Gray hadn't dared tell his peers the reason behind his trip to America. He would be a laughingstock amongst them. That's if they believed the Earl of Montegut would go in search of a bed covering to undo his late father, Pierce's, unwise investments.

Dark with despair and fury, Gray's mood matched the rapidly blackening skies. He eyed the chipped wooden door with irritation. A man on a mission, he'd arrived in Natchez, Mississippi, only three hours ago in search of his great-grandmother's quilt, which sported the ridiculous name of Mary's Fortune.

Gray's blood raced with indignation. Thanks to his witless cousin Rochester, Gray had endured an infernally long and boring three-month journey across the Atlantic. Roc went to London last year to meet Gray for the first time and return the few possessions Pierce left behind in America from his childhood. While in London, Roc, the bloody fool, had given Mary's Fortune to a man by the name of Lincoln Marshall.

Gray hadn't thought much of the incident. A musty old quilt wouldn't enrich his life. But then he'd read the letter his great-grandmother left behind. Somewhere within the pattern of Mary's Fortune lay a map leading to a treasure.

The fading scrawl of an annoying riddle within the letter came to mind. *If you have the measure to search for my treasure, it will line your pockets with gold. Decipher Mary's Fortune and let your pleasure unfold.*

More than once he wondered why someone else had never opened Mary Dunston's letter, which had been addressed to his father. Was this a bloody hoax? Desperate to save the Dunston family fortune, Gray couldn't leave any stone unturned. Taking a chance and going on a wild-goose chase for the musty old quilt that he'd never seen couldn't be avoided.

Straightaway from the grueling journey, he'd gone to meet his American relatives. A more quaint bunch of con-sanguines didn't exist. And now the run-down hovel he stood in front of hinted that the same breed of people lived on the other side of the half-broken door.

His temper on edge, Gray snorted in aggravation. He looked at the slip of paper in his hand and rechecked it against the address on the shack, hoping for a small bit of salvation, praying that the numbers didn't match. They did, just as they had minutes ago when he'd arrived.

Deciding the time had come to take action and get the hell out of this godforsaken country, he pounded on the door. Anger goading him, he didn't care if it splintered into tiny pieces.

He stood fully prepared to buy the quilt back from Lincoln Marshall if he must. Or if Marshall refused to sell, Gray would simply make him an offer no sane man could refuse. Besides, it held no value for Marshall. Only Gray knew its secret.

Just as Gray raised his fist to bang on the door again, it swung open. Unprepared for the sight of the stunning girl who stood there, he felt as if the wind had just been knocked from him.

Her gaze looked him up and down, taking in his fine

clothes and polished boots. She looked past him to where his palomino grazed on a grassy slope near the river. Swallowing hard, she smiled with uncertainty, the pulse point at the base of her slender throat pounding.

"Can I help you, mister?"

Her soft words emphasized her common speech, grating on Gray's aplomb. Considering her place of residence, a cultured tone was hardly to be expected.

For a moment he forgot Mary's Fortune existed as he stared at the girl, her beauty entrancing him. Thick, black lashes fringed green eyes exuding vitality. Her carelessly upswept black hair framed a heart-shaped face, and alabaster skin accentuated fine bones.

She placed reddened hands on slim hips, her clean but simple gown unable to hide her supple curves. "I don't have time to be standin' here. You lost or somethin'?"

He didn't have time to stand there either, scrutinizing someone who could only satisfy his lustful needs. Whatever label given him, he didn't steal the innocence of young misses, poor or otherwise.

The spell broken by her annoyed tone, Gray affected his most intimidating pose. His eyes narrowed. This always worked when dealing with his tenants. "I'm looking for Lincoln Marshall. He has taken possession of a quilt that belongs to me."

A flicker of recognition lit the girl's clear green eyes before she masked her expression. "I don't know what you're talkin' about, mister. I don't know a body named Lincoln Marshall!"

She made to slam the door shut, but Gray jammed his tall, muscular frame into it.

"Do you know Roc Dunston?"

A barely perceptible nod forthcame. She shifted her weight and met his eyes, appearing unintimidated by his size and obvious wealth. "Everybody knows Mr. Roc, mister. The Dunstons are the richest family in these parts."

Roc's wealth was one of the few distinctions setting him apart from this creature. In all likelihood, this young woman probably possessed more wits than the entire clan of American Dunstons. One *needed* wits to survive Under-the-Hill.

Gray bit back the disdainful remarks, realizing anger fueled his unforgiving thoughts. Nevertheless, he couldn't wait to retrieve the quilt and get back to England, and away from *her,* this stranger with the lively eyes and animated features.

He cleared his throat, determined to temper his uncharacteristic reaction to her. "I see. Well, it was Mr. Roc who said Lincoln Marshall lives here. Dare you say Roc is wrong?"

Her chin shot up. "I do. Just because Mr. Roc is rich doesn't mean he's smart," she snapped.

"Touché, my dear," Gray said, unamused at her response and his unrelenting awareness of her. "I wholeheartedly agree." Still, he hesitated to give in so easily. He hadn't left the comforts and culture of England for disappointment. He would get that blasted quilt back if it killed him. "Maybe you can tell me where this Lincoln Marshall resides?"

"I surely couldn't."

Gray pulled his mouth into a thin line. Instinct told him she lied. Someway, somehow, he would pull the truth from her small, red lips. "You can't or you won't?"

"I *can't,*" she stressed, glaring at him. "Now, if that's all you want, leave me be!"

She slammed the door as thunder grumbled in the sky. Gray's temper snapped. He barely refrained from breaking the door down, but intimidating her wouldn't be a good idea. Charming the truth from her would be a much more satisfying diversion, but he had to tread carefully. She was lying for a reason, and more than likely fright guided her. He'd had enough experience with the poor to know fear of reprisals made them prevaricate at certain times. Nothing in this girl's mannerisms suggested she feared him, however only warmth and exuberance asserted itself, along with a good amount of wariness. In comparison to the sophisticated, cool Englishwomen he was used to, the little ragamuffin he'd just met was a breath of fresh air.

Gray hardened his thoughts. A *lying,* unsophisticated breath of fresh air. Something told him, however, that she held the key to finding Lincoln Marshall as well as Mary's Fortune. The instant attraction he felt for her came to mind, and he smiled with grimness, caught in a snare he couldn't escape. *Charming* her could very easily turn into seduction.

∞

BAINES MARSHALL WATCHED THE beautiful man as he turned on his heel, mounted his golden horse, and started down the road. Her heart pounded as she watched him leave. He sat with arrogant pride upon his fine mount, commanding, riveting Baines's attention. He was a tall man, much taller than herself. His body seemed muscular, powerful, beneath his gray trousers, matching topcoat, and blue silk shirt. Inky and fine, his hair reminded Baines of coal dust, and she felt the oddest need to touch it, to touch *him.* But it was his eyes—sad, remote, and dangerous—that called to her. They burned with intensity and hinted at secrets that left Baines unsettled.

Thunder rumbled again, followed by a flash of lightning, and she jumped, hating the rain. The stranger was nearly out of sight. She struggled with her conscience not to open the door and shout for the man to return and wait out the approaching storm. But she couldn't. Her uncle came before anyone, and she refused to put him in further jeopardy so a complete stranger could stay dry. No matter how lonely, how in need of understanding he appeared. His presence posed a threat to her and Uncle Lincoln somehow.

As far as she knew, real people didn't melt when a little rain hit them. If the fancy dress of the stranger was any indication, Uncle Lincoln had gotten himself into a mess of trouble again.

With a sigh Baines retreated from the small window, affected by the stranger for reasons unknown, reasons she suspected had to do with much more than only her uncle Lincoln.

She frowned as lightning sliced through the house. Because of the cost of candles, the interior of her home wasn't as well lit as she liked it, especially now as thunder grumbled again, and hesitant drops of rain banged against her roof. Her gaze fell on the quilt Uncle Lincoln had brought to her several months ago. He'd sworn Mr. Roc had given him the beautiful covering. Apparently Uncle Lincoln had lied. Again.

Exhausted from her long night of working in the Horse and Mule Tavern, she decided that her tiredness probably had a lot to do with the way the man had affected her, and made her way to the quilt. A huge covering, jewel tones dominated the blocks where funny patterns were woven within each one. Age yellowed the pearl-white borders, which had frayed all around. Still in very good condition, the quilt's four corners had strange designs on them. Whoever created the quilt had Baines's respect. Months of work had to have gone into the making of it, along with a good deal of patience and a wild imagination.

Sometimes Baines studied the patterns and thought she detected a map within them, but then she ultimately decided it was she with the wild imagination.

Before Uncle Lincoln brought it to her, she'd only had a threadbare cover for herself. She had been dirt-poor her entire life. Even if there wouldn't have been a price to pay for this bit of Uncle Linc's thievery, she couldn't have given up her quilt. She remembered her parents catching their deaths, two years apart, her father from working long and hard on the waterfront, and later her mother due to the frigid weather, and she didn't want the same fate to befall herself.

It might have been selfish of her to want to keep another man's property if Uncle Lincoln stole the quilt that the stranger was searching for, but she refused to dwell on it. She wanted time to study the strange quilt further so she could duplicate it for sale.

With determination and hard work she would use her skill at sewing the latest fashions and stitching quilts and other necessities to make a better life for herself and her uncle. Perhaps then she could stop worrying about him so.

Perhaps then he wouldn't do some of the things he did for her benefit. Maybe one day she would even have as much money as the Dunstons and the stranger who'd appeared at her door.

To the world, she was Baines Marshall, happy and always smiling. In private, she felt old beyond her nineteen years and wary of what her future held.

She wanted wealth and a better quality of life for her and Uncle Lincoln. She wanted acceptance by the rich class instead of the disdain she suffered every day dealing with ladies of leisure in Miz Annabelle's shop.

No matter how many years of hard work she had to endure, she would be accepted in that elite world. She would have graceful days and charmed evenings to define her life, instead of constant anxiety about her uncle's lifestyle and her own well being.

Pulling off her worn shoes, she dropped down on the jewel-toned quilt, which covered her small cot, and took the pins from her hair, letting it ripple down her back to her waist.

For a moment she imagined it was the handsome nabob there, tangling his long, elegant fingers through her hair. She smiled with bitterness. As if he would really take an interest in her, a poor girl from Rivertown.

A moment of resentment flashed within Baines, but she immediately chided herself. Through no fault of his, he'd been born into wealth; but she could blame the nabob for his arrogance and uppity manner. She could blame him for making her pulse pound and her knees weaken.

The rain began in earnest, the heavy torrents loud on the tin roof. Thunder sounded on and off, a drumroll across the sky. Flashes of lightning followed, illuminating the small house.

Hands behind her head, she laid back on the cot and stared at the ceiling, telling herself to forget her visitor. But it was impossible. He wanted Uncle Lincoln. Surely the man would return.

The day Uncle Lincoln brought the quilt to her came to mind.

A smile dimpled his ruddy cheeks as he beamed at her and handed over the coverlet.

"Baines, honey, I done brought you a warm coverin'. Ever since that old quilt's been tearin' and wearin' out, I been powerful worrit you would catch your death like your mommy and daddy done."

Suspicious about how he acquired the expensive-looking quilt, Baines eyed her uncle with skepticism, doing her best to ignore the heavy covering. It was cold then, and because of the cost, they had to ration the wood needed to light their potbellied stove to keep warm. Because of the time it took to create a quilt, and selling the ones she did make to bring in extra money, Uncle Lincoln probably thought she'd never get around to stitching one for herself. Still, they didn't have money to waste to get him out of trouble if he'd been at his thieving again just to get her a better quilt.

"I thank you for your concern, but I'm just fine, Uncle Lincoln," she lied.

"Take it, Baines," Uncle Lincoln insisted. "You need it for the cold nights."

Placing her hands on her hips, she glared at him, displaying authority to get the truth from him. "And where did you take it from?"

Comprehension dropped into Uncle Lincoln's features, and he shook his grizzly head. "I guess I'm deservin' of your distrust, honey," he grumbled. "But I didn't steal this. Mistah Roc done gave it to me when he seed me in London. He said he was there to meet his cousin and he was sure Mistah Gray wouldn't care to be rid of some old quilt. . . ."

That scene occurred six months ago, and Baines couldn't believe her gullibility. She would have to have a talk with Uncle Lincoln. His thieving would one day be the death of him.

With a groan Baines rolled over and folded half the quilt over her body. The other half she used as a cushion to soften her lumpy cot. She would rest a spell before she fixed herself some breakfast. Afterward she would work a little more on the quilt she was stitching for Uncle Lincoln's birthday. He'd taken her worn coverlet when he'd brought her the jewel-toned quilt, but Baines wanted to do something special for him. After all he'd done for her, she felt Uncle Lincoln deserved better than her leavings, so Miz Annabelle graciously offered Baines the scraps of material from the shop for the birthday quilt.

Though working the night shift at the tavern always drained her, especially since she didn't do it very often, the excitement of anticipating Uncle Lincoln's surprise kept her going.

She'd better get used to her lack of energy. For the next month it would be a constant with her. She'd agreed to help out Luther until he could find another tavern maid. It would be a big help to her, too, what with supplementing the pay she received for helping Miz Annabelle at her sewing shop. In another month she could even buy herself a decent dress for the summer.

Her thoughts again fled to the stranger. Was he Mr. Roc's London cousin, Mr. Gray? If so, maybe she could reason with him if he decided to press charges. Mr. Roc had always been fair and kind-hearted. She hoped his cousin was, too.

The hard planes of the stranger's face came to mind, and Baines frowned. She doubted he would listen to her pleas. People like him didn't understand what drove people like her and Uncle Lincoln to do what they did.

A chill of foreboding assailed Baines. With annoying certainty, she knew Uncle Lincoln lay somewhere, passed out from drinking. She hoped he would soon be sober and return to the refuge of their shack before the beautiful man with the lethal blue eyes and black hair to match her own found him.

She knew she hadn't seen the last of the stranger.

2

"BAINES MARSHALL, YOU'VE MISSED your callin'," Annabelle Shepard said the next morning. She examined the half-completed quilt Baines was making for her uncle as Baines removed their breakfast dishes from the small table. "You might not have any fashion sense 'bout clothes, but you're a natural for stitchin' a quilt together."

"Thank you, Miz Annabelle." Stifling a yawn, Baines smiled. Pouring more coffee into her and Miz Annabelle's cups, she felt mighty proud to receive such a compliment from her friend, the best seamstress in Natchez. The shapely, red-haired widow was also like a mother to Baines, and she valued her opinion. "Seems I know what makes a quilt pretty more than I know how to make a dress pretty."

Miz Annabelle took a sip of her steaming coffee, then set it on the table. "It'll all come in time, honey. Never you fear. No matter what you're sewin', your stitches are always perfect. I took you under my wing 'cause you like all kinds of sewin', although I haven't given up on your dressmakin' abilities yet. I have a new consignment comin' in two days, and I'm assignin' the task to you. When I'm done with you, there'll be none better under or over the bluff, savin' myself, of course."

"Of course." Baines forced a laugh. She knew she could never compete with Miz Annabelle's dressmaking skill.

When Miz Annabelle arrived at Baines's door right after Baines returned from her shift at the Horse and Mule, the seamstress hadn't seemed in a hurry to leave. So Baines whipped up some buttermilk pancakes and coffee for their breakfast. Dead tired, she needed to sleep, but Miz Annabelle had been kind enough to bring some more scrap material for Uncle Linc's birthday quilt. The very least Baines could do was entertain her friend.

She walked over to the quilting frame Uncle Lincoln had made for her, where the half-completed quilt hung. On her cot next to it lay the small pile of scraps to add to Uncle Lincoln's cover. Less than two weeks remained before Uncle Linc's birthday; eleven days to be exact. If she worked on it all day today with the additional material, she would be that much closer to seeing it done.

"Here, Baines, honey."

Miz Annabelle knew her too well, Baines thought with a reverent smile. She accepted the scissors that Miz Annabelle held out to her and divided a large scrap of material. While the Widow Shepard cleaned the dishes, Baines added the newly cut scrap to her crazy quilt, so called because of her uneven patches haphazardly sewn together.

She'd considered stitching a perfectly made quilt for Uncle Lincoln, but decided he would appreciate something more closely associated with his personality, something wild but capable of being warm, as warm as the cotton interlining she planned to use.

Thoroughly enjoying her task of adding her patches, she hummed a lively tune, wondering when Uncle Lincoln would return. Luther had told her last night that her uncle was in New Orleans. Whenever her uncle showed himself again, she would have to have a good talk with him about yesterday's visitor.

Taking a deep breath, she closed her eyes briefly. She had passed a restless night thinking about him. A part of her had a powerful need to see him again, and another part, the part of herself with sense, wanted him to stay far, far away from her and Uncle Lincoln.

Her draw to the stranger bewildered her, while her uncle's actions with the quilt and the feeling that the stranger would never consider her good enough for him and scorn her attraction if she ever revealed it troubled her.

Confused, tormented, she sighed and returned to her task. At least she'd discovered Uncle Lincoln hadn't been out getting sotted yesterday. But still he had lied to her about the quilt, then left her to deal with the consequences of his actions—consequences that might prove to be trouble in more ways than one.

Irritated now, she finished applying another block to the quilt, then studied it with a critical eye and measured it for length and width.

"You're doin' a grand job, Baines," Miz Annabelle repeated. "I think your quiltin' is far better than mine."

"Go on, Miz Annabelle." Glad to focus on something other than the nabob, Baines wondered if Miz Annabelle spoke truthfully or just said the compliment to boost her ego. *Her* better than Miz Annabelle? Impossible! "I'm pleased for the regards, but nobody's better than you."

"I guess you're right, but you're the only one close." She glimpsed the quilt on Baines's cot. "Now, that there quilt's got perfect stitchin' and square, even patterns. Think you could make one like that?"

"I been studyin' it ever since Uncle Linc gave it to me. Why, I bet I could make one just like it from scratch if I had the proper materials."

Miz Annabelle's blue eyes shone with motherly pride as she dried the last dish and placed it in the cupboard. Done with her cleaning, she sat down on the soft-cushioned bench. "I know you can."

Baines studied Miz Annabelle. Taking a deep breath, she spoke. "If you'd agree to supply the material, after I finish Uncle Linc's quilt, not only will I duplicate the one he gave me, but I'll put it up for sale in your shop, and we can split the profit."

"Why, darlin', that's a capital idea! But, of course, I wouldn't takes half your earnin's." When Baines opened her mouth to protest, Miz Annabelle raised her hand for quiet. "If you insist on payin' me, just repay me the cost

of the material. Lord knows it's gonna be difficult to find
that same material. Of course, if we can't, I've got plenty
of other scraps, so it may turn out just a bit different.''

Baines went back to her task, excited by the prospect,
though adamant in her decision to use the exact materials.
Or at least the exact colors. But there would be time enough
to discuss that with Miz Annabelle. Baines wondered why
she hadn't thought of such an enterprise sooner, and decided there had been nothing to inspire her. Although she
loved sewing and dreamed of having her own shop, when
she'd seen the special quilt with the strange designs, she'd
felt a desire to complete something just as remarkable. The
assignment would prove challenging, a refreshing change
from the simple templates she performed when sewing the
other quilts.

Thinking of the beautiful quilt again brought yesterday's
visitor to mind. She debated with herself whether she
should tell Miz Annabelle about the nabob who'd come
looking for the quilt.

Although the Widow Shepard knew of Uncle Lincoln's
thieving ways, Baines wasn't ready to part with the quilt,
nor did she have a desire to see her uncle in jail for theft.
Knowing Miz Annabelle's honesty, she would insist Baines
give up the quilt. Not that Miz Annabelle wanted to see
Uncle Lincoln in jail. She would only want to see the quilt
returned to its rightful owner.

And that's where Baines had a problem. The danged
quilt's rightful owner seemed mighty determined and altogether without compassion. He would have Uncle Lincoln in jail for thievery quicker than the sun could make a
hoot owl blink. No, she would just figure this one out using
her own wits. And when she saw the fancy stranger again,
she would be as cool and distant as he was. Her strange
fascination with him was only a fleeting thing and something she would control once she was assured he was gone.

He was rich and handsome and foreign. In sum, every
woman's fantasy. But he was forbidden to her because she
was poor without the proper social graces. And underedu-
cated. And a lowly seamstress.

Resentment for him and his wealth and heritage that people like him clung to surfaced within her. Her family was as important to the city's founding as the Dunstons. The Marshalls might have been in these parts longer, having settled there when Natchez was little more than a trading post, plagued by Indians.

But no one thought about that. Folks only recognized the importance of the Dunstons with their wealth and English kin.

"You seem mighty deep in thought. You sure your mind is on what you're doin'?" Miz Annabelle asked suspiciously. "You know I promised Lincoln to watch over you, along with Luther and Eli. And what those two men might miss, I can sure detect."

Baines shifted in her seat and stared at her friend. Sometimes Baines didn't appreciate Miz Annabelle's discerning ways. "What do you mean, Miz Annabelle?"

"You're nineteen years old now, and I know girls your age sometimes have their minds on more than just work. Or in your case quiltin'. What's troublin' you, child?"

"I'm beholden to every kindness you've given me, especially your worry over me. But there ain't no need." Even as she spoke, an image of the handsome stranger flashed before her mind's eye. Her blood warmed, and the pit of her belly clenched. She reminded herself that she didn't like her visitor. It was only his lifestyle and male beauty that had her thoughts fixated on him. "I'm just fine," she said with an assurance she didn't feel.

Rising from her seat, Miz Annabelle laughed. "I reckon you are, Baines. And I believe I've distracted you long enough from your stitchin'. I'm gonna run along so you can finish your chores."

Miz Annabelle gathered her parasol and reticule, then walked to the door. Baines followed close behind.

"You just slowed me down a bit, is all."

"Well, even slowin' you down a bit is a caution, since you got other things to do. Go on with your chores, and I'll see you down at the shop tomorrow." She hugged Baines. "If Luther works you too hard, let me know."

"Yes, ma'am."

Standing on her small, creaky porch, Baines watched Miz Annabelle trudge down the dusty road until she disappeared from view.

Back inside, she went to the alcove and studied the beautiful quilt Uncle Lincoln had stolen for her. Staring long moments, Baines noted her own work sported every color of the rainbow; even black was sprinkled here and there. But only white, mulberry, emerald green, rose, and sapphire blue dominated the even-squared quilt Uncle Lincoln had given her, all perfectly uniformed. She determined that the quilt she would duplicate to sell would be just as perfectly beautiful as this.

Too tired to return to her stitching, she went to the window and gazed out. At almost noon and quite warm, the area where she lived near the river was practically deserted. From where she stood, the river looked clear. It beckoned to her, and she decided to answer its call. Maybe the water's crispness would wake her up. Checking again out the window, she saw no one around.

Quickly she shed her garments for one of Uncle Lincoln's big shirts and rushed out the door.

∞

HELL AND DAMNATION!

Gray couldn't believe the sight greeting him. The girl from the day before stood inches from him, her hair dripping wet, an oversize white shirt her only covering and bloody plastered to her lithe body.

The Mississippi lulled lazily behind her, and she appeared a river sprite, just out from the water to charm and beguile the humans around her. Never mind that he was the only other human about at the moment. She'd obviously chosen a time when she thought she would be alone to frolic in the river.

Suddenly he wished it were storming, or at the least he could be anywhere but there. Maybe he would just leave and let Mary's Fortune go to hell. He snorted. He could never leave. He felt obligated to fight for his family's heritage.

Only a flicker of surprise crossed her features at seeing him, but quickly vanished.

"Well, what can I do for you today?"

Her resigned tone annoyed him. He'd hoped for a better reception to his presence. Yet it seemed she expected to see him again and wasn't at all happy about it. His suspicion that she had knowledge of Lincoln Marshall increased. Gray narrowed his eyes, fire surging through his veins at her appearance. With effort, he decided not to comment on her state of undress. The wisest course would be to speak his business and get back to Dunland, Roc's plantation just down the road. "You can direct me to Lincoln Marshall."

Dismounting, he held on to the reins of the palomino he'd ridden to the girl's house.

Brief disappointment clouded her eyes, and she stiffened, her nipples defined against the wet cloth. He hoped her reaction was from his nearness. Her words said that it was not.

"Mister, I told you I don't know a body named—"

"I have cash," he interrupted, lustful images flaring to life against his better judgment. He refrained from telling her that he came to see if she was as beautiful and refreshing as last night's dreams led him to believe. He was there for one reason, and that was to get the quilt. Indecision vied with worry on her face, and Gray wondered what was going through her mind. Yet the play of emotions reinforced his suspicions.

"Are you Mr. Roc's London cousin?" she finally asked, her words soft and throaty.

Gray nodded, glad for the headway. "I am." Ignoring the pleasant tingles coursing down his spine at the tone of her voice, he bowed. "I am Lord Grayling Dunston, the Earl of Montegut, at your service."

Her eyes widened at his display. She stared at him, her look unfathomable, but compelling all the same, then she broke into contagious giggles, breaking the spell that she seemed to have cast over him. "I never thought you the type to bow to anyone, Mr. Gray."

She said his name as if she'd known him forever.

He chuckled, unused to such unabashed amusement. She seemed unconcerned that she faced him in that bloody shirt. Gray felt grateful that the sun was beginning to dry the fabric, but still he could have been there to do her harm. Was she always so trusting? Or was she just naive?

When she met his gaze, he thought he could lose himself in the warmth radiating from her green orbs. He felt a powerful draw to her, and an overwhelming urge to pull her into his arms and kiss her fervently.

"I suppose I should tell you my name?"

She sounded questioning, unsure.

"I suppose you should," he agreed.

For a moment she remained quiet and stared at him, as if assessing his true character. He must have measured up.

"It's Baines," she stated simply.

Unbidden, another smile crossed his face. Baines. A quaint name for a quaint girl. It seemed befitting and just right for her.

"Baines," he repeated, testing the name for himself.

Gray's heart hammered. Her exotic beauty made him feel as breathless as a schoolboy with his first infatuation. He itched to run his fingers through her wealth of black hair and discover if the fine mass felt as soft as it appeared. What bloody madness possessed him? He had a host of experienced women available to him. He certainly wouldn't be irresponsible enough to bed a girl such as Baines, then be forced to marry her out of honor. He hadn't journeyed across the Atlantic just to fulfill one duty to his father, only to neglect another.

"Mr. Gray, I need to be goin' in," Baines announced.

Mary's Fortune returned to his thoughts at the wary regard on her face. "Aye, well, this will only take a moment, Baines." Before she could protest, he continued. "I'll give you a gold eagle if you tell me where I can find Lincoln Marshall."

Irritation flew into her eyes. "I told you—"

"I know what you've said." Gray's patience ebbed, and his desire rose. Despite all of his reasoning, the draw he felt to her hadn't lessened. "But I don't believe you."

"That's not my fault, Mr. Gray."

He went into his pocket and pulled the ten-dollar piece out, ignoring the heaviness in his loins. "Take it. If you can't lead me to Mr. Marshall, maybe you can get the quilt I'm in search of. I'm paying you beforehand for your efforts."

Baines did the last thing Gray expected. She broke into peals of laughter. "You sure are a caution, Mr. Gray. If I don't know Lincoln Marshall, how am I supposed to know where to find your quilt?"

Gray wouldn't be deterred. "Take the money, Baines. You may hear a tidbit about town and lead me to Mr. Marshall."

He didn't miss the longing that crossed her features as she stared at the money. But instead of taking it from his still-outstretched hand, she shook her head and lifted her chin, pride in every move.

"I can't."

"Damn it, Baines!" Gray sighed in frustration but dropped his hand to his side, deciding to change his approach. The determined set of her small mouth suggested she was as stubborn as she was naive.

She started past him, her fresh, sun-dried scent wafting to him. "Evenin', Mr. Gray—"

"Call me Gray," he instructed, hoping familiarity would loosen her tongue.

With a shrug of her dainty shoulders, she nodded but didn't comply, intent on walking away.

"I would like to escort you to the ball Roc is hosting for me this Saturday," Gray blurted before he realized what he offered, his only thought to halt her departure.

It worked. She stopped in her tracks, an incredulous look marring her exquisite features.

"What did you say?"

What indeed? Bloody hell, he couldn't believe he'd made such a cruel offer. He would have to recall his invitation, but sensed this might disappoint her greatly. By social standards, she would meet with undue and harsh criticism at the ball. The hope on her face, however, made recanting the invitation an impossible task.

He cleared his throat. "Will you accept?" he asked, guilt pervading him at his ulterior motives. To discover the location of Mary's Fortune, he reminded himself, he had to do this. He had to use Baines and subject her to an evening she would never forget, but not for the fun she expected to have.

"You're serious?" she whispered in awe. "You're invitin' me to Dunland as a guest?"

"Aye," Gray responded huskily, pushing aside the possible repercussions for more practical matters. It didn't matter that to her it seemed the most important thing in the world to attend a ball at Dunland, Natchez's most prestigious plantation. Saturday night would be another tactic to get the truth about Mary's Fortune from her. "I am."

Baines laughed wistfully, disbelief shining in her beautiful eyes. In response, he curved his lips into a hint of a smile, the effect she had on him disturbing.

All of a sudden it seemed most important to him that Saturday night be a genuine success for her. He would take on every member of his social class who disparaged Baines and offer her the best night of her life. It would ease his conscience about using her to gain knowledge about the quilt if she truly enjoyed herself.

"I'll be honored," she whispered. Suddenly shy, she looked at him one last time and fled.

After watching her go inside, he remounted and urged the horse to start off.

A whistle screeched as a steamboat approached lazily around the riverbend. Smoke belched from the two identical smokestacks on either side of the boat, leaving a black trail in the wake.

Allowing the palomino to take the lead, Gray perused his surroundings. A mule-drawn cart clattered down the dusty road. Baines's shack sat in no better condition than the other cabins near the river's edge. But unlike the others,

hers had a chinaberry tree in front of it. Something else that seemed fitting and just as right for her as her name.

The branches of the tree appeared thin and delicate, and the lilac flowers blooming amongst the leaves were sweet-smelling and elegant, a burst of color against the lush greenery.

A fleeting picture of him and Baines sitting under her tree and taking in the soporific sights of the day rose in his mind. He shook his head slightly, convinced that he'd lost his wits.

Guiding the horse off the loamy path that led to Baines's house, Gray urged the palomino onto the road away from Natchez-Under-the-Hill. The city's waterfront, located at the foot of the bluffs, was a bloody abominable stretch of saloons, taverns, and whorehouses. Roc warned him to be careful in this section and to look out for the rough and raffish crews from the flatboats and keelboats that frequented the area.

The weight of his gun pressed securely against his waist gave Gray some semblance of safety. Under the hill now, he couldn't wait to get *over* it.

Odd feelings for the beautiful Baines coursed through him. She didn't belong there, among cutthroat rivermen and loose-moraled women. Despite her display of undress and proper lack of indignation at his approach, he felt her character to be superiorly chaste.

He drew in a deep breath. How could he have been so deuced impulsive and invite her to his ball? The girl appeared feisty, but she was bloody unlearned. He hadn't even thought of proper attire for her for a party. One look at her surroundings and it wouldn't take a genius to know she didn't attend fancy functions.

Well, even if she wore a pair of britches, he wouldn't bloody care. That's if she came. She had the answers to his questions. He vowed to himself that after the introduction party, Baines . . . Baines . . .

Pausing, he frowned. Had she revealed her last name?

He shook his head, unable to believe how remiss he'd been. He should have been more alert. Instead, he'd been caught up in her beauty and hadn't asked for her last name.

Well, no matter. At the end of Saturday night she would reveal a great deal more than her last name. She would reveal the whereabouts of Mary's Fortune.

Feeling a modicum of satisfaction for the first time since setting foot on American soil, he steered his horse onto the path toward Dunland.

∞

BAINES TWIRLED AROUND THE little shack, feeling like one of the fairy princesses Uncle Lincoln had told her about. Mr. . . . Gray . . . Gray had actually invited her to one of the Dunstons' parties. He'd seemed as surprised by the invitation as she had, and she'd fully expected him to say he'd only been teasing. But he hadn't. He'd actually been serious.

Laughing in pure delight, she twirled again. A fairy princess she felt like indeed, and Grayling Dunston, the Earl of Montegut, was her knight in shining armor. He was inviting her into that elite world that for so long had shut her out and trampled upon her esteem. He seemed not to care about her background, and she had been wrong to assume that he was like all the other nabobs.

A flicker of worry pierced her happiness. Her mother and Miz Annabelle always taught her honesty above all else. Instead of adhering to those lessons, she was repaying Gray's kindness with deliberate deception. Telling herself that she could possibly learn more about the quilt and its maker didn't ease her conscience. Neither did it help when she considered that one day she might even be able to take lessons from the creator of the quilt.

Thinking of her uncle, however, allowed her to continue with the course she'd set for herself. Briefly she wondered if her duplicity was any better than Uncle Linc's thievery. Suddenly she feared she would confess all to Gray and lose the chance of a lifetime.

But she couldn't. Nothing could stand in her way, not

her gratitude for Gray's fairness, or an attraction to his good looks.

With that decision, she turned her attention to her attire for Gray's ball.

Never in her life had she been invited to a fancy party. With the less than fashionable clothes she owned, she doubted she would even be able to get through the door.

She eyed her small surroundings, searching for something that she could use as material for a new dress. The one lone curtain would hardly pass as a chemise. There was nothing, absolutely noth—

Her thoughts halted midsentence. There was *something*. Her gaze fell on the quilt Uncle Lincoln had given her.

She smiled with satisfaction. No one at the Dunston ball would be clothed in a quilted gown! She would be unique, special, and set apart from every other woman there.

3

SPANISH MOSS SWAYED IN the warm breeze, scenting the air with the smells of the magnolia blossoms, azaleas, camellias, gardenias, and roses growing in abundance on Dunland's grounds. The river glimmered bronze as the sun begin to sink into the horizon.

Gray stood on the top gallery, the French doors leading to his bedchamber gaping open behind him, and allowing him to see the clock on the fireplace mantel clearly. 5:40. He had two hours and twenty minutes before the ball began.

The five days since he'd extended the invitation to Baines had passed with agonizing slowness. On several occasions he'd thought about going back to her shack, but he refrained from doing so. He didn't see the point. She would still deny she knew Lincoln Marshall as well as the existence of the quilt.

Shaking his head, Gray sighed. His father had meant well. Pierce had only wanted to extend the family fortune. Instead, he'd just about ruined them, and Gray had only six months left to save their fortune.

He hated the obligation he felt, an obligation that forced him to search for Mary's Fortune. That same obligation forced him to stay when it seemed Mary's Fortune was gone for good.

He wouldn't give up that easily, however. He wouldn't

see his heritage stolen away from him without a fight.

Not for the first time since discovering Mary's Fortune existed, Gray wondered what really drove him. Was it truly obligation to his family name? Or his innate fear that he would end up poor, an impoverished lord left to be pitied as he now pitied his tenants?

He considered himself fair and generous to those who depended on him for their livelihood. In spite of everything he did for them and gave to them, the people of Montegut still lived in poverty. Would he soon end up like that, depending on the generosity of others for survival?

Baines came to mind. For whatever reason, she'd refused his gold. He couldn't help but admire her for that. To many, she would have been considered foolish for not taking the money and running with it, whether she had the information he wanted or not. But she'd followed her own counsel and hadn't taken the ten dollars.

Why? Was it because she really didn't know anything about either Lincoln Marshall or Mary's Fortune? Or maybe because she had lied to him, she felt guilty about taking the money. Could she be as carefree and innocent as she appeared?

She seemed to take everything in stride: her unpretentious existence, her disreputable uncle, her residence in an undesirable section of town, her beautiful face.

Gray leaned against the lacy iron-worked banister. Her beautiful face would haunt him to his dying day. How strange that she'd affected him; but she had, and if he dared to be honest with himself, he would admit that he'd wanted to go back to her shack to see *her*, not necessarily to ferret out the truth about Mary's Fortune.

"There you are, Gray."

Roc's voice cut into his thoughts. Gray glanced over his shoulder. His cousin stood there, already dressed in his formal attire, a brandy snifter in his hand.

The Dunston genes carried through to Roc. He appeared to be Gray's replica, with his black hair and blue eyes, but the resemblance ended there. While Roc was rather liberal, Gray was most conservative.

".What can I do for you, Rochester?"

Knowing how his cousin detested his given name of Rochester, Gray pushed his troubling thoughts away to tease Roc. Now that his anger was subsiding and his resignation setting in over Roc's actions with the quilt, Gray realized that Roc was actually an intelligent, fun-loving chap.

"You mentioned you had an escort for the evening, but you neglected to tell me her name."

Gray smiled. "It's Baines," he stated the way she had in her introduction to him.

Roc halted next to Gray, his blue eyes alive with mischief. "Baines? Well, that's an odd name." He sipped his drink, affecting a casual pose. "How'd you meet her so quickly, and more to the point, where'd you meet her?"

He wanted to say in a place where she didn't belong, in a den of squalor and iniquity. But who was he to say where Baines belonged? He couldn't rescue her from her meager existence while his future was so uncertain, even if he wanted to. Which he insisted he didn't.

For as long as he remembered he'd helped the poor of Montegut and got naught in return but a fight to save his own wealth. No, Baines would survive on her own however she chose to do so.

Uncomfortable with his thoughts, his decision, he shifted his weight. "I met her in Natchez-Under-the-Hill when I went in search of Lincoln Marshall."

"You invited a whore to your party?" Flabbergasted, Roc's eyes bulged.

His unyielding introspection disintegrating at Roc's harsh tone, Gray's body tensed.

"To *my* home?" Roc continued, not noticing or not caring about Gray's rising anger. "Where my wife lives? What will she think?"

Gray thought of Baines, beautiful, young, innocent, and the insane urge to call Roc out crossed his mind. "Baines is *not* a whore," he snarled, offended that anyone would even consider her such. His defense of her seemed natural and not the pretense he'd assumed it would be when he extended the invitation to her. "And if you or your wife have a bloody problem with her attending, then I won't be attending, either."

"Whoa, Gray!" Roc retreated. "It's your party. Invite whomever you please. I didn't mean to offend you."

What was bloody wrong with him? The girl was a complete stranger, and if not for his wont for answers regarding Mary's Fortune, Gray told himself he would never have considered inviting her to Roc's home. Only his upbringing now dictated that he defend Baines, not the fact that she was so bloody desirable.

Frowning in disgust, Gray questioned his own prejudices. As the Earl of Montegut, he'd never communicated with a young lady outside his class in a social setting. He wondered if this were England would he have responded as Roc had. Without too much thought, he knew he would have, and the realization bothered him.

The abject poverty in which Baines lived jarred his conscience. He had never realized that he suffered such an extreme feeling of condescension toward the poor. Aside from not wanting to become *one* of them, he'd never dwelled on their plight or their treatment by society.

But again he reminded himself that he didn't know Baines, and once he had Mary's Fortune back, he would be on the first ship back to London.

Besides, he didn't want to know how Baines survived. He was a peer, destined to marry a nobleman's daughter. Baines represented nothing more than a means to an end for him.

"I'm the one who's sorry, Roc. My temper is at the end of its tether as I search for Lincoln Marshall and the bloody quilt."

"That quilt sure means a lot to you," Roc observed. "Is there something I should know about it?"

Was there something Roc should know about Mary's Fortune?

Gray snorted, seeing the first star of the evening appear in the sky. Just as he couldn't trust Baines with the secret the quilt held because she was a stranger, neither could he trust Roc for that very same reason.

From Mary's letter, Gray knew the quilt had been made nearly a hundred years before.

Apparently she'd had a whimsical sense of humor and decided to bury a fortune somewhere and weave the map leading to the treasure within her quilt, aptly naming it Mary's Fortune. She'd bequeathed it to her son, Gray's grandfather, who met and married an American woman. Together they immigrated to what was now Natchez, Mississippi, and took the quilt with them. Their union produced two sons, Gray's father, Pierce, and Roc's father, Reginald. The quilt, along with the English titles, automatically went to their firstborn.

Pierce, as the elder son, decided to return to his native England and reclaim his title as the Earl of Montegut. Either on purpose or by accident, that bloody quilt was left behind.

Yet Gray refused to divulge any of that. He refused to put his complete trust in anyone ever again. He had once, and it nearly destroyed him as well as his reputation.

"There is nothing to know about it other than its sentimental importance to me." His explanation sounded ridiculous and lame, but he didn't care. He would do anything to save the family fortune and to restore dignity to Pierce's name.

Roc nodded, apparently not finding anything wrong with Gray's response.

An idea hit Gray. "You're the one who gave me that address for Lincoln Marshall. Yet Baines insists she doesn't know anyone by that name. Could you have been mistaken?"

"No, I couldn't have been," Roc said.

The assurance of his words convinced Gray that it was Baines who lied. It also gave him another excuse to pursue her beyond tonight if he needed to.

"This Baines may be his niece."

"What?"

"Lincoln has a niece. I've never seen her nor do I know

her name. I stay out of Natchez-Under-the-Hill for fear of my life.''

''Well, how do you know Lincoln?''

''He came around once looking for an odd job. We have slaves here to do everything, but I felt sorry for him, so I hired him to help do certain repairs around Dunland. He's very good and is here at Dunland whenever he's not at sea.''

''So I just need sit back and wait, and eventually he'll walk into my lair?''

The problem facing him was a three-month journey back to London, which meant he only had three months to find the bloody quilt. Lincoln Marshall could take forever to show himself, especially if he were at sea again.

''Exactly. But I have to get back down to help DeEdria attend the early arrivals. I came in search of you because this Baines sent a message for you.''

Gray frowned. It never occurred to him that she could read, let alone write. But then again, why would it? His only interest in her was her access to the quilt. ''Baines sent me a note?''

''No, a verbal message from a young boy. She wanted to let you know that she's going to be a mite late because the alterations on the gown she's stitching for the ball aren't quite complete.''

Dread, the likes of which Gray had never known, dropped into the pit of his belly. He imagined Baines traipsing through the magnificent doors of Dunland clothed in her finery that had once been Mary's Fortune.

She wouldn't . . . would she?

4

A BREEZE FROM THE river blew through Baines's open door and window, cooling the house to a comfortable degree and bringing in the smell of frying catfish from some unknown location. The incessant barking of dogs from nearby droned on. In the distance the rowdy sounds of drunken riverboat men blared through the house.

Listening to Miz Annabelle's disapproval over the gown Baines would wear to Dunland, Baines ignored the scents and sounds that told her the daily nightlife in the district was coming alive.

With a sigh of frustration she realized the contradiction of her talent. She was an excellent quiltmaker, but her fashion sense seemed seriously hampered.

Miz Annabelle turned her this way and that, inspecting the much-decorated ecru gown she wore. "Baines, darlin', I gave you that gown to save you the trouble of ruinin' your pretty quilt and the heartbreak of matrons' waggin' tongues. But you've ruined the dress. Why in creation would you stitch bows and flowers and buttons over the *entire* gown?"

"Well, Miz Annabelle, it was plumb plain, and I wanted to liven it up," Baines said defensively. Tears burned the back of her eyes, but she refused to let them fall, and her throat ached with the effort. She'd so wanted to look pretty and feel special, but according to Miz Annabelle, she'd just assured herself that she would be a laughingstock amongst the high class—which wouldn't do at all, if she expected to be taken seriously in their world.

"My word, my word, Baines Marshall. How far did you expect to git wearin' that thing?" Miz Annabelle threw her hands up in exasperation, seeming almost apoplectic. "I've never seen a body make a more perfect quilt than you, but I realize your work is cut out for you if you expect to make it on your own as a dressmaker. You've practically ruined this dress!"

Baines glowered at Miz Annabelle, unaccustomed anger rising within her. Hadn't Miz Annabelle already said she'd ruined her pretty gown?

She realized her anger was more at herself than at Miz Annabelle. Baines so wanted to make an impression on Gray. If a man like him could see her as beautiful and acceptable, then surely the other members of his class would as well. Yet it seemed as if he suddenly was the only important thing in her life. The widow's gentle chiding only increased Baines's worry and frustration.

But why should it matter to Baines what Grayling Dunston thought? When had she decided that his approval was all-important to her? She couldn't blame everything on her gratitude or even her need to be accepted. Part of it had to do with the way she felt when she was near him, the awareness of herself as a woman and of him as a man.

"First rule, Baines, is the plainer a gown, the more attractive it is." She pulled flowers and buttons and bows off the gown as she spoke. "You're too plumb pretty to need anythin' more than silks and satins to call attention to yourself."

"Miz Annabelle!" Baines squeaked in horror, watching her patient handiwork come apart and the fruits of her labor litter the floor. Despite her sudden worry that she would be ridiculed, eagerness to begin her journey over the hill to Dunland Plantation and Grayling Dunston assailed her. "I'll be late for the party."

"Hush, Baines," Miz Annabelle ordered, then sighed. "I

can't blame you for your fashion sense. Your poor mama taught you all she knowed about quiltin'. Too bad she knowed nothin' about fashion. But I do, and for the past two years I've only let you sew what I create. Well, darlin', I'm not gonna be around forever. Your dream of havin' your own shop might come true sooner than you expect, so I'm gonna learn you what you need to know about dressmakin'. Ain't much more I could tell you about quiltin', since you're so good at that.''

Baines glanced down at the Widow Shepard's neatly coiffed red hair, its fiery highlights glinting in the dim light. Tall and fine-boned with a well-rounded figure, Miz Annabelle's elegant style and no-nonsense attitude kept her business thriving. In her late forties the seamstress's looks remained attractive.

Because of that and the respect Baines had for the lady, on any other day Baines would have been dancing for joy at Miz Annabelle's offer. At the moment she didn't give a dang. Until Gray's invitation, getting out of poverty had been the most important thing to her. Now, however, all she could think of was being in the grand manor house that she'd only seen from afar, attended by the most handsome man she had ever laid eyes upon.

The first star of the evening showed itself in the twilight, and Baines wanted to get to Dunland. She didn't want to show up late for the first and possibly only ball she would ever attend.

Baines peeked at her gown and closed her eyes against the sight. Bits of thread and fluff hung from nearly every inch of the material. She should have followed her own mind and made her quilted gown; but, no, she had to let Miz Annabelle talk her into taking the ecru gown that no one had ever bought.

Huffing in irritation, Baines eyed Uncle Linc's crazy quilt. Since Tuesday, she'd added only one other patch to it. She should have been ashamed of herself, but instead Grayling Dunston and his ball consumed her attention.

Images of cold blue eyes and inky hair haunted Baines. The last time she'd seen him, he'd been standing next to his horse, tall and proud. An air of isolation surrounded him, but still he commanded authority just by looking down his aquiline nose.

Remembering that scene, an inkling of doubt hit her. Not for the first time since her disbelief at his invitation had left her, she wondered what went through his mind that day. A gnawing suspicion that he'd only invited her to Dunland to gain knowledge of the quilt clamored at her.

What other reason could there be? With all the society ladies he could choose from, he certainly hadn't invited Baines because he fancied her.

Resentment welled inside her, but she decided to use him to enter his world, as she believed he thought to use her to get the quilt. Still, she was excited about going.

"Mr. Roc's cousin will be expectin' me to be on time," she complained. "Now I'll be lucky if I get there at all!"

"Never fear, darlin'. Those things last on into the night. You'll get there, even if it's ten o'clock," Miz Annabelle reassured. "Now, I'm gonna show you one more time the difference between my fashion sense and yours. And this time I expect you to pay attention."

Folding her arms across her chest, Baines tapped her foot impatiently. She admitted that the gown hadn't been all that impressive with the adornments. Until Miz Annabelle stopped by to see how she looked for her big night, however, Baines had been danged certain it would have been the most outstanding thing at the ball. She glared at her second mother and mentor. "What are you plannin' to do to it?"

"Make it presentable for you and the kind of affair you is going to," Miz Annabelle said. "You just sit yourself down on that lovely quilt there while I straighten out your mess."

∽

"GRAY, IT LOOKS AS if your lady has declined your invitation after all."

Gray scowled at Roc. The bloody blighter didn't sound

one bit disappointed at Baines's tardiness. If the relief he heard in his cousin's voice had been a bloody beacon of light, Gray would have been blinded by it.

He should have been relieved that Baines hadn't come. He wouldn't have been able to enjoy himself because he would have had to defend the ragamuffin against the whole of society. Yet all he felt was acute disappointment and incipient anger. In his arrogance, he'd never considered she might decline his invitation. "What time is it, anyway?" he growled.

"Nearly eleven," Roc answered. "Never fear, old boy. There's no shortage of lovely young ladies at your discretion as of now."

Lovely young ladies Gray had been avoiding the entire evening. That's why he stood secluded in a far corner of the dancing salon, nearly concealed by a huge planter. Unfortunately Roc had discovered his hiding place. "One would have to be bloody blind not to notice, Rochester," he grumbled. It seemed the ladies on both sides of the Atlantic all had the same thing on their minds—marriage—and they were all deuced blatant about their intentions. Well, matrimony was not his goal at the moment. Finding the blasted quilt was!

He couldn't wait to get his hands on Baines. To think he'd worried over her hurt feelings and vowed to take on anyone who offended her. He'd even vowed to make this evening special for her.

Her absence smelled of guilt. She'd missed a once-in-a-lifetime chance to enter a prestigious home as a guest, and she'd snubbed him; *him,* a peer of the realm, an upstanding lord who was widely sought by many a maiden.

Her innocent disbelief at his invitation came to mind. He cursed her, and then himself, and then that bloody quilt. Because of it, he'd met a lying, stealing little ragamuffin with hair like onyx and eyes the color of emeralds. Brilliant eyes. Happy eyes. Innocent eyes.

Could their owner really be the person Gray branded her, merely because she hadn't shown for this blasted party?

In all honesty, he wished *he'd* never shown for it. Baines

had probably come to the same conclusion as he—that she wouldn't fit in amongst his class.

Gray snorted derisively. Not that his class proved anything special. Nearly everyone present, including himself, was a self-serving, self-righteous idiot, looking with favor upon a person merely because of the luck of his or her birthright.

Still, Baines's snub annoyed him. He'd had such a wonderful evening planned. Then at the end of it, in her gratitude, she would have told him where to find Mary's Fortune. Or, at the very least, Lincoln Marshall.

"Should I send for the little beggar, Grayling?"

Gray had forgotten Roc's presence. The bloody mischief sparkling in his cousin's eyes made Gray consider doing so again.

"Why? I never really expected her to show," he lied. He'd told himself that he invited Baines to gain information about the quilt, and indeed, that remained partly the reason. But now with Roc's goading he wasn't at all sure of the primary reason.

In the days since he'd met her, he'd vacillated between resentment about her poor state, guilt over using her to gain knowledge about the quilt, and lust for her person.

Part of his problem was that he desired her, but he didn't trust her.

A collective gasp rose amongst the guests, preventing any more words between him and Roc. Gray looked toward the entrance of the dancing salon, the sudden focus of everyone's attention, and blinked.

Baines? He blinked again.

She floated toward him. That was the only way to describe her advancement to him. Clothed in an ecru gown, she looked absolutely stunning! Light tan lace barely showed from under the hemline, where beige bows circled the bottom. Puffed sleeves sported similar bows, and the plain, scoop-necked bodice brought attention to her beautifully formed bosom.

Her hair fell to her waist in deep, shining waves, its color enhanced by the ecru gown. The natural color in her cheeks and her dancing eyes in her beautiful face made her look like a walking dream.

By the time she reached him, his fingers itched to touch her alabaster skin.

"Evenin', Gray," she said softly. "I'm so sorry I'm late. Hope it ain't too ill-mannered of me, but it couldn't be helped." Smiling, she extended her hand.

Gray found himself momentarily speechless. Had this been their first meeting and she'd remained silent, he wouldn't have guessed her true origins. Her accent gave her away, but it didn't stop his heart from swelling with pride as he brought her hand to his lips. He noted how work-roughened it felt, but ignored the pity that observation brought about.

Suddenly it came to him that he'd expected Baines to embarrass him by showing up looking like the ragamuffin he'd met. The fact that she didn't bewildered him. He knew he would have responded to *that* Baines with protectiveness and patience.

But the beguiling beauty she'd turned into made it even more obvious to him that she didn't belong in Natchez-Under-the-Hill. It also changed his mind and made him want to help her find a way out of her poverty.

Accustomed to helping poor people, Baines simply would be added to his charity list. Yet he wondered if it was just lust guiding him in this situation. Ordinarily only his tenants were the recipients of his generosity.

His own plight came to mind. He would help her, that is, if he wasn't also living in poverty in a few months.

All there assessed Baines, and the blatant disdain on some of the women's faces brought to mind the grand task he faced tonight. But seeing Baines dressed thusly would make every protective word he had to offer on her behalf worth it.

"I had no doubt that you would come," he lied. "After all, you did send word that you would be late."

She smiled, and Gray's loins stirred. Wondering what she would feel like quivering beneath him, he returned her smile with a spark of eroticism in his.

Subconsciously she placed one small, worn, black-shod foot over the other. Until that moment, Gray didn't think Baines realized that she was the center of speculation.

"I wouldn't have missed comin', Gray," Baines said shyly. "I figured since you invited me, you must have wanted me here."

"Yes, I did, Baines."

Her old shoes barely peeked from beneath her lovely gown, and he glanced around the room at the curious and, aye, amused faces. His temper pricked at the lustful looks the men gave her and the petty, scornful stares of the women. At the moment he didn't like himself very much. He had used this lovely waif for his own gain.

Inviting her to Dunland was like dangling a carrot in front of a starving rabbit. For a taste of luxury, she would jump at the chance. All this because he wanted information about Mary's Fortune. What was he thinking?

Yet he doubted that she was totally unaware of the consequences of this evening. She had to know that she would be foreign to this atmosphere and considered less than desirable by the other guests.

Still, his guilt won the battle. He couldn't have her humiliated because of a deuced quilt! "Baines—" he began, intending to invite her out on the veranda, then escort her back to her house. Roc's and DeEdria's approach interrupted him.

DeEdria Rowley Dunston halted before them in a swish of watered-silk skirts. She hailed from one of Natchez's oldest families, and had been married to Roc for ten years. Pretty in the classic sense, she had medium-length blond hair and velvety brown eyes. Her take-charge, genteel ways served as the perfect complement to Roc's easygoing manner.

"My, my, Cousin Gray," DeEdria drawled, eyeing Baines critically. "I don't blame you for choosing your own partner for your ball. She is absolutely breathtaking." Approval beaming in her gaze, she extended a delicate hand. "Hello, my dear. I'm DeEdria Dunston. Welcome to Dunland."

Baines didn't miss Miz DeEdria's friendly attitude. Instead of feeling welcomed by it, however, she felt intimidated. If she didn't measure up to the lady's standards,
would Gray regret his invitation?

Seeing him and the heated looks he gave her, she was
no longer sure that he'd invited her just because of the quilt.
Although he knew of her place of residence when he'd
extended the invitation, Baines didn't wish to disappoint
him.

But how could she measure up to DeEdria Dunston?
While she had quite a task running this huge household,
Miz DeEdria still lived a life of leisure.

Her upbringing, her experiences, her very existence were
worlds apart from Baines's. Baines had merely to look at
DeEdria's soft, pale hands for evidence. Her own were red
and work-roughened in comparison. She smiled hesitantly,
waiting for a gesture that would prove DeEdria's friendli-
ness to be false.

"T-Thank you, ma'am."

"You're welcome, I'm sure," Mr. Roc interjected.
"Gray, keep a firm grip on her. Every gentleman in this
room has his eye on her. Two or three of them will probably tap you on the shoulder for a dance from her."

Gray forced a grin. "Perhaps you're right. And, judging
from their leers at Baines, a dance is probably the last thing
they want from her," he snarled.

Gray's fierceness surprised Baines. He sounded decidedly protective—and decidedly jealous. Her heart pounded
maddeningly at the prospect. His strong jaw taut and his
firm mouth held in a grim line, he looked dangerous and
predatory.

Dark gray trousers clung to his long legs and looked both
elegant and seductive on his tall frame. His white, ruffled
silk shirt added to his masculinity and accentuated his
tanned complexion and inky hair. Massive shoulders filled
his midnight-blue topcoat, making the blue of his eyes
stand out.

An unwelcome surge sparked through Baines. She had
her dreams to pursue, and a romantic involvement with

anyone, especially *him,* would only stand in her way. Men
from his world seldom took women from her class as mistresses, and marriage to them broke every rule of protocol
ever written. Not that it never happened. But Baines wanted
to make her own way in the world, to create her own
wealth.

She couldn't do that with a husband. She also had to
remember her obligation to Uncle Linc. Suddenly she worried whether it had been a mistake to come here.

An attraction to this mysterious man would be a caution
to her peace of mind, but she doubted her logic had a say
in the matter.

When Gray cleared his throat, she remembered her manners. Heat crept up her cheeks.

"I-I can't dance," she revealed in a low, embarrassed
tone.

"Then you won't have to, Baines," Gray assured her.
"At least not tonight." Smiling in relief, he turned to Roc
and DeEdria. "Dancing is not a requirement, is it?"

Shaking his head, Roc laughed. "Of course not, Gray. I
don't know much about you, Cousin, but I could see your
previous smile hadn't been genuine. I pity the poor sot who
would have asked for a dance. I'm kind of relieved Baines
can't dance."

DeEdria laughed. "Oh, Roc, don't tease. Pay him no
nevermind, you two. Baines, honey, there are ways other
than dancing to enjoy a party."

"Aye, there is," Gray agreed.

"I'd like to introduce you to some of my friends,"
DeEdria said pleasantly.

"Oh, no, Miz DeEdria, I couldn't—"

"Call me DeEdria." Her mood was playful, her words
genuine. "Unless you want me to call you Miss Baines."

"Go with her and call her DeEdria," Gray said, grateful
to his cousin's wife. "She seems to like the sound of her
name without the 'Mrs.' before it, anyway." Hoping to put
Baines at ease, he winked at her. Maybe she wouldn't be
intimidated by the gentry. As Roc's wife, DeEdria wielded
a lot of social power. With her help, Baines would gain

acceptance that much quicker. Still, DeEdria's attitude of embracing everyone equally was a new experience for Gray.

Uncertainty in her green depths, Baines looked at him.

"It'll be just fine," DeEdria assured her. "Come." She took Baines by the arm, leaving her no choice.

Hating to leave the protection of Gray's nearness, Baines walked beside the mistress of Dunland. They left the dining room and crossed into the ballroom. She tried not to gawk at the fine furnishings surrounding her, but she had never seen so many delicate things. Beautiful crystal chandeliers, silk draperies, linen wallpaper, Oriental carpets, and marble fireplaces entranced her. She'd barely recovered from her awe when DeEdria halted before a tall, thin woman with the coldest black eyes Baines had ever seen.

"Baines, I'd like you to meet Belinda Myers," DeEdria said softly. "Belinda, this is Baines . . . ?" She looked at her expectantly.

"Marshall," Baines mumbled. Gray had never asked for her last name, but when he discovered it, it would take him no time to figure out the truth.

"So you're the woman who's come between Roc's handsome cousin and all the other lovely young ladies whose hopes of becoming a countess have shattered." Miz Myers looked down her long nose at her and imparted those words between thinned lips. "Including my own," she spat with a tight grin.

"Don't rightly know what you're talkin' about, Miz Myers," Baines responded. Unprepared for such malice, she felt self-conscious and out of place. Maybe tonight *had* been a bad idea. But she hadn't done anything to Belinda Myers. "Seems to me, Gray'd be the one doin' the shatterin', since he'd be the one doin' the askin' if he had a mind to. And I'm hopin' you didn't expect to get asked to become a countess tonight. Why, he's just barely got his boots on our soil." She leaned in closer to the lady, who stood red-faced and speechless. It hadn't been Baines's intention to embarrass her, but neither would she let the woman mock her. "Maybe if you were not so eager to get yourself married to Gray, yours and the other ladies' hopes wouldn't be shattered.''

Visibly shaking, Belinda's mouth dropped open. Fury radiated from her like steam from boiling water. "Well, I never!" she said with a gasp. "I do declare, De De. She is quite an offensive little thing."

"Linny, do hush!" DeEdria imparted. Her fine eyebrows drew together in a frown. "Baines is refreshingly charming and innocently unaware of any offenses she may have uttered, deserving though they might have been."

Another woman stepped into what was becoming a gathering of disapproving ladies of society. With diamonds glowing from her ears, neck, wrists, and gloved fingers, she announced her wealth in a shameless display.

Her ample body stiffening in outrage, she blared out, "So she's witless, then."

From their sudden disdain, Baines assumed the other husband-hunters, whose hopes she'd shattered, overheard what she'd whispered to Miz Myers.

I ain't shattered anybody's hopes, because Gray hasn't asked me to marry him. And I surely have all my wits. It's those husband-wantin' women who seem to lack wits.

"Baines, is it?" another woman sneered. She was an older woman, with graying hair and exquisite features. "Your gown is lovely, dear, but your sense of coordination is appalling. Your shoes don't match."

At the mention of her worn, black work shoes, Baines covered one foot with the other in embarrassment. Her heart sank. What could she have been thinking to come here?

But perhaps she deserved what she was getting. She'd thought merely to use Gray, but he and his family went out of their way to put her at ease. They couldn't be faulted for her overwhelming desire to enter their world. Neither could they be faulted because the others were treating her so badly.

Because she had defended herself, she was being humiliated. It didn't matter that DeEdria was giving the rude woman a good dressing down on her behalf. She had to do it for herself.

Baines raised her chin in defiance. "It's not what's below a body's ankles that's important, ma'am," she said with a sniff, "but what's above the neck. I may be poor at the moment, but I won't always be. I am a quiltmaker and a seamstress, and I can learn coordination just as I learned to quilt." She paused, taking in the many faces that had joined the little group. "Besides, it takes more than a costly gown and a fancy pair of shoes to create a lady."

"Exactly my sentiments!" a richly gowned matron exclaimed from the back of the crowd. Her dark hair gleaming in the brightly lit room, she walked forward. "Baines, my dear, I am Evelyn Dunston Middleton, Rochester's sister. I agree wholeheartedly with you. Some of us are smothered in our own self-importance. You are indeed a breath of fresh air. Allow me to apologize for any insult you may have suffered here this evening."

"Thank you, Miz Middleton," Baines piped in and smiled at the lady. "I'm not insulted, though, just a little irate. But I realize some folks can't help showin' their ignorance at times." She caught sight of Gray striding toward them, like the very Devil possessed him, cold fury on his features. Wondering what she had done, her smile faltered.

"That they do, my dear. That they do," Evelyn agreed with a laugh. "I want to see just how good a seamstress you are, Baines. I would like you to return here one day next week and fit me into a new day dress."

Eagerness and satisfaction soared through Baines, and she opened her mouth to shout that she would be available whenever the lady wanted her presence. Instead, she shocked herself and said, "I'm mighty appreciative of your offer, Miz Middleton, but I'm in the middle of stitchin' a birthday quilt, so I'll have to take you up on your offer in a couple of weeks."

This was the chance she'd been waiting for, and Baines almost recalled her words. She almost said she would take the lady up on her offer immediately. She'd worked with Miz Annabelle long enough to know how fast potential customers changed their minds.

But she wouldn't give up her goal just to make some

quick money. It didn't matter how badly she needed it, especially since she needed help where her fashion sense was concerned. Although she had to admit the gown Miz Annabelle had given her as her latest assignment for the shop was turning out quite nice. Baines only hoped their customer, one Miz Roberta Franklin, thought so.

If she accepted Miz Middleton's work right away, however, her ultimate goal of duplicating the special quilt might be lost for good. Anticipation at using her quilting skills on the replication and images of the quilt dancing before her mind's eye made her lack of time for her uncle's quilt all the more acute. Baines felt confident she could start her replica from memory. Of course, having it near her would help whenever she forgot a small detail.

"That's a marvelous idea, Evie," DeEdria said. "Please count me in on the fitting, Baines, whenever you're able to attend us. I could use some new gowns myself, and maybe even a new quilt for the Rose Chamber."

Gray reached her side and took her hand in his own, his possession unmistakable; his anger palpable; his nearness breathtaking.

"Are you all right?"

Baines nodded, unable to do more than that as she realized he was angry *for* her, not *at* her. She exalted in his strength, his beauty, his appeal. Longing tugged at her, and her knees felt like jelly.

Everyone watched them, breathless, waiting, expectant. But she didn't care. And neither did Gray.

He took her hand into his own. His fingers were long and well manicured, his touch gentle. Her breath caught in her throat, and her pulse raced. Hand in hand, they started for the door. He had invited her here as his guest. Surely that had to account for something.

Belinda Myers blocked their exit. An unfathomable expression written in her features, she smiled blandly. "I meant to belittle you, Baines," she said, capturing everyone's attention. "I guess most of us did." She looked at Gray with depthless black eyes. "You needn't have worried. She gave better than she got. And we deserved it."

She extended her hand to Baines. "Can we bury the hatchet and you add me to your list of clients?"

Baines grasped Belinda's hand and found it clammy and cold. When she met the woman's gaze, a calculating, mocking expression crossed her face so briefly Baines wondered if anyone else noticed.

"And me, too?" the diamond-bedecked woman asked. "At least we know you do have a brain in your head."

"And I thought her a bit of a mouse," an unrecognizable voice called out. "But she kind of grows on one, all at once."

Before Baines could respond, Gray leaned down. His warm breath caressed her skin.

"May I escort you outside, my dear, so we can enjoy the breeze on the veranda?"

5

BAINES DREW IN A breath of balmy night air and whiffed in the mingled scents from various night-blooming flowers. She easily recognized her favorite, night jasmine, and breathed in deeper. The shame she felt at her knowledge of the quilt's true location didn't allow her to relax, and the awareness of Gray's devastating appeal made her heart thump uncomfortably. He stood inches from her, bold and powerful. Still that air of loneliness surrounded him.

She wanted to somehow breach the emotional mantle he had placed about himself. But she reminded herself that he was a stranger and would soon leave.

Perching herself on a wrought-iron lace bench, she stared out into the darkness. The darkness concealed Dunland's parklike surroundings and her turmoil.

Drifts of music floated from the manor through an opened window. Gas lanterns lined the stately double gallery, and she watched as Gray gripped the railings of delicate ironwork, his black hair gleaming in the soft light. He, too, stared over the dark land, and she wondered what went through his mind. When he turned to her, she still found no clue to his thoughts. His expression was masked.

They stared at each other for a moment, and his eyes impaled her, seeming to probe to the very core of her. Baines couldn't look away. Light from the lanterns flickered

in his eyes, reflecting brilliantly within his sapphire depths
and revealing his desire, his interest, his suspicion.

"Excuse me for a moment, Baines."

His accented voice sounded deep and husky, sending
warm tingles through her body and unladylike thoughts
through her mind.

She forced a coy smile and willed herself to ignore her
uncertainty. "Sure, Gray. Take your time."

Alone, she leaned back and listened to the shrill whirs
of cicadas competing with the crickets as they chirped their
nighttime songs. An owl hooted, and the sound of water
lapping reached her ears. Nothing, however, could soothe
or relax her senses.

Every kindness he'd shown her tonight hadn't seemed
anything but honest. Why had she believed that his motives
were anything but genuine?

Because she'd had enough experience with the rich not
to just blindly trust their good intentions. If it hadn't been
for the quilt, Gray never would have gone to Rivertown.
But that was no excuse for what she was doing now. Was
it her own guilt over her deception about the quilt or her
use of Gray to gain acceptance at Dunland that made her
mistrust him so thoroughly?

Unable to answer her questions, she counted the huge,
pedastaled Doric columns on the gallery and found six. She
wondered what Gray would think if he discovered she knew
how to read and write. She could even count, she thought
proudly. Uncle Lincoln had seen to it that she'd gotten
schooling.

But listening tonight to those ladies speaking with the
proper language made Baines realize she still had a lot more
learning to do. Thinking further, she decided Gray wouldn't
care one way or the other about her ability to read and
write. It didn't matter how he'd treated her tonight. More
than likely his interest in her only extended as far as her
knowledge of that danged quilt. Besides, she wouldn't better herself for Gray's benefit. She would do so for her own
satisfaction.

"I've brought you something."

At the sound of Gray's voice, Baines nearly jumped out of her skin, alarmed, anticipating, electrified.

"You scared me half to death, Gray," she scolded, accepting the tall glass filled with mint leaves and a cool, green liquid that he handed to her. Their fingers brushed, and her body grew tight with tension. Her breathing uneven, her heart pounding, she stared into the glass and frowned at the contents. Gingerly she sniffed. The potent smell of gin assailed her senses. "What is it?"

"It's what the Southern ladies of leisure and class drink, Baines. It's called a mint julep." Taking a seat next to her, Gray sipped from his glass of bourbon.

"Oh, really?"

His words, spoken so casually, made her remember why an attraction between them would be harmful. Humiliation coursed through her, sickening and familiar. His description of Southern ladies sounded callous and out-of-hand to her. Perhaps she wasn't a lady of leisure, but his words made it seem as if she didn't have class, either. Yet she wouldn't show her annoyance. She refused to let him know that he'd pricked a nerve.

Forcing a deceptive calm about herself to mask the renewed resentment coiling around her insides, Baines laughed. "It looks so pretty and smells wonderful. Like mint." She took a tentative sip and sighed at the delicious taste. Her genuine pleasure surprised her. "Umm! It tastes good, too. I don't recall ever fixin' a mint julep at Luther's. Of course, no fancy ladies ever come in there. All I ever serve is watered-down beer and rotgut whiskey to that river hoard that slithers in." Involuntarily her scorn towards him asserted itself through her words.

Gray cleared his throat, his eyes questioning, his firm mouth curving into a hint of a smile, beckoning to her. Her gaze held his, and her hands trembled. She dared him to mock her, to mention the differences in his class and hers. Yet his features showed neither ridicule nor scorn, but deep concentration and genuine interest. It intensified her earlier thought that she had misjudged him.

A moment of silent combat, of mutual awareness, passed between them, then Gray spoke.

"Exactly what is it you do, Baines?"

She wanted him to find her beautiful and desirable and acceptable. But she couldn't tell him that. So she lifted her chin, her heart quickening further at the double meaning to his words.

"I'm a quiltmaker, Gray," she answered proudly, softly. She added as an afterthought, "and a seamstress."

His gaze traveled over her face, searching her eyes, then moving slowly over her body. Finally his regard settled on her mouth, his thoughts all too clear.

Instead of leaning over and kissing her, however, he asked in a hoarse voice, "Did you make the gown you're wearing?"

Baines shook her head, entranced by the moment, the man. "No, it was already made, but it was quite plain, so Miz Annabelle helped fancy it up. She says I know how to quilt, but I don't know what fashions to sew. Says I don't have an eye for fashion."

"With some time and teaching, I'm sure you'll get the hang of it," he said with encouragement, caressing her, undressing her, with his eyes. "Is quilting all you do?"

He scooted closer to her, nearly impossible on the small bench. She was barely able to keep her wits about herself, barely able to remember that she resented him. One glance at his sharp, confident expression told her it would be wise to flee his presence while she was still capable of doing so.

Yet running away wasn't in her nature, and she wouldn't give in to that thought now.

Nervous at being so close to this man, she took a gulp of her drink, then responded. "Oh, no. Sometimes I give Luther a hand. He owns the Horse and Mule Tavern down at the end of Silver Street."

"So living alone, you have to eke out a living any way you can. Even in a place like the Horse and Mule."

"I never said I live alone," Baines snapped, not liking the censure in his tone. Ready to defend herself, she paused and faced him, then wished she hadn't.

He seemed distant and even somewhat cold, as though he allowed himself to relax only so much before retreating. She mustn't allow herself to answer the pull of attraction she felt for this puzzling man. His changeable moods told her she could be hurt.

Still, he was her knight in shining armor who'd allowed her entrance into a palace. Although she hadn't been treated like a fairy princess by the other guests, *he* had championed her. But what had she done for him in return? Nothing. Absolutely nothing. Worst of all, she had started off by lying to him and resenting his wealth, as if he'd chosen his birthplace—and hers as well.

The smallest reminder of his good breeding felt like a blow to her pride. But even that couldn't control the tingling she experienced at his nearness. Her confused emotions tormented her.

Unable to understand the feelings he stirred inside her and wanting to atone for her lies, she cleared her throat. "Why do you want that quilt so badly?"

Gray swallowed and leaned closer, his mouth inches from hers. "It belonged to my great-grandmother and had been handed down to my grandfather, then my father, and finally me. Roc didn't know how badly I wanted it, so thinking it was useless, he gave it to Lincoln Marshall."

He sighed, sounding weary, and Baines felt his pain down to her toes. Her guilt deepened. Before she could confess, he continued.

"I guess my search will end in failure."

A sad smile crossed his handsome features, and Baines's throat closed. She had never seen a man more miserable, and it was all because of her. She wasn't sure which was greater—her pity for him, her guilt over her dishonesty, or her happiness that Uncle Lincoln hadn't lied. Mr. Roc had really given him the quilt!

Clearly Gray pined for his great-granny's quilt. What was she turning into? She'd lied to Gray about it, then refused to believe Uncle Lincoln's story about how he'd come by the quilt. Well, Uncle Lincoln deserved her apology, and Gray . . . poor Gray. After all his good will toward her, he deserved to get back his family quilt.

She hoped the understanding man she had glimpsed beneath Gray's cool appearance surfaced and listened to her reasons for doing what she did. Taking a sip of her drink, she mustered up her courage and released an anxious cough. "There's somethin' you need to know about that quilt, Gray."

"Don't trouble yourself, my dear," Gray whispered.

His husky words carried on the soft breeze and wrapped around her, settling into the core of her. When he began to toy with her hair, she leaned her head into his hand. He seemed to move his fingers to the rhythm of the soft music floating around them. Each place he touched invited more. But they were on a bench in the darkness at his relatives' home with a world of differences and the location of a prized quilt between them. This could lead to nothing but disaster.

Yet she had to give up the beautiful covering. Among all the reasons why she couldn't keep the quilt, the most outstanding was she could no longer lie about it, especially since Uncle Linc wasn't in danger of being arrested. Still, she wished she could remain silent. In giving up the quilt, she might well have been giving up her dream. She would rely on her memory as best she could, however.

"It's really not your concern, Baines."

"It is, Gray," she blurted, closing her eyes against the tingling sensations his scalp massage caused. "I lied to you about not knowin' Lincoln Marshall and—"

"You did? Why?"

His voice soothed, mesmerized, and sounded far, far away. Although she still felt the movement of his fingers, Baines opened her eyes to see if he remained near her. He did, with flushed skin and darkened eyes. In all the time she'd been working down at Luther's, she never saw a man give a lady a more lustful look than the one Gray now gave her.

She warmed under the heat of his shocking gaze. He seemed to be mentally undressing her, as if he were moments away from carrying her off to his private chamber and having his wicked way with her. The thought sent waves of excitement through her. He leaned toward her, and her heart lurched wildly.

But then, suddenly, abruptly, he closed his eyes and groaned audibly. To Baines he sounded in pain. Worried, she brushed his arm with a feather-light touch, and he flinched. Long moments passed before he opened his eyes again, and when he did, his remote look had returned.

She sighed, disappointed, and unsure why.

"Why did you lie, Baines?" he asked without anger.

His hands seemed to move to the cadence of his voice, hypnotizing and bewitching.

"Because I-I misunderstood your reason for wantin' to see him."

Gray untangled his fingers from her hair and looked at her. He quirked an inky eyebrow, and sharp mockery invaded his stare. "Really? My mistake. Although I'm sure I told you the reason for my visit. Do you in fact know Lincoln Marshall?"

His expression had turned brutally frank, and Baines licked her lips nervously. "He's my uncle, Gray."

In the silence that followed her hoarse announcement, she faltered under his steady scrutiny. But she wouldn't regret her decision. Even if he hated her for her deception, she felt her confession was ultimately for the best.

"I see," Gray said, not as friendly, although he didn't seem too surprised by the revelation. He stood and walked the short distance to the railing before facing her again. "Then you have knowledge of the quilt?"

"I *have* the quilt. I am so sorry I lied before." Baines didn't want to tell him the true reason for her falsehood. She didn't want Gray or the other Dunstons to know that her uncle was sometimes light in the fingers. Although he did steal occasionally, she didn't want *them* branding him a thief. They wouldn't have a thief working at Dunland, and the extra money helped.

It didn't matter if Gray had already discovered that she was Lincoln Marshall's niece. It was the principle of the situation. She had lied to him.

"I am so sorry," she repeated miserably.

He released laughter rich with satisfaction, and Baines widened her eyes in surprise.

"Don't be sorry, Baines. You've made me a very happy man."

Relieved, Baines sagged and laughed with him. "A body can tell the quilt's old, Gray, but it's beautiful."

"I'm sure it is, Baines," Gray said. "Let's enjoy our drinks before going to get it. Where exactly in your house is it?"

"Why, where would a quilt be, silly? On a bed, of course." Baines laughed, then turned the tall glass up and drained it. "You surely are a caution, Graylong."

Shaking his head, Gray turned an amused look to her. "It's Grayling."

"Well, whatever." Baines set the empty glass on the gallery floor. "You can't make me believe you don't know where a quilt is suppose to go."

Gray chuckled and, walking to her, pulled her up off the bench. "Baines," he said as she swayed against him. "Is your last name Marshall too?"

"Well, of course. What else would it be? I'm not married or anything."

"I think you should allow me to take you home, Baines," Gray said, changing the subject. "Even though you work in a tavern, it's obvious you don't imbibe."

Baines leaned against his solid chest, the brushed velvet of his coat tickling her cheek and the scent of his spicy cologne making her senses spin crazily. "And don't you forget it, Lord Montygoo."

"Can you walk?"

" 'Course I can walk. I got two legs, don't I?" She pushed herself away from him and gingerly took a first step, following that with another. Abruptly she stood stock-still, dizziness nearly making her fall to her knees. Her head swam, and she giggled. "I-I guess maybe I can't walk without a little aid."

Back at her side instantly, Gray placed his big hands around her waist and led her back to the bench. "Sit down, little mouse. I'm going to arrange for a buggy to take you home.''

"I'm sorry I ruined your evenin', Gray," Baines slurred, the reason he called her a mouse at the fringes of her memory. "Leastwise, it won't be a whole loss. You can get your quilt when you see me home.''

Walking to the entrance, Gray didn't respond, but stopped in the imposing doorway to gaze at her. Her heart beat rapidly against her breast at his intense look.

"Ruin my evening? Just your mere presence has enhanced my day." He stopped, as if he caught himself before he said something more. Smiling, he cleared his throat and changed the subject. "I have nothing against my relatives, mind you, and I know they're anxious to show me off with this obligatory ball. They mean well, too, so you understand that I will merely have time to get the quilt before I return here? I think I owe them that since I'll be returning to England in a few days.''

Too overcome to speak, Baines nodded, her joy evaporating. She damned her honesty. Because of it, Gray would be getting his quilt back, and she would probably never see him again.

6

AS GRAY PULLED THE horse and buggy to a stop, an odd sensation of being watched engulfed him. He glanced around, but found nothing that suggested imminent danger.

Dark surroundings and boisterous noises in the distance mocked the peaceful serenity they'd left behind at Dunland. The moon cast tree shadows against the hard earth, and Gray searched for any untoward, human movements around them. When he realized he didn't have Roc's gun with him, he cursed. He didn't relish being in this area without protection.

Deciding it was only uneasiness at being in this notorious part of the city, Gray glanced at Baines, not wanting to unduly alarm her. Tenderness surged within him. Baines's head bobbed, and he felt a moment's guilt that he'd given her the gin-laced drink. He'd only wanted to introduce her to something new; he'd never meant to get her sotted.

Gently he shook her. Her eyes fluttered open, and then she squinted before opening her eyes in full awareness.

"I-I fell asleep?" she squeaked, sounding mortified.

Gray smiled, ignoring the impulse to pull her into his arms. "Aye," he said softly. "You were utterly entrancing."

A pleasant smile crossed her lips, and Gray swallowed hard, wondering if Baines had any idea of how beautiful she was. As unpretentious as she seemed, Gray doubted it. He doubted she knew she could make a man's body hard with need or fill his mind with only thoughts of her.

He also doubted he could return to the party once he got back to Dunland. Knowing how deeply he had played on Baines's conscience as well as her innocence, he felt like a complete cad. Somehow, with him moments away from claiming Mary's Fortune, the happiness that should have pervaded him eluded him. The only persistent thought was that he would never see Baines again.

Maybe that would be for the best. Maybe Mary Dunston's letter was a bloody hoax, and the quilt led to nothing at all.

A sigh of irritation escaped him at his wandering thoughts, and Gray got to the ground, then helped Baines out of the buggy. She wobbled unsteadily, and he snaked his arm around her waist to steady her.

"Are you all right, my dear?"

Baines nodded, and the feel of her warm body so close to his wrecked his resolve to get the quilt and leave. In silence they made it to her door.

Unfortunately his disquiet hadn't dissipated. That annoyed him. He prided himself on his composure. But at the moment he felt like plundering the surrounding darkness to discover if the danger he detected actually lurked in the shadows.

"Where's your uncle, Baines?" he asked, not liking the idea of Baines being here alone.

Swaying slightly, Baines shrugged, seeming unconcerned. "He said he was goin' over to Louisiana. New Orleans, I believe. He's gone to see if he can get hired out on another ship."

"You stay here all alone at night?" Gray asked incredulously, already knowing the answer.

"I'm not scared," Baines answered quietly. "I know just about everybody around here. There's none brave enough to tangle with my uncle Lincoln. He's warned them to treat me like a lady." She added that last bit almost defiantly.

Gray hadn't yet met Lincoln Marshall, but his regard for

him went up considerably. It seemed Marshall took his responsibility of protecting his niece seriously. "You are indeed a lady, Baines Marshall," he said. He wondered how much of her boasting of being unafraid was truth and how much was bravado.

After unlocking the door, Baines pushed it open, revealing a darkened interior. She staggered past him, and Gray listened to her movements, but remained in the doorway. Within moments two candles gave off their meager light inside the small house.

Nerves on edge, he walked farther inside, his gaze taking in every detail of his surroundings that the measly lighting allowed. A table with two chairs stood against one wall and a big, black potbellied stove against another. He noticed a small alcove with a little cot and decided this was where Baines slept. Next to it stood a finely finished quilting frame, over which a half-completed quilt in an array of colors hung. If that was Baines's work, Gray admitted she was quite skilled. One lone curtain covered the only window of the spotless little house.

Nothing out of the ordinary. No bogeyman awaited in the corners to jump out at him. A sense of relief washing over him, Gray almost laughed at his active imagination.

"It's n-not m-much," Baines slurred without a trace of apology for the appearance of the poorly furnished room, "but it's my home for now. I plan to live on the bluff one day."

"I believe you will succeed with that dream, Baines." He stood looking at her. Her eyes brightened from the effects of alcohol beckoned to him. The door remained open, and the light from the moon added to the lumination inside the room. It bounced off her hair and made it shine like black silk.

He needed to feel it again, to slide his hand over its soft texture. He'd controlled himself on the gallery at Dunland when he'd been nearly witless with desire for her. He could control himself again.

Drawing her closer, he touched her hair, and the thought that he might never see her again crossed Gray's mind. His good intentions became lost in a muddle of confused regrets and unsated passion. Bringing her against his chest, he slanted his mouth over hers.

She tasted of mint and gin, and it intoxicated him as much as the feel of her unresisting body in his arms. Standing on tiptoe, she wrapped her arms around his neck. He traced the outline of her temptingly inviting, small red lips with his tongue, and she sucked in a breath. When his tongue entered her warm mouth, she melted against him, and Gray's manhood hardened. Sensations swirled through his body as she continued to kiss him greedily, holding on to his lapels as if he were her lifeline.

Thoughts of bringing her into the small alcove, laying her gently on the cot, and making her his ran amok in his brain. But he couldn't. He was leaving and he refused to steal her innocence, then abandon her.

Gray moaned softly. "Baines," he said against her lips. She was too bloody desirable by far. And too deuced innocent by half. The physical state she'd put him in would leave him miserable for the rest of the night.

He set her away from him. Her eyes closed, her cheeks flushed, she swayed toward him. Black, sooty eyelashes curved against her creamy skin like an upside-down rainbow. Her lips, swollen from his kisses, beckoned to be kissed again. He slid his hands down her narrow waist to steady her, the feel of her torturous.

"Baines," he croaked. "Little mouse, you should rest. I will take possession of my quilt and will more than likely leave for England in a day or two. You have my deepest gratitude for returning it to me."

She opened her eyes, and the emerald depths threatened to consume him. Had they been a pit of fire, they would have.

"W-Will I get to see you before you leave?"

"Most definitely," Gray answered. It would be for her sake as well as his own. When he returned to England, he wanted to bring a lifetime of memories with him. "I will make it a point to come here and tell you farewell."

Baines smiled shyly at him, then went to the small alcove. Her hands flew to her flushed cheeks, and she raised her gaze to Gray, a horrified look on her face.

"What's wrong, Baines?" he asked with concern, an inkling of dread hitting him. He thought for a moment Baines would go into apoplexy. He wondered if his earlier sense of danger had been warranted.

"The quilt, Gray," she barely whispered. "It's gone!"

7

HER WORDS SLAMMED INTO Gray's senses like a sledgehammer to his middle.

The quilt gone? Had someone indeed been lurking about? Was this person there to do Baines harm?

"What else is gone, Baines?" he asked worriedly.

Her gaze roamed around the shack. "Nothin'," she answered. "The quilt's the only thing."

He glanced at her, his demand that she accompany him back to Dunland catching in his throat. The shock, the unease on her face sickened him. She was lying to him. He knew it, could feel it in his very soul. *Only* the quilt had been taken? Gray couldn't credit that.

In quick strides he reached the alcove and looked down at the cot, then stared at her in disbelief. But instead of spewing his anger, only his alarm showed itself.

"W-what are you talking about?" he managed. The small hope he harbored disintegrated, and his last chance to avenge his father's name and save their fortune crumbled.

"The quilt, Gray, has disappeared."

She felt all over the cot, as if that would bloody prove her wrong. When it didn't magically appear, she got down on all fours and looked under the cot, her small backside round against the material of her dress. She stood and dusted off her lovely gown, then faced him.

"It's gone."

Gray threaded his hand through his hair, frustration and incipient hostility burrowing into him. Roc should have been the target of his resentment. It had been Roc who'd been inspired to give away Mary's Fortune. Instead of Roc, however, Baines garnered most of Gray's antagonism.

Baines, who had set his blood afire and made him want to know her better. Baines, who had lied to him from the very beginning.

His innate mistrust overtook his sense of fairness.

"How could it be gone?" he snapped. "You said it was *here*. On your bed. Apparently you lied."

Anger lighting her eyes, Baines threw him a withering stare.

Of all the bloody cheek! Gray could hardly credit that she had the blasted gall to lose her temper, when he should have been tearing this ramshackle hut down to find his quilt.

"I am not a liar, Mr. High-and-Mighty," she huffed, appearing more sober than she had in an hour. "You take that back!"

"Oh, no?" Gray laughed nastily. He barely refrained from shaking the truth from her lovely little lips. "You lied to me from the beginning, Baines, pretending you had no knowledge of Lincoln Marshall. And you lied to me tonight! Now, where's the bloody quilt?"

"I don't know!" Baines shouted, stamping her foot in frustration. "Someone must have broken in and stolen it!"

"How? Materialize through the deuced walls? Baines, your door was latched! Please explain to me, mistress, how someone could *break* into your house, then take the time to bolt the door on his way out after stealing only *my* quilt?"

Glowering at him, Baines moved to the long cushioned bench that also served as her uncle's bed. Maybe Uncle Lincoln had come in and borrowed it for the night, she thought as she searched the area, but found no sign of her beautiful quilt. She bowed her head and admitted she made up wild excuses for the unexplainable disappearance of the quilt.

Uncle Lincoln had brought it for her, and he'd never once even wrapped it around himself, even when she wasn't using it.

It was one thing to freely give the quilt to Gray, but to have it snatched from both of them proved almost unbearable. Out of guilt she had decided to do the right thing and return the quilt to Gray. She'd put aside her own dreams and aspirations. For her good intentions, she received this treachery.

What had happened to the quilt was a mystery to her. How could it disappear from a locked room? Who could have been in here to take it? The thought that her private sanctuary had been invaded frightened her, and she almost asked Gray to let her come back to Dunland with him. Almost.

She had her pride and she refused to allow anyone to accuse her of a crime she didn't commit. One peek in Gray's direction told her he blamed her for the disappearance of the quilt.

Her head pounded from the Mint Julep she'd drunk; and her fog of desire had been forced to ebb in a most unappealing way. But she refused to suffer Grayling Dunston's accusations. Hands on hips, she glared at him and raised her chin.

"Just because I fibbed about my uncle doesn't mean I've lied to you now. I only thought Uncle Lincoln was headed for a heap of trouble for havin' your old quilt—"

Drawing in an agitated breath, Gray narrowed his eyes at her. "Why should I believe you now? Especially since you have no justifiable explanation for what has happened to the quilt?"

Baines stalked to the door, unwilling to admit how much his words hurt. And to think she'd believed she would miss him when he left. She wished he did have his quilt, so he could be on the first ship back to England and leave her be.

"Get out!" she barked. "I'm not a thief and I'm not a liar!" She brushed away a renegade tear. "I refuse to allow you to stick those labels on me. I aim to find your quilt and make you eat those awful words. Now get!" With all the strength she could muster, she pushed him out and slammed the door.

Taken by surprise, Gray went sprawling over the small porch and down the steps. He landed on his face in the dust.

"Bloody witch!" he snarled, raising himself to his full six feet four inches. Dusting himself off, he stomped to his horse and buggy. He should have her arrested for theft, but it would be his word against hers.

Regardless of his anger toward her, the thought of having her arrested didn't sit well with him. He climbed into the carriage and pulled the reins, turning the horse in the direction of Dunland. Fury ran hot in his blood, but for the time being he would squelch his anger to appear gracious to his hosts and their guests. The party had been for his benefit, and the guilt he'd felt over the manner in which he finally got Baines to confess evaporated completely. The thought of that guilt only made his anger deepen.

Pushing the horse to its limit, Gray reached the manor in no time. He halted the beast and disembarked from the carriage, then started up the wide gallery steps as a slave rushed to get the horse and buggy.

As he reached the gallery, laughter echoed from inside the house. He hesitated. In all honesty, he didn't want to return to the party, not without Baines. Tonight she'd been the envy of every woman and the fantasy of every man. She positively sparkled and had handled herself as a most respectable lady, with a whimsical charm that dared anyone to mock her. Just as she dared him to malign her, but he had done so anyway.

Weariness crept into him, and he sat heavily on the bench he'd shared with Baines. He thought about their time together and searched for any reasons why she would lie to him about owning Mary's Fortune. She could very well have been telling the truth. But why should he trust her?

What reason had she given him to trust her? She lied to him when he met her, claiming she had no knowledge of Lincoln Marshall or the quilt. Not only did she have the quilt in her possession, but also the man in question was her uncle! Yet what other reason did she have to lie to him? He saw the quilt she was stitching, proof that she didn't need *his* quilt.

Harshly he reminded himself that Baines wasn't his one-time best friend, James McKay. But Gray could hardly credit that. If Jamie taught him nothing else, he'd taught Gray not to trust anyone, besides his father, ever again. And Pierce was dead.

Gray laughed harshly and stared out into the darkness. "Jamie, you bloody bastard."

But he didn't want to think about his friend. He didn't want to remember how the person he'd loved as a brother had almost gotten him kicked out of Eton. If not for Pierce's unswerving belief in him and fatherly love, Gray's life would have been ruined.

He wanted to do no less for his father, posthumously though it would be. He'd tried everything, however, and Mary's Fortune had been his last hope. The insane urge to weep possessed him, but a disturbing thought surfaced through his misery.

If Baines told the truth, then that meant in spite of the bolted door someone had managed to get inside her house. But how? Gray straightened in his seat. "Bloody hell!" The window! The person could have gone through the window. If that proved correct, that meant she could possibly be in danger if the thief returned. Perhaps he had been nearby when Gray felt someone watching him.

Remembering Baines's meager belongings, Gray could think of nothing he considered valuable enough for anyone to steal. Still, concern ate at him. One man's trash was another's treasure; and Baines was the most valuable treasure of all. Baines Marshall a treasure? Aye, most definitely, and he would have to see to it that the treasure was guarded.

His inner doubts returned to taunt him. Baines Marshall could very well be the thief herself, in cahoots with her uncle. Gray could well have imagined being watched. Maybe she'd taken so long to come to the ball because they'd been devising a scheme to get money from him. Maybe their plans had gone awry when he'd brought the mint julep to Baines and gotten her sotted. Maybe . . .

"There you are, Gray. We've been searching for you and Baines."

The tone of Roc's voice irritated him. His cousin sounded so deuced *happy*. "Baines has gone home," he gritted out.

"So soon?" Roc laughed wickedly. "You two have a lover's quarrel?"

Gray stood, his concern over Baines's safety at war with his doubt about her honesty. He turned a quelling look to Roc. "I'd temper that bloody amusement of yours, Rochester," he barked. "I'm in no mood for it."

Roc's laughter deepened. "Of course, Grayling. Didn't mean to offend." He turned on his heel and started off. "The ladies will be ecstatic to know that you are no longer preoccupied with the little pretender."

"What did you call Baines?"

"It's not what *I've* been calling her. It's what Belinda Myers has been calling her."

Gray glowered at his cousin. The thin face of the tall redhead surfaced in Gray's mind. He'd thought her apology to Baines sincere, but it had been given merely to impress him. The bloody, lying—

"Whoa, Gray, Belinda is still a lady," Roc defended.

He hadn't realized he'd spoken his thoughts out loud until Roc's gentle chiding.

"DeEdria defended your lady well enough and summarily dismissed Belinda from Dunland for the evening."

Clenching his jaw in an effort to control his agitation at Belinda Myers and ignoring Roc's reference to Baines as "his lady," Gray changed the subject. He would deal with Belinda later. At the moment Baines's safety was more important than the other woman's prejudices.

"I believe someone has invaded Baines's home, Rochester. Send a watchman to guard her place and to see that no harm befalls her tonight.''

"Is she all right?" Concern laced Roc's voice.

"She seemed fine when I left," Gray answered. Not exactly fine, he thought, more like bloody fuming and wanting his head on a platter. But he wouldn't go into detail. "Send someone as soon as possible to guard her house."

Roc nodded. "It's as good as done, Gray. Anything else?"

Gray glared at Roc, his mischievous tone and knowing look galling him. "No!"

But when Roc made to depart, another question surfaced.

"What did Belinda mean when she called Baines a pretender?"

"Belinda says Baines is pretending to be a lady of class, when she's only an impoverished wretch born on the wrong side of the hill." Roc remained silent for a moment, apparently awaiting Gray's response. When none came forth, he shrugged and took his leave.

Gray couldn't answer. Rendered speechless, he watched his cousin walk away and enter the house.

He should have still been thinking of Baines, alone in her shack. He should have been thinking to pay Belinda Myers a visit and warn her not to hurt Baines. Instead, he focused his thoughts on himself.

A sick feeling went through him. The same censure that Baines faced every day of her life from the upper class loomed before him. Added to that censure, however, would be pity for the Earl of Montegut, whose father had ruined the family name and fortune. Elite circles that had once thrown their doors wide open for him would now shut those doors tight against him and whisper behind his back.

Unless he found Mary's Fortune and it actually led to a valuable treasure.

Walking into the entrance hall and returning to the festivities, Gray vowed to resume his search for the quilt tomorrow.

8

FURIOUS AT GRAYLING DUNSTON, Baines stalked around her small house. To think she'd felt sorry for him and offered the quilt in good faith. She didn't *have* to give it to him. Uncle Lincoln had come by it honestly, which made it hers by right.

Mr. Swell Elegant had the nerve to call her a liar and a thief. She would prove to him that she was neither.

To think she'd thought him different. What a fool she was.

An odd chill engulfed her, and she glanced around the dimness, searching for the source of her discomfort. Everything appeared in place, and she sighed heavily, suddenly wishing she hadn't thrown Gray out. The quilt had done a disappearing act, and she wasn't all that brave, since she felt certain a body had helped it to disappear.

Disrobing down to her chemise, she didn't like the fear she felt. This was her home. She shouldn't have been scared to fall asleep. Uncle Lincoln had made it a safe haven for her. He'd warned everyone to leave her be. What idiot had the nerve not to listen to him?

Despair ran hand in hand with her anger, and she sat on her cot, more tired than she'd ever been. "High-and-mighty drink for high-and-mighty ladies," she grumbled. "They have the time to sleep off the effects."

In spite of her unease, her eyes drooped, and she stretched out on the cot. She reached for her quilt and remembered its fate.

"Dang," she whispered, flinging her arm across her throbbing forehead. She wondered if she would have missed the quilt as much as she did at the moment if she'd given it to Gray as she'd intended. Without thinking too intently on the matter, she knew she would have. It had kept her warm on cold nights and occupied with ciphering the secrets it seemed to hold on boring days.

Images of the Earl of Montegut rose in her mind. He was just about the handsomest man she'd ever seen with his blue eyes as clear as a summer sky and his black hair as dark as night. But she remembered his cruel words, and her goodwill toward him evaporated. She didn't want to think about him anymore. He upset her balance too much.

Well, she sure wouldn't let him upset her! If she never saw him again, it wouldn't matter. She didn't need him in her life interfering with her plans anyway.

Forcing her mind away from Gray, Baines ran her sleepy glance around the perimeter of the room as another chill assailed her, almost as if cool night air crept in through a crack. She still found nothing out of the ordinary, only the window. . . .

With a frown, Baines sat up abruptly and stared at the window. It was raised slightly, and just then another breeze blew, ruffling the curtain. Sliding off the cot, she went for a closer look.

"Dang!" she said aloud, shutting the window tightly. "Someone did come in through the window." Queasiness churned within her stomach, fear and mint julep mixing and threatening to spill out. Again she cursed the fancy drink, and Grayling Dunston as well.

He hadn't believed her, then she'd hastily forced him to leave. But hadn't she always faced her fears alone? At an early age she'd learned to allay her own fears. Uncle Lincoln was gone so much she doubted he would know *how* to comfort her when she had a rare nightmare.

Nightmares, however, were altogether different from

this. Once she awoke, the nightmare ended, but who knew if a thief would return to get something he suddenly remembered.

She considered going to Miz Annabelle's or even to the Horse and Mule to see if Luther needed a hand tonight, but quickly decided against it. She didn't relish roaming about Rivertown in the dead of night on her own.

Rubbing her hands up and down her arms in an effort to calm herself, she walked around the room. Before she could sleep, she needed to feel sheltered, but she needed to sleep so the aftereffects of the alcohol could wear off.

Her dilemma identified, she dragged a chair to the door and pushed it under the knob; then she went to the window. What could she do to make it safe?

Baines sat at the small, weak-legged table and drummed her fingers on the surface. Feeling vulnerable for the first time in a long time, she wondered how she could make herself feel secure again.

She shook her head in amazement. She had nothing worth stealing. That quilt had probably been the most valuable thing in the house, and it had already been taken.

Her gaze fell on the poker that she used for their pot-bellied stove. She could use the poker to wedge between the top and middle part of the window to prevent someone from raising it again.

Silently applauding her astuteness, she got the poker and did her task, then she rechecked the door latch and the soundness of the chair beneath the knob.

Starting back to her cot in the alcove, she detected a brass-colored button near the window. Picking it up, she frowned. It was just a button, perhaps one she and Miz Annabelle failed to notice when they'd tidied up their sewing mess. Hmm. She had no brass buttons on her gown.

Holding the button next to the candlelight, she examined it more closely. It looked familiar. Where had she seen it before? But who paid attention to buttons? It didn't belong to Uncle Lincoln, so who . . . ?

A scene flashed into her memory. Just last week Uncle Lincoln and his friend, Eli Washington, had sat at the table

to eat the meal her uncle bought for her to fix. A button
on Eli's shirt came undone, and Baines offered to tighten
it for him. Eli had promised to bring it by later because he
hadn't wanted to expose his bare chest to her.

He never came back. Until tonight.

The thieving riverworm. She knew it was the same button because the surface had an *E* scratched on it, the way
this one had.

Uncle Lincoln trusted him, and so did Baines. But Eli
stole her quilt, and it wasn't even cold out! Why would Eli
steal her quilt? Was there something special about it that
he knew? Maybe there was. Otherwise, why had Gray been
so determined to retrieve it?

Baines walked back to the alcove and sat on the cot,
placing the button beneath her pillow. She had some thinking to do.

Eli would probably be at the Horse and Mule tomorrow
evening, as he was every Sunday, acting as innocent as a
newborn babe. Baines glowered at the ceiling. She planned
to render him as helpless as a babe if he didn't produce the
quilt. And then, after she took advantage of her much-
wanted chance to study it, she would *sell* it to His Lordship,
for five thousand dollars!

For his unwarranted accusations and the loss of her quilt,
she decided to make him pay. The money would go to good
use. Five thousand dollars would be enough money to get
her and Uncle Lincoln out of Rivertown, move them up on
the bluff, and still leave enough for her to open her shop.
Then no high-and-mighty rich man could ever accuse her
of being a thief or a liar again.

She reckoned Gray could afford her price. If he wanted
that danged quilt bad enough, that is.

A small niggling of doubt entered her mind, but she
shoved it aside. And she dared not think of the kiss he'd
given her. He'd probably kissed a hundred women, but she
felt certain she had been the only woman he'd kissed in
America.

Still, that didn't give her a great deal of satisfaction, especially since she figured out *why* he'd kissed her so pas-

sionately. He hadn't really felt anything special for her. He'd only wanted her to give him the quilt.

The way she'd felt in his arms had been the sweetest and most intense experience she'd ever had. But she wouldn't let that deter her again. She wouldn't let *him* deter her again, with his handsome face and tempting words.

Grayling Dunston was a swine, with one goal in mind—that bloomin' quilt. Well, he would get it, and she would get more money at one time than she ever thought she would.

Still, she regretted the day she ever laid eyes on that quilt. She had never been made to feel more aware of her poverty than she had been tonight. If Gray hadn't wanted the quilt, he never would have invited her to Dunland, and she wouldn't have gotten measured up by that bunch of witches.

Tears stung her eyes, and she blinked them away. She hated Gray, and she disliked herself. He hadn't really wanted her as his guest at Dunland. He'd only used her. Consumed with getting out of poverty and wanting to live the way that his family did, she'd naively believed him.

9

"GOOD MORNING, GRAY," DEEDRIA chirped as he made his way to the dining table. "I trust you had a pleasant rest?"

"Pleasant enough." Without elaborating, Gray paused beside the table and stared outside, doing his best not to think of Baines and her role in the disappearance of Mary's Fortune.

The sun gleamed through the open draperies, the spotless window framing the front gallery and the lawn beyond in all its glory. Crimson splashes of azaleas and camellias posed a striking contrast to the green grass. Slender pines stood tall and erect, and massive oaks bearded with Spanish moss lined the drive leading to the gallery. A mockingbird landed on the lacy iron railing, and Gray tensed in this serene setting. His thoughts were anything but serene.

He admitted to being quite impressed with his American relatives and their home. In the short week he'd been at Dunland, he could hardly credit how his perception had changed about his family. Remembering that he'd considered them a quaint bunch of consanguines, he shifted his weight uneasily. He wondered at his change of heart.

Maybe Baines was responsible, or maybe the fact that he was facing poverty himself helped. With a self-pitying sigh, Gray discredited both thoughts. More than likely his bone-deep weariness from sitting up the entire night worrying about Baines and wondering about Mary's Fortune softened his attitude.

"If I die and wind up in hell, Gray, it'll be your fault."

DeEdria's soft, teasing voice reached his brain. Her words sinking in, Gray smiled politely. "And how is that, my dear?" Turning his attention to her, he remained standing. He had no appetite to eat. However hard he tried to deny it, Baines's welfare was uppermost in his mind.

"Because of your party, I missed church this morning. I just couldn't remove myself from bed when Roc went to preside over the slaves' service."

"I'm sure your indiscretions will be forgiven, DeEdria, so don't fret." Gray turned his look indulgent and squeezed her hand gently. It was a delicate, soft hand, pale and unmarked, and so unlike Baines's small, reddened hands that a shudder passed through him.

As the mistress of a large household, DeEdria worked as hard as Baines. But where one worked hard at giving orders, however kindly said, the other actually *worked*.

"I sure hope you're right, Gray." She raised a speculative brow. "You're not going to sit?"

Gray considered her offer, then thought of Baines once again, alone with her fears and anger. In spite of last night and his suspicions, he wanted to see her. Until he did, he couldn't relax. "I have an errand to run, DeEdria, so I'll skip breakfast. I expect to join you later today for evening repast."

DeEdria laughed softly, her velvety brown eyes twinkling. "She surely must have made a mighty impression on you, Gray," she teased, and nodded to the mahogany dining chair to her left. "Do sit down. Your Baines is safe. Since you were so adamant last night about having someone watch her house, Roc followed your instructions to the letter."

He expelled a breath of relief, both at hearing of Baines's safety and because he didn't have to face her this morning. At odds with his feelings about her, he wasn't sure what he would do if he saw her. Hug her tightly to him to assure himself that she was indeed fine or shake her thoroughly to get the truth from her?

He seated himself, and DeEdria rang for a servant. "She isn't *my* Baines," he grumbled, irritated that he couldn't camouflage his desire for the girl, and also at DeEdria's jesting. "She's merely a young woman who appeared in jeopardy and deserved to be protected. Since I was unable to rush back down the hill, vigilance by Roc's workers was the next safest solution."

A slave girl appeared, carrying a tray loaded with platters of thickly sliced ham, steaming grits slathered with butter, freshly baked buttermilk biscuits, apple jelly, scrambled eggs, and hot tea. She smiled at Gray as she set each dish before him. When she was done, she asked, "Would ya like anythin' else, Masta Gray?"

"No, thank you, Sally."

Sally scuttled away, her empty tray dangling from her hand.

His appetite still hadn't returned, and Gray scowled at the massive amount of food. When he wondered if Baines ever saw this much food in a week, his scowl deepened. Why did he suddenly associate every bloody thing with that blasted girl?

Against his will, he asked his next question. "Did anyone approach her house?"

"No, Gray. Roc's men said Baines emerged from the house this morning and went over the Bluff."

"Over the Bluff?"

DeEdria nodded, a curl in her upswept tawny blond hair bouncing. "It's a place most folks from Rivertown move to when they can afford to leave Natchez-Under-the-Hill. Mind you, it's nothing like what we have here on the hill, but it's a sight better than where they come from."

He wondered who Baines knew on the Bluff. Was it a suitor or someone who had the quilt?

"How well do you know Baines Marshall?"

"Why, Gray, I never saw her before last night." DeEdria laughed. "Have you become smitten with her?"

Gray ignored her good-natured goading and said instead,

"I only thought you could tell me why she would go on the Bluff."

"Maybe to visit Annabelle Shepard. She's the seamstress for most folks in the area," DeEdria clarified at Gray's questioning look. "She's done sewing for some of the ladies in my church group."

"I recall Baines telling me about a 'Miz Annabelle' who helped fancy her dress up. Since some of your guests asked Baines to make them new gowns, my guess would be that she went to see this Annabelle Shepard."

"Could be you're right," DeEdria agreed. "I am sure she'll be safe enough there, so relax and enjoy some breakfast. If you truly wish to get hold of Baines, I can have her up for afternoon refreshments."

Gray considered DeEdria's offer and admitted how badly he wanted to see Baines today. But he wanted to see her away from the probing eyes of his family. "It won't be necessary to disturb her, my dear. If she is in fact at Annabelle's, I'm sure I'll see her sometime later."

DeEdria shook her head. "A man of confidence. That's what I like about the Dunston men. They're all so sure of themselves." She laughed. "Take Roc for instance. He's so sure you will be available to entertain Belinda tonight that he didn't bother to ask your plans."

Tonight Gray planned to interrogate Miss Baines Marshall again about his missing quilt. Roc shouldn't have been so presumptuous of his time.

"Roc should have asked," Gray imparted. He hated the crestfallen look that crossed DeEdria's features, so he relented. Besides, he did have a thing or two to settle with Belinda Myers. He smiled gently. "Perhaps Belinda will agree to return another time. I do have plans tonight."

"Oh, Gray, you're just going to love Belinda. She's a widow, but with a most wonderful sense of humor. She's also a very competent hostess and—"

"Enough!" Gray commanded, his patience coming to an end as he listened to DeEdria drone on about Belinda's fine points. "I have no wish to hear about Belinda Myers anymore. I do not like hypocrites, DeEdria." He raised his hand to still her protest. "She pretended to apologize to Baines and then maligned her behind her back. I appreciate your defense of Baines, but the only reason I wish to see Belinda again is to warn her away from mocking Baines further. Do I make myself clear?"

DeEdria nodded, but a speculative gleam lit her eyes. "Of course, Gray," she said gently. "As soon as Roc returns from his obligations in town, I will inform him of your other plans."

"Very good." He took a sip of his now tepid tea and stood, moving restlessly to the window. The scenery should have soothed him, but it didn't. He wondered what kind of plans beyond asking Baines once again to tell him what really happened to his quilt did he actually have.

Last night he'd been ambiguous about her explanation, and perhaps overly concerned about her safety. But his attraction for her was certainly not in question. She was as much on his mind as Mary's Fortune.

"Do you think you'll find your quilt soon, Gray?" DeEdria asked, as though she'd read his mind.

Gray forced his attention back to the talkative woman. "I hope so."

He wanted to hear no more talk of Belinda and the bloody matrimony trap Roc was setting for him. The quilt and only the quilt was his priority while in this country. Not Belinda Myers and the countless others like her. And especially not Baines Marshall, whose face could haunt a man's dreams and invade his conscious thoughts.

He admired her pluckiness and couldn't forget her kiss. Baines . . .

Bloody hell! He must endeavor to remember the next time he saw her that she wasn't pertinent to his situation. Only Mary's Fortune was.

10

BAINES'S VACILLATING EMOTIONS OVER the stolen quilt and Eli's treachery, coupled with her hurt feelings over Gray's accusations, prevented her from sleeping.

Finally, at the crack of dawn, she gave up her battle, and sunrise found Baines sitting down to work on her uncle's crazy quilt, a piping-hot cup of coffee on the table before her. Her door ajar to allow fresh morning air inside, Baines listened as the riverfront slowly awakened.

The sun crept lazily from the horizon, turning the sky a deep rosy red. A rooster cock-a-doodle-dooed, and a dog barked in answer. A donkey cart clattered down the lane, and on the river Baines noticed a keelboat heading for the landing not far away.

Still, her tiredness and annoyance didn't allow her to enjoy the sights and sounds. Sipping her coffee, she sighed and picked up her quilting needle.

Avoiding any black strips, she pointedly chose a batch of colorful patches to stitch together, hoping to brighten her mood. The betrayal she felt by both Eli and Gray cut deeply. She knew Eli was a thief, a man who stole every chance he got. But she never thought him capable of stealing from his friends, especially her and Uncle Linc.

And to steal her precious quilt, of all things! The good-for-nothing snake. Family was important to Baines, and she thought of Eli Washington as such. In return, he'd misused her trust and Uncle Linc's as well.

Not wanting to admit how crushed she was, Baines swiped away an angry tear and sewed a green patch to a blue one, then added that to the crazy quilt. She set her quilting needle down and picked up her cup, taking a generous swallow of coffee. The warm liquid felt good going down and helped to keep her energy up, if not her spirits.

A steamboat whistle blew, and she returned to her quilting, sewing strips and patches together in mindful disarray. When she got a big enough block, she stitched it to the quilt.

For three hours she worked with furious vitality, trying not to think of Gray, trying only to picture Uncle Linc's surprise when she handed him his quilt.

Gray had deceived her, after all. Why would she want to think about him? But she had allowed herself to be deceived, hadn't she? At the chance to enter the fancy world of the wealthy, she'd lost all perspective. Deep down, she'd known why Gray invited her to Dunland. Yet she'd denied the quilt had been the reason, denied everything but the undefinable pull she felt toward Gray.

Well, she sure wouldn't allow her emotions to interfere with her plans to move to the Bluff. Not ever again. Gray's deceiving interest in her suited her just fine, leaving no complication in the way of her goal. He'd made his intentions gospel clear, and she wasn't included in them.

Well, *she* had a dream, too. A purpose. And it wasn't Lord Grayling Dunston, the arrogant Earl of Montegut. Since meeting him, he'd only enforced her desire to get out of poverty.

Nothing or no one would prevent her from attaining her goal.

With staid determination, she gulped the last of her now cold coffee. Glancing at the battered clock on the wall above the cushioned bench, she realized she would be late for work at Miz Annabelle's if she didn't hurry.

After quickly tidying up her mess and laying the quilt

back on the rack, she grabbed her tattered reticule and rushed out the door, closing it firmly behind her.

∞

MIZ ANNABELLE PLACED A straw bonnet on her head and smiled at Baines. "You sure did a grand job on Miz Franklin's day gown, darlin'."

Still on its dress form, Baines picked up the striped gown and followed Miz Annabelle through the breezeway as they left the sewing room that also served as a fitting area and kitchen. The shop was one of the older buildings on the Bluff and fashioned in the dogtrot style.

Reaching the receiving room, the scent of floral potpourri assailed Baines's nostrils. Painted in a lemony yellow, it was cheery and warm, reflecting Miz Annabelle's good taste. Bursts of flowers graced the walnut sofa table and counter. A cream-colored damask settee sat by the big side window. The opposite corner held a table with patterns and color swatches, among other things. Directly behind the counter stood a rack filled with ready-to-wear clothes and Baines's stool. Dress shapes with frilled gowns and elegant evening wear stood before the front window, beckoning to customers.

"She'll be in directly to fetch it. Make sure you box it real pretty for her. That is, after she inspects it as she's always wont to do."

Baines set the gowned dress form behind the counter and shook her head. "She's a caution, that Miz Franklin. Real full of herself. I don't reckon you like her much, Miz Annabelle."

Tying the emerald ribbon on her bonnet into a bow beneath her chin, Miz Annabelle narrowed her eyes. "Well, I declare, Baines Marshall," she huffed with indignation. "How would you know that? I never said how I felt about her one way or another. Have you gone and become a mind reader?"

Brushing an imagined wrinkle out of the gown's skirt, Baines shrugged. "I'm not readin' your mind, Miz Annabelle," she answered calmly, "just your actions. Seems to me you're fixin' to leave. You always make a point of not bein' here whenever Miz Franklin is due to arrive. I sure didn't mean my words to offend you."

Miz Annabelle ruffled a red curl peaking from under her bonnet and burst out laughing. "You're the caution, child, and you knows me like a book. I can't stand that woman's uppity ways," she admitted. "Always lookin' down her nose at everyone. You know, she even did it to her own husband when he was alive? A man nicer than Sam Franklin couldn't be found." She pulled on a white lacy glove, her agitation obvious with that gesture. "The only reason I accept that woman's business is because she's a good customer and she pays my price." She walked to the door. Hand on the brass doorknob, she looked at Baines. "I'd better leave before I run into her. If I don't get back before closin' time, darlin', just lock up, and I'll see you tomorrow. Remember, there's sweet biscuits and coffee in the kitchen if you get a hankerin' for somethin' to eat."

"Thanks, Miz Annabelle," Baines called as the woman stepped out the door.

Alone in the shop, Baines gave Miz Franklin's gown another inspection. Pride filled her. This really was one of her finer pieces of work. It had taken her all of three days to complete, and although Miz Annabelle instructed her on how it should be finished, this time she'd allowed Baines to use her own judgment.

Yet the widow's skill at sewing intimidated Baines. She knew if she was ever to be as successful at sewing as she was at quilting, she would have to overcome her fears that she would never be as good as Annabelle Shepard. The more she worried, it seemed the worse her gowns turned out—as was the case with the ecru gown for Gray's party.

After all of Miz Annabelle's work on it, the society ladies had still disdained Baines. What would have happened if she'd gone there wearing it as she had fashioned it? She shuddered to think.

She was glad that night was over, glad that she would never have to be subjected to such treatment again. In the cold light of day, she still hated Gray for inviting her into his world.

He'd known exactly what would happen. But he hadn't cared. To get that quilt back, he would have seen her burned at the stake if it had been called for.

Cursing his heartlessness, she went to the table where the patterns and other sewing notions lay. Scissors, thread, dress patterns, and material sat in orderly arrangement. Baines insisted on keeping it that way because it was easier for her to pick things out without a hassle, and Miz Annabelle seemed to like the tidiness.

Going right to the partially finished bodice, Baines pulled her stool from behind the counter and began stitching white lace onto the front.

Making small, delicate stitches, Baines admitted that her sewing skill showed itself in every gesture. She smiled grimly. With every needle puncture, she imagined Grayling Dunston the recipient of each prick.

Uppity nabob.

She *would* lift herself out of poverty. But only because she didn't want to be poor, not because she wanted to be one of them. She would *never* become one of them. Cruel and insulting with no thought to another person's feelings. Bettering herself wouldn't mean looking down her nose at folks less fortunate than she.

Like that Belinda Myers. The snooty witch. She'd made the kind gesture only to impress Gray, not because she sincerely meant it. Wondering if Gray believed the woman's display, jealousy sparked through Baines, and she lost her concentration. The needle jabbed her finger, and she cried out in surprise, then popped the injured digit into her mouth.

Baines's head snapped up at the sound of someone clearing her throat.

"How long do you intend to let me stand here, girl?"

The imperious female voice nearly wrecked Baines's aplomb. Heat suffused her cheeks. It was just her luck that Miz Franklin would find her nursing her injury.

Baines stood. Head held high, she flipped her long braid

over her shoulder. "Why, Miz Franklin, ma'am, I didn't hear you come in. I was rather absorbed—"

Miz Franklin placed her hands on her hips. "I don't want your excuses, Baines," she declared. "Nothing's more important than your customer. Remember that. Now. I am here to fetch my new day gown. Where is it? And where is Mrs. Shepard?"

Baines drew in an agitated breath before answering. Miz Annabelle had the right idea when she left. Baines wished she had gone with her. She sincerely wanted to tell Miz Franklin a thing or two, but knew she had to hold her tongue. The huffy woman was one of Miz Annabelle's best customers, and Baines could ill afford to offend her.

Miz Annabelle would never forgive her if she did. She swallowed her intended retort. "Miz Annabelle was called away unexpected, Miz Franklin," she explained with a tight smile. "She regrets she couldn't be here. I'm truly sorry I didn't hear you come in. Let me show you your gown, ma'am."

Gritting her teeth, Baines hurried to the gown. How much more scorn could she tolerate from the likes of Gray and this woman? Would she, too, forget her beginnings if she ever became rich? Or at most, realized her dream and lived on the bluff?

If not for her uncle, she would give up her dream of leaving Rivertown, if she thought such a move would change her. Yet even if she discovered a change in herself was inevitable, she couldn't stop fighting to make a better way, because she wanted her uncle to live easy and free of crime.

She promised herself she would never become a Belinda Myers or a Roberta Franklin.

"What do you think of it, Miz Franklin?" she asked, watching as the woman fingered the gown on the busty form.

Miz Franklin looked at it from back to front, then up and down. "Well, I can find no fault." She sounded disappointed at that discovery.

"Shall I put it in a box for you, Miz Franklin?"

Her expression turned derisive. "I'll certainly not accept it unpackaged, girl," she snapped. "I'll wait in my carriage. Bring it out when you're done." With that, Miz Franklin bustled out the door.

Baines surprised herself at the pity she felt for the woman. She should have been angrier, but she couldn't help herself. If Miz Franklin didn't have money, she would have nothing, not even a personality. She needed to throw her weight around to get noticed.

Retrieving a cardboard box from the other room, Baines took the gown off the form and boxed it. Then she brought it outside to the waiting carriage and handed it to Miz Franklin.

"Thank you, girl." Miz Franklin pressed some gold coins into Baines's hand. "This is the price I agreed to pay Mrs. Shepard. See that she gets it." Without waiting for a response, she commanded her driver to move.

"Now, there's a woman used to having her way," a masculine voice said with wry amusement.

Baines turned to the accented sound. A tall, golden-haired man smiled down at her. It was windy today, and the breeze blew through his long hair, setting it askew. "I beg your pardon?"

The man laughed, briefly illuminating his pale eyes. "I meant no offense, mistress. I overheard the tone of the woman's voice and thought her rather rude."

The stranger could quite possibly be good-looking, although she couldn't tell because he had a thick mustache and a beard covering most of his jaw.

He seemed friendly enough, but the black shirt and breeches he wore gave him a rakish appearance. Standing with an air of confidence, he looked as if he prided himself on his well-proportioned body.

"It's just her way, mister," she answered, regarding him with curiosity. He was too richly dressed and his voice too finely educated to be a riverboat man. "She knows no other way to be."

"I see."

"Are you from England?" she blurted, unable to temper the question.

Again that devil-may-care smile crossed his features. A cloud rolled by and covered the sun for a brief second. "Born and bred."

"Well, what are you doin' here?"

He reminded her of Gray. Especially those sad, remote eyes, as if he had secrets that ached to be revealed. Like Gray.

"Just . . . um . . . looking for someone."

"I know just about everyone in these parts." Baines told herself she didn't care what gnawed at Gray. The quicker she forgot him, the easier it would be for her. "Maybe I can help you."

"Maybe," the man agreed. "But I wouldn't want to put you through the trouble. Besides I want to surprise the person I'm seeking. That woman who just left here, I suppose, is one of the gentry of this region. Who is she?"

"Why, that's Miz Roberta Franklin. She's the widow of Samuel Franklin. He was a sugar planter and left her well off when he passed away. But still she ain't the wealthiest nabob in these parts."

"Oh?" A blond brow shot up when Baines didn't continue. "Then who is?"

"Why, it's the Dunstons."

The stranger's interest piqued. "Really?"

Baines nodded proudly. "They're even wealthy enough to have English kin. Well, at least *one* English kin."

"I see," he said with a laugh. "So, being wealthy and having English relatives sets one in a category all by itself, huh?"

Baines giggled at his amused observation.

Regarding her casually, he stroked his beard. "I suppose you wouldn't know the name of the Dunstons' English kin, would you, mistress?"

"I suppose I do," Baines retorted. "him bein' an English lord and all that. It's Graylin' Dunston, and he'ain't no better than any other wealthy snob."

At the mention of Gray's name, Baines thought she detected a hint of recognition in the bearded face. Quite possibly, the man knew Gray. They were both English, and he seemed mighty interested in the Dunstons.

"How would you know he's a snob? Unless you and he—"

"I don't like where you're headin' with your speculation, mister," Baines asserted.

He assumed she was a woman of loose morals simply because she had hinted at knowing an English lord. In doing so, he suggested a woman of her status was only good enough for one thing with a man like the Earl of Montegut.

Lately, it seemed at every turn, someone was reminding her of her poverty, she reflected with bitterness. She stiffened her resolve, but the desperation she always managed to hold at bay lurked in the shadows, threatening and foreboding. But she wouldn't be defeated. She wouldn't show her vulnerability.

She was nearly trembling with newfound determination. She glared at him, hoping the reproach she felt for the stranger burned in her eyes.

"I don't reckon it's your business how or what I know about Graylin' Dunston," she spat out. "If you're aimin' to buy somethin' from the sewin' shop, I'll sell it to you. If not, just get on your way and leave me be."

"My mistake," he said with a sly smile. "I don't suppose you have any pearl-studded reticules? I promised to bring someone back a gift when I returned to England."

"No," Baines said icily. "We only make reticules on special order." She shot him a cold look. But worry for Gray overtook her anger at the stranger's insinuation. She should have cautioned her information, but now unease swept through her.

Could he be searching for Gray for a reason? Did it have anything to do with that blasted quilt? Was Gray in some kind of trouble? And if he was, was this man there to help him or hurt him?

"Thank you for your time, mistress." The man dipped his head slightly, then sauntered off.

Baines watched him as he walked to the tavern just down

the block and disappeared through the doors.

Sunshine beat down upon her, but a hesitant drop of rain hit her cheek, and she frowned, gazing up at the sky. Except for a cloud here and there, the sun was indeed shining, and rain was beginning to fall, the sight odd and beautiful as always.

On her way back to the shop, Baines wondered if the sunny rain foretold a sign of things to come.

11

BAINES TRIED TO PUT the strange man out of her mind, but she couldn't because of Gray. She sat at her work table and folded her arms, rapidly tapping her foot in frustration. Last night had left no doubt about her attraction for him. This morning, leadened with fatigue and hurt, she was still attracted to him.

Her anger at Gray had lessened a mite, replaced by misgivings for his safety. Although Grayling Dunston's safety shouldn't have concerned her after his treatment of her, she felt even an animal deserved some worry over its well being.

But Gray was a human being, stunning in his maleness. She doubted, however, that he would caution himself over *her* safekeeping.

Grabbing the bodice that she had been working on when Miz Franklin interrupted her, Baines tried to concentrate on her task. She still had three more lonely hours ahead of her at the shop before heading to the Horse and Mule, and the silence was deafening. She wished Miz Annabelle would return, but experience told her that the widow was gone for the day.

Jabbing the needle into the material, Baines pricked her finger for the umpteenth time that day. "Dang!"

A deep, husky voice snapped her head up. "Good afternoon, Miss Marshall."

Her regard fell on Gray, and her heart sped up foolishly. He practically filled the doorway as he inclined his dark head. Aristocratic as always, buff-colored riding breeches and a dark blue topcoat covered his tall frame.

For a moment surprise took away her ability to speak, and she blinked, then narrowed her eyes. Her resentment returned in full force, and she forgot her concern as well as her attraction. Had he come to finish debasing her?

She threw the bodice aside once again and stood from her seat. Head high and shoulders stiff, she walked toward him, deciding to treat him simply as a customer.

"Can I help you, sir?" she asked frostily.

Dipping his head slightly, Gray chuckled without amusement and fixed his icy blue gaze on her. But Baines saw beneath his annoyance and anger. She saw the naked fear that his eyes revealed and the unmistakable hurt that marred his features.

She swallowed a gasp, her throat closing at his expression. He seemed lost and without hope. What could possibly cause such grief? Surely it couldn't be solely his loss of the quilt?

At that thought, she faltered. But he had accused her of having something to do with its disappearance. He had also used her thoroughly. How could she feel sorry for him?

She did, however. She wanted to reach out and wipe the sadness away. Yet she couldn't. For whatever reason he'd come, she doubted his interest was genuine.

Gray stepped fully into the shop, and Baines's pulse pounded as he stopped inches from her. She told herself it was because she didn't want another argument, but she knew her reaction was caused by his nearness.

Baines raised her chin. "Well?" she asked, successfully controlling her roiling emotions, wondering if he had come to purchase something for Belinda Myers. "Is there somethin' I can help you with?"

"No," came the husky reply.

An electrifying shudder rocked her body at the sound of

his voice. She stood very still, waiting to hear what he would say next, hating the hope that she felt, knowing it was misplaced.

But Gray remained silent, and she wondered if he was ill or drunk. He didn't appear drunk, however, yet his actions at the moment were so unlike the bold, powerful man she'd grown used to.

"Why are you here?" she finally asked, her curiosity overtaking her best intentions to dismiss him.

"I'm here because I've been remiss, Baines," Gray explained. "It wasn't very chivalrous of me last night to leave you alone—"

He stepped even closer to her, and his hard thigh brushed hers. She inhaled sharply and stepped back slightly, needing distance between them if she wanted to keep her head. "You must be believin' I was robbed, then," she whispered, hope welling within her. But she wouldn't show it. She couldn't allow him to know what power he had over her.

Instead of agreeing with her, however, he said, "What I believe is irrelevant. I saw to your house being guarded last night. But I realized today that I needed to see for myself that you are truly safe."

Her lips parted in surprise, and his words nearly sent her reeling. Of all the reasons she'd expected to hear from him about his being at Miz Annabelle's shop, concern for her wasn't one of them. She searched his face for the truth, but saw no reason to doubt him.

The quilt was gone, and Gray couldn't know that she suspected Eli of stealing it. So what other reason except genuine worry about her well being could there be?

Her heart danced in delight. "Y-you had my house guarded?"

"Aye," Gray answered, taking a step nearer. "It had nothing to do with the quilt. I am not a fickle man, Baines. One has nothing to do with the other."

Didn't it, though?

Gray sounded so tormented. Dang! Doubt intruded upon Baines's sudden happiness. If the quilt hadn't been stolen, he wouldn't have had to see to her safety. Yet he had sent a watchman, and Baines attempted to understand his reasoning, his humble demeanor.

After last night she'd thought his only interest in her lay with the quilt. But today she wasn't so sure. Could he possibly be interested in *her* as well?

"Why did you send a guard to my house?" Baines questioned. "Somethin' I was unaware of till this moment."

"A necessary precaution," Gray replied, pulling her into his strong embrace. "Nothing is worth putting you at risk, not even the obligation I have to find the quilt."

He locked his mouth with hers, and Baines's pulse spun out of control. His behavior as well as her emotions bewildered her. Last night he accused her of stealing; today he worried about her safety and now kissed her with need and desperation. Likewise, she thought to stay angry with him and distance herself from what could only hurt her in the end, but her resistance melted the moment she gazed into his eyes. She locked her arms around his neck and barely clung to the reality that stood between them. She savored the feel of his demanding mouth against her own. He nibbled at her earlobes and moved along the column of her throat. Desire sizzled through her, and she wanted to linger in his arms and surrender to him.

When Gray ended the kiss, he enfolded her within his embrace and kissed the top of her head. For a moment Baines rested her head on his chest, her mind racing. What type of obligation forced Gray to search for a quilt? Did it indeed hold the secrets she sensed within the design? If so, did the other nabob who'd come sniffing about know of the quilt and what the patterns meant? Even as those countless questions plagued her, an amazing sense of contentment spread through her. She pressed a kiss to the hollow of his neck and stepped back, barely standing on her own power.

The pained look on his handsome face touched her soul. Smiling hesitantly, she caressed his clean-shaven jaw with her hand. Abruptly, as if by magic, all traces of Gray's despair disappeared from his expression. He gave her a long, smoldering look, melting every other emotion except hot anticipation.

"I'm grateful you're well," he said. He opened his mouth to say something else, but hesitated and glanced over her head. He sighed. When he looked at her again, his demeanor was rigid once more. "I'd best go now and leave you to your chores." Walking swiftly to the door, he stopped at the entryway. "Do your later plans include that . . . tavern?" he asked scornfully.

"Y-Yes," Baines managed, weak-kneed, disappointed, and hurt at his abrupt change.

"I see," Gray said. "Good day, Baines."

Gray hurried out of the shop, his manhood hard with need. He had to get away from Baines before he seduced her. After he'd spoken to DeEdria, he thought the matter had been decided. When Roc returned from the slaves' sermon, the two of them had gone riding over Dunland's vast grounds, not deterred by the rainfall that had come while the sun still glistened in the sky.

Still, thoughts of Baines plagued Gray, and he knew he had to see her. Without questioning his need in depth, he'd gone hell-bent-for-leather to the shop.

Then he saw her, so perfect, so beautiful, and he'd realized how thoroughly he'd used her; he realized, too, that not only did he want to assure himself of her safety, but he wanted to apologize to her. Yet he hadn't. Not really, anyway. His pride—and mistrust—had stood in the way of him saying anything other than he'd been remiss.

Once he'd spoken to her, however, he should have gone, but he'd had to taste her sweet lips and feel her soft body. If he were less principled, he *would* have seduced her.

Gray released a self-deprecating laugh. Exactly how principled was he after he'd misused Baines so totally; if he toyed with her emotions, knowing there could be nothing between them other then shared passion; if he still held back his complete trust in her?

After their kiss, he'd almost told her about Mary's Fortune and its secrets. But he hadn't been able to reconcile his cynicism about her integrity with his need to share his problems with her.

As he returned to the palomino and mounted it, he stared one last time at the shop. The rain had ceased, but droplets of water from the earlier showers clung to the flowers in the boxes outside the inviting building. He saw Baines move back to her work space, and his heartstrings pulled.

In that instant he decided he would pay a visit to the Horse and Mule during Baines's shift tonight.

⁓

FIVE MINUTES LATER BAINES still sat at her worktable, staring out of the window, tapping her foot on the floor. Gray's actions puzzled and bothered her. His kiss told her his disturbing visit had more to do with her than the quilt. That should've made her deliriously happy, but still she couldn't fully relax or trust his intentions.

Gray had seemed on the verge of telling her something, but somehow wouldn't. Or maybe couldn't. He had a powerful amount of pride, and that probably made him tongue-tied. And although he tried to hide it, his sadness reached the core of him. The mere loss of a quilt wouldn't cause such turmoil to a man's soul. Could there be another reason?

In spite of the unpleasant circumstances surrounding the quilt, Baines's heart still sang. Gray had made a special trip to assure himself of her well being. He didn't apologize for his actions last night, but that didn't matter. His visit spoke a whole dang library of volumes.

Should she read something into that visit? In the short time she'd known Gray, he'd never seemed more sincere to her than he did today. Not only did he make her more aware of her attraction for him, but he'd made her more aware of *his* feelings for *her*.

In spite of all his raging, he had thought to protect her. Baines drew in a shaky breath. Of course, all this was speculation on her part. Maybe even wishful thinking.

But one thing was true. Gray knew she didn't have the

quilt. What he did last night wasn't for the quilt. It had been for her!

For a fleeting moment he'd allowed Baines to glimpse another side of him—a side that was tender and vulnerable—and she felt with all her heart that *she'd* touched that part of him.

She doubted that she would ever again see that emotion in him or that he would ever mention it. His primary goal was still the quilt, but the gesture he made toward her today heightened her feelings for him. Nothing would change that.

Her bewitching encounter with Gray didn't raise her expectations regarding him, however. Just as she was certain he wouldn't call attention to his strange behavior, neither would she when next she saw him.

That he came at all was deserving of her discretion.

Taking up her needle again, she sighed. She only hoped he wouldn't completely revert to his old self again and cause her to lose her temper. Although she rarely lost her self-control, she usually regretted her actions when she did.

Not that he wouldn't deserve to be called a dang riverworm for his uppity ways.

Smiling to herself, she hastened to finish the bodice she was working on in order to leave on time to go to the Horse and Mule. She couldn't wait to confront Eli again, and afterward she would go to Dunland and tell Gray about her discovery.

12

"WHAT'S YORE PROBLEM T'NIGHT, Baines?"

Luther Shelton stood behind the long wooden bar where he served drinks at the Horse and Mule. Part Natchez Indian, his intelligent chocolate-colored eyes studied Baines closely as she wiped away the drink she had spilled.

"You been grumpy ever since you came in."

Baines wouldn't explain what a tumultuous day she'd had after suffering a miserable night. The only thing she felt proud of was the work she'd done on Uncle Linc's quilt this morning, accomplishing more than she had in six days.

Gray's visit earlier today still dismayed her, even as the thought of his concern warmed her and the remembered feel of his lips against her own sent feverish urges through her body. The more she thought about him and the type of man she suspected him to be, the more she realized that he'd come as close to an apology as someone of his standing could.

Now, however, after such a long, emotional day, she was tired and irritable and not just a little vexed with Eli. It seemed the passing hours only increased her anger, and the appearance of the blond stranger hadn't helped.

At the time she hadn't thought to ask for his name, but now she regretted not doing so. It could have been useful if anything untoward occurred. Each time she remembered his casual interest, a wave of unease swept through her.

Gray was possibly in danger, and she couldn't let her emotions over Eli's treachery stand in the way of warning him to take caution. After today's encounter with the Earl of Montegut, Baines's desperation to find the quilt became even more acute. She wanted to help Gray any way she could, and something told her finding the quilt would be a big help, which only added to the disappointment she felt because she hadn't seen Eli tonight. Just where was he? Baines smiled grimly. More than likely, he was enjoying the comforts of her quilt—that's if he hadn't already sold it for quick cash.

Yet it wasn't fair for her to take out her problems on Luther. He was her friend and deserved some explanation. She settled on the easiest one.

"I'm sorry, Luther," Baines answered tightly, her nerves on cdgc. "It's just that I cxpcctcd to scc Eli—"

"Oh, he ain't comin' in t'night. He done gone down to New Orleens to ketch a ship. He's hopin' he can git there and connect wit' ole Linc."

"What!"

Baines's furious shout attracted unwanted attention.

A man she'd never seen before leered at her from his spot at the bar. "Don't fret, missy. I kin keep comp'ny wit' you as good as yore Eli." Getting up from the stool, he started toward where she stood.

"Territorial encroachment is a dangerous offense, my friend," a voice low, challenging, and edged with steel announced.

Baines gasped at the sound, amazed, shaken, and momentarily stunned that Gray was standing inches from her.

"Then don't encroach," the seedy man with the leer snapped. "I seen her first. Yore fancy dress don't give you no special favors."

"Take another step toward the lady and several days from now, you'll still feel the effects of your rash move." Gray's tone remained low but was now menacing.

"Gray!" Baines got over her surprise at seeing him there.

More shaken than she cared to admit, she exulted at the sight of him, yet hated the joy she felt that he was there. A war of emotions raged through her at his bewildering behavior. She'd thought not to see him again today. Yet here he was, ready to defend her, announcing to all and sundry his wealth with his powerful presence and expensive clothing.

Was this his reason for asking where she would be tonight? So he could come and shame her? Rich men like him usually had one interest in a woman with her background. Baines knew by his words and the other men's leers they'd jumped to the wrong conclusion about their relationship.

How dare he! How dare he hint that the two of them had something going.

Stark anger etched his features as he looked from Baines to the dirty, unkempt riverman. Although the man was huge, outweighing Gray by several pounds, to Baines his bulk appeared to be mostly flab. She stared at Lord Dunston, and her traitorous heart sped up.

Against the backdrop of the Horse and Mule, he seemed out of place in his fine riding clothes and expensive leather boots, his black hair trimmed neatly and his face clean shaven.

The chipped tables and battered chairs sat on a dingy floor, and the air smelled of smoke, cheap whiskey, and sweat. Filthy, bearded men with stained clothing eyed Gray with contempt and served to make the difference between the place where Gray came from and Baines's background all the more outstanding.

Baines's nemesis assessed Gray, uncertainty on his face. When Baines walked over to where Gray stood at the end of the bar, the big man slunk back to his seat, amid taunts and laughter from other customers.

"Hank done let a proper-talkin', fancy nabob from over the hill scare him down!" a voice boomed.

"I ain't scairt," Hank insisted. "Don't get a hankerin' to test my patience, Cal. Remember, I'm half horse an' half alligator jist like you, but you'll thinks I'm a hurricane after the whuppin' I give you if you so much as glance at me cross-eyed."

Baines closed her eyes in horror. Half horse and half alligator? That was a sure sign a fight was near to hand. She only heard the term used when the boatmen referred to themselves in a boast to an opponent.

Hank pointed a meaty finger at Gray. "This uppity gent'man here is lucky. I heared her call him by name. Seems she was expectin' him. I ain't nevah comed between a man and his woman."

"Aww, you's jis' scairt!" another voice goaded. "If you be a real man, that fancy dresser thar would be fish bait by now."

"Ain't nobody gonna be nothin'. I'll show y'all half horse and half alligator," Luther declared, coming from behind the bar holding a shotgun. Keeping his eyes trained on the rivermen, he said, "Baines, it appears you knows this man. Ain't he got sense 'nough to know he's on the wrong side o' the hill?" He frowned and sidled a look at Baines. "What's he doin' here anyway?"

Gray's gaze swept the large, crowded room with a disdainful, fearless look before turning to Baines and not allowing her to respond to Luther. "We have an important matter to discuss, Baines. May I escort you home?" he asked. "Whenever you're ready to leave."

Thinking it would be best to leave now, Baines stared at him, her spirits crumbling at the sight of his rigid stance. Like this afternoon, was this visit because of concern for her? Or was there another reason? His words suggested that he'd merely come because of the quilt.

Unlike his humbleness of earlier today, his cool manner irked her; she'd felt such happiness when he appeared, but she resented the distaste in his features. She pushed her feelings aside for more practical matters, however. If Gray remained, his life might be in danger from the clods who seemed danged bent on fighting.

She glanced at Luther, and he nodded.

"You kin leave now, Baines. I think it best, while I tell the newcomers here 'bout yore uncle Linc's policies. You sure that fella can be trusted?"

"Yes, Luther," Baines answered. "I know Lord Dunston. He was taught to respect ladies."

Wondering why Gray had sought her out and angry with him because of his mysterious demeanor, Baines raised her chin in haughty defiance. Not wanting to put him in danger, she would unleash her temper when they were well away from the Horse and Mule.

He never ceased to amaze her.

If she refused to accompany him, a brawl could ensue. Grayling Dunston didn't look like a man who would back away from a fight, even with the odds against him. Here he would be fearfully outnumbered.

Why should she be concerned about his safety anyway? She doubted his sudden appearance tonight had been merely to save her honor. He sought to save the quilt he thought she still had knowledge of, despite whatever he'd told her at Miz Annabelle's.

"Mr. Dunston, jis' you make sure you remember what you been taught," Luther warned. "That girl ain't no easy mark."

Gray dipped his head slightly, his expression masked. "I'll remember, sir," he said. "Her ladylike manners are evident in more ways than one. Shall we go, Baines?"

Without waiting for her response, he took her by the arm and guided her through the door and out of the place.

Warmth flowed through Baines like hot molasses, both at his compliment and his touch. She scolded herself for enjoying his nearness and for giving any credence to his words. Already she figured out why he'd invited her to Dunland. But was it the same reason he'd come to the Horse and Mule, and the same reason he now guided her away? Were his pretty words nothing more than a farce and his sweet touch an act? If so, she would show him and make him pay for every insult he'd directed at her.

She shook off his hold and faced him, angry with herself for still being so concerned with his safety and needing to vent her feelings. "Either you're the stupidest man or the bravest," she huffed. "I can't yet tell which. You were no match for that bunch in there."

Gray ignored the green fire burning in her eyes and reclaimed her arm. He led her to the horse and buggy waiting on the far side of the street and stopped beside it.

The uneasy sensation of being watched once again overtook him. He glanced over his shoulder, expecting to find the riverboat men descending on him, but he saw no one. The feeling left him, and he frowned, calling himself an ass for his unnecessary wariness.

He wondered what he was doing there, in the company of Baines. She was so bloody unappreciative and too deuced tempting.

When he'd left Dunland, he hadn't thought about the consequences of going to the Horse and Mule. He really hadn't thought about how Baines would react to his appearance.

Earlier at the sewing shop, concern had truly motivated him. But tonight? He wasn't sure *how* she should feel about his visit. He didn't know how to explain himself.

Was it still concern? Or was it really mistrust?

"Release your hold of me," Baines demanded. Suddenly a stricken look crossed her beautiful features. "Territorial encroachment?"

"Baines—"

"I'm not your territory—"

"Baines, listen to me—"

"I'm not stupid, either."

Baines's suspicions and overwhelming emotions left her bewildered and unable to contain her misgivings. The feeling that Gray's interest at being there was as much for the quilt as it was for her angered her. She'd already told him that she would search for the quilt on his behalf. Unless he still believed she was involved in its disappearance, why couldn't he wait for her to follow through with her plans?

The thought that he was only using her because of the quilt resurfaced.

"I know when I've been insulted. You came lookin' for that dang quilt and couldn't wait for me to get in touch with—"

He was kissing her again. Gray told himself he kissed her to quiet her down, not because he really wanted to feel her soft mouth against his own; not because he'd worried about her the entire time since he'd last seen her; and certainly not because he couldn't get their previous kiss out of his mind.

He had tried earlier to explain to her his relief this morning when DeEdria had assured him the watchman Roc sent to Under-the-Hill had reported that Baines remained undisturbed the entire night. Yet how could he tell her how sorry he was he'd accused her of being a liar and a thief, especially when he still was uncertain about her innocence? But most important, how could he explain to her the urgency of finding Mary's Fortune before it was too late?

This afternoon, apparently, his visit hadn't explained any of that to her. It only intensified his emotions for her, and probably confused her about his true intentions toward her. Intentions he wasn't even sure of.

Tonight the words to further explain any of that to Baines eluded him, so he gave in to his overwhelming urge to kiss her senseless—an urge he'd had ever since he'd walked into that disreputable tavern and saw her standing at the bar.

She wore a simple green dress that enhanced the color of her eyes. The hemline barely reached her ankles and allowed Gray to notice her black boots, the same ones she'd worn last night to his party.

Now, kissing her unhurriedly, that same simple dress allowed him to feel every supple curve of her body. Her tongue twined and mated with his. He withdrew from her sweet recesses, then delved in again.

Baines clung to his lapels, allowing him to have his way with her. He yearned for all of her and he yearned for his

life to be on an even keel once again. Then maybe he and
Baines would have had a chance.

Yet even if he retained his wealth, he wondered how
anything between him and Baines could be possible.

They were worlds apart—how could she ever fit into his
world? It was a world that had been most important to his
father. He'd championed Gray through his youthful woes.
Pierce had gone to Eton and insisted on an investigation
when Jamie's lies seemed to have convinced everyone that
Gray was amoral and depraved, not to mention a thief and
a fabricator.

Gray had no doubt that Pierce expected him to marry
well to carry on the Dunston family line. Just because his
father was no longer alive didn't mean Gray would shirk
his responsibility because of Baines's beautiful face and
tempting body.

"Gray," she whispered softly.

Desire flushed her cheeks and made her body pliant
against his.

"Gray?"

"Aye, little mouse?" Gray murmured, his body heavy
with need, his thoughts in turmoil. "You must learn to
control your temper." He rained a circle of kisses around
her face. "Why are you so angry?"

Baines left his embrace and gazed up at him. A curious,
deep longing stood clear in her eyes.

"I'm angry because of your highfalutin manner and your
callin' me a liar and a thief. I'm neither!"

Gray sighed, then smiled. He wished he possessed her
unpretentious nature. Maybe then things would have been
easier for him.

"You've every right to be angry, Baines," he said honestly, surprised at how easy the words came. "I was hasty
in my judgment. I apologize for my remarks."

Baines ran her hand across the leather seat of the buggy.
"Why did you come here tonight?" She didn't turn his
way. "Was it for the quilt?"

How could he answer that?

He drew in a great intake of breath, not willing to explain

that it was as much for the quilt as it was to see her. He didn't see the point. There couldn't be anything between them, and such an explanation would give her undue expectations. So he remained quiet.

Glaring at him, she climbed into the buggy, her movements stiff and angry. "You said you came to escort me home," she snapped. "I'm ready."

Regretting the change of mood between them, without a word Gray climbed in beside her.

13

THEY PASSED THE SHORT ride back to Baines's house in silence. There were no spacious grounds with avenues of live oaks surrounding fine homes and scents of magnolias in the air to distract her. There were only dirt roads, dilapidated houses, and businesses, the loamy bluff jutting out from the earth on one side of them and the lazy Mississippi on the other.

Tonight her surroundings added to her melancholia. Before meeting Gray and being invited to Dunland, she'd only had her imagination to fuel her dreams. But she'd actually seen how the Dunstons and the others of their class lived. It should have been of no consequence to her, but it was.

Baines's resentment of Gray deepened. The only thing of concern to him was the stupid quilt. He didn't have to worry about eking out a living for next month's meals. He didn't have to worry about being warm on cold nights or cool on hot days.

At the least she'd wanted to hear that he came to see her. Instead, she'd heard his great intake of breath. A regretful sound if ever there was one and the only answer she needed. Climbing into the buggy, her anger had deserted her, leaving her as she was now, dejected and alone.

She really had no one to rely on. Not Uncle Lincoln, as much as he tried. He was always gone. And not Gray. His only interest in her was the quilt. Again she chided herself for even caring, when it was apparent that he didn't.

To get out of Rivertown she would have to make her own way. Sewing some gowns for those ladies wouldn't go a long way in helping her to achieve her dream, but duplicating the beautiful quilt would have. Now, however, more immediate needs, like a new pair of shoes and a new gown—and another bed covering—took precedence.

When she laid eyes on Eli Washington again, she would throttle him. Without his thievery, Gray would have been long gone—before he'd spoken so horribly about her and before he'd kissed her so thoroughly.

Gray reined the horse to a stop in front of Baines's house. She stiffened as she viewed the pitiful little shack with the lonely tree in front of it. Certainly nothing like the lush greenery at Dunland.

Stop it, Baines Marshall. This is your home, and you have every right to be proud of it.

Yet since meeting Gray, she was anything but proud of it. Whether or not he intended to make her feel so inadequate, she didn't know.

He remained quiet, gazing at her as if he tried to cipher every thought in her head. Finally he spoke.

"Baines, we have to talk."

"Indeed we do," she agreed. "I haven't had supper yet. You can join me if you like."

"Sounds like a sterling idea, Baines."

Gray's accent sounded thicker than she'd ever heard it, but she wouldn't comment on it. Instead, she allowed him to hand her down from the buggy and escort her to the door.

Once inside, Baines lit the lamps and made a mental note to check the supply of oil.

She indicated the padded bench with several pillows along the back. "Have a seat. I haven't got any good whiskey, but I have what Uncle Lincoln drinks if you'd like," she explained.

"No, thank you, my dear." Gray had an idea of the kind of alcohol Lincoln Marshall drank and didn't wish to have a hole burned in his stomach. He sank down on the seat. Its comfort surprised him, and he wondered if Baines had used her sewing skills to fashion the thick pad and pillows. If one were to recline on it, it could very easily become a cozy bed, perfect for lovemaking.

He shoved the enticing thought aside as Baines moved about, first firing up the potbellied stove, then opening the window and door, leaving it slightly ajar. She took a few meager foodstuffs from a corner shelf and set about preparing dinner.

Turning away from the sight, Gray studied his surroundings more closely. A seaman's trunk sat in front of the bench, and he had the insane urge to throw the thing open and search for his quilt. But surely Baines wouldn't have invited him in with so obvious a hiding place out in the open.

Shaking off his suspicions, he realized the house had more furnishings then he'd noticed last night. Next to the potbellied stove stood a washstand with a pitcher and basin on it. Near it was the weak-legged table with the two chairs pushed under it.

His gaze shifted to the quilting frame and the unfinished quilt atop it. The silence deafening, he asked the first question that popped into his head. "Are you making a quilt, Baines?"

She looked up from her chores and narrowed her eyes at him, then glanced at the quilt and nodded.

"When you're finished with it, are you planning to sell it?"

"It's for my uncle Lincoln's birthday," she answered tightly. "I plan to surprise him, although he believes I'm makin' it to sell."

Hoping that she'd forgiven him for going to the Horse and Mule, Gray smiled. He wanted to continue the conversation to discover everything he could about her. "I'm sure your uncle will be surprised and very pleased. It's quite beautiful," he said sincerely. "You're very talented."

"Thank you." With those polite words, Baines went back to her cooking.

Gray sighed. Her polite dismissal told him she hadn't gotten over her pique. His heart twisted in his chest as he finished his perusal of her house. He had never been this close to such poverty. At Briarwood, his home near London, the poor always came to him, and he was always there to give them aid, for any reason.

Would his little mouse accept his aid? He chuckled ruefully. His little mouse indeed. Baines was her own person, belonging to no one. But she didn't belong in this hellhole. The quilt was rightfully hers, so when she recovered it, he'd offer to buy it from her. He hardly had it to spare, but he would offer her fifteen thousand dollars. At one time such money would have been a mere pittance, but not anymore. Yet Baines needed it more than he did, and maybe as a result of his charity some deity would take pity upon him and help him save his family fortune.

Within half an hour he was seated across from Baines at the weak-legged little table, eating flaky biscuits and orange marmalade, and beans flavored with crisp bacon served on cracked plates. The scent of boiling coffee filled the air.

"It's not much," Baines said apologetically as she filled his glass with water.

He sensed her embarrassment and wondered what to do to ease it. He didn't have a ready answer, so he merely said, "It's wonderful. You're a fine cook, and I'm enjoying your meal."

Totally at ease with her, he hadn't lied to her. She *was* a fine cook. Never in his life had he eaten beans, but he enjoyed them immensely. Beans reminded him too much of the poor, so he always chose not to eat them.

He hoped she hadn't depleted her larder on his behalf, but he vowed to remedy that as soon as possible. He smiled warmly at her, and she smiled back, seeming to be enjoying this meal as much as he was. Yet as much as he wanted to avoid a confrontation at this serene moment, he had to broach the subject of Mary's Fortune.

"Tell me, Baines, have you word on the whereabouts of the quilt?" Waiting for her reply, he spread a dollop of marmalade on the warm biscuit.

She rose and went to the stove to get the coffee. "That's what we have to talk about," she announced as she returned to the table and poured them each a measure of the steaming brew.

Gray frowned at the mysterious note in her voice. His biscuit forgotten, he stared at her.

Reseating herself, she took a sip of the aromatic coffee, then calmly met his gaze. "Eli's in New Orleans to get a ship out to sea."

Gray couldn't help the tinge of envy he felt. Eli must have been the reason Baines seemed so at odds about her feelings for him, despite her passionate response to his kisses. "And who's Eli?"

"Eli's the one who stole my quilt," Baines scoffed. "He came through the window."

His thoughts went back to the seaman's trunk. Could it be that she told one outrageous story after another because she had hidden the quilt in there? "How do you know he's the one?" Gray asked, his interest roused.

"I have my reasons for knowin'," Baines answered cryptically. "I'm goin' to get that quilt back."

"How?"

"I'm goin' down to New Orleans, that's how. I'm goin' to ask Luther to lend me the fare."

He was amused at her feisty determination and relieved at her adamancy. Certainly she wouldn't be so hell-bent about going to New Orleans if she had the quilt in her possession. Would she?

"That won't be necessary, little mouse. We both have an interest in that bloody quilt, so allow me to accompany you to New Orleans. All expenses paid."

"That's mighty generous of you, Gray." She eyed him with uncertainty, then raised her chin. "But there's somethin' I should tell you first, and after hearin' it, you just might change your mind about payin' for me."

"Really?" Gray raised a speculative brow. "Now what could possibly make me change my mind?" The thought that had come to him moments ago returned, and he hated the jealousy he felt that compelled him to ask his next question. "Is this Eli something special to you?"

"Me and Eli?" Baines released a peal of laughter. "I'm not intendin' to marry a ne'er-do-well and a thief, and Eli Washington is both." She paused and met his steady gaze with a defiant look. "I aim to sell you the quilt, Gray, for five thousand dollars."

"I beg your pardon, mistress, I don't think I heard you correctly."

"I believe you did," Baines shot back.

The larcenous little witch! She wanted to *sell* his own quilt back to him! Her audacity infuriated him, and his gullibility outraged him. Never mind that he had contemplated buying the quilt from her for three times that amount.

He'd thought her different from anyone he'd ever met, but she wasn't any better than his one-time friend, James McKay. Baines would use his misfortune for profit. What a bloody fool he'd been.

He was glad he'd never deemed her trustworthy. Her duplicity felt like a dull ache and reinforced his lack of faith in human nature. He met her determined stare with an icy one of his own.

"Very well, Miss Marshall," he said, gritting his teeth. "If I must pay to recover my property, I will. Right now, we'd better make arrangements to leave posthaste. We must find Eli before he sets sail to some distant country."

14

BAINES SPENT THE REST of the night preparing for the trip to New Orleans. She told herself Gray's changed attitude toward her didn't matter. The fact that he barely spoke two words to her after he'd announced his plans to make their arrangements didn't matter. Nor did it matter that he'd left an hour ago, stalking away like an angry mountain lion, silent, dangerous, and predatory.

She insisted she'd done what she had to do. Five thousand dollars would get her away from Natchez-Under-the-Hill; it would assure her of Uncle Lincoln's safety. No longer would he have to steal, or work for the Dunstons, or even go sailing if he didn't have a mind to.

Gray didn't need the money, but she and Uncle Lincoln certainly did. If a man could travel across an ocean just to get a quilt back for sentiment, than he could afford to pay for that same quilt.

With a sigh she glanced around her house, searching for something to pack a change of clothes in, since she didn't own a traveling bag. Unsure of how long they would be gone, Baines decided to take the only four casual dresses she owned; she would wear her ecru gown aboard the ship. The journey to New Orleans couldn't take more than two days, and she didn't expect them to be there for more than a day, so her wardrobe would be sufficient.

After all, how long would it take to search the docks of New Orleans?

She eyed the pillow coverings on the bench. Brightly colored with various flower patterns, they would make a wonderful pouch bag. Removing the coverings and her sewing bag, she set about her task, a task she would gladly trade for a few hours' work on Uncle Linc's quilt.

Just as she settled herself into her work, a knock sounded on the door.

"Darlin', are you in there?"

Miz Annabelle's voice came through the thin walls loud and clear. Worried, Baines rose from her seat at the table and rushed to the door.

"Baines Marshall! Open this door—"

"What's pesterin' you, Miz Annabelle, to be here at this hour?"

Miz Annabelle swept past Baines, leaving a scent of lavender in her wake. Baines closed the door and frowned at the other woman's disapproving demeanor. Not bothering to seat herself, the seamstress folded her arms and tapped her foot. Fashionably dressed, her apricot-colored gown revealed more cleavage than Baines would have ever felt comfortable showing. Nonetheless, Miz Annabelle looked fabulous, with her red hair upswept and her blue eyes sparkling.

"Where is he, Baines?"

"Where is who?"

"Don't play games with me, young lady," Miz Annabelle snapped. "You know who I'm talkin' about. The fancy nabob who took you from Luther's. I assume he's this English lord who invited you—"

"Luther had no right to discuss Gray with you." Baines glared at her friend.

Miz Annabelle harumphed. "Didn't he? Luther was worried about you and intended to come check on you himself, but I told him I would do it on my way to supper with Mr. Foxe."

On another occasion Baines would have questioned who Mr. Foxe was, but tonight she felt too dispirited to do so.

On another occasion she would have also questioned what Miz Annabelle had been doing at the Horse and Mule. Proper ladies weren't allowed in taverns as customers, and Miz Annabelle certainly had never expressed a desire to go into the place.

Then she recalled Jesse, Luther's unreliable assistant, who sometimes served as Baines's escort home when her shift ended. She'd thought him out to sea again, but detected his handiwork in Miz Annabelle's pique. When he was in port, the big oaf sometimes spied on Baines for Uncle Linc and even Miz Annabelle and Luther. The trio meant well, but they left Baines no privacy.

Light from the full moon glimmered through the window, and muted sounds reached her. Until she'd met Gray, she didn't realize she desired privacy.

Quietly Baines went back to the table and reseated herself. Her recent encounter with Gray fresh in her mind, she was in no mood to answer Miz Annabelle's questions.

She couldn't get Gray out of her mind. Not only had there been anger in his gaze, but disappointment, too, as though he'd expected better from her. Remembering that wounded look, guilt pervaded her, and she wondered if her request was justified.

"Baines, honey, talk to me." Miz Annabelle sat on the seat next to her. "I don't want to see you hurt."

Miz Annabelle's gentle words almost started Baines's flow of tears. How could she tell the widow that he'd already hurt her? His accusations still stung, and because of them she'd asked Gray for an outrageous amount of money for a quilt that was rightfully his.

"Oh, Miz Annabelle," Baines whispered, miserable. "I'm already hurtin' inside and I don't know what to do about it." She explained why Gray had come to her house in the first place, why he'd invited her to Dunland, then the subsequent disappearance of the quilt and his accusations.

"When I told him about the quilt at the party, I was willin' to give it to him then and there. I felt his pain and I wanted to do something to ease it."

Miz Annabelle took Baines's hand into her own. "But

his accusations hurt, so you decided to sell him his own quilt.'' She stared at Baines with motherly tenderness. ''Tell me, is your hurt pride an excuse to sell him a quilt you were willin' to give him?''

Baines bowed her head. ''My hurt feelin's got nothin' to do with it. My reasons are a mite more practical than that. If I don't sell the quilt to Gray, only through years of workin' will I achieve my goals. By then Uncle Lincoln could be dead from stealin' one time too many or even from *his* years of hard work.''

''That's just the thinkin' of a defeated person,'' Miz Annabelle scolded, ''and you ain't been defeated yet. You got a good head on your shoulders.''

''But—''

''No *buts*, Baines. If Gray had never come, you'd still have to stick to your plans for getting out of here.''

''Yes, but the quilt was going to be my way to get out faster, and now it's gone. I just know I could have copied it.''

''So it's gone. You can still follow through with your plans and replicate it.''

Baines shook her head, unsure of her memory. The shock of her loss blurred the quilt's detail. ''I don't know if I can remember every little detail.''

''In time you will,'' Miz Annabelle reassured her, ''so don't start doubtin' yourself. Now, what are you takin' these pillow casin's apart for?''

''To make some travelin' bags. Me and Gray are goin' to New Orleans—''

''Baines!''

Heat crept up her cheeks at Miz Annabelle's scandalized look. ''I promise I'm not goin' to do anythin' I shouldn't, but I have to search for that blasted quilt to prove to Gray how wrong he is.''

Instead of the lecture she expected, Miz Annabelle hugged her tightly. ''Darlin', why does his opinion matter so much if you're never gonna see him again after he gets his quilt back?''

Before Baines responded, Miz Annabelle continued.

"He may never forgive you for tryin' to blackmail him, and I don't want you more hurt than you already are."

Baines's heart twisted. To hear what she'd already concluded hurt more than she thought possible. "Miz Annabelle, you need to be goin'." Her words sounded abrupt, but she needed time to sort through her muddled feelings. "I don't want you to keep Mr. Foxe waitin' on my behalf."

Miz Annabelle hugged Baines tightly. "I expect to hear from you as soon as you return, young lady. And if that man so much as harms one hair on your head, forget Lincoln—this Gray will have me to deal with. Do I make myself clear, darlin'?"

Comforted by Miz Annabelle's protective instincts, Baines nodded. "Thank you," she said softly. "Now, go on with you. Go enjoy the rest of your night."

With one last motherly hug, the Widow Shepard departed. Alone once again, Baines returned to her sewing. Bits of the conversation with Miz Annabelle swirled through her mind.

Jamming the needle through the thick material, Baines admitted that Uncle Lincoln's well being wasn't the only reason she'd asked Gray for the money. Her own well being mattered to her as well.

Secretly she wished for a sewing room, her own private sanctum that housed the latest inventions for quilting and sewing. She also wanted a card room for Uncle Lincoln. Realistically she knew he would never give up his hell-raising ways. But at least she could monitor his activities if he gambled at their house; a big house, with a drawing room and a dining room, and a nursery with hers and Gray's offspring.

Her practical side knew she had to pursue her dreams at any cost, not only for herself but for Uncle Linc as well. And Gray would only stand in her way. What husband, especially an English lord, would allow his wife to have her own business, one that he had absolutely no involvement in?

That logic was well and good. But the other part of herself, her emotional side, insisted she would do herself an injustice if she wasted her life working. She could at least try to win Gray—

To what end? Suddenly furious with her feminine nature, she laughed bitterly. If she didn't have a chance with him before, she certainly didn't now. Gray despised her because of her blackmail. Yet could she blame him? Would she have reacted any differently if the situation had been reversed? She doubted it.

Besides, how could she overcome her deep-seated resentment for the wealthy and her inferior feelings when she was in their company?

She'd never given these feelings much thought. In mere days her life, her entire attitude, had been changed forever.

Listening to the sounds of the house, an aura of loneliness enveloped her. Wood creaked from some unknown place; the wall clock ticked the time away; the chair squeaked as she shifted her weight in restless agitation. Before meeting Gray, she'd never contemplated how alone she felt when Uncle Lincoln was away. But even if Uncle Lincoln had been there, she doubted she would have felt much different. She still would have felt alone and lonely.

Gray was little more than a stranger to her, but he had given life to her womanly dreams. Shaking her head, she drew in a breath.

"What is it about Gray that has affected me so much?" She frowned. "As if it really matters to him how I feel about him."

Most of the night had passed when she finally completed her pouch. Gazing at the straps she'd added, as well as the assortment of buttons for fastening, she nodded in satisfaction, quite proud of her efforts. She neatly folded her clothing, then placed them in her bag.

Next, she took off her boots. They really were beyond repair, but she cleaned them as best she could. Done with that, she disrobed and went to the washstand. Pouring water from the pitcher into the basin and taking the soap and a towel from the shelf that shared space with the food, she scrubbed herself thoroughly. She refused to go to the river at this hour, so this would have to suffice. The cool, early-morning air raised chillbumps on her skin, and she hurried to complete her task. Soon she was dressed in the gown she'd worn to Gray's ball along with her boots. By that time sunshine gleamed through the window. Too nervous to eat breakfast, she sat on the bench and awaited Gray's arrival.

Barely five minutes passed before Gray strode up the path to her door. She didn't give him a chance to knock. Picking up her pouch, she rushed to the door and threw it open. She stopped dead in her tracks. The green leaves on her Chinaberry tree glistened with morning dew and swayed in the river breeze. A horse and buggy sped by but didn't deter Gray as he moved toward her.

Impeccably dressed, he appeared every bit the remote lord as he halted his stride and nodded. "Good morning, Miss Marshall."

Baines swallowed, hating the brittle sound of his voice. He stood before her, all muscled tension and cold disdain. Nothing of the friendly man she had known existed. Shifting her weight from foot to foot, she met his gaze, his eyes an impossible blue, frigid and distant. She couldn't find her voice to greet him, and the silence between them stretched.

"Come along, mistress. We'll miss the ship if we don't hurry."

On leaden legs Baines followed behind Gray. He didn't offer to carry her bags as they started toward the docks, and his rudeness offended her. Despite his anger, she'd expected better from him. He was a gentleman. He knew how to treat ladies, but apparently he really hadn't considered her a lady, so it was easier for him to slight her so thoroughly.

The walk to the boat landing was short and miserable. He pretended she didn't exist, but try as she might, Baines couldn't ignore Gray. His presence filled the space between them. He walked close to her and inadvertently brushed his arms against her breast. Heat spiraled through her. Her senses sang at the scent of his cologne, and her heart beat frantically.

Chaos met them at the docks. Steamers filled with cargo

lined the landings. Drays and carts loaded with bales of cotton moved cautiously toward the town. People rushed in various directions, and dogs loped about, barking furiously at the activity.

Gray caught Baines's arm and guided her through the bustle, propelling her in the direction of the *Natchez Belle*. The black steam billowing from its smokestacks and its sheer size made it look like some great beast. She stiffened. Before her fear overtook her surprise, Gray pulled her up the gangplank, onto the main deck, then up the wide, curved stairway. They passed beneath a sign liberally trimmed with gingerbread with the name of the boat carved in bright gold lettering.

Finally he halted before a lean whiskered man Baines assumed was the captain.

"Lord Dunston," the man greeted. He placed a pipe in his mouth and walked forward. "I'm glad you made it. We're near ready to take off."

"If you'll just show me the way to your daughter's stateroom, Captain Cordair," Gray said. "I would like to get Baines settled in."

"Of course, sir," Captain Cordair said and started forward.

Baines couldn't imagine that a captain was required to act as a porter and escort anyone to their quarters, but that's exactly what Captain Cordair did. She suspected Gray's rank as an English lord earned them such special treatment.

Intimidation invaded Baines. Already she'd been subjected to the spitefulness of society matrons at Dunland. Just how would she be treated here on this boat, with its wide promenade, numerous spittoons, and fancy doors and skylights, as the companion of the Earl of Montegut?

If she encountered anyone of her acquaintance, her reputation would be in shreds. Her reputation, however, was well worth the risk if she could prove to Gray how wrong he was about her.

The captain opened the door to their room, and Gray stepped aside, allowing Baines to precede him into the cabin. Her breath caught just as Captain Cordair spoke again.

"Is it to your satisfaction, my lord?"

"I think we should ask the lady that, sir. My dear, is this to your approval?"

Baines blinked at Gray's sardonic tone. Surely he had to be joking. She'd never stood in a bedchamber as fine. It was bright and cheery, decorated in delicate furnishings. A sleigh bed and chest of drawers stood against one wall, while a sofa covered in light green silk sat against the opposite wall. A porcelain commode, rosewood washstand with pitcher and basin, and a large table with two chairs completed the richly furnished room. Gray had asked her if this was to her approval! She narrowed her eyes at him, sure he *was* making sport of her.

"It's fine," she mumbled, disliking him and his great wealth.

"If that'll be all, then," the captain said, a little uncomfortable, as if her tension was rubbing off on him.

"Aye." With the captain gone, Gray watched as Baines's gaze swept the interior once again. Trepidation was clear in her features, and the urge to draw her into his arms and reassure her nearly consumed him. But he couldn't, her betrayal and blackmail still too fresh.

Yet he was angry with himself for being angry at Baines. He had no right getting upset with her for offering to sell him Mary's Fortune. It was hers to do as she saw fit. He also knew of her desire to move from Under-the-Hill. *He* wanted as much for her. With the money she'd asked for, she would be able to do it.

It would certainly be a relief to get her away from that blasted tavern and Luther. He wondered if Luther was stepping in for her uncle, protecting her from the river scum, or for himself. No, Gray concluded, the Horse and Mule exuded danger, and Baines seemed all too trusting. In spite of her surroundings, she was a lady who deserved better.

She was also innocent and beautiful. He halted his thoughts before they ran amok and took a more amorous turn. Gray closed the door.

"Would you like some breakfast?"

She stared at him. "This is a beautiful cabin, Gray," she whispered. "Is it yours or mine?"

Shock registered in his brain. He'd forgotten he hadn't explained the circumstances about the room to her. "This room belongs permanently to Cordair's daughter. At the moment she's visiting friends in Vicksburg. Ordinarily the room remains empty in her absence, but Roc is friends with Cordair." He sighed and looked at her levelly. "This was the only remaining stateroom left, so it's *ours.*"

In an instant, anguish replaced Baines's apprehension. She started for the door. "I'm afraid I can't share this room with you, Gray. It ain't proper."

When she reached for the doorknob, Gray covered her small hand with his. Surprising warmth flooded him. He hadn't expected to feel any reaction to her touch. He'd believed himself too angry and hurt. But he realized that in spite of the chasm between them, she still affected him.

"Baines, I would never impugn your honor," he said softly.

He brushed a silky lock of hair behind her dainty ear. The temperature in the room exacerbated the heat of desire growing within his body.

"But I—"

"Please sit down, little mouse, so I can explain."

Baines hesitated. Her eyes were large and liquid, and he knew she was as affected by him as he was by her. The thought cheered him, even as a part of him insisted she was naught but an opportunist.

Silently Baines walked to the sofa and sat.

"Roc secured this cabin for us, Baines," Gray began quietly. "Since this was the only one available, he had us listed as being married."

"Oh!" Baines jumped up from her seat. "You—"

"It's the only way, Baines," Gray insisted. "If we are to recover the quilt, we go together or not at all. Besides, we both have a stake in this."

Baines swallowed hard and sat back down. "You're right, of course, Gray. If you went alone, you couldn't identify Eli. And I know you wouldn't pay passage for me to go alone. . . ."

When her voice trailed off, Gray wondered if she was thinking what he was. For them to be alone for two days in the same room together would be sheer torture. Bloody hell!

She smiled timidly. "Yes, I guess this is the only way."

Her gaze went to the bed, and Gray combed his fingers through his hair. The libidinous thoughts running through his brain didn't matter. He wanted to ease her mind. "I'll sleep on the sofa, Baines. You take the bed."

Grateful green eyes met him. "Thank you, Gray."

"There's no need for thanks, Baines. It's how ladies are treated." Her eyes reminded him of unrefined emeralds, dazzling and warm. He knew then why some men fell privy to any demand their woman made of them. He grinned and changed the subject. "I haven't had breakfast yet, and I'm sure you must be hungry. Shall I order for us?"

Baines stifled a yawn. "I know it's mornin', Gray, a time to be gettin' up and doin' chores. But I'm awful tired—"

"You are?" Gray interrupted, puzzled. His concern ate away the last of his anger. "Didn't you sleep last night?"

"I was busy gettin' ready for the trip, and daylight just snuck up on me," Baines answered without elaborating.

She looked tired and dejected, and Gray's heart swelled with a tenderness he'd never experienced before. That same compelling urge to take her into his arms and just hold her returned.

Realizing he hadn't been very nice to her, he drew in an agitated breath. He vowed to remedy his actions toward her. Even if naught else came of his efforts, he wanted to at least be her friend.

"It is morning indeed," Gray finally said. "But when the body's tired, time is irrelevant. Why don't you get some rest, and I'll go to the dining salon for breakfast."

She went to the bed and stretched out on it, so tired she fell asleep before her head hit the pillow.

Gray stooped next to her to rid her of her shoes. They were practical but terribly worn. Suddenly he wanted to clothe her in silks and satins and buy her the latest fashions. But he knew her pride wouldn't allow her to accept such gifts from him.

Trying to ignore the soft feel of her legs as he removed her stockings, he straightened himself and gazed at her lovely face. He'd come searching for a quilt and found a fascinating, exotic, rare flower.

Although Baines was not unaffected by her poverty, neither did she grieve over it. Instead, she made the most of her situation.

Her courage and quiet strength was growing on him. In the short time he'd known her and in the few occasions he'd been in her presence, he'd learned a lifetime of lessons from her.

If he had to, he would summon the courage to live in poverty, and he would do so with Baines's dignity. But if he had her at his side . . .

No, Baines deserved better. If he suddenly lost his fortune, he would become nothing but an albatross around her neck. If he couldn't save his family's fortune, he would be a poor man alone.

15

LINCOLN MARSHAL GUZZLED THE last drop of his watered-down whiskey.

He sat in the bar of the riverfront hostel on Tchoupitoulas Road, where he was staying in New Orleans. The acrid smell of smoke and the dim light, as well as the cheap women hiring themselves out to the patrons, didn't improve his mood. He'd paid for a week's lodgings in this rat hole, hoping to get hired on one of the merchant ships heading out to sea from the busy port.

Europe remained his preference, so he'd held out for a ship going there. Finally he got lucky today and was hired on the *Eagle's Pride,* which would set sail tomorrow.

It annoyed him that he wouldn't be able to see Baines before he left. But his deceased brother's only child had lived with Lincoln's spur-of-the-moment departures for most of her life and had adjusted better than he'd expected.

He would never forget Baines's grief when her momma died. Lincoln had felt grief as well at Lizzie's death, but he also felt fear for the first time in his life. Scratching his long beard, he hooted with laughter. Even now, his fear was unimaginable for a barrel-chested, strongly built man such as himself. Yet he hadn't known what to do with a nine-year-old child. He'd made many mistakes along the way where rearing Baines was concerned. But she'd always been such a good child, and they'd adapted well to each other. Over the years she'd become the daughter he never had, and he wondered where he would be without her.

As she grew older, she kept him on the straight and narrow. Indeed, he still supplemented their income with gambling and even stealing at times. Because of Baines, however, he'd straightened up more than he'd ever thought possible.

Her parents would have been proud of the lady she had become. He certainly was.

Eager for the night to end, he stood from his seat. His gaze meandered around the run-down room, not much better than the one he slept in. The boisterous place hosted ragged, unwashed, unkempt occupants, making Lincoln feel decidedly out of place. He *was* clean, and Baines saw to it that his clothes were never torn.

Disgusted and feeling out of sorts, he directed his steps toward the large room that housed the beds.

Baines deserved better than the life she had, relying on his income and serving at the Horse and Mule to make ends meet, besides working in the sewing shop. Lincoln knew her dream was to become a fancy seamstress like Annabelle Shepard, so he'd seen to it that Baines was hired there five years ago. He'd also seen that she'd learned to cipher letters and numbers, and talk better than him.

Now his task was to see to it that she made a better life for herself, and if he had to stay out to sea for two years, he'd see that she got everything she wanted and deserved. With her skill at quilting, she could become famous. With the money he expected to make, he could buy her a small shop to set her down that path.

Up till now the nicest thing Lincoln had ever given her was that quilt Mr. Roc gave him in London. He was even prouder of it because he hadn't stolen it!

Tonight, for some unknown reason, he was worried about his niece. Wondering if he was doing the right thing in sailing away, he reached the doorway to the sleeping room and went in quietly, going straight to the bed he'd been assigned.

A double row of about forty cots, twenty on each side, stood in the room, and a rank, musty odor filled the air. Loud, drunken snores echoed from the men, grating on Lincoln's nerves. Baines probably had to listen to the same thing from him most of the time when he was in Natchez, so he was receiving his just rewards.

Only about twenty beds were occupied tonight, which was good, considering the rowdy lot that stayed here. Dead tired and bone weary, he wanted to get some rest. Had there been more men housed there, that might have been impossible. Their bad habits and sleeping noises would have kept him awake. One or two would have even attempted to sneak a willing woman in here to whore the night away.

Praying for the day he had an easier life, Lincoln sat on the side of his cot and took off his work boots, giving a cursory glance to the sleeper in the next bed. Something familiar caught his eye in the dimly lit room, and he looked again.

Facing the wall, the man slept in the end cot. But the quilt he used as a pillow commanded Lincoln's attention. Cursing under his breath, he shot up and shook the unidentified, sleeping man.

"Wake up!" Lincoln growled.

"Hey . . ." The man turned over, ready to defend himself. "Linc!"

"Eli?" Lincoln narrowed his eyes, familiarity breeding disgust. "What in tarnation you doin' here wit' Baines's quilt?"

Apprehension on his scraggly features, Eli sat up, a whiff of alcohol reaching Lincoln's nostrils.

"I kin explain, Linc," Eli began.

"It betta be good." Lincoln sat back down on the bed and waited. Endless minutes passed without further response from Eli. His best friend had stolen the one thing he'd ever given Baines. His patience ended at the thought. "What d'ya have to say for yourself?"

Eli cleared his throat but didn't meet Lincoln's eye. "Baines knowed I was comin' to hook up wit' you on a ship, an' she done sent the quilt to you fo' safekeepin'."

He laughed nervously, exposing several missing teeth. "I sure is glad I done found you. I wouldn't want to dis'ppoint Baines." Reaching for the quilt, he handed it to Lincoln. "You betta take it afore it gits stolen from me. You knows what kinda place we's in."

Grabbing the quilt from Eli's shaking hands, Lincoln laid it on his cot. He knew Baines and Eli as well. Eli Washington was nothing more than a thief like him, but Eli enjoyed thieving. Lincoln didn't. Eli'd even taken a couple of things from Lincoln, but he thought he'd made it clear to everyone that Baines and her possessions were off limits.

He gave Eli a hard, penetrating look. "You done stole it from Baines, didn't you, Eli?" He hoped his tone convinced Eli not to lie to him again.

"I done tole you what happen, Linc. I don't go aroun' lyin' for nothin'."

"That's all you ever do is lie for nothin'," Lincoln countered. "I wants the truth, Eli. Now!"

Eli bowed his head and sighed. "Yeah, Linc, I took it," he confessed. "But I never intended to steal it. I went to yore shack to check on Baines, jis' like you said I should. But she weren't there, so I went aroun' checkin' the doors an' winda. Well, it was unlatched, so I jis' opened it an' went in. I was only intendin' to git somethin' to eat, but I seed the quilt on Baines's bed—"

"So you took it!" Lincoln sneered angrily.

"It ain't even cold, Linc," Eli whined, meeting his eyes for the first time since the conversation began. "I figgered by the time the weatha changes, you be done got her anotha one. I ain't meant no harm. Besides, you done got her old one. And I seed the new one she was makin' hangin' on the quiltin' frame you made for her. I swear she don't need this one."

Lincoln glared at him, barely restraining himself from pummeling Eli. But he couldn't. The captain of the boat warned him he wouldn't tolerate such behavior. "Where was Baines when you stole her quilt? Iffen she wasn't at Luther's, she shoulda been home."

"She weren't at Luther's, Linc. She were at them Dunstons. Some nabob come a-callin' fer her the day b'fore.''

Not liking the sound of that, Lincoln eyed him curiously.
"Who?"

"Dang iffen I knows."

"Don't think jis' 'cause I'm concerned 'bout who was
wit' Baines I'm forgettin' you,'' Lincoln snapped, annoyed
at the relief in Eli's tone. He stood. "You's goin' back to
Natchez."

"I cain't do that!" Eli protested, standing also. "I got a
ship leavin' tomorrow. The same one's you's gon' be on.''

Later Lincoln would question how Eli had found him
and gotten recruited for the same ship as him, but now there
were more important matters at hand. He paced the length
of the small area. "I trusted you wit' my niece's safety, an'
you go an' steal from her. An' me. I knowed you was a
thief, but I thought I made it clear to stay away from
Baines."

"Aww, Linc—"

"Shut up!" Lincoln ordered, still pacing to release his
anger. "I ain't finished." He didn't worry about waking
the others. Their continued snoring suggested nothing
would rouse them. "You's goin' back to Natchez to bring
Baines her quilt, an' tell her how sorry you is for stealin'
it. An' you's gon keep a eye on her till I gits back." Eli's
treachery decided Lincoln. He would sail to Europe. That
was the only way he would get Baines away from snakes
like Eli. "*I* cain't go 'cause I'll miss my ship," he continued. "It's important for me to make decent money so I kin
git Baines outta that hole. You an' the res' of my friends
will take care of Baines till I gits back. Iffen any harm come
to her, I aim to crack heads. Startin' wit' yourn.''

"How you expeck *me* to live, Lincoln?" Eli threw his
hands up in frustration. "That ship was my chance to make
money, too—"

"You done loss yore chance. You shouldna stole from
me an' mine. Go see Mista Roc Dunston. He might fin'
somethin' for you to do. That's iffen you kin stay sober
long 'nuff, an' keep yore fingas in yore pockets an' off the
Dunstons' things.''

Sitting dejectedly back on the bed, Eli sighed, long and weary. "I guess I deserve yore scorn for what I done. But I'm powerful sorry 'bout it. I'll neva do it again."

"Not iffen you want to continue walkin' you won't. You's s'ppose to be the one keepin' the scum away from Baines, an' you turn out to be one o' them!"

"You's right," Eli mumbled. "Ain't nothin' I can say to dispute you."

"Git some rest. We git up wit' the sun tomorrow. I aim to see you headin' back to Natchez wit' Baines's quilt afore I board my ship."

"You kin trust me. I ain't gonna lose yore friendship over no quilt. I hopes you forgives me."

"This time only," Lincoln emphasized. He sat at the edge of the bed, some of his anger deflating at his friend's contriteness. But Eli had betrayed him. Added to his anger was worry about Baines. Who was the nabob courting his precious niece?

He hoped she kept her head and didn't fall for any sweet-talking the man might do to her, filling her with pretty promises in the hopes of seducing her. More than one beautiful young lady had lost her innocence to some lying son of a rich man, only to be abandoned with the consequences.

"I surely wish I could git that ship, Linc," Eli said quietly. "I needs the money. It'll soon be too hot to use a quilt. Cain't we take it wit' us? We'd be back in time fer the winta."

Lincoln sighed. Despite his thieving, Eli really was a good sort. Maybe if he could make some decent money and stay sober, Eli would straighten up. Besides, Luther would look after Baines. He wouldn't let anyone, especially some pale, smooth-talking nabob, harm her.

"I s'ppose keepin' you from yore chance to make some money is too much punishment for yore thievery. I don't want to know why you was too dumb to realize I'd recognize the quilt when I seed you wit' it." Stooping down, he placed Baines's quilt on top of his traveling bag. "I'll jis' hold onto it for safekeepin' an' send word to Baines that I got me a ship. I reckon she'll be glad to see her quilt again when I git home, jis' in time for the cold season.'' He laid on his cot and stared at the dirty ceiling. '' 'Bout six months from now!''

16

UPON AWAKENING, BAINES FOUND herself alone in the beautiful stateroom. The fading sunlight gleamed through the porthole, and she realized she'd slept most of the day away.

Yet she was grateful to be alone, grateful to have only her thoughts as company. She needed this time to herself, without Gray's disturbing presence to cloud her thinking.

Unable to forget Miz Annabelle's gentle chiding, she shifted on the comfortable bed. Somehow Baines needed to find the right words to tell Gray how sorry she was for asking for the money. Somehow she had to find a way to make him forgive her.

She was cheeky to assume that Gray had that kind of money to hand out, or even that he wanted the quilt back for sentiment. Baines really had no idea what Gray wanted the quilt for. He'd never told her.

Sitting up, she swung her legs over the side of the bed. Realizing that her shoes weren't on her feet, she supposed Gray had taken them off. At the thought of Gray touching her, her heart beat wildly in her chest. She only wished she had been awake to feel his fingers on her flesh, and to see his eyes darken with passion for her. Heat flushed her skin at her unladylike thoughts.

She had to get her thoughts, her feelings, in hand. Too

much hostility existed between her and Gray for them to have any future together.

In that moment she stopped fooling herself that it wouldn't matter when Gray left Natchez. She felt something for Gray; something powerful and exciting; something uncontrollable and frightening.

But she couldn't believe she loved him. How could she? She was opposite of everything he was—wealthy, remote, and reserved. Yet she knew there was more to him than his outward behavior suggested. She had seen glimpses of his caring manner and passionate nature.

There was something locked inside him that he refused to release, however. She wanted to reach out to him and let him know that she was there for him.

Stooping to pick up her shoes, Baines stopped. Years old and pitifully worn, her shoes reminded her that worlds stood between her and Gray, even if anger hadn't. The plight of her belongings gave her a rude awakening. For the first time in her life, pure shame hit her. No wonder Gray insisted she stay and rest. He was ashamed to be seen with her.

Her shoulders stiff and proud, she made her way to the sofa in her stockinged feet. Until now, she hadn't seen herself as Gray and the women at his ball must have. To them, she was nothing but a poor, classless tavern maid from Under-the-Hill. And she'd added to Gray's negative thoughts when she'd asked for the money.

For a brief second a lump formed in her throat, and she swallowed. She was here on the boat on her way to New Orleans with Gray for the same reason she'd gone to the ball—because of that danged quilt!

Her speech was improper, her clothes were simple, and she was poor. How could she actually have hoped that his interest in her could go beyond her knowledge of the quilt?

Remembering his kiss, she brought trembling fingers to her lips. Why did his mouth against her own haunt her so, when she knew he hadn't been sincere? When everything he did was because of the quilt?

But had she been any better? Just as that quilt appeared

to take over his life, it was doing the same to hers. She'd happened on it by mistake, then decided to profit from it. By right, it wasn't hers because it hadn't been Mr. Roc's to give away in the first place.

Baines sighed. She wouldn't use Gray's mishap to line her pockets. She couldn't live with herself if she did. At the moment she was powerless to correct her situation. Overcoming her self-pity, she again vowed to make her plans a reality.

The door swung open, and Gray sauntered in. He wore a smile that made Baines's heart skip a beat.

"Good evening, Baines," he said cheerily. "I suspect you are well rested."

Returning a shy smile, Baines drank in the sight of him. "I can't believe I slept all day. You must think I'm the laziest person around. I ain't, however."

Gray laughed, and sat beside her. "It *isn't*," he said, "that you're lazy. It's just that you were tired. I would never think of you as lazy."

She applauded the shrewd way he'd corrected her speech. Looking at her hands folded in her lap, she didn't respond. She wondered at his high spirits, but supposed his expectation of finding the quilt was the reason.

The silence between them turned Gray's laughter into an embarrassed cough. "You must be famished. There's very good fare in the dining salon. If we leave now, we can assure ourselves of a good table."

Go into a fancy dining room and risk the censure she'd received at Dunland? Absolutely not. But she couldn't tell Gray of her fear and humiliation, not now, not ever. So she settled for a partial truth.

"I thank you for the offer, Gray, but I don't have p-proper shoes to wear."

Gray cleared his throat. "If you would allow me, when we get to New Orleans, I should like to remedy that." He gave her a cavalier bow. "Until that time, however, you would do me a great honor by accompanying me to the dining room. I assure you, little mouse, I would be most proud to have you on my arm."

She stared at him, unsure if she should trust his words. But nothing in his manner suggested he jested with her. When she remained silent, he continued.

"The price of whatever you purchase in New Orleans will be considered a loan to be deducted from the money we agreed upon when the quilt is recovered."

Here was her chance to tell Gray how very sorry she was for asking for the money. Minutes fell away, easily accountable by the ticking of the clock. But she was afraid to speak, afraid this moment between them would be lost forever. He mentioned the money as if it had been *his* idea to give it to her, as if he genuinely wanted her to have it.

Tears threatened to spill down her cheeks. Refusing to let them fall and unable to trust herself to speak, she couldn't believe what he'd just said.

Gray met Baines's dewy, dreamlike gaze and nearly lost himself in the lustrous sheen of her beautiful eyes. For long moments he absorbed her loveliness, held spellbound by her irresistible charm.

"Don't worry about your attire," he said, getting control of his emotions. "I promise you, Baines, you won't meet with the kind of pomposity you encountered at Dunland. DeEdria's friends were certain you stood in the way of their aspirations."

"Aspirations?"

Gray smiled. "Aye, Baines. They went to the ball with matrimony on their minds."

Baines laughed softly. "And their hopes were shattered."

"Exactly," he responded, proud that she deciphered the meaning of the word from his simple explanation. "So will you join me?"

"If you're certain—"

"Perish the thought before it surfaces," Gray ordered. "I'll be the envy of every man there."

She stood up, going toward the bed. "I'll be just a minute. I just have to put on my shoes."

As she sat on the edge of the bed and pulled on her bluchers, Gray studied her. Something tugged at his heart.

He insisted it was nothing more than compassion for her plight—and the fact that she was utterly entrancing.

"There," Baines said, her engaging spirits intact. "All done."

"Splendid, my dear."

Gray held out his arm to her, anxious and honored to show her a world beyond her own.

17

BAINES SWEPT HER GAZE around the magnificent dining room. Never in her entire life had she been surrounded by such elegance. She'd thought Dunland highfalutin, but this boat was a grand place.

Huge, crystal chandeliers blazed, lit by hundreds of small candles. Gilt-framed, crimson-colored chairs surrounded intimate dining tables topped by pristine white tablecloths. Red carpeting provided a lush walking space. Dressed in impeccable black-and-white uniforms, food servers rushed about with precision.

Ladies clothed in splendid gowns took notice of only the fancy-dressed gentlemen who sat with them.

Surprised that she felt so relaxed in these dazzling surroundings, Baines deemed to enjoy her meal. Her feet planted firmly under the table assured her that no one would see her shoes. Her ecru gown, though not as showy as the other grand dames', was indeed pretty and passable. Feeling quite the lady herself, she smiled at Gray.

"Thank you," she whispered. She thanked him for his stout insistence that she dine with him. She thanked him for his fairness and his kindness. Yet she didn't feel the need to elaborate. He appeared to understand her simple words without explanation.

Gray returned Baines's alluring, artless smile. Her

beauty, her astonishing composure, enthralled him. In the presence of princes or paupers, she would remain marvelously natural. She would remain Baines.

"You're most welcome, my dear."

Their gazes met and fused. In the short time he had known her she had become a fire in his blood, threatening to consume him. Yet only his rigid self-control kept his desire in check.

But he wanted to send his discipline straight to hell and make passionate love to her. In all honesty, even if he had been assured of his ability to care for Baines, he wasn't sure he would have pursued her.

Before this crisis, he had never given marriage much consideration. The only thing he'd been sure of was that one day he would marry to continue the family name.

But this wasn't London, and Baines wasn't one of the young ladies bred to be the wife of a lord.

He cleared his throat, uneasy with his thoughts. Could he dare to be alone with her? Could he *bear* to be alone with her and not touch her?

He must remember his mission as well as his predicament. He hadn't counted on meeting anyone. The simple plan of coming to America to get Mary's Fortune was far from simple now. The engaging beauty sitting across from him complicated matters in more ways than one.

From the beginning he'd needed her to recover his quilt, but another need for her slowly emerged; something powerful and tantalizing; a need he found increasingly difficult to ignore. But he *would* ignore it. The only thing he planned to bring back to England was Mary's Fortune.

Unless he could have been certain that his wealth would be saved. Then, in spite of everything else running through his mind, he and Baines might have had a future.

He didn't want to explore why he considered such a thing. Maybe the lust he felt for her gave him such impractical thoughts.

"Is you ready to order, suh?" The waiter stood over Gray, wearing a pristine white coat and apron. A wide grin lit his chocolate-colored face.

"Shall I do the honors for you, my dear?"

Baines gave the waiter a quick glance, then nodded her agreement to Gray. After taking Gray's menu selection, the man departed.

They waited in silence for the waiter to return with their orders. Baines contemplated the consequences if they didn't find the quilt in New Orleans. She wondered what Gray would think of her. She also wondered again why the quilt was so important to Gray. It was important enough for him to willingly give her five thousand dollars!

She strained her memory, wanting to recall the quilt. When he saw the covering, he might decide it wasn't worth the money.

But hadn't she decided she wasn't going to take the money? Hadn't she concluded that her honesty, and Gray's opinion, was worth more?

The waiter approached them, carrying huge silver trays loaded with dishes of food. With a deftness borne of long practice, he soon had steaming plates and bowls of delicacies placed before them. Baines drew in a satisfying whiff.

"Mmm. It smells just wonderful."

If they had been alone, Gray would have pulled her into his arms and kissed her witless. He chided himself for the direction his thoughts took. But the pleasure on her lovely face at the delicious aromas was bloody appealing. Hell! Everything about her was appealing.

He reached for his napkin as the waiter took his leave. "I hope it tastes as good as it smells, Baines."

Watching him pick up the correct utensil and proceed to eat, Baines mimicked everything Gray did. Halfway through the meal, Gray realized what she was doing and guided her through the rest of their dinner, with the utmost patience.

From that moment on, Baines detected that an unspoken agreement had occurred between them. Gray would teach her social etiquette with the same subtlety he taught her the correct way to eat in public.

Finished with dinner, they started for their stateroom.

Baines was just mildly uneasy about being alone with Gray. But he was a gentleman, so she had nothing to fear, she reassured herself. With a self-deprecating sigh, she questioned if she feared Gray more or her traitorous body, which longed to be embraced by him.

Upon reaching their room, another realization hit her like a slap in the face. Once they arrived in New Orleans, she had no idea where to go on the docks or who to talk to there to find Eli. If she couldn't find Eli, that meant she wouldn't find the quilt. Would Gray accept that?

Baines didn't know which would be worse—sleeping in the same room with this magnificent man, or facing his wrath once again if the quilt couldn't be found.

18

WATCHING BAINES STANDING IN the center of their stateroom, Gray had never felt more awkward. He knew the outward calm she displayed belied her true fear at being alone with him. Not wanting to cause her any more anxiety, he decided to put her mind at ease.

Grinning at her, he shrugged out of his evening jacket and waistcoat. Her eyes rounded at the sight of him standing there in naught but his trousers and white shirt. He ignored her unconscious assessment of him, but felt warmed by it. His sense of awareness heightened, and his loins pulsed to life, heavy with need.

It didn't help matters that she looked as aroused as he felt.

"I'll not have it said that I wasn't gentleman enough to let you choose your sleeping spot, Baines. Which will it be? The sofa or the bed?" As soon as he'd asked the question, he realized the matter had already been decided. Yet he hoped inane conversation stopped the rising tide of passion between them.

Relief vied with the rising blush on Baines's lovely features, and he realized she'd felt as nonplussed as he did.

Her innocence amazed him. He'd expected her to be more worldly, working as she did around rowdy riverboat men at the Horse and Mule.

She smiled brightly, and a warm glow flowed through Gray at her cheeriness.

"Well, I had not given it too much thought, Gray, so I'll take the sofa. Since you're payin' for this trip, it don't seem fittin' that *you* sleep on it."

Gray chuckled at her impish tone. "That's quite an unselfish gesture, but no gentleman worth his salt would deny a lady the comfort of a bed, even if it *doesn't* seem fitting."

"But—"

He held up his hands, amused by their playful diversion. "I insist you take the bed." His grin widened. "Unless you've a mind to share the sofa with me."

"Thank you, Gray." Ignoring his goading, Baines went to the sofa. "If you ain't ready to go to sleep yet, can . . ." Her voice trailed off, and she looked at him expectantly.

"*May* asks permission, Baines," Gray explained tenderly. "Correctly used, the word *can* means to know how to do something."

"May I sit on the sofa until you're ready to go to bed?" As she spoke, her gaze never left his face.

Swallowing tightly, Gray exalted in the proud, spirited young beauty. He wondered if her sudden interest in correcting her speech was because of an interest in him. Wishful thinking, he told himself. Baines's pride in herself went way above par. Any improvements she accomplished would be for her own esteem. Of course that would please him, but he couldn't deny the twinge of disappointment coursing through him at the thought that *none* of her efforts were for him.

"For such an honor, my dear, I may sit up all night."

Baines laughed softly as she settled into the comfort of the sofa. "I won't be sittin' that long."

He gazed with longing at her. Patiently he awaited an invitation to join her, but she remained silent, lost in her thoughts. His blood heated. His interest stirred. He wanted to know everything about her; he wanted to hear that he had a place in her life, with his riches or without. At that thought he reminded himself that Baines lived day in and day out with her poverty. For her it was survivable. For him it was beyond comprehension.

"May I join you, Baines? You do look lonely there all alone."

"I'm not lonely," Baines murmured. She regarded him with an unfathomable expression. "But you may join me if you wish."

Her small mouth moved provocatively as she spoke. Only his years of practicing social graces helped him follow the gist of the conversation.

Gray settled next to her. Intense anticipation filled his entire being. "I can't imagine you being lonely, Baines," he commented. "But I suppose if you live alone most of the time, loneliness does occur."

"Sometimes I get lonesome, Gray, without a body to talk to." She shifted herself and twirled a long strand of hair. "Since my mama passed away, I kinda have gotten used to bein' all by myself."

Empathy for her loss replaced Gray's indifference toward the conversation. "How old were you when she died?" Sympathy laced his tone.

"Barely nine years old when my mama died. My papa, Uncle Linc's baby brother, died two years before my mama."

"Is Marshall your only living relative?"

Baines shrugged, resigned to her fate long ago. "So far as I know, Gray. He came back to Natchez just days before Mama died. Uncle Linc promised Papa he'd take care of me and Mama. Before my mama died, we hardly saw him. He was always away on some ship."

Gray frowned. "What did he do with a little girl to care for? He couldn't bring you on a ship with him."

"Uncle Linc gave up seamanship for a spell. Mr. Roc allowed him to work at Dunland, and he did other work, too."

"Your uncle is to be commended, my dear. It seems he took his responsibility as a proxy parent very seriously."

"He does," Baines agreed proudly. "He even saw to my schoolin'. I don't know where I'd be without Uncle Linc.

About five years ago he took to the sea again, but he warned every mama's boy around Natchez-Under-the-Hill to leave me be.''

"And just like that, they left you be?"

Baines laughed. "Not quite. Not at first. Uncle Lincoln had to convince some of the menfolk that he meant business."

"How'd he do that?"

"He busted a few heads. Them that got their heads busted turned out to be the ones to watch over me for Uncle Lincoln."

Unbidden, Luther came to Gray's mind. He wondered if the tavern owner truly saw Baines as a younger sister or if Lincoln Marshall's warning held him back. "When did you become a tavern maid?"

"Three years ago. I took the job mostly to help Uncle Linc make ends meet. He was powerful upset that I had to work there and thought he'd failed at rearin' me. But I was sixteen and I should've been pullin' in a better wage than what I was earnin' at Miz Annabelle's. She's like a second mama to me. But I aim to be as good as her or better so I can build up my clientele. I aim to make my own way in the world without havin' to rely on anybody else for survival. Nobody is gonna stand in the way of my dream," she said, almost defiantly.

Gray didn't like the sound of that. It was almost as if she dared him to gainsay her. Yet what right did he have to question her motivation for making such a brash statement? How could he ask her if she sincerely meant what she said or if she only spoke the words because she saw no other way for herself?

If he thought she sincerely didn't wish to work, he would've done everything in his power to see that she didn't. Likewise, if he thought she wanted her own sewing shop, he would've moved heaven and earth to see that she attained her dream.

Recalling her demand for his money in return for the quilt, he refrained from saying what he was feeling. He wasn't still angry about her request. Indeed, he admired her grit. But he felt the chasm between them had widened with her stout words, one that he didn't like, and one that he didn't know how to bridge. So he merely asked, "Did you have any other option besides working in the Horse and Mule at sixteen?"

" 'Course I did. I could've married Luther. He offered for me, but Uncle Linc left it up to me to accept."

"Why didn't you?"

"Because I didn't love him as a wife should love her husband," she stated simply. "When I told him no, Luther seemed relieved, and we never spoke of it again. I haven't thought of his proposal until now."

Gray didn't know why he felt such relief over her last statement. It shouldn't have mattered to him if she spent her days pining for another man.

But it did. Vainly he wanted it to be for himself if she was pining for anyone. He wanted everything she was willing to offer a man, her beauty, her innocence, her charm, and especially her determination. But it was that same determination that could ultimately come between them, even if he settled his father's debts satisfactorily and overlooked his responsibility to marry a well-bred young lady.

"I quit Luther's for a spell, but I just recently started there again to help him out for a month, which is gonna help. This past year, Uncle Linc's only been out to sea twice."

"The last time was when he acquired Mary's Fortune," Gray remarked, the quilt coming to mind.

"Mary's Fortune?"

"The quilt, Baines. My great-grandmother Mary made it and named it Mary's Fortune," Gray explained.

"Oh," Baines said in a small voice.

She'd forgotten again why she found herself in this stateroom with Gray. Fool! It was because of that danged quilt that Gray was holding court with her; because of that quilt, flames of desire burned in his sapphire gaze. How many times would she have to tell herself that he didn't have any true interest in her? What would it take to finally convince herself of that truth?

He was only using her to locate Mary's Fortune—

What an odd name. Mary's Fortune? Baines wondered what the name meant. Was it really just an old quilt? If it was, why would Gray go to such lengths to recover it? Could his sentiment for his great-grandmother's handiwork really bring him across an ocean and beyond?

She searched her memory. The lost quilt flashed before her mind's eye for a brief second. Even the square patterns had odd, mysterious designs on them. Was it in fact a secret map? Or was the fortune woven into it?

Gray had called her a liar. She was beginning to suspect that he was the one who'd lied to her. What secret did Mary's Fortune hold to drive Gray the way it did to find it? If it was some kind of fortune, Baines could only imagine what he would do if he never recovered the quilt.

Until he'd mentioned the quilt, she'd enjoyed talking to Gray and telling him about herself. He'd seemed genuinely interested to hear about her life. But it had all been pretense.

She swallowed tightly, his nearness tormenting. He was beyond handsome in his dark evening attire. He was regal and noble, doing justice to his proud heritage. His black hair shone with bluish highlights, thick and straight, tapering neatly to the white collar of his shirt. A massive chest led to a slim waist and flat stomach. A more perfect specimen of masculinity she had never encountered. She doubted she ever would again.

She pretended to stifle a yawn, hating the attraction she felt for him. If only she was back at her house, completing Uncle Linc's quilt, and away from Grayling Dunston.

"Baines, my dear, I fear I am keeping you awake." Gray stood from the sofa and stretched. The muscles in his arms and legs rippled with his sensuous movements. He eyed her for a moment, his eyes sparkling. "I'll step outside to allow you some privacy so you can prepare yourself for bed."

Baines stood. Her heart hammered, and her pulse roared in her head. "I hope you don't mind, Gray," she managed, proud of how unaffected she sounded. "I really am tired."

"Of course not, Baines. Despite your nap, this day has

been rather trying. The quicker it's over, the closer we'll be to Mary's Fortune.'' He strode to the door and placed his hand on the knob. ''Take your time. I'll be gone awhile.'' With that, he stepped out and closed the door behind him.

She slipped out of her ecru dress and, keeping on her chemise, got into bed. She wondered if Gray would remain clothed while he slept. Having no desire to find out, she determined to keep her face to the wall the entire night.

That, however, wasn't her main worry.

The quilt, Mary's Fortune, gnawed at her, and the true reason Gray pursued it so doggedly.

19

THE NEXT MORNING BAINES slid from the bed and padded across the floor to the ornately carved washstand. A large white ceramic bowl sat on the marble surface, with two pitchers, one metal and one ceramic, on either side of the bowl.

Baines smiled at the arrangement. The metal pitcher held hot water, while the other one held cold. Wondering if Gray had even slept on the sofa and not knowing how long she'd be alone, she put aside her delight and quickly completed her cleansing.

Sunshine gleamed through the porthole, promising a beautiful day, the prospect filling her with momentary serenity. Gray came to mind, and her heart took a perilous leap.

She wondered how long she could deny her attraction for him, how long she could pretend a mere friendship with him would content her.

Until she'd met Gray, she never thought about marriage or having kids, which was all a girl her age should have had on her mind. So she'd never really considered the type of man she wanted to spend the rest of her life with. But the more time she spent in Gray's company, the more she realized he was everything she wanted in a lifemate and more.

From the first, he had been her knight in shining armor. Come what may, he was proud of her and interested in every little aspect of her life.

Some of her happiness fled as she thought of the quilt, Mary's Fortune. Doubt intruded. Surely Gray's interest in her wasn't solely because of that blasted quilt. Although she'd thought that last night, in the warm light of day she just couldn't believe it of him. Not when he so honorably left her to her own devices to complete her dressing. Not when he so chivalrously gave her the bed for her comfort, when he was paying for this entire trip. And certainly not when his bold features and admiring blue eyes danced in her head.

Still uncertainty plagued Baines as she dressed in a gown she had packed for the trip, then sat on the sofa, waiting for Gray to make an appearance.

She wished she could understand Gray's attachment to that quilt. The closer they got to New Orleans, the less sure she became that it would ever surface again.

Thoroughly irritated with the turn her life had taken, Baines tapped her foot rapidly on the floor.

In a week's time her honesty had been questioned, her routine had been changed, and she was bound for New Orleans to search for a quilt that she'd thought was her salvation but could very well be her downfall. She was sharing a cabin with Gray, the Earl of Montegut, and the most magnificent man she had ever met. Wicked heat coursed through her body, and the kisses they had shared came to mind.

Shamefully she wanted him to take her into his powerful arms again, to kiss away her doubt and fears. Last night, during dinner and afterward, they had forged a bond, one that was fragile and thread-thin, but one that could only grow stronger if allowed. Baines wondered if he felt it, too; she wondered if he was as attracted to her as she was to him.

Abruptly she stood and went to the door. She was hungry and confused and didn't want to wait for Gray any longer.

Viewing her attire once more in the cheval mirror, she

hesitated before stepping outside her room, knowing her attire wasn't the standard for the ladies of class. But Gray wasn't like the others, and his opinion was all that mattered.

Baines stiffened her spine at the loathsome look a passing lady gave her. Her nerves tensed immediately, and a cold knot formed in her stomach.

Swallowing her anxiety, she closed the door, refusing to allow a fancy dress and insulting scowl to intimidate her.

The lavender gown she wore was old and worn. Years out of style, it hung loosely about her. Unlike last night, she now attracted attention as she walked along the promenade deck. Matrons heading in the same direction as she sniggered and sneered. Even the gentlemen's gazes taunted her.

Baines almost returned to her cabin. She almost screamed at them that they were no better than she. Perhaps it had been a mistake to leave the security of the room. Besides, she had no money to pay for breakfast, and Gray might not be in the dining room.

With remarkable resolve, she continued forward, head held high. Swallowing a determined sob, she ignored the taunts. Reaching the dining salon, she stopped in the doorway. Her eyes scanned the room.

She gasped, and her heart slammed against her chest, her shock almost overtaking her.

A beautifully dressed woman sat at the table with Gray, and they seemed lost in conversation. The lady wasn't much older than Gray, her mahogany hair fashionably styled. Very attractive, she only had eyes for Gray and was most attentive to his every word. Her ringing laughter sounded, punctuated by a caress of Gray's arm.

He didn't seem to mind. He laughed right along with her and seemed to pretend not to notice the way the lady's hand lingered.

Baines thought to retreat. She was a pitiful comparison to the woman's grace and style, and she didn't want to intrude on what seemed to be a private conversation. It didn't matter that Gray was supposed to be *her* husband. He had obviously forgotten their pretense as well. Although she'd heard rumors that wealthy men kept mistresses, she couldn't believe they would be so blatant.

She told herself Gray's actions didn't matter. She *wasn't* jealous, and the emotion she felt certainly wasn't betrayal. After all, their attraction and closeness was only in her mind. Gray was a single man who could do as he pleased.

Then why did she feel like crying? Why did she feel like aiming something at Gray's inky head to vent her frustrations?

"Pod'n me, miss. Is you sure you in the right room?"

Lost in her thoughts, the scornful tone surprised Baines. She looked up. A black waiter stood there, disdain clear on his face.

"Perhaps you should show her the way to the galley," a woman loudly scoffed as she glided pass Baines. "It seems she has this room confused with the kitchen."

All eyes turned to her, and her cheeks heated. It was a humiliating, deflating moment, made worse by the hurt she felt at Gray. She felt sick and faint and wanted to run far, far away. But for the life of her she couldn't make herself move. Rooted to the spot, her gaze clashed with Gray's as he strode toward her and reached her side immediately.

Yet she didn't want him near her. It was on the tip of her tongue to tell him to return to the mystery woman. Baines only wanted to be left alone, to nurse her embarrassment in private. That Gray had witnessed this was bad enough, but he'd witnessed it with an attractive woman in a beautiful gown. When the lady's hand flew to her breast, sympathy clear on her face, tears of despair burned Baines's eyes.

Her throat ached with her refusal to let them fall. She wouldn't cry. She wouldn't! Yet there wasn't much to smile about, either. The happiness and contentment she'd felt in the cabin was gone completely, replaced by wounded pride and heartfelt anguish.

Gray took her into his arms and hugged her, then brushed his lips across her own in a lingering, passionate kiss. Stepping away from her, he met her gaze. His eyes were brilliant, as blue as a summer sky, and filled with tenderness and longing. He smiled with encouragement.

Baines blinked rapidly, trying hard not to let him see her tears, and trying even harder not to stare at him. From the contact of his mouth, fire burned in the pit of her belly. Yet he was there for her, embracing her with no shame for all and sundry, including that woman at his table, to view. She straightened herself with dignity.

"Baines, my dear, pay the witch woman no mind." His voice was hard, and his glower penetrated the room at large. "It is she who is confused, missing the turn to her cave. Come, little mouse, join me."

With a gentle tug he pulled Baines's hand through the crook of his arm and escorted her to his table.

Nearly overcome with astonishment at Gray's chivalry, Baines moved automatically to where he led her. Looking over her shoulder, she saw that the "witch woman" rushed red-faced from the dining room.

A smile of satisfaction crossed Baines's lips. She knew the other diners, though pretending disinterest, watched her out of the corners of their eyes. She wondered if she alone garnered their interest, or was it the sinfully handsome man whose arm she held on to?

When Gray pulled out a chair for her next to the woman who still sat at his table, Baines's smile faded. Face-to-face with this paragon of femininity, Baines's self-esteem disappeared. The woman's smile, however, was bright enough to lighten the darkest day.

"That was positively gallant what your husband just did, my lady," the woman beamed in a British accent. "And who can blame him? You are quite the prettiest thing on this boat!"

Baines frowned, her gaze going from Gray to the lady and back to Gray again. Who *was* this woman, and what had Gray told her?

An uncomfortable look in his eyes, Gray seated himself across from the two women. "My dear, permit me to introduce Penelope Anderson-Wallingford, a fellow citizen of my native land."

"H-how do you do, ma'am?" Baines stammered. She

didn't want to shame Gray and hoped she responded properly. Since she was supposed to be his wife, she would try to act the part.

It had apparently been easy enough for him if the way he'd walked up to her and kissed her was any indication. The aftereffects from it still warmed her insides. He was unlocking her heart and awakening her body, and she wondered what she would do when he left her.

"Ma'am?" Penelope chuckled. "My lady, you must accustom yourself to being married to a lord of the realm. It is *I* who should address *you* as ma'am or lady." She touched Baines's arm. "Never you mind. You've only been married a few days. You'll get used to it."

"I'm sure she will," Gray put in, his gaze secretive. He smiled intimately. "Baines, I hope you don't mind, but I gave Penelope—"

"Oh, my lady Baines," Penelope interrupted dramatically. "Lord Montegut told me how your trunk got left behind on the docks in Natchez with all your lovely clothes inside. It's just dreadful! He said you ended up with some poor person's traveling sack."

Gray wouldn't make up such an outrageous tale about her. No, surely not. In all of their acquaintance, he had never expressed shame at her attire. *He* had championed her constantly against everyone else. She turned to him.

One look at him left no doubt in her mind that he'd said those hurtful words. His skin was flushed with heat, and he was glowering in Penelope's direction.

Baines smiled coldly and permitted herself a withering stare. "And just how did I end up with some poor person's travelin' sack, Gray?"

Baines's brittle tone was like the sound of pebbles slamming into a marble floor, and the coldness in her green eyes almost caused Gray to shiver.

"Baines—"

Her abrupt rise from her seat interrupted him.

"Save it," she spat out. "It's been a pleasure meetin' you, Penelope." With that, Baines hurried from the dining room. And him.

He hadn't meant to hurt Baines. He'd only sought to help her with his wild story. Penelope appeared to be the same size, and he'd offered to buy a gown from her for Baines, since they still had yet another day and night on the river before reaching New Orleans.

Penelope, the foolish woman, had repeated everything he'd said, but not the *way* he'd said it.

When Gray returned to the stateroom last night, Baines had been asleep, just as she was this morning when he'd left to give her the privacy he knew she needed when she woke up.

He'd been sipping his coffee, wondering if enough time had gone by before he could escort Baines to breakfast. But Penelope's approach had sidetracked his intentions. She'd apparently made it her business to discover his marital status and had introduced herself to ferret information about his wife. It was then that the idea to tell that ridiculous story had hit him.

As an earl's wife, Baines wouldn't have been dressed in anything but the utmost finery. Still, that really didn't matter to him. He was an *earl*, and if his wife wanted to traipse around in a bloody sack, that was no one else's concern.

He'd merely thought to protect Baines. Try as she might to hide it, other people's opinions mattered to her, and he knew how spiteful society women could be. As she was undoubtedly learning.

Yet he wouldn't have Baines think he'd made light of her poverty. "Will you excuse me, Madam Wallingford?"

"It's Penelope, remember?" she purred. "Of course, I'll excuse you, my lord. I hope it's nothing serious with your wife. Do tell her what a pleasure it was meeting her."

"I'll do that, Penelope. It's been a pleasure meeting you," he said with forced politeness and started away from the table.

Making his way to his stateroom, he cursed Mary's Fortune for the dozenth time. If it hadn't been for the deuced quilt, he wouldn't be on this bloody boat. He wouldn't be on his way to a beautiful enchantress to ask forgiveness for his thoughtlessness.

But without the treasure Mary's Fortune had to offer, it was anyone's guess where he would wind up when the deadline to pay his father's debts came due in six months.

Reaching the door, he paused a moment, inhaling an agitated breath. Mary's Fortune. His nemesis or his salvation?

The door swung open to his knock, and he stepped inside the cabin.

20

GRAY TOOK IN THE stricken look on Baines's face as she stepped aside to allow him entrance. His heart twisted. He wanted to explain to her that she'd taken Penelope's meaning the wrong way. Truly, he wasn't ashamed of her or the fact that she was poor. Yet the words wouldn't come. Explaining away his actions was not in his repertoire. He was an earl, a peer, who was used to having others answer to *him*.

They stood facing each other for long moments, their gazes locked.

He took in her pale face and searched her eyes. He hated the hurt he saw, especially since he was the cause. He walked toward her. She stepped away from him.

"Baines," he began. Her name sounded like an entreaty. He realized he felt as vulnerable as she looked. "Baines—"

"Don't!" Baines said, the word bursting from her.

Red-hot anger replaced the despair in her features. He watched as she grappled with words and fought some inner turmoil.

"It's obvious you're not comfortable with the likes of me around you." Green eyes gripped him like talons. Her words were raking, accusing. "I'll try to stay out of your way, Gray."

His temper flared. She stood unwilling to listen to him,

believing the words of a stranger without giving him a chance to tell his side. "Mistress, perhaps it is you who's uncomfortable in my world," he said coldly. "Do not blame me for your own insecurities!"

Blood siphoned from her face, and she went stock-still, as though she had turned to stone.

"Bein' poor ain't my choice!" Her voice was high and strained. "For the time bein', I just am. The one thing I don't do is make up excuses for my plight. You would oblige me if you didn't do so on my account."

She didn't remark upon his words. It was a glaring omission. Obviously he had touched a nerve, and suddenly he regretted it.

"Dammit, Baines! Let me explain—"

"There ain't no need to explain, Gray," Baines responded. "You were pretty clear in your meanin'. Now go away and leave me be."

Gray gave her a penetrating look, trying to decipher her thoughts and discern how to reach her. But he could find none. So he stalked out of the room and slammed the door behind him.

Baines sank down on the sofa, her anger at Gray dissipating. Why should she have been surprised at his actions? He'd given her no indication that he'd truly accepted her for what she was. Over and over, he showed in every way possible that he only wanted her for what he thought she could do for him. Each time, the reason was that dang quilt!

Well, she hated it! Temptation to become dishonest had never presented itself until she'd received that quilt and Gray came looking for it. She had to come to terms with the fact that she might live the rest of her days in poverty. Her talent didn't matter. There were bodies out there a lot more talented than she, and she doubted they were wallowing in riches.

If she'd still had the quilt in her possession, there was no guarantee it would lead to the kind of money or success she desired.

Yet Gray's words, even more than his actions, rankled. They cut deeply because of their brutal honesty. He had touched a nerve, one that she'd tried so hard to cover up.

Hadn't she masked her worry, her fears, with laughter? Didn't everyone see that she accepted her plight until her luck took a turn for the better?

Baines brushed tears from her eyes. For the first time in her memory, she thought it was okay to cry over her lack of wealth. As much as she worried about Uncle Linc, she realized he wasn't the driving force behind her goals. It was her and her foolish dreams—and her jealousy.

Was she so obvious? Did everyone see how tired she was of being looked down upon by the wealthy class? Could anyone detect her worry over her plight and the fact that she didn't want to end up working herself into an early grave like her father had, or dying of lung fever like her mother?

How could she bear to leave the cabin again? How could Gray have been so insensitive?

She couldn't give up her dreams. She had lived with them for months, and they had been her guiding force. Dreams were hard to sustain and make come true, but one day she would do both. She knew no other way to feel or to think.

How dare Gray try to rip her hope from her?

A knock sounded on the door. She sniffled, refusing to acknowledge it, knowing instinctively who it was. After a few minutes the door opened slightly, and Gray peeked in.

"Baines?"

He walked fully into the cabin and stared at her, his expression unreadable. She looked at him out of tear-stained eyes and hoped he didn't comment on her state. He swallowed hard, as if he fought not to inquire about her anguish.

"You must be hungry," he said quietly. "I have ordered breakfast to be brought to our room."

"That's mighty generous of you, Gray," Baines said, and sniffed with rancor. Her hackles raised, despite the fact that she'd just considered staying in the cabin herself. "At least if I am hid away in this cabin, I won't shame you with my appearance—"

"Stop it, Baines!" Gray flared. He sat next to her, stiff and ramrod-straight, his tension obvious. "I don't care one bloody whit what you're wearing."

"Don't you? Don't mock me, Gray."

His long fingers drummed against his thigh. Baines wondered if he ever relaxed enough to wear comfortable breeches and simple shirts. She wondered how she didn't realize that every time she saw him he was dressed in elegant and formal clothes, as if he took great pains with his appearance.

He'd been proud to have her on his arm last night, but that was only because she'd looked as presentable and fashionable as the other ladies in the dining salon. Even though he'd run to her rescue today, she doubted he'd been sincere. He'd only been guilty of maligning her as the others did, and thought to ease his conscience.

"I'm not senseless," she hissed shrewishly. "I'm only poor."

"Aye," he gritted. "You're poor. But you seem to have more of a problem with that than I do."

She inhaled sharply, his words like a knife in her chest, twisting her pain deeper. That was the second time he'd told her that. Yet how could she dispute him, when he only spoke the truth?

He touched her cheek, his caress soft, coaxing, and so very tender. She remained still, not moving a muscle, increasingly aware of him. A battle raged within her, one that she knew she was destined to lose.

The hard truth was that she was a simple quiltmaker from Rivertown, who had only her dreams to sustain her, and who had no right to have feelings for someone in Gray's position. He was an English lord who was on some mysterious mission to retrieve an old quilt and anxious to return to his country. Without her.

"Baines . . . little mouse," he murmured. "My only thought was to put you at ease. I never meant to insult you. I certainly never meant for my words to be repeated so callously."

"Then why did you do it?"

Baines stiffened her shoulders and raised her chin in haughty defiance. His warm fingers against her skin was affecting her more than she wanted to admit. Her blood was stirring, and her senses were awakening. She was no match for his experience, no match for his seductive intent. Not when her heart was so tangled with emotion for him.

"Why, Gray?"

Gray sighed and moved his fingers through her hair, which seemed to be his favorite spot.

"It was my intention to buy a gown from Madam Wallingford for you," he confessed. "I wanted you to walk freely about the boat without being self-conscious. I have not mocked you. I merely used poor judgment."

Baines risked a glance at him. His hot look scorched her and burned away the last of her anger. He smiled that intimate smile that made her belly clench. She wanted him to kiss her again and feel his firm mouth as it possessed hers.

Her pulse banged against her chest, and she summoned her courage. Leaning toward him, she pressed her lips against his.

It was all the encouragement he needed, and it seemed as if he had been barely containing the same impulse. He kissed her greedily. Guiding her back on the sofa, he moved his hard body over hers and trailed his mouth over her chin, down the long column of her throat and finally the bare expanse of skin left visible in the bodice of her gown.

She felt his raging hardness pressing against her skirts, and liquid fire rushed to her secret place. He moved against her, provocatively, sensually.

Her emotions whirled and skitted to a halt. This had happened so fast. One moment they had been arguing, and the next desire was raging out of control. Yet she wanted to answer the passion flaming in her body. She clung to him and caressed the strong planes of his back. His hand slipped beneath her bodice and caressed a hardened nipple.

She raised her hips to meet his, the gesture instinctive—

A knock sounded on the door.

Gray cursed at the intrusion, and he cursed his weakness.

He had been moments away from taking Baines's innocence. Good God, how sweet she'd felt in his arms.

His body aching for release, he stood as the knock sounded again.

"Just a moment," he called, more sharply than he intended.

Slowly Baines sat up. She looked dazed and flushed. Her gaze was bright and limpid, and he wondered how he would stop himself from taking her into his arms again once they were alone.

Readjusting his clothes and waiting until Baines did the same with hers, he opened the door and stood partially behind it to shield his raging desire. A waiter pushed passed him into the room with a serving cart and quietly placed the contents on the table, then left without a word.

There were scrambled eggs, sausages, biscuits, marmalade, a pot of coffee, and milk.

"I'm powerful hungry," Baines said huskily, then blushed as the double meaning of her words sank in.

Gray was hungry as well. But not for food. She smiled at him and wet her lips. The agitation between his thighs increased.

"I reckon there's enough food there to last until we reach New Orleans," Baines commented with a nervous laugh.

"Sit down, my dear." He pulled a chair from under the dining table.

She seated herself, and he watched the pulse point pounding at her throat. He watched the rise and fall of her lovely breasts. She was as aware of him as he was of her.

He brushed his hand across her shoulders, and she inhaled sharply.

Some semblance of sanity remained, possibly because his years of responsibility took over. He had obligations to fulfill. He couldn't overlook that fact again.

If he got Baines with child, he would have to marry her. Never mind his father's expectations. His honor dictated no less. If he didn't find Mary's Fortune, he would be hard-pressed to care for himself, let alone someone else.

He seated himself, not interested in the food. His gaze

roamed over her beautiful face, once again animated.

"I would be proud to escort you on deck, little mouse. Or to the dining salon. Or anywhere on this boat you care to go." He thought it necessary to inform her of that and erase any lingering doubt from her mind.

"Thank you, Gray," Baines said softly. She scanned his face. "If you don't mind, I would rather finish the trip here in this beautiful stateroom."

Unsure of how to keep from touching her, he poured himself a cup of coffee. "Are you sure?"

"Aye," she teased. "I'm bloody sure."

She giggled when he threw his napkin at her. Laughter welled in him at her playfulness, and he chuckled.

He didn't want friction between them. Soon he would have to return to England and he wanted to leave as Baines's friend. But while they were together on the boat, he wanted her to enjoy the trip.

He could very well spend the rest of their journey making scalding love to her, and he would need some distraction from her to take that thought off his mind.

How could he bear to be in such constant proximity to her for the next twenty-four hours after what had transpired between them?

"Gray," Baines began, pouring out a cup of coffee for herself, "I don't expect you to sit out the rest of this trip in here with me."

It was as if she'd read his mind. Gray smiled at the thought, images of the two of them entwined naked on the bed turning in his mind. He cleared his throat.

"Are you throwing me out? I thought you enjoyed my company."

He gave her a wounded look, and Baines laughed at his theatrics.

"I do," she said. "But I would feel plumb better if you wouldn't lock yourself away in here just to oblige me."

"Very well, my dear." Grateful for her consideration, Gray nodded and stood. He would use this time wisely, to get his thoughts in order and his passion under firm control. "I'll leave you to your musings for a while and go out on deck."

21

WEARING HER ECRU GOWN once again, Baines stood on the deck, taking in the various sights New Orleans had to offer, and guarding her and Gray's traveling bags. She was waiting for Gray to hire a carriage.

Keelboats, flatboats, and steamers ladened with cotton and cane lined the wharves as far as the eye could see. People of all nationalities and colors crowded the docks and sprinkled the air with the local dialects and thick accents. Barrels of grain, flour, and coffee beans waited for transport along with crates of oysters, shrimp, and crabs. Their scents mingled and carried on the river breeze.

Early May sunshine gleamed on the scene, creating an aura of sultry grace the city was so famous for. It was warm today, and Baines hoped Gray completed his task soon so they could be on their way.

The past day had been a sheer delight for her. It seemed as if they'd called an unspoken truce since the argument and ensuing passion of two days ago.

She still hadn't told him she didn't want his money, afraid that their happiness would end if she brought up her blackmail scheme. So she allowed herself to be carried away by Gray's charm and honor.

She hadn't seen him the entire day after he'd left her at breakfast, but yesterday she and Gray had explored every inch of the *Natchez Belle*. She realized she was sorry to see the trip come to an end.

Here in New Orleans, reality would certainly intrude.

The uncomfortable sensation of being watched made Baines glance around the docks. A tall man stood not far away from her, a wide-brimmed hat covering his head. Recognition dawned immediately and her heartbeat increased.

She would remember that arrogant, bearded face anywhere, and she wondered what he was doing in New Orleans. Then the answer became obvious—he had followed her. Or more to the point, he might have followed *Gray*.

Her eyes widened in alarm, and she locked her gaze with the stranger's. A lazy smile curving his full lips, he tipped his hat at her and sauntered off toward the landing.

She searched the area, looking for Gray.

A slave woman dressed in brightly colored garments pushed a cart laden with flowers in every color of the rainbow in front of Gray as he started toward Baines. She watched, fascinated, her worry momentarily forgotten.

Dressed in a silk shirt and gray trousers, Gray appeared a god, put here solely to torment and beguile unwitting young women. Ever the nobleman, his fine clothes bespoke his wealth. Yet he seemed relaxed and at ease. A thrill of excitement shot through her.

Gray sauntered up to her, a small bouquet from the flower woman in his hand. He held it out to Baines.

"Flowers for a rose." Desire glittered in his blue eyes. "Although I know of no flower, including roses, that can touch your beauty, Baines."

Heat, scalding and unrelenting, crept up Baines's neck and invaded her cheeks. She tingled at the way he murmured her name. It sounded personal and intimate, as if he alone had sole right to her. Swallowing hard, she accepted the flowers.

"Thank you for those nice words, Gray."

He smiled, his teeth perfect and white against his tanned skin. "My pleasure."

He started to guide her away, but she grabbed his hand and halted him.

The feel of her soft skin was like a flash of fire to his senses. But the alarm in her eyes worried him.

"There's a man, Gray," she began, her voice reed-thin with fright. "He was at the shop the other day, and I saw him again just a few moments ago." She searched his face. "I think he's after you."

Gray frowned, his anger flaring at the thought of anyone shadowing Baines. After all, who in this country knew *him?* For that matter, who in England had a vendetta against him?

But whoever he was, Gray would bloody tear him apart for frightening Baines.

"Describe him to me," he snarled.

"He's tall. A-and blond with p-pale eyes and a devil-may-care smile. His visit at the shop worried me, but it just slipped my mind. But seein' him here I realized he's trouble, Gray. I can feel it in my bones."

Gray barely heard her, could barely follow the thread of conversation. Indeed, Baines was right. The man she described was trouble, and miles away from home.

Jamie.

From her description, the stranger could be no other. Yet what could he possibly want with Gray? After all these years without a word, an apology, why would Jamie follow him across an ocean?

No, there had to be another excuse, one Gray couldn't care less about. He was in no danger, of that he was sure. Jamie might have been a liar, but he wasn't a murderer.

He smiled without warmth. "Never fear, little mouse. I'm in no danger."

"Gray—"

He propelled her in the direction of the waiting black carriage. "We will endeavor to enjoy our stay here. Forget about this man. If he is who I think he is, he is merely an old friend I would rather forget. Jamie knows this, which is why he refuses to approach me."

"Jamie?"

"Aye, James McKay—"

"Who—"

"Cease your questions, Baines!" Gray snapped. "I would prefer not to discuss him."

"Fine," she huffed.

Gray smiled at her indignation.

In his memory he had never been more at ease than he had in the past two days with Baines. But he couldn't be distracted from his goal. Once he had the quilt in hand and his family's good name restored, he would examine his feelings about Baines further.

After a few moments of silence she asked, "Where are we goin', Gray?"

"*You* are going to the Tremoulet House, my dear. I, on the other hand, will remain here and try to garner information on this fellow Eli."

"B-but you won't be able to recognize him, Gray, since you've never seen him."

"If someone knows him, little mouse, he will point him out to me," Gray reasoned. "Now go. By the time you reach the hotel, everything will have been all arranged. Captain Cordair sent a message ahead and settled things for us. I asked him to secure a suite with two bedchambers."

Digging in his traveling bag, he retrieved a pouch and handed it to her. "There are several double eagles in there, along with a goodly amount of picayunes—" He smiled at her surprise, stemming the urge to kiss her inviting mouth. "Rochester apprised me of the money difference between our two countries," he interrupted himself to explain. "Now, as I was saying, your room should be situated right next to mine. You must pay the carriage driver with the smaller denomination of picayunes. . . . Why are you smiling?"

"This is my country, Gray," Baines explained lightly. "I know how to use money here."

Gray laughed, her easy manner contagious. "Forgive me, Baines. It must be the prospect of reclaiming Mary's Fortune that has me so forgetful."

A slight breeze rippled through Baines's hair, gently lifting it about her shoulders. It fell below her waist like a silken mantle. Gray longed to run his fingers through it and savor its soft texture. He longed to spread it on a pillow like an exotic fan while he made love to Baines.

She was everything he wanted, soft, sweet, determined, and proud.

"I've been told there's a couturiere a few doors from the hotel, Baines," he said. "There's enough money in the pouch for a few gowns if you care to make use of it while I'm gone."

An enigmatic expression crossed Baines's features. She looked as if she were about to speak, then decided against it. She cleared her throat.

"I would be plumb proud to, Gray. But maybe I should go with you. Eli might not want to give up the quilt to a body he never saw before."

Gray snickered evilly. "I have ways of making him give it up. Besides, Baines, I don't want you on the docks. It's no bloody place for a lady!" He delivered that statement with stern finality. His vehemence surprised even himself, but the worry he felt over her safety convinced him that he did the right thing. Yet he wouldn't allow Baines to see his concern. She might get the wrong idea.

Not liking Gray's tone, Baines thought to gainsay him and insist she accompany him. Seeing the worry in his eyes, she decided against it. She knew that worry was for her.

She had no idea what Gray would do to Eli if Eli refused to relinquish the quilt. But that would be Eli's misfortune. She wouldn't dwell on it.

"Whatever you say, milord," she jested, giving Gray her most dazzling smile.

"Get on with you," Gray said to the driver after helping her into the carriage.

Baines felt Gray's gaze on her as the livery man commanded the horse forward. It took every effort not to turn back to him, but she couldn't. Not while such intense feelings churned within her.

Pretending a serenity she didn't feel, she faced forward, nearly bursting with eagerness to explore the city. The carriage clattered past rows of shanty houses and into the heart of the Vieux Carré so quickly, Baines hardly had enough time to see anything. Soon the driver pulled the carriage to a stop before the Tremoulet House, located at the corners of Old Levee and St. Peter streets.

It was an old moresque structure. Huge planters filled with blooming flowers graced each side of the entrance doors. Slaves liveried in scarlet and white served as doormen and rushed forward to assist her from the carriage.

Baines smiled and paid the driver, then allowed herself to be assisted down. She drew in an awe-inspired breath, feeling dwarfed by the imposing structure and out of place by the elegance. But she had weathered her insecurities on the boat and she would do so here.

Looking down the street, she saw a neatly trimmed red sign with the word *Couturiere* written in black letters. Something else was written beneath it, but she was too far away to discern what. She stood contemplating whether to visit the little shop or go to her room in the hotel.

"*Pardonnez-moi*, mademoiselle, may I help you?"

In surprise, Baines turned to the sound of the man's voice. She found herself staring into a pair of dancing black eyes set in the face of a young man who was appraising her appreciatively. She had no doubt that he was considered handsome by many. When she compared him to Gray, however, he seemed naught but a boy severely lacking— in what, she wasn't certain.

"I am Jacques," he said with a smile. "I can assist with your belongings, if you so desire."

"Why . . ." She hesitated, glancing again at the sign in the next block. Quickly she came to her decision. "Thank you, no. Not at the moment, Jacques. But please take my belongin's up to Lord Dunston's rooms." Smiling politely at the man's helpful mood, she began walking toward the dress shop.

The words she was unable to discern from afar leaped out at her at close range. *Couturiere: Dresses ready-made and made to order.*

Hardly able to contain her excitement at the prospect of new garments, she drew in a quick breath and pushed open the door to the little shop.

22

LATER THAT EVENING, ATTENDED by Mimi, a chambermaid, Baines relaxed in the marble tub in her bedchamber, enjoying the most luxurious bath she'd ever experienced.

The suite Captain Cordair had procured for her and Gray was well appointed and elegant. A four-poster canopied bed dominated her private chamber, along with a matching dressing table, an armoire, and a dining table with two matching chairs. A crystal chandelier gleamed, casting soft light against the pink walls. A colorful arrangement of fresh flowers sat in a silver vase and stood on the mantel of the unlit marble fireplace.

The elegance that she was subjected to in Gray's presence continued to astound her. By now she should have been used to it. Every little detail shouldn't have mattered.

For as long as she could remember she'd dreamed of living this way. But she couldn't do so with a clear conscience as long as her uncle struggled to make ends meet. And she couldn't do so at Gray's expense.

Tonight she would summon the courage to apologize to him. She would explain that her misguided attempt to swindle money from him had been foolish and selfish.

Thinking of the money he'd given her, she smiled. There had been three hundred dollars inside that pouch, but she would inform him that she considered it a loan. She'd thought to refuse the money when he'd handed it to her, but decided against it. And she was glad she did. Now she had a wardrobe to make herself presentable to His Lordship.

She loathed to end her bath, but the water had grown cold. Standing from the tub, Baines allowed the water to drip from her body. Rose oil, put in her bath by Mimi, beaded her skin.

She felt sensual and alive, as if she could conquer the world. But the world seemed easy to conquer compared to the daunting task of trying to win Gray.

Some of her happiness evaporated at the thought. Even now Mary's Fortune had probably been returned to his possession. While she passed the time dreaming of him, he was more than likely securing passage on a ship bound for London.

"Madame will wear the black-and-gold gown?" Mimi smiled slyly as she assisted Baines with her toweling. "It is a creation just for you, and you are a creation to drive a man senseless with desire. Your husband is a lucky man."

If only Gray were her husband. If only this wasn't a pretense created by Gray and unwittingly prolonged by Captain Cordair.

Baines laughed with forced merriment, but her cheeks felt heated. She'd never heard such talk from a woman before. Not even Miz Annabelle, who Baines deemed quite scandalous at times.

"Then maybe I better not wear that one, Mimi."

She thought of how she had gone overboard at the couturiere. She'd been unable to resist the beautiful gown and another wine-colored one, plus two day dresses. Her true sense of fashion seemed to come alive the minute she entered the dress shop.

With fabric and colors filling her senses, she concluded her sense of style had been stifled around Miz Annabelle. The widow's knowledge of fashion and style had Baines thoroughly intimidated. But never again.

Not even for Miz Annabelle or Uncle Lincoln would she

unintentionally hinder her real skill. She *knew* fashion and style, just as she knew quilting. She just hadn't concentrated on dressmaking they way she did quilting.

"Either gown you wear, madame, will place you in a very entrancing position with many a gentleman, which may cause your husband to fight a duel," Mimi said. She helped Baines with the brand-new soft linen chemise Baines had also treated herself to. "A position envied by most women."

When the chambermaid finished with her task of dressing Baines, she released an excited gasp at the completed product of her labor. "Oh, *Mon Dieu!* You are what every man imagines a woman should be. You are—"

A knock at the door interrupted Mimi's glowing comments.

Going to the door, she placed her ear against it. *"Oui?"*

"Is Baines ready to depart?" Gray asked from the sitting room of the suite.

"Noooo!" Baines squeaked. "Don't open the door. I'm not all together yet. My hair—"

"Oui, madame. I'll fix it," Mimi replied with glee. "Monsieur," she shouted through the door, "Madame will meet you in the atrium. Wait for her there *s'il vous plait."*

"Mimi!" Baines cried. "I thought you meant my hair."

"I will fix that, too!"

∽

GRAY GLANCED AT THE timepiece on the wall above the bar as he stood in the atrium of Tremoulet House awaiting Baines's pleasure. Ten minutes had already passed, and still there was no sign of her. If he hadn't been in such a hurry to see her again, he would have been happy to have this chance to ponder the events of the past hours.

He'd learned that Eli Washington and Lincoln Marshall had missed the ship they signed up for and would possibly hang around New Orleans to hire out on the next one going to the Caribbean. Gray's informant, a man known only as Tic, told him they were more than likely on Tchoupitoulas

Road in one of the hostels that dotted the area.

Convincing Gray that that part of town at night was no match for a fancy dresser such as himself, Tic promised Gray he would call for him in the morning. For a price, he would personally accompany him to Tchoupitoulas Road and Eli Washington.

Against his better judgment, Gray took Tic's council, but only because of concern for Baines. Her passage back to Natchez was already paid, and he'd given her three hundred dollars in gold, so she wouldn't be strapped for money. His concern was if he *were* to turn up missing, she would go to that rat-infested placed looking for him. Goodness knows what end she would come to there. No, he would be patient and wait for the clear light of day.

Absently Gray glanced toward the center staircase, catching sight of the cause of appreciative murmurs rippling throughout the atrium. The most exquisite creature he'd ever seen glided slowly down the stairs. He'd thought his little mouse beautiful, but this woman who commanded every eye in the place stole his breath.

She reached the bottom of the stairway, as regal as any queen. The black bodice of the black-and-gold gown she wore seemed to caress her impossibly tiny waist. The woman stopped and looked around the chamber.

When her green eyes settled on him, shock scorched through Gray's body. Smiling happily, she proceeded toward him.

Gray thought everyone would hear the thumping in his chest. He thought everyone would discern his passionate response. How could he not recognize her? How could a mere garment cause such a magnificent change?

"Evenin', Gray," Baines said, reaching his side. "I'm sorry to keep you waitin'. Seems to me when a body has a maid to help dress it, it takes longer. That maid had a real knack for sayin' things. I reckon it's 'cause she's French. But she sure burned my ears."

Gray burst out laughing. "What a delightfully refreshing creature you are, Miss Marshall," he said. "Come, little mouse, your carriage awaits."

Outside, a team of magnificent black horses attached to a sleek black carriage awaited them. Stars winked at them from a cloudless sky, glittering like diamonds. The air was warm and filled with scents of jasmine and honeysuckle. Fireflies buzzed around them, lending to the magic of the evening.

"My lady?"

Gray held out his hand, which Baines accepted. His fingers felt cool against her heated skin. Too excited to speak, she allowed him to assist her into the carriage. He climbed in beside her, then commanded the driver to move with a tap on the ceiling of the conveyance.

Gray's burgundy topcoat added to his masculinity and served as stark contrast to his white shirt. The fit of his black trousers made unladylike thoughts race across her mind.

At a loss for words, she remained quiet during the rest of the ride to the restaurant in which she now sat. Their order had already been placed and wine set before them. A serene, exotic atmosphere pervaded the place. This was the perfect time to tell Gray about her decision not to sell him his own quilt, she thought as she tasted her wine. Already entranced by her surroundings, Gray's heated, tender looks further mesmerized her.

While she was declining the money she'd insisted on, she would ask about the location of the quilt. She hated to hear his answer. It would break her heart to hear that he would be leaving. But she realized he would tell her nothing until she asked.

Gray couldn't drag his attention away from the vision that sat across from him. Her unaffected naturalness enthralled him. Her incredible beauty bewitched him.

Suddenly he wondered if he could keep his hands off of her. Maybe his battle was already lost and his fate decided, despite his honor and his responsibility to his father and their heritage.

Luckily tonight he and Baines wouldn't return to their suite until late. He planned to surprise her and take her to the theater to see a late play after dinner.

Reaching across the table for her small hand, he brought it to his lips for a kiss. "You're so very lovely. I wish . . ." He stopped and drank from his glass. It wasn't time yet to make rash statements or bold commitments. But would there ever be a time?

Eyeing him innocently, she sipped her wine. "What do you wish, Gray?"

Her soft voice was low and throaty. It brought to mind whispered words and heated passion. Gray chuckled softly, lustful images flaring to life. "I wish the waiter would make haste with our order. The night is young, and I have a surprise for you."

He barely finished his sentence when their waiter set two plates of oysters baked in wine sauce before them. Gray made a subtle gesture, picking up his small fork. Baines smiled and followed suit, tentatively tasting a forkful.

"Like it?"

Baines nodded and drained her glass. "Very much. It's very good."

"I can see you found the couturiere's shop all right. Your gown is beautiful, Baines. Is that the only one you bought?"

"No, it isn't." She paused and shifted in her seat. Swallowing visibly, she met his stare. "Gray, about the money."

Gray stiffened, his good mood bursting. He should have known better than to let his guard down. Despite how badly he wanted to see her with the money, his doubt persisted, exacerbated by his lack of success today. "What about it, my dear?" he asked tightly, his mistrustful nature taking over his better judgment.

She waited until after the waiter refilled her wine glass and departed before speaking.

"It was wrong of me to expect you to buy back your own quilt. Please forgive me. Takin' money from you is no better than stealin', and I'm not a thief."

"Of course you're not, Baines," he replied with amusement. Relief washed through him in waves. He needed to reevaluate his propensity to judge so harshly so quickly. "I fully expect to pay your price, however. You deserve it. Your efforts brought us here. I want you to take the money with my blessing.'' He wanted to haul her across the table and into his arms. Out of the goodness of her little heart, she wanted just to *give* him the quilt.

It was one thing to be ordered to give her the money. It was quite another to give it to her of his own accord.

How could he continue to resist her? At every turn she chipped away his defenses, until only his honor would remain to ward off his desire for her.

''I can't accept your reasonin', Gray. The only effort I put into it was discoverin' who the thief was, and where he could be found. You got your quilt back without me havin' to point Eli out to you. It sure is a pretty quilt, ain't it?''

''*Isn't* it.'' Gray winked at her and finished his wine.

''Isn't it,'' she repeated. ''It may take a spell, but I'll learn the proper way to talk, even if it kills me.''

''Good for you, little mouse. Just remember to practice.'' He cleared his throat and pushed his plate away, finished with his delicious appetizer. ''I haven't seen the quilt to know how it looks.''

Baines held a forkful of food inches from her mouth.

''What?'' She placed the fork back on her plate.

Gray swore he saw relief in her gaze, but decided he must have been mistaken. ''I'm sorry, Baines. I should have told you earlier.''

''B-but couldn't you find Eli?'' She finished her food and set the plate aside, then washed it down with wine.

''Now, now, there's no cause to worry. I've been told Eli, along with your uncle, can be found on Tchoupitoulas Road. A place too dangerous for strangers to traverse at night. I'll set out first thing in the morning. In the meantime, I command you not to be concerned and enjoy your visit in this exotic place.''

Any further comment was halted when the waiter came and cleared away their dishes to make room for their entree, a delectable dish of fish with a delicious cream sauce, braised potatoes, and fresh peas with miniature onions. After their food was settled, Baines spoke again.

"Gray, I hadn't intended to take any money from you, but when you gave me the money this mornin', I decided to put it to good use as a loan. I need a couple of presentable dresses to go over the hill and do business with the wealthy plantation mistresses. And although I don't expect to get invited to a fancy function again, if by chance someone do—"

"Does."

"Does. Someone does, I'll be ready. I reckon with my quiltin' and dressmakin' I can pay you back in half a year." Her gaze held his. "I don't want your charity, Gray. If you can't make it a loan, I'll just return my purchases and give you *all* the money back."

"I'm the envy of every man here," Gray responded. "How could I let you return that beautiful gown? I'll leave a forwarding address and I'll expect my money in six months."

Baines smiled and shoved a forkful of food into her mouth. "Lord a-mighty this food is delicious," she said, after chewing and swallowing. "Those French folks sure know how to whip up some fancy cookin'. I don't reckon I need to know the name of this dish I'm eatin', not knowin' French and all. But I sure would like to, so I can brag to Miz Annabelle."

Glorious wasn't a strong enough word to describe Baines. Gray would have to settle for it at the moment, however. She seemed to have scattered his wits, leaving him unable to do anything but drink in her loveliness.

"It's called Trout Mueniere. I'm pleased that you're having such a wonderful time, Baines. Maybe you'll be allowed to take along a menu and other mementos when we depart. Would you like that?"

At the moment Gray would give her the stars if she desired them.

"Now what would I be wantin' with mementos, Gray? I don't need mementos to remind me where I been or where I'm goin'. I aim to come back here one day and I don't

need mementos to tell me what I know is a plumb fact,"
Baines stated with absolute certainty.

Gray didn't respond. He just knew, felt as certain as she,
that she would succeed in her endeavors. His heart began
its rapid pounding again as his pride in her swelled near to
bursting. Bloody damn! He couldn't be falling in love with
the little beggar, could he?

By the time they were preparing to depart the premises,
they'd consumed a bottle of very expensive wine, pecan
pie for dessert, and after-dinner liqueurs. Gray remained
unaffected, but not so Baines.

Deciding to call it a night, he was only mildly disappointed that they couldn't proceed with the plans he had
made. With his desire for her on the precipice of snapping
his control, he thought to drop her off at the hotel and go
explore the city. Or *something*. Anything would be better
than staying near her tonight.

"Tomorrow evening, little mouse, we'll go to the St.
Philip Street Theatre to watch a musical," he said, hoping
his wayward thoughts weren't transparent. "We'll dine *afterward*."

Baines chuckled softly. "It seems every time I get
dressed up for you, I end havin' to be brought home. I'm
sorry, Gray. That liquor can do powerful things to a body."

"I know. But that's only if you let it." Gray rose from
his seat and went to her, helping her out of her own.

Steadying herself, she leaned against his enormous chest.
Remembering where she was, she stiffened and stood
straight.

"I'm all right," she said.

Gray nodded, but took her arm anyway and guided her
toward the exit.

23

"THERE'S NO WAY I can accuse you of ruining the evening, Baines," Gray assured her. This was the time to leave and get away from the temptation she presented. She stood a little apart from him in the sitting room of their suite, all dewy-eyed and inviting. He shrugged out of his jacket. "Seeing the way you enjoyed yourself was all the entertainment I needed."

Her smile was devastating, irresistible.

"I did have a great time, Gray. Thank you."

Currents charged between them, hot and sizzling.

"Did you?"

In an instant, Gray closed the gap between them, encouraged by her words. He merely wanted to be closer to her; to better view her small mouth as she spoke; to watch the shadow of the candlelight dance across her alabaster skin, turning it golden; to smell the floral scent from her skin and hair. Instead, he gathered her into his arms and kissed her with all the passion in him.

Her hungry response surprised and encouraged him, shattering his willpower. Their tongues met, mated, intertwined. She was a feather in his arms, soft and supple. His greedy exploration of her mouth turned into savage intensity as days of frustrations exploded.

His hands traveled across her back and down to her

rounded derriere. He held her in place against the over-whelming demand of his swollen manhood. Innocent and instinctive, her body moved against his, and Gray groaned harshly. She ran her fingers through his hair and gasped.

He rained kisses over her cheeks, her eyes, her face, her slender throat. "Baines, my beautiful, rustic treasure," he croaked, bringing his hands to her bodice.

In seconds, he'd freed her breasts. Round and proud, he cupped one in his hand and lowered his head to it.

Baines whimpered. Her breath nearly lost, sensations rocked her, and the heat nearly consumed her. She gladly gave herself to his demands. Shivers engulfed her at the feel of the bold hardness of his maleness. His tongue danced over her nipple and she tossed her head back in surrender.

She needed succor. There was no other end to the un-bearably sweet torture. Gray brought his lips back to hers, kissing her over and over. Clinging to him, she felt every corded muscle, every lean sinew of his body, even through his garments.

"Gray," she whispered through her fog.

Breathing rapidly, he willed himself to stop kissing her.

Too much wine had made her vulnerable; and the atmosphere was so far removed from *her* reality. He held her face between his large hands and met her darkened gaze. Her features were flushed with passion, and her lips were red and swollen from his kisses.

He swallowed hard, intending to be honorable and do the right things.

But she stared at him, her fog of desire obvious, and pressed her mouth to his. She hugged him fiercely, posses-sively, crushing her small body against his and moving against him erotically. His honor deserted him in stunning swiftness, and the last vestiges of his resistance and sanity fled.

"Baines, I need you," he murmured.

Her response was a barely perceptible nod of the head. Scooping her up into his arms, Gray carried her into her bedchamber. Smothering her with ravishing kisses, he set her on her feet and brought his hand to the hooks on her gown. With trembling fingers, he unfastened them and slipped her bodice below her breasts.

"Oh!" Baines cried softly as cool air hit her skin.

"It's all right, little mouse," Gray said in reassuring tones, reminding himself not to rush. "Let me view all of you."

Slowly, seductively, he peeled away her garments, trailing his lips over each inch of skin he bared, until finally her naked form stood before him, glorious to his adoring eyes.

Her heart pounding, her mind filled only with Gray and what was about to happen between them, Baines stared at him. Gray knelt before her, his tongue warm against her belly, his hands caressing her curves.

Then his fingers were *there*, touching her woman's place, befuddling her, bewitching her.

Then his mouth was there, too, kissing her moist heat, and she cried out, her knees buckling. Sensations rocked her, and she thought she might die from the pleasure, the intensity. She tangled her hands within his thick hair and threw her head back, crying out his name, pleading with him for an end to her torment. But he was relentless, until she moaned senselessly, until she collapsed against him.

Her pulse pounding, her breathing labored, Baines squeezed her eyes shut, fighting the acute embarrassment she felt, overwhelming heat pervading her.

"Open your eyes, Baines," Gray commanded softly.

She did so, and her gaze locked with his.

"There's nothing to be ashamed of."

Silently he took her hands and placed them on the buttons of his waistcoat. He undid the first button. "Disrobe me, my lady."

In a trance, Baines unfastened his waistcoat and slid it over his muscled arms. Her gaze never leaving the bold angles of his face, she did the same to his silk shirt. She caressed his smooth chest, felt the hard planes of it and his flat stomach.

Gray stepped out of his shoes and took off his stockings,

then slipped out of his trousers. He stepped a little away from her, his arousal blatantly demanding.

Weakness overpowering her at the sight, Baines gasped. Her gaze roamed over his sculpted body again, then back down to his imposing maleness.

He embraced her again and lifted her face to his. Bringing his mouth to hers, he kissed her hungrily, and Baines melted against him, matching his passion, moving, grinding her body to his.

Guided only by passion and desire, ignoring the warning taunting him in the back of his mind that he wouldn't take Baines's innocence and desert her, Gray lifted her and brought her to the bed, laying her gently on it.

Teasing her rounded breasts, Gray slid his tongue over each cherry-tipped bud, lavishing feather kisses and tiny nips over her heated skin. He delighted in her low moans and soft whimpers. She was a treasure beyond all price. And, in spite of the thoughts returning to prick his conscience, he would make love to her tonight.

He would make love to her slowly, with maddening tenderness. And then with fierce desire.

Breathless and beyond reasoning, Baines writhed and moaned. Her small hands moved over his chest. "Make it stop," she murmured in a heated whisper.

Only too eager to comply, Gray lowered his body over hers and kissed her with deep longing. He guided his manhood to her center and met the barrier of her innocence. She whimpered again.

Sweat beading his brow, he held on to her rounded bottom and, before she had time to wonder what was happening to her, pushed into the heated core of her with one powerful thrust.

Baines cried out and gritted her teeth, fighting the pain. "It's all right, little mouse," Gray croaked.

Good God, she was so hot and ready for him. With expert finesse and exquisite slowness, he moved within her. She relaxed again, yielding and warm in his embrace.

Baines lay beneath him, clinging, searching, burning like a red sun. She moved to his rhythm, faster now, raising her hips to meet his explosive thrusts. A hot tide of passion raged through her, ebbing and flowing with his masterful touch. Shivers racked her, and fire burned in her veins. She gasped, arching her back, seeming to rise on an explosion of fire and light, of pleasure and ecstasy, until there was nothing left but surrender.

Gray clung to Baines, feeling her release, yielding to her burning sweetness. With a harsh groan, he found his own shuddering release and knew then why it was called *le petite mort*. He felt as if he had died and gone to heaven. In Baines's arms. Lost inside her soft body. With little thought to the consequences of his actions.

Bloody damn.

He wished he could die and go to hell.

"Little mouse," he said hoarsely as he withdrew from her and pulled her into his arms. "My precious angel."

Baines sighed breathlessly and snuggled closer to him. "So that's what it's like."

Gray didn't respond. He brushed aside the hair that had fallen into her face and kissed her forehead. Regret filled him.

He'd thought honor was the one thing he had left, besides the duty to his family. The full force of what he had done tonight hit him. He'd prided himself on his honor and his iron control.

But he'd compromised Baines because of his lust, and his raging arousal suggested he could do so again. Yet he couldn't ask her to become his wife. He couldn't ask her to give up her fervent dreams for him. She would only grow to hate him for taking her away from everything she held dear, and that he couldn't bear.

Unless Mary's Fortune was found and the treasure discovered.

Gray pushed her from him and held her at arm's length. "Are you all right?" Her face was a flushed mask of confusion. He wondered if it was from embarrassment or from passion.

"Y-yes, thank you."

"Little mouse, this should not have happened. It was

irresponsible of me. Please forgive me.'' He knew this wasn't the time to bring this up, not after the overwhelming passion they'd shared, but his guilt wouldn't let him remain silent.

Hurt glittered in her eyes. ''Of course,'' Baines said in a small voice. Long moments passed before she spoke again. When she did, her voice was void of emotion. ''Maybe you should go to your private chamber, Gray. I'm awful tired.'' With that, she turned away from him, at once remote and untouchable.

Gray breathed in deeply. He wanted to wash away the pain and indecision in her features. He wanted to assure her that he wasn't a cad, that they had a future together. But he couldn't. He didn't know what his future held. To him, *this* was where Baines belonged—in luxury and elegance, showered with whatever her heart desired.

But was he being fair? She could walk with the finest or live with the poorest, and the essence of her personality would remain the same.

''I'll be leaving early tomorrow to get to Tchoupitoulas Road. I'll see you whenever I return.'' He moved out of the bed and dressed quietly. It would be a long night for him. ''Have a good rest. Good night, Baines.''

She gave no indication that she heard. With a heartfelt curse, he departed.

For long moments after Gray departed, she stared at the closed door. Finally, with her body still feverish and tingling, she got up and secured the latch.

Something had happened to her tonight. Something deep and incomprehensible, to her mind, to her body, to her soul.

She crawled into bed and curled into a miserable ball.

Gray's kisses and caresses affected her deeply, and his lovemaking rendered her senseless. Even now, she couldn't believe that what had happened between them was a mistake. Even now, his regret and his words cut deeply.

In spite of his callous use of her in the beginning to obtain Mary's Fortune, Baines couldn't fault him for all that had transpired between them since.

She never meant to, but against her will she'd fallen in love with him.

But he was going to leave her. He wouldn't have regretted making love to her if he felt as she did. He would want her with him if he loved her.

Now she must face the consequences. Yet in the end, she would see to it that he never discovered her true feelings.

24

GRAY'S RECKLESS BEHAVIOR MADE sleep impossible for him.

After leaving Baines's room, he went to his private chamber and folded his topcoat neatly over the chair there, then returned to the sitting area and poured himself a brandy.

Unable to forget the taste of Baines's sweet mouth, the feel of her soft body as she clung to him, and his senseless desire as he drove into her, he drank deeply. Yet he was angry, with her, himself, and that bloody quilt.

Only one time before had he felt so out of control. Then, as now, his honor had been in doubt, his duty and responsibility questioned.

That other time, however, was different. He'd been a mere lad. And he'd been innocent of the crime he'd been accused of.

True enough, he and Jamie had snuck away from their dormitory to rendezvous with a doxy. But when they returned, the headmaster awaited Gray in his chamber.

Jamie, the bastard, had dissembled and swore he'd been in school the entire day. He hadn't once seen Gray, he'd said.

In the end Gray's name was cleared, and he was reinstated at Eton because of Pierce. His father had hired a Bow

Street Runner to find the doxy, and when he did, he'd given her five hundred pounds to come forward and tell the truth.

Gray had never forgotten his father's faith in him. He'd never forgotten his obligation to Pierce and his duty to his family.

Until tonight. All because of his damnable lust.

Not only did he have his irresponsibility to contend with as well as his confused emotions about Baines, however, for the first time in years, he wondered what had driven Jamie to betray him so shockingly. They had been as close as brothers until that fateful day. In an instant everything had changed.

Like the dynamics of his and Baines's relationship. They had crossed the thin line that separated friends and lovers, and they could never turn back now, not even if they wanted to.

He supposed he would never know the answers to the questions about Jamie crowding his mind. He finished his drink. Not that he really wanted to.

But *he* was the answer to his and Baines's dilemma. He and Mary's Fortune.

He considered going back into Baines's chamber to talk to her. But what could he tell her until that blasted quilt was found? No, for the time being he would let everything remain as it was. For the time being, he'd said enough.

His temples throbbed from the weight of his problems, and he turned his thoughts to his search for Eli Washington.

Suddenly he saw a light at the end of his despair and he smiled.

He *had* to find Mary's Fortune. When he did, he would ask Baines to become his wife.

∞

ANTICIPATION GUIDING HIM, GRAY hurried through his morning ablutions, then left his bedchamber and walked into the sitting area. He paused, thinking of Baines and glancing at her closed door. The insane urge to peek inside her chamber and look at her crossed his mind.

Swallowing hard, he fought the impulse. He worried that he would crawl into bed with her and make passionate love to her again. Desire for Baines rode him hard, and he wondered how much longer he could go without succumbing to it again. He was a mere man, who could suffer only so much. Besides, she would soon be his wife. This was the day he would get Mary's Fortune.

Going to the door and closing it quietly behind him, he laughed, the sound relaxed and happy.

When he reached the dining chamber five minutes later, he ordered breakfast and coffee and ate hurriedly. Twenty minutes later he stepped into the cloudy morning and saw the lanky figure of Tic walking toward him.

"Mo'nin', Lord Dunston, suh," Tic greeted as Gray approached him. "Sure hope I didn't keep you waitin'."

"Your timing is perfect, Tic." Gray tried to ignore the constant twitch in the man's left eye, but the feat was nearly impossible. "We'd best get started. I'd like to get this over with as soon as possible."

"I'm all for that, my lord. But ain't you forgettin' somethin'?" Tic held out his bony hand.

Gray raised an imperious brow, his disdain for the unkempt, fetid-smelling man barely hidden. "I don't believe I am."

Tic narrowed his eyes, his twitch all the more apparent. "You done promised to pay me iffen I brang you to Tchoupitoulas Road to find Eli Washington."

"And I shall, Tic. I am a man of my word. I've been told Tchoupitoulas Road is dangerous to outsiders, however. I am not carrying any money. In order to get paid, you'll have to see to it that no harm comes to me for want of my purse and you'll have to accompany me back here."

Gray didn't trust Tic one whit. The man was a product of Tchoupitoulas Road and would think nothing of bludgeoning him for his money, after falsely claiming to have knowledge of Eli Washington.

He figured he would have a better chance of leaving Tchoupitoulas Road alive if Tic, and any henchmen of his acquaintance, believed Gray wasn't carrying any money.

"Well, that ain't right," Tic grumbled. "How do I know you'll pay me?"

"Because I said so," Gray growled impatiently. He wanted to get the blasted quilt back and enjoy the remainder of the day with Baines. "The more time you waste protesting, the less money I'll pay you."

Tic held up his hand. "Awright, awright, I'll go, but it ain't fair," he said. "How much you payin' me, anyway?"

"That depends on how quickly we find Eli," Gray snapped. "You could earn a half eagle. Now let's get started."

Tic didn't need to be told twice. Five dollars! That was all the incentive he needed.

First Tic brought Gray to the docks, where they'd met yesterday. They spent most of the morning traversing the docks in a gentle rain. Toward noon the sun burst through the clouds, signaling an end to the showers. They headed for Tchoupitoulas Road. All along the way Tic complained of being hungry, and Gray held on to his temper by a thread.

When they went into their fourth tavern, Gray was thoroughly vexed. Yesterday he'd believed Tic knew exactly where to find Eli. But he saw that wasn't the case.

"Do you bloody know what you're doing?" Gray snarled. He watched as Tic craned his scrawny neck and squinted his good eye, searching the dingy interior.

"You want Eli, don'tcha?" He gave him a rotten-toothed grin. "Well, he could be in any one o' these here places." He swaggered to a huge, bald-headed man, a totally disreputable-looking creature complete with hooped earring, leather vest, and a black patch over his right eye. "Hey, Mongo! Is you done seed Eli Washington anywhere?"

Holding a glass half filled with a brownish liquid of undiscernible origins, Mongo looked with annoyance at Tic. He shook his head and gulped the drink down. His eyes watered, and he belched contentedly.

"No, Tic," he finally answered. "I ain't seen him. When I do, though, I aim to bust his head. He stole my spare pair of shoes."

"Name a price, sugar. If I agree, I'll give you pleasure like you've never had. But I warn you. I get paid first."

All three men looked toward the throaty sound.

A woman clad in a garish gold chemise, cloying perfume surrounding her, stared at Gray suggestively. Her features were faded, her curves well rounded.

He smiled tightly.

"Off with you, Edna!" Tic said sharply before Gray could respond.

Edna looked at Gray one last time. He turned his back on her and listened as she stomped angrily away, a sharp curse falling from her rouged mouth.

Mongo eyed Gray with contempt. "Who's the fancy dresser?"

"He's who I'm a-huntin' Eli for," Tic answered. "He's my friend. So don't get no ideas. 'Sides, he was smart 'nough to leave all his money at the fancy French roomin' place."

Mongo laughed evilly. "That there sure was smart thinkin'. Pass the word, Tic. He ain't carryin' no money, so there ain't no point in bustin' his head."

Gray touched his hand to the pistol he carried under his coat and glared at the men. He knew threats wouldn't intimidate Tic, so he simply appealed to his avaricious nature. His pistol held only six shots, by God, and this section of town was overrun with river vermin. Six shots would hardly protect him from the river horde if they decided to use him as fish bait.

"Tic," he gritted, "if you don't bloody get your arse out of here, all bargains are off!"

"Awright, Mr. Dunston," Tic quickly said. "We kin try another place. See you, Mongo."

All along Tchoupitoulas Road, in seedy taverns and run-down hostels, one after the other, Gray followed Tic in pursuit of Eli Washington and Mary's Fortune.

He wondered if this was all worth it. Maybe the quilt would never be found, and then what would he do? Could he come to terms with that? Not only would he fail his father, but Baines as well.

He had taken her innocence and he felt obligated to make amends. He felt wholeheartedly that Pierce would understand Gray's duty to marry her, outside of their class as she was.

By the time they entered Seaman's Rest, night was approaching, and Gray's mood had become dangerous. He hadn't eaten since early morning. He was fighting off whores like Edna from one end of the road to the other and he was tired.

A withered old hag sat behind the bar. She laughed with a toothless cackle and gave Gray an appreciative glance.

"What can I do for a fine gent'man like you?"

Tic laughed. "Ain't you the dreamer, Mama Nell? The onliest thing you kin do fo' him is point him to Eli."

Mama Nell looked startled. "Eli? Eli Washington?"

"Yeah," Tic said. "One and the same."

"Eli and Linc done ketch a ship t'ree days ago," Mama Nell said. "They're on their way to Europe."

Gray reached her in angry strides. "What!" he thundered.

"Ain't you heered me, mister?"

"He heered you, Maw," Tic answered. "It jist ain't what he wanted to hear, that's all. Him comin' all the way from Natchez an' all to fine Eli."

"I was led to believe they missed that ship."

"Natchez?" Mama Nell tsked, ignoring Gray's comment. "You shoulda asked old Linc's niece afore you comed all this way. He done sent her a letter tellin' her he was leavin' after some fella write it for him."

Gray told himself to wait and listen to Baines's story. He told himself she wouldn't lead him all the way to New Orleans knowing Eli Washington and her uncle had put out to sea.

He tried to calm the seething anger and raging humiliation. He tried and failed. His last chance to save his fortune had sailed away, *if* Eli really had the quilt. Gray had never pressed Baines on how she'd concluded Eli was the thief.

They had left three days ago. Three bloody days ago!

Did Baines know her uncle had left for sea duty? Aye.

She *had* to know. As seriously as Lincoln Marshall took his responsibility toward his niece, he wouldn't leave the country without telling her beforehand. Gray couldn't believe that of the man.

The lying little—

He couldn't finish the thought. She'd duped him. Again. And then seduced him. How could he have been so foolish and trust her? Never again would he trust her, and neither would he forgive her.

The thought that she had known how this trip would end became a blazing inferno threatening to consume him. More than likely, seduction had been her intent all along. To think he'd considered marrying her. To think he'd felt guilty over his actions.

He almost shook with his fury, and prayed someone in there would provoke him so he could unleash his rage on that unwitting person. But it didn't happen.

Stalking out of the place, he began his journey back to the hotel. He was aware of Tic following close behind.

When he reached the docks close to the hotel, he went into his coat pocket and came up with several coins. He picked out the half eagle and handed it to Tic.

The man gaped in surprised. "I thought you said—"

"I lied," Gray snarled and headed toward the *Mississippi Lady*, where even then passengers were walking up the gangplank in anticipation of the boat raising anchor.

25

WHEN BAINES AWAKENED, IT was to the pitter-patter of rain falling on the slate roof. Laden with heartache, her mood matched the gray skies.

The soreness between her thighs made her blush, and her and Gray's remembered intimacies sent heat spiraling through her. But for Gray their lovemaking had been a mistake. For her it had opened a flood of passion and love she would never overcome.

For one insane moment, she hoped she carried Gray's child, but just as quickly realized how foolish she was. The baby would be born a bastard, and not only would they live in poverty, but also mother and child would be shunned by society.

A tear slid down Baines's cheek, her heart sore with wanting Gray.

The mahogany clock ticked loudly in the quietness of the room, that single sound unnerving—as if she could hear herself being brought closer to impending disaster.

"Gray!"

How could she have forgotten that he was leaving for Tchoupitoulas Road this morning? That should have been uppermost in her mind. Instead, she focused on her unrequited feelings and their shared passion.

Shoving the covers aside, she jumped out of bed. She

wanted to see Gray before he left, to remind him to be careful. She pulled one of her new day dresses over her head and threw open the door leading to the sitting room. It didn't matter that her buttons were unfastened. Her concern made her forget modesty.

Crossing the room, she went to Gray's chamber and knocked on the door. When there was no response, she cautiously opened it. Her heart sank. She was too late.

The draperies were opened, revealing the clouds outside. Gray's topcoat from last evening was folded neatly over a wing-back chair. The bedcover was barely crumpled. Everything in the room was in perfect order, but Gray was gone.

Quietly Baines backed out of the room. She paced, her thoughts running amok. How could he have left without telling her goodbye? What would she do if anything happened to him? Why hadn't she insisted on going with him? And just what, pray tell, would happen if he didn't find Mary's Fortune?

She realized she had to get out of there. Her worry wouldn't do either of them any good. Gray would be fine. He knew how to take care of himself and certainly wouldn't want her to waste her day sick with concern for him.

With that in mind, she rang for Mimi. Baines ate breakfast and stared out at the horizon. She was happily relieved when the sun peaked through the clouds. Soon afterward she left the chamber to explore the city.

The clip-clopping of a horse being ridden across the cobblestones by a finely dressed gentleman greeted her. In the next instant a mule-drawn carriage clattered by. A mulatto, her head wrapped in a brightly colored tignon, peddled fresh cheese in broken French. She smiled as Baines passed her.

Enthralled with the sights and sounds, Baines walked along at a sedate pace. On the corner of Decatur and Toulouse, she came across a material shop called Boats of Bolts. Intrigued by the odd name, she went inside. Bolts of material sat in displays shaped like boats. She giggled at the owner's cleverness and decided she would have to be as clever with a name for her shop.

"May I help you?"

A short, dimpled lady rushed up to Baines.

She smiled. "Not at the moment. Can . . . *may* I look around?"

"Feel free. If you need assistance, let me know."

With that, the lady hurried away.

Slowly Baines walked about the shop, discovering material of every description and color. Mary's Fortune was in there. Flashes of the quilt rippled through Baines's mind, and her heart leaped. Along one aisle, she saw replicas of colors and materials for the quilt.

Not thinking twice, she called the shop attendant over.

"I wish to purchase ten yards each of the mulberry cotton, the emerald green flannel, the rose cotton, the pearl white linen, and the sapphire blue flannel. I also need ten yards of wool to be used for interlining." Baines also purchased thread for the trimmings, which made up the strange designs in the corners of the quilt, and the templates she would need to cut the blocks. "Pack everything securely so they won't be damaged on my journey back to Mississippi."

She felt proud of herself and beholden to Gray's kindness. Because of the money he'd loaned her, she didn't have to impose on Miz Annabelle's generosity to make the quilt.

She was anxious to get back home and begin work on her own Quilt of Fortune. A part of her wished they were already on their way back to Natchez. At least now she had something more than Gray's departure to focus on. She loved quilting. She would immerse herself in it, not giving herself time to think about Gray once he left for good.

Tired from her day of exploring the city, Baines returned to the Tremoulet House. Now, relaxing in her chamber, she looked at the clock and found it nearing four o'clock.

Baines itched to open her packages and finger the material. But she dared not. She didn't want to trouble herself with reclosing the box.

She wondered what time Gray would take her to the theater. Should she start preparing herself now?

Her earlier fears returning, she walked around the room, fidgeting nervously. Was Tchoupitoulas Road as dangerous during the day as Gray said it was at night?

As time slowly consumed the light of day, Baines grew frantic. She was too nervous to eat, too nervous to wait in the sitting room. Had something awful happened to him?

Just as she thought to go down and inquire about him to calm her fears, the door burst open.

"Get your things," Gray snarled. "There's a boat leaving for Natchez in thirty minutes!" He glared at her. Stark anger and cold disbelief lined his features.

"We leave tomorrow on the *Natchez Belle,*" Baines protested.

"The quilt is gone! What's the point of waiting for the *Natchez Belle*?"

Gray's curt voice lashed out at Baines. Panic invaded her. Wide-eyed, she stared at him. "G-gray, you're frightenin' me. What's wrong? What has happened to you?"

The reproachful, contemptuous look he gave her tore at her insides.

"Don't, Baines! How could you take me for such a bloody fool? You knew all along that Eli and your uncle had sailed away the day we arrived."

"What?" Baines's shock yielded quickly to anger, and she was furious at her own vulnerability to him. "How could I have known such a thing and still make the journey here? And for what motive?"

"What motive? What motive? How badly did you want those dresses? Telling me you wouldn't accept the five thousand dollars was just a ploy to throw me off." He laughed harshly. "Apparently five thousand dollars must have pricked your conscience as too much money to deliver exactly nothing to me. Thanks a lot, Miss Marshall, for the ruse. I hope your three hundred pieces of silver allow you to sleep at night—"

The slap she delivered to him interrupted his merciless

tirade. Baines stood there, shocked at her actions, her anger gone as quickly as it had come.

"Gray, I—"

"Get your things, Miss Marshall, and meet me downstairs in ten minutes." He stalked across the room to his private chamber.

For an endless time Baines remained staring at the empty space where Gray had stood. She was unable to understand what just happened. His anger frightened and shocked her, but she also noted panic in his eyes.

Realizing she'd better gather her belongings, she started toward her bedchamber to pack her gowns in the new traveling bag she'd bought especially for them.

"Madame?"

Startled at the sound of the male voice, Baines looked up to see Jacques standing in the open doorway. "You startled me, Jacques."

"So sorry, madame," Jacques said quietly, as if he knew of her turmoil. "On his way up your husband asked me to come and give you a hand with your belongings. A cabriolet is waiting out front."

"I'll be a second, Jacques." Numbly Baines went to her room. Gathering her gowns, she stuffed the beautiful dresses inside her bag, then fastened it with trembling fingers.

Before long, she was being helped into the carriage for the short ride to the docks to board the *Mississippi Lady*. They passed the trip in tense, brittle silence.

Gray didn't speak to her again until they were on the boat.

"Your stateroom is on the main deck."

"Gray—"

As if he didn't hear her, he walked down the deck and stopped one cabin away. Going inside, he closed himself in.

Baines thought her chest would explode with pain. Gray had snubbed her more effectively than anyone ever had. He had pretended she didn't exist.

26

BAINES SAT ALONE AND dejected in her cabin. Bewilderment increased her misery. Hours had passed since Gray had guided her to her room, then walked away as she tried to speak.

She still didn't understand why Gray had turned on her so viciously. She'd realized he hadn't found Mary's Fortune, but why did he take his disappointment and anger out on her in such a manner? He'd gone so far as to accuse her of tricking him out of his money.

At the spur of the moment she'd decided to use the three hundred dollars as a loan. Until then she'd determined she was wrong in the first place to ask Gray for money for the return of his quilt. He'd labeled her a thief once, and now he implied she was dishonest.

How could he? After the time they'd spent together and all that they had shared, he should have known of her morals by now. If only he cared about her, he never would have accused her of such dreadful acts.

Attempting to calm her hurt and building anger, she paced the length of the room. Its meager appointments didn't matter to her at the moment; nor did the sound of the terns warbling from shore and the drone of the boat's engine. Neither did it matter that dawn was presenting itself through the porthole.

She wanted to see Gray and ask him to be reasonable, to explain what was troubling him. Certainly he wouldn't have gotten so powerful angry at her if Mary's Fortune merely held sentimental value for him. The panic wouldn't have been in his eyes for the world to see, either.

Well, she double dang wouldn't allow this to continue. They'd shared too much over the past few days. Baines stomped to the door of the small, cramped cabin and swung it open. Stalking to Gray's cabin, she banged as hard as she could on his portal. It swung open so suddenly, she fell forward into his arms.

Strong, powerful hands caught her by the shoulders. They stared at each other. In confusion. In regret. In longing.

A breeze blew across the deck of the boat, a short relief to the warm night. The single lamp that lit Gray's cabin gave the room a soft, romantic glow. The buttons on his silk shirt were open, revealing a smooth chest and flat stomach.

Pity filled her. Because of a reckless request she'd made, she'd lost Gray. She'd thought to find an easy way out of her poverty; and she'd wanted him to pay for his insult. In the end she'd destroyed everything between them.

Brusquely he set her away from him. His eyes turned as hard and cold as a frozen river. "Haven't I made it plain enough that I want you out of my sight?" Blazing with fury, his low voice chilled Baines. "What the bloody deuce do you want, Miss Marshall?"

At his icy scrutiny she almost withered. He hated her. Whatever he'd discovered had turned him soundly against her. But she couldn't give up that easily. Gray needed her. If only she could break through the barrier he'd erected around himself. If only she could convince him that she wasn't the enemy.

Mustering up her courage, she folded her arms and raised her chin. She met his stare and glowered at him, refusing to allow him to know how much he'd intimidated and crushed her. "I want you to talk to me, Lord Dunston."

"I've said all I want to you, Miss Marshall, and I bloody

sure don't want to hear anything more you have to say. I suggest for the remainder of this voyage you stay as far away from me as this small craft will allow.'' He made to close the door, then stopped. ''One other thing. This isn't the *Natchez Belle*. I don't know the caliber of this boat's passengers. I've made arrangements to have your meals brought to your cabin. Don't venture on deck alone. And *don't* dare come to my cabin again. Good night, Miss Marshall.''

His anger would prevent him from listening to her, but she felt she'd been dismissed as though she were a naughty child. She frowned at him and flounced back to the cabin. It wasn't until she'd closed herself inside did she hear the faint click of the latch on his door when he closed it.

∞

ALONE IN HIS CABIN Gray stiffened his resolve, adamant in his decision never to forgive Baines Marshall. He refused to become ensnared in her tender trap again. He'd allowed himself to believe her, and she'd betrayed him, not once but twice. How could he have been such a bloody fool?

His anger turned into scalding fury and contemptuous humiliation. Baines had known when they arrived in New Orleans that Gray was chasing a rainbow that would lead to nothing—no quilt, no Eli, and not even that bloody Lincoln Marshall.

How could she? How could she let him believe in her? She must have been in her cabin having a good laugh at his expense. Then she'd come to his cabin, playing havoc with his resolve, pretending remorse and concern.

It had taken every bit of willpower not to haul her into the cabin and make love to her with all the confused desire and frustrated anger roiling within him.

Aye, she had betrayed him. But still he loved her.

That realization dawned on him as she'd stood in his doorway, hurt and determination in her rigid body. Her hair fell around her shoulders to below her waist, inviting his touch. Wariness sharpened her eyes, making them appear as brilliant as emeralds. The pity in her features made him want to bellow with rage.

He hated her pity. Deep within his being, he'd known all along that eventually it would come to this. How could she not pity him when he was about to lose everything he'd known in life, everything his father held so close to his heart?

Her pity exacerbated his failure, and she had been an accessory to it, then witnessed his defeat.

∽

THE NEXT TWO DAYS could have been the most tortuous of Baines's life. Instead, they became the most creative. She made sketches of what she recalled of Mary's Fortune. A sketch would make it easier for her to assemble the quilt.

Determined to make an exact replica, she went over in her mind how each square was assembled. Often as her memory worked, she told herself she'd seen a map within the design of the quilt. But when she thought further, she decided there really wasn't one there.

A map, however, would explain the quilt's odd name. It would also explain Gray's reaction to it being gone.

After her encounter with Gray she didn't seek him out the remainder of her time on the boat. Nor did she want to. She would give him time to get over his anger. She missed his companionship, however, his virile presence, his scalding kisses, and felt lost without him.

But she had to make him see reason and talk to her.

He would be lost to her forever if he left Natchez to go home immediately after they docked. After all, Gray's mission was complete. He'd come for the quilt and hadn't found it. What other reason did he have to remain?

By the time the boat docked early on the third morning, her mind was pretty much made up about how she would proceed with the quilt's beginnings. About Gray she remained unsure and worried.

Helped by a crew member off the boat, she stood with

her belongings on the pier. The day was warm and sunny, but the new buttercup-yellow day dress she wore offered cool comfort. Hoping to hire a carriage, she swept her gaze around the busy shore. She had too many parcels to carry, or she could have walked home.

Her heart swelled with anticipation. Perched atop a buggy, Gray came toward her, guiding the brown horse to where she stood.

Gray pulled the horse to a stop and glanced down at her. His haggard appearance shocked her. Stubble lined his square jaw and strong chin, sharpening his rakish appearance. His black hair sat askew, one lock falling over his forehead in careless disarray, and sorrow clouded his eyes.

For the first time since she'd met him, he didn't present himself as a noble lord. Instead, he appeared an ordinary man, looking quite vulnerable.

Baines thought her heart would break at such wrenching sadness.

Turning his gaze away from her, he looked straight ahead, not uttering a sound. Before she could break the tension between them, an ebony man walked up to them. He looked up at Gray.

"This be it, suh?"

Barely perceptible, Gray nodded, and the man loaded Baines's things into the buggy. She climbed in next to Gray, and he stiffened, but commanded the horse to move.

In a short spell they reached Baines's house.

Without ceremony or sound, Gray climbed from the buggy and took Baines's possessions off the carriage. He placed them on her porch and waited for her to get down from her seat.

He stood there filled with male pride. She was glad that he didn't touch her, glad that he kept his distance. If he hadn't, Baines felt sure she would have crumpled at his feet and begged him to forgive her.

But poverty-stricken man or powerful lord, she begged no one.

Standing next to her belongings, she watched as he

climbed back in the buggy. Glimpsing her one last time, he urged the horse away.

But the image of his eyes cracked her resolve. They seemed misty blue, as though he had forced tears to remain at bay. Surely she had to be mistaken.

Later she would go to Dunland and comfort him. At the moment she had to get control of her spiraling emotions. After unlatching her door, she brought her things inside.

Leaving the door ajar, she opened the window. She wanted to let in fresh air and light. After being closed for so many days, the house smelled musty and needed airing out.

Before taking the trip with Gray, she had been satisfied to live here for the time being. Now she felt as if the walls were closing in around her. For six days she had been exposed to comfort and elegance. Even her cabin on the *Mississippi Lady*, as small as it was, was luxurious compared to this.

With a sigh she went to the alcove and placed her packages on her cot. Then she regarded her sanctuary. Uncle Lincoln's quilt was still on the rack, waiting to be finished. The place was always as clean as she liked it. It was also familiar.

What was she turning into? This was her home. It had been fine for her before, and it would have broken Uncle Lincoln's heart to know how she disparaged the place. He did the best he could for her, and she should have been ashamed of her ungrateful thoughts.

Feeling a little more settled, she raised the lid on the seaman's trunk. Carefully she packed away her gowns and dresses, both old and new. After reclosing the trunk, she started back to the alcove where her material lay on the cot.

"Knock, knock! Can I come in, darlin'?" Without awaiting Baines's answer, Miz Annabelle opened the door wider and stepped into the house. The river breeze gave it a cool atmosphere.

"Miz Annabelle!" Baines exclaimed happily. She rushed to the older woman and threw her arms around her. She needed Miz Annabelle's guidance and motherly protection. "How in heaven did you know I was back?"

"I have my ways."

Baines looked at her in question.

Miz Annabelle harumphed and glided to the padded bench, her lavender skirts floating around her. "Bad news travels fast when an ill wind blows about."

"W-what do you mean?"

"I mean that quilt done sailed away with Eli and Lincoln."

Baines widened her eyes. "How would you know that?"

Patting the space next to her with her satin gloved hand, Miz Annabelle said, "Sit down, darlin'."

Her senses filling with trepidation, Baines lowered herself to the seat next to Miz Annabelle. Seeing the worry on her face, the widow chuckled.

"I would know by readin' this letter Linc done sent you over to my house, that's how."

"Miz Annabelle!" Baines squeaked. "You weren't supposed to read my letter."

Fingering a red curl, Miz Annabelle harumphed again. "How am I supposed to know what's goin' on with you otherwise? Quit findin' fault and read it for yourself."

Baines all but snatched the letter from her friend's hand. The words popped out at her, and Baines wanted to shout with joy. She felt vindicated.

Baines, honey,

Eli done slinked to New Orleans with yo' quilt. I foun' him quite by accident. I ain't gonna go into detail, but I wanted to let you know that I ain't trustin to send the quilt back. Some thief might up an' take it. I'm gonna keep it wit me fer safe keepin'. I thought I would be home in three months, but the ship I wanted to ketch done left witout us. Instead, I'll be sailin' the Caribbean an I'll see you in 'bout six months. My crewmate, Albert, is the only one here know how to write more than his name. So he's writin' my words an' will see to some-

body gettin it to Annabelle's, since you's always over
there.

  Keep a smart head on yo' shoulders, Baines honey.
Stay away from that fancy nabob Eli done tole me 'bout,
an help the good Lord to stay you safe.

                                          Uncle Linc

Baines put the letter on the trunk. "How long have you
had this letter, Miz Annabelle?"

  "Since the day you left for New Orleans. Ain't you seen
the date on it?"

  Baines shrugged and glanced at the parchment again.

  "What kept you, Baines?" Miz Annabelle asked, stud-
ying her intently.

  "I didn't know about Uncle Linc's letter," she responded defensively, ignoring Miz Annabelle's question.
"Why didn't you bring me the letter and stop me from
leavin'?"

  "Because it came that evenin'. And I reckon you were
quite a way down the river by that time."

  "I reckon I was," Baines mumbled.

  "Baines, darlin', there's somethin' I have to ask you,
and I reckon you'll be honest."

  Baines picked imagined lint from her dress and shifted
in her seat beneath the other woman's firm scrutiny. "I
ain't . . . I have never lied to you before, have I, Miz Annabelle?" she asked in a small voice.

  "No, Baines, you haven't," Miz Annabelle answered
proudly. "I trust you won't start now. You didn't do anythin' with that English Dunston you'd be ashamed of, did
you?"

  She thought about Gray's lovemaking. "No, Miz Annabelle, I didn't," Baines quickly responded, not in the
least ashamed or regretful about her actions with Gray. But
she couldn't tell Miz Annabelle all that had transpired between them. The widow was like a mother to Baines and
would demand Gray do the honorable thing by her, even if
that meant informing Uncle Linc to see that happen.

The widow narrowed her blue eyes, her gaze keen and assessing. "There's somethin' you ain't tellin' me, Baines Marshall!" she scolded. "What are you hidin'?"

Tears pooled in Baines's eyes, and she flung herself into Miz Annabelle's arms and wept.

"Now, now, darlin'. Ain't nothin' so bad it can't be fixed," Miz Annabelle soothed. "Have you gone an' got yourself in a mess with that nabob?"

"Not that way, Miz Annabelle," Baines sobbed. "But I think I love him fiercely, and he hates me!"

Once that got past her lips, Baines related everything to the Widow Shepard. As Baines spoke, Miz Annabelle rocked her back and forth, like a mother would a tiny child.

"Weep no more, Baines. Your Englishman loves you as fiercely as you do him."

Baines straightened herself and glared at the other woman, angry at her coddling tone. "How can you say that after what I've just told you?" she flared.

"Didn't you hear *yourself*? He showed you he loved you, and you couldn't recognize it!"

"And how did he do that?" Baines gritted.

"He told you not to walk the boat alone and didn't close his door till he was sure you were safe inside your cabin. Baines, darlin', he could have left you alone on the docks to fend for yourself. Instead, he saw you safely home. His actions spoke volumes. He didn't have to talk to you. Don't let your pride ruin your chance at love."

"But why is he so angry with me if, as you say, he loves me?"

"It ain't that he's angry with you, darlin'. Somethin' else is eatin' at him. I'm thinkin' it has to do with that quilt." She harumphed once more. "Whoever heard of puttin' a name to a quilt, like it was a livin' thing."

A weight lifted off Baines at Miz Annabelle's logic. She smiled. "Miz Annabelle, if Gray truly loves me the way you said, I won't let him get away. I'm goin' to Dunland and make him listen to me."

Laughing, Miz Annabelle stood up. "You're talkin' like the Baines I know. I'll walk to the bluff with you, honey."

"I love you, Miz Annabelle. Thank you for makin' me see reason." Baines closed the window, then went outside with Miz Annabelle. After locking the door behind them, she started out for Dunland.

Whatever it took, she would make Gray listen to her.

27

"I'LL EXPECT YOU IN the shop tomorrow, darlin'," Miz Annabelle said when she reached the sewing shop on the edge of the bluff. It sat next to the widow's modest house, both structures lined with flower beds. Marigolds, periwinkles, and roses bloomed in colorful perfection. "The work's really pilin' up. I pretty much need you full time, but I understand about your other obligations."

"I'll be there," Baines replied. "I prefer workin' in the sewin' shop rather than the tavern. But the extra money I make at the Horse and Mule sure helps. Since Uncle Linc won't get back before six months, I plan to put his quilt aside for a spell. So I guess I can swing both you and Luther."

"We'll see," Miz Annabelle said. "Go on with you now. Go see the fancy nabob so's you can go home and rest. I know you're a hard worker, darlin', but there's lots to do in the shop. And only the good Lord knows what Luther has in store for you. Well, if he works you too hard, *I'll* give him notice, an' you can work for me full time."

Baines laughed. "You would, too." She hugged the older woman. "Thanks, Miz Annabelle. I'll see you tomorrow."

Leaving the other woman standing in front of the shop, Baines quickly made her way over the hill. Crisp, morning air blew against her cheeks, and she decided to enjoy the sunshine and light. She turned off the road and onto the Trace.

Wearing her newly purchased buttercup-yellow day dress, she felt beautiful. Lace surrounded the three-quarter-length sleeves in abundance. The frilly bodice went up to her throat, covering it with a soft lace collar; and her hair hung down her back, bouncing with every determined step she took.

Stately tupelo and bald cypress trees rose majestically, forming shady umbrellas above her. Wildflowers filled the morning air with their sweet fragrances. A mockingbird landed on a low-hanging branch of a beechtree, but Baines paused briefly to watch a woodpecker chip away at bark with its sharp beak. A pair of playful raccoons zoomed past her, startling Baines out of her reverie.

This was the quickest way to get to Dunland from Under-the-Hill, but she'd been warned of the Trace's danger. Thieving brigands hid amongst the thick stands of trees and dense vegetation, robbing unsuspecting travelers of their possessions every chance they got.

Miz Annabelle and Uncle Linc would have hissy fits if they ever found out she traversed the Trace alone.

With that thought Baines hurried her steps. After walking a quarter mile on the Trace, she finally reached Plantation Lane. The closer she got to the plantation, however, the more apprehension she felt.

Suppose Gray refused to see her? Suppose she was refused entrance? Dressing up in fancy new clothes still didn't make her one of them. A few of the society matrons might have grudgingly accepted her at Gray's party after they discovered her plans for opening her own shop, but that didn't mean they would willingly socialize with her. She was of yeoman class, and Gray and his family were aristocrats who ruled the town. Many of the Natchez nabobry even owned country houses across the river in Concordia Parish in Vidalia, Louisiana. And one of their supreme codes of conduct prevented the two classes from mingling and marrying.

But Baines didn't believe DeEdria would turn her away. The woman's remembered kindness heartened Baines and made it easier for her to continue along.

After twenty minutes of walking and convincing herself she did the right thing, Baines finally reached the imposing mansion. With stout determination, she opened the elaborate iron gates and walked through, daring anyone to turn her away. But no one roamed about to notice her arrival. A stone walkway wound through neatly manicured lawns, which stretched before her like an emerald carpet. Flowering magnolia trees and pitch pines dotted the land. Baines noticed the two story kitchen wing attached to the side of the house. Curls of smoke rose from the chimney, and she wondered what delight was being prepared.

Hesitating for a second more, she commanded herself to move and marched up the walkway to the gallery. Firmly she knocked on the door.

A few moments passed before the door was opened by a house slave.

"Mo'nin', ma'am," the man greeted.

"Mornin'." Maybe she'd ask to see DeEdria first. After all, this was *her* home. Despite all of Miz Annabelle's encouragement, Gray might turn her away, but DeEdria wouldn't. Her good manners wouldn't allow her to do so.

The slave cleared his throat and smiled, friendly and warm. "Kin Ah he'p you?"

Baines nodded and shifted her weight. "I'm Baines Marshall. Ca . . . um . . . *may* I have a word with Miz DeEdria?"

He smiled brightly. "Yes'm. They's in the parlor. Folla me."

Baines stepped inside the entrance hall, and the man closed the door. She followed him across the plush beige rug, passing a small round table standing in the center of the floor, a beautiful arrangement of fresh flowers in an antique vase on top. A long, curving staircase sat opposite the doorway the slave led her through.

The sight that greeted her in the parlor made Baines consider retreating. Belinda Myers sat across from DeEdria

Dunston. Both women looked elegant and sophisticated in
expensive day dresses, their hair fashionably styled even in
early morning. A silver tea service sat on the sofa table
with fresh pastries and fruit. Neither woman noticed the
two new arrivals. DeEdria raised her porcelain cup to her
lips just as the slave spoke up.

"Miz Baines Ma'shall is heah to see you."

DeEdria looked up, her cup inches from her mouth but
untouched. Baines swore DeEdria's golden eyes sparkled
like sunshine at first sight of her. Was she happy to see
her?

"Baines!" DeEdria set her cup down, its contents forgotten. "Oh, my dear!" She rushed from her seat to meet
her, then hugged her warmly.

Hardly able to contain her relief and happiness at De-
Edria's display of affection, Baines smiled. "Hello, De-
Edria."

"Why, Baines Marshall, you're just the prettiest thing
under or above the hill," DeEdria chimed. "What a pleasure it is to see you again." Holding on to Baines's hand,
she pulled her fully into the room. "Look who's here,
Linny."

Belinda Myers glared at Baines. She hadn't stood, and
now looked down her long nose at Baines.

"I can see, De De. And she came on her own, uninvited
and everything."

"Oh, Linny!" DeEdria said patiently. "I like Baines and
I hope she knows she doesn't need an invitation to visit
Dunland."

"Thank you, DeEdria." Baines ignored Belinda Myers
and her hateful stares and spiteful words. Baines's gown
might not have been as expensive as hers, but it was fashioned in the latest style. She was every bit as presentable
as Belinda Myers, or any other Dunland guest.

From the sole of her new shoes to the crown of her head,
she felt every bit the lady.

"What can I do for you, dear?" DeEdria asked, taking
Baines's arm and leading her to a seat. "Would you like
some tea?"

"Tea?" Baines asked. She preferred coffee, but wasn't sure if it was proper to tell that to DeEdria.

DeEdria laughed. "It's what Gray likes," she explained.

Remembering the time when Gray had sat in her house and drank the coffee she'd brewed, Baines frowned. Had he drank coffee merely out of good manners or because he liked it as well? She didn't believe that. Not with all the other times he'd drank coffee, when he could have had tea.

"We expect him down shortly, if you'd care to join us."

"I'm sure little Baines didn't come here to socialize, De De," Belinda snapped with ill-concealed resentment. "Let the girl state her business, so she can get on with her affairs."

"Oh, posh, Linny!" DeEdria chastised. Her mouth thinned with displeasure. "One cup of tea is hardly socializing."

"Well, then, maybe two is." Roc's voice floated through the room. All three women turned to see him standing there in buckskins. He nodded in Baines's direction. "Hello, Baines. Very nice to see you again."

"Hello, Mr. Dunston—"

"Roc," he interrupted, his blue eyes twinkling with mischief.

"Roc," Baines repeated. Her confidence grew. She felt as though she were about to be accepted into an entirely different world from her own. The fact that they were accepting her for who she was, not what she was, made all the difference in the world.

Roc Dunston didn't seem at all surprised to see her. Had he been talking to Gray?

"Roc, where's Gray?" DeEdria asked.

"He's packing, DeEdria. I can't talk him into staying longer. He'll be down for breakfast when he's done. Afterward, we're going to purchase a ticket on a steamer that leaves tomorrow. He hopes to make connections with a passenger ship to Europe."

Desolation cut into Baines at Roc's words. Gray was leaving. But hadn't she suspected as much? Hadn't she realized that the quilt was the only reason he remained in Natchez? Her vision blurred, and she blinked rapidly to clear the tears from her eyes. She'd lost Gray. He certainly wouldn't remain at her request.

She opened her mouth to speak, to tell them that there was no reason for her to remain. Gray had decided to leave, and she doubted he would have told her goodbye.

Belinda Myers's words kept her silent.

"I can't let him get away," the redhead drawled. "He's the kind of man I've been looking for all my life." She looked at Baines and narrowed her eyes. "Exactly why are you here, Baines? This isn't the time to peddle your wares. You did that well enough at Gray's party. Lord Dunston has just returned from a grueling business trip. I'm sure he wants to relax with just his family. And me, of course, since De De and I are as close as sisters."

At first Baines thought to put the woman in her place, but when Belinda went on about Gray's grueling business trip, Baines wanted to burst into peels of laughter. Obviously Belinda didn't know Baines had accompanied Gray to New Orleans.

No one needed to respond to Belinda's venom, however. Someone cleared his throat, and Baines looked to the doorway. A dark frown marring his handsome features, Gray stared past Baines to where Belinda sat.

"Well, Miss Myers," he growled. "You appear to have appointed yourself spokeswoman for my needs and wants. Are you always that presumptuous?" Although not sure why, he felt obligated to defend Baines.

Her face turning an unsightly deep red, Belinda gasped. "Why, Gray!"

Baines's heart hammered at the sight of him. Wearing dark blue trousers, a snow white shirt, a blue waistcoat shot through with silver threads, and a dark blue topcoat, he had regained his noble bearing. His jaw was clean-shaven and smooth, and the sorrow that had clouded his eyes was gone, leaving them the lethal blue that Baines remembered.

His highly polished boots were the same color as his hair.

Shining like onyx, it fell loosely to his shoulders. Baines thought it outshone her own. His sensuality mesmerized her. Remembered passions bewildered her.

Her sense of urgency returned.

He couldn't end their blossoming love before it had a chance to bloom.

"I-I apologize, Gray, if I have offended you," Belinda spoke into the charged silence.

"Not *me*, my dear," Gray imparted icily. "You should direct your apology to Baines. I'm sure you meant to offend *her*."

"Why, I would never do that," Belinda protested sweetly. "In all honesty, Gray, I merely meant to be courteous."

"Did you?" Gray raised an inky brow in question. "And how's that?"

Belinda pursed her lips. "Well, sometimes De De makes it hard for someone to come and go as they plan. She insists on having a repast. How can anyone politely refuse such unrestrained kindness?"

Gray's mouth curved in wry amusement. "How indeed?"

"Anyway, after De De's invitation, Baines couldn't graciously reject her. So I merely thought Baines should state the reason she came and save a bit of awkwardness." Belinda laughed nervously. "Such as we're experiencing now."

"Oh, Linny, sometimes you can be so exasperating," DeEdria complained. "Gray, it's just her way. She's harmless, but she's right. I should have asked Baines whether or not her visit was social." She turned to Baines. "Is it, Baines?"

Baines met her clear, brown eyes and smiled. "It's a social call."

"How wonderful! I'm so glad you felt free to come calling. You have an open invitation to Dunland and will always be welcome."

"Thank you, DeEdria," Baines responded shyly, "but I didn't come callin' on you. It's Gray I came to see."

"Well-ll," Roc sniggered.

Gray glowered at him, then transferred his attention to Baines. He stared at her a moment, his expression blank.

"I'll see you in Rochester's drawing room, Baines." He regarded the others. "Will you excuse us?" With that, he took Baines by the arm and led her away.

28

GRAY INDICATED THE RED leather armchair across from the matching sofa. "Have a seat."

Meekly Baines sat, her stomach churning and her heart pounding. If she could only stop her pulse from racing so frantically, maybe she could talk to Gray without a shaky voice.

He stood over her. "What can I do for you, Baines?"

He was close enough to her for her to easily smell his fine cologne, and close enough to her for him to clearly hear the sound of her pounding heartbeat. That's why she felt so intimidated.

"You can sit down to begin with," she said with irritation. "Please," she added, relenting under his glare. He seemed as angry as he had been when she last saw him.

Gray hesitated a moment before seating himself on the sofa. Seconds ticked by in silence. Tired of the charade, he smiled without warmth. "Tell me, mistress," he began coolly, "are you so desperate to leave Natchez Under-the-Hill that you schemed that whole fruitless trip?"

Baines gasped and looked at him incredulously.

He chuckled nastily. "Was it your intention to have me compromise you and force my hand in marriage, Miss Marshall?"

Her eyes blazed at him, but he ignored the look. His

anger goaded his unforgiving words, and he felt powerless to hold them back. Later he might regret speaking to her so harshly, but he didn't at the moment. Not when he could think of no other way to save his family's fortune and restore dignity to Pierce's name. And not when his heart lay like an open wound in his chest each time he thought that Baines had betrayed him.

He continued with his diatribe, hating his mistrust, looking for any sign that Baines hadn't deceived him.

"Or are you just a lying, scheming, little gold digger, intent on marrying a man of means?"

"You think too much of yourself, Lord Dunston," Baines said harshly. "Maybe you have charmed other women into thinkin' they need you and your money, but I aim to help myself *alone*. Until a week ago you didn't exist for me. My plans for my future haven't changed merely because I've made your acquaintance."

Gray eyed her coldly, unwilling to fully digest her words. "I'm relieved," he said sarcastically.

"I didn't come here for your insults, Gray," Baines snapped, but her lower lip trembled, and her eyes filled with suspicious moisture.

"Oh?" Ignoring the despair creeping into her eyes, mockery laced his tone. "You're too intelligent to believe I would welcome you with open arms. Pray, what did you come here for?"

Swallowing hard, she tilted her chin, then met his icy stare without blinking. "I can make that quilt for you, then ship it to you in England if you're already gone when I'm done."

A gamut of perplexing emotions engulfed Gray, but he refused to allow Baines to glimpse the hope her words caused. He refused to let her know that she had such power over him. He merely lifted one inky eyebrow, ignoring the pounding of his heart.

"Why should I trust you now, mistress?" he said with a sneer. "Everything you've done thus far has been to deceive me."

"I would choose my words real careful, Gray," Baines

warned. "You might come to regret them. You have no choice but to trust me. You have no quilt now. I'm offering you a duplicate."

He hesitated, then asked, "Why?"

"Because I feel obliged to you. My uncle has your great-granny's quilt, so I'll do what I can to rectify that." Regarding him with suspicion, she waited to see if he would accept her offer.

Gray's jaw tautened. "How long will it take you to make it?"

"Only slightly longer than usual. I must make sure I remember every little detail."

"Very well, Baines," he said coldly. "I'll accept your offer."

Baines fingered Uncle Linc's letter, which lay secure in her pocket. She was glad she'd thought to bring it with her. Maybe it would help her to convince Gray that she spoke the truth. Her eyes searching his, she regarded Gray levelly. "Do you really think I tricked you into givin' me that money, Gray?"

He observed her. All his faculties seemed gathered together in intense thought, but he remained motionless, as if one gesture would burst his concentration. Finally he shook his head. "No," he answered grudgingly.

Baines drew the letter from her pocket. Until then, she hadn't realized she'd been waiting to hear his answer before she revealed it. "I'm glad," she said softly. She handed the letter to him.

Taking the letter, Gray peered at her in question.

"Read it," she instructed. Relaxing slightly, she leaned back in her seat and watched as he unfolded and read the letter.

When he finished, he looked at her, his eyes suddenly shadowed with pain.

"Forgive me, little mouse," he said, reaching the letter over to her. "I know I hurt you and I'm so sorry."

Slipping it back into her pocket, she sat quietly. Now that they were alone, the noble bearing remained, but was only a thin facade for his sorrow. Yet she had breached the wall he'd erected around himself. Now her task was to penetrate it fully, so he would stay in Natchez with her.

Breathing in deeply, she broached the subject. "You're leavin'?"

"Aye. I must."

"Why?"

His expression turned grim and remote.

"Do you hate me so much?" she blurted.

An unreadable emotion darkened Gray's eyes. She thought he wouldn't answer her, but he did. "Don't ever think that I hate you, Baines."

"Then why are you leavin' me? Has it got anything to do with the quilt?"

Gray laughed bitterly. "Everything," he retorted.

"Such as?"

"Go home, Baines," he commanded, standing abruptly. "*My* quest has ended in failure, but I am confident that your dreams will all come true."

If he left, one of her dreams would instantly die. She would still open her shop and eventually get a house for her and Uncle Linc on the bluff. But it would take her a long time to repair her heart if Gray walked out of her life.

Well, she wouldn't let him. Not without a fight. She popped from her chair and stood before him. Hands on her hips, she glowered at him. "I won't leave until you tell me about that quilt, Gray. About Mary's Fortune. Surely you must know that I'll send it over to you on the next ship crossing, when Uncle Linc brings it back." She paused as realization dawned. "It holds some kind of secret, doesn't it? But wouldn't it still be the same when you get it back? Why do you need it now, instead of later?"

Gray laughed—rich, warm, and genuine—at her ceaseless questions. The moment didn't last long. Within seconds he grew serious once more. "Secrets," he said. "It can get lonely with no one to share them with."

She grabbed his arm, feeling his strength beneath her fingertips. Her senses leaped to life, and she froze. The attraction between them grew stronger in that instant. An irrepressible, incandescent bond pulled them ever closer.

"You have someone to share your secrets with, Gray," she whispered. "Me. Tell me, what could possibly have you so bothered?"

Moving away from her, Gray walked to the window. He owed her an explanation. She *wasn't* Jamie McKay. She was sweet and beautiful and caring.

But more than that, she had become his friend. He would have to settle for that because he would never take her to England with him. His worst fear had come to pass, and he refused to let her wallow in poverty and disgrace with him.

Her future belonged here, without him. In time, she would forget he ever existed. But what would she have in England? Naught but pity and scorn as the wife of the once powerful Earl of Montegut. Enemies would say his family received what they deserved, but they wouldn't believe that Pierce hadn't been guided by greed. They wouldn't believe he'd been guided by the thought to merely secure their wealth.

What an irony that was. Instead of securing the family fortune for succeeding generations, Pierce had assured them of poverty forever.

Gray's failure tasted like bitter bile in his mouth. Better for Baines to believe he wasn't interested in her than for her to insist she leave with him.

With the crook of her little finger, she could convince him to take her with him. He would never let her know of that power. In the end it would only destroy her. And the love he believed she bore him.

Drawing in an agitated breath, he perused the surroundings outside. "I'm a proud man, Baines," he said without facing her. "I don't relish exposing my plight to the world."

"I ain't the world, Gray." Too late, Baines realized she'd used incorrect speech. Heat rose in her cheeks.

Gray turned and smiled. "No, little mouse," he agreed. "You're not the world. And for that I'm grateful. I think, however, you deserve to know the truth about Mary's Fortune and why I'm so desperate to recover it." Pacing across

the room, he opened a humidor on the desk and took out
a cigar.

Occasionally he enjoyed a good cigar, but mostly after
eating. In all honesty, he didn't want one now. This was
just a stalling ploy to get his confused thoughts in order.
Giving Baines a cursory glance, he noted the expectant look
on her flawless features.

Unable to resist, he pulled her to her feet and hauled her
against his chest, kissing her fervently. Urgent and explor-
atory, his mouth ravished hers. Her lips felt soft and moist
beneath his own, and her response touched his very soul.

"Perhaps if Mary's Fortune had smiled on me, *you* could
have been my world," he croaked before releasing her.

Baines sucked in a breath and steadied herself. "W-what
do you mean, Gray?"

"I mean I'm almost penniless," he answered without
further hesitation. "My father made some unwise investments before he died, and now the creditors are calling in
the debts. Because my father was a highly honorable and
respected peer of the realm, his creditors extended my time
by six months before foreclosing on my estate."

"What does Mary's Fortune have to do with your creditors, Gray?"

"Mary's Fortune was my last hope, little mouse. It has
a map to a fortune woven somewhere within its pattern.
But now that hope has faded."

The colors of the quilt rose in her mind. Four mulberry
corners sitting on the pearl white border. Blocks of emerald,
rose, and sapphire in crisscrossing patterns. She remembered Mary's Fortune as surely as if she had created it.
Briefly she considered the ramifications of helping Gray.
That meant her dreams would have to be put on hold a
while longer. Maybe in the end he would still walk away
from her, but she was coming to realize that money wasn't
everything. For her, it would mean nothing without love.

She laid a comforting hand on Gray's arm.

"I've been studyin' the pattern, Gray. I know I can make
the quilt from memory."

"Make Mary's Fortune, and you'll have my gratitude for

life." He slid her down the length of his body and kissed her again.

Her thoughts scattered to the four winds, Baines could hardly respond. She didn't want his gratitude. She wanted his love. And she wanted him to stop kissing her like that. Well, not really stop, just give her warning.

"I-I can start t-today," she said breathlessly. "But to-morrow I have to go to Miz Annabelle's. Tonight I have to go to the tavern."

Gray pushed her away and glared at her. "I don't want you in that putrid hole, Baines," he declared as though he had a right to dictate where she should and shouldn't go.

"I have to go, Gray. I already gave my promise to Luther."

"I'm learning of your honor, Baines, and I'm proud of you. But the Ox and Donkey is no place for a lady." He gave her a teasing look and a grin that would melt butter in a cake of ice.

Baines giggled. "It's the Horse and Mule," she corrected.

"I knew it was a couple of dumb animals." Gray laughed. "Just like its bloody patrons."

Baines laughed with abandonment. "Except my uncle Lincoln," she corrected.

"Except your uncle Lincoln," he agreed.

He lifted a lock of hair and caressed it, swallowing hard. His gaze traveled over her face and searched her eyes, soft as a caress.

"I . . . um . . . better go so I can get started, Gray."

"Of course," Gray said huskily. "How did you get here?"

"Walked."

"All that distance?"

"Oh, I took the shortcut. I came by way of the Trace. It's beaut—"

"Are you daft? The Trace, Baines? Even *I* know not to traverse there if possible. You could have been killed. Or worse!"

Baines laughed. "What can be worse than bein' dead?"

"Never mind, little mouse," he answered in exasperation. Her naiveté didn't surprise him. As a young lady, she could have been ravaged. But she seemed not to realize that. "I'll take you home."

"No, Gray, it wouldn't be right. Your family is eager for your company. As is *Linny*." Baines said the name with amusing sarcasm and giggled at Gray's disapproving scowl. "Besides, you have to tell them you'll be stayin' a while longer."

He contemplated her exuberance but didn't remark upon it. "You're right, of course. I'll see to someone taking you home. Promise me you won't take that dangerous path alone again."

She couldn't stop the rush of heat that invaded her body. He cared about *her* and her safety. Miz Annabelle was right. He did love her.

"I promise," Baines said demurely.

Gray sighed in relief. "Good. I'll stop by your house later if that's all right."

"Of course," Baines responded serenely.

Her whole being tingled from his touch, his kiss, his nearness. She needed time to gather her wits about her, before their next encounter.

Still she wondered if the accusations spoken today would hang between them in the days to come. She hoped the time she anticipated with him would be enough for him to realize his love and confess it to her, however.

Yet she couldn't hold back the time she needed for that to happen, any more than she could the rushing waters of the Mississippi.

29

LATER THAT AFTERNOON BAINES laid a yard of material out on the weak-legged table. Measuring the new template on the cloth, she proceeded to cut her first perfect square. She continued the process until an entire yard of mulberry material had been prepared.

Mary's Fortune's patchwork began with the color mulberry at each corner. Emerald, rose, and sapphire followed, and a pearl white border surrounded it. Each color was repeated all the way to the bottom.

Four mulberry corners. Baines went to her cot to check the sketch she'd drawn from memory. Since she didn't have the appropriate colored chalk to mark the squares on her sketch, she wrote in the name of the colors for each row.

Stitching the colors in their proper order would be easy enough for her. What suddenly became daunting was the size of Mary's Fortune. It was a large quilt, and Baines had failed to procure its measurements. Would that present a problem with its accuracy?

Dang! Gray was depending on her to come through for him. She couldn't fail him. Not only because he was depending on her, but because she didn't want to disappoint him.

Closing her eyes, she pictured the quilt in her mind.

The ends had been a mite frayed, and, if the colors were

situated correctly in her mind, the quilt was as wide as it was long. That wouldn't be a hindrance. Its length and width would fall into form with each block she stitched.

But suppose the quilt itself held the fortune? Then what? If only Mary's Fortune were here, she could open it now to discover if the interlining was made from cloth or bank notes. The feel of paper, however, would be significantly different from the feel of cloth. Unless it was disguised somehow.

Baines sighed. Gray apparently believed otherwise. He wouldn't have been so plumb happy if he'd thought there was a possibility that the treasure was within the quilt. Therefore, she would recreate it and help him to look for a map within the design.

She reckoned getting everything together for stitching would claim a right good amount of time. She still had nine more yards of mulberry cloth to cut, and that didn't include the lining. But she would cut that after she finished with the colored cloth.

Stacking her blocks together, she carefully laid them on the long, padded bench. Then, collecting her scraps, she put them in her sewing sack with the other scraps Miz Annabelle had given her for Uncle Linc's quilt.

She loathed to remove his birthday quilt from the rack, but deemed it necessary. Maybe she would ask Miz Annabelle to let her use the empty rack in the back of the shop for the crazy quilt for the time being.

Again Baines searched her mind for any little detail she might have overlooked. She wanted to make a perfect quilt for Gray. He would be so happy with her because she'd helped to save his family fortune. He would never want her to leave his side. In his love and contentment he would ask her to become his wife.

Pushing her fanciful thinking aside with effort, she cleared the table once again and spread the second yard of mulberry cloth out on it. Using her template for measurements, she proceeded to cut another square.

Gray stood in the open doorway, watching Baines. She

appeared deep in thought, so set in her task that she was oblivious to his presence. He was glad for that. It allowed him time to bask unashamedly in her beauty.

Too occupied with his own plight this morning, he'd failed to recognize how lovely she looked. He hadn't *commented* on her loveliness, he amended. Always he recognized her beauty, as was the case at this moment.

She'd changed out of the fashionable creation she wore earlier into a buckskin dress. On any other woman, the dress would have appeared drab and unappealing. Baines was the exception. It clung to her curves, accentuating her creamy skin. Her hair fell loose down her back and reminded him of fine silk. He ached to let it ripple through his fingers again. He wanted to taste her sweet mouth; to hold her close and feel her warm softness. He wanted to

"Gray! You came!"

He smiled, brought to his senses when Baines abruptly glanced up from her work. Her emerald eyes brightened with enjoyment, and Gray's mood lightened.

"Aye, little mouse. I promised you I would. I see you're making preparations to put the quilt together. 'Mary's Fortune Two.' Or maybe I should call it 'Baines's Inspiration'."

Walking from around the table, Baines chuckled merrily. "So, I inspire you? Or is it that quilt?"

Gray grinned enigmatically at her and changed the subject. He would never confess that she was his inspiration and the quilt his salvation. "Are you hungry, Baines? Cook fixed a basket for you. Would you like to stop and eat?"

"Dang!" Baines glanced at the clock and saw that it was nearly three o'clock. "I became so excited over my quiltin' I forgot about eatin'. Is there enough for two?"

Her high spirits were like an aphrodisiac to him, entrancing and bewitching. Eating was the farthest thing from his mind.

Images of her facing him in a wet shirt that clung to her curves after she'd frolicked in the river sprung to his memory. His loins stirred, and he shifted his weight.

"Gray?"

"Er . . . aye, Baines. I could never let you eat alone. I wouldn't be much of a gentleman if I did."

"Um, well, I'm workin' at the table, but if you don't mind, there's a shady spot under the chinaberry tree. And a patch of grass in a beautiful shade of green like you never saw before."

Oh, aye. He would stake his life that he had seen a more beautiful shade of green. He merely had to gaze into her eyes and he would find a brilliant green, as clear and sparkling as emeralds.

"It sounds perfect," he murmured. "Besides, I have no intention of hindering your progress for want of a table to eat on."

Baines fetched her one tablecloth from her food larder and bade Gray to follow her as she brushed past him and went out the door.

Reaching the shade of the tree, she spread the tablecloth along a spot on the grass, then sat down.

Standing over her, Gray held the basket. "I must say, you're quite expedient, Baines." He joined her on the grass and sat the basket on the tablecloth.

Opening the container, Baines laid out the plates, then took out the food—fried chicken, warm bread, cheese, and fruit. "Mmm. Smells mighty temptin'."

Gray picked up a drumstick. "Let's see if it tastes as tempting as it smells." He took a generous bite. His senses heightened by Baines's nearness, the chicken tasted delicious. It was well seasoned and crispy, cooked to perfection.

Unaware of how erotic she looked, Baines took a dainty bite from her piece of chicken and ran her tongue over her small red lips to lick away the crumbs. He saw the pleasure she derived from each bite she took and each piece she swallowed.

He wanted to make love to her again then and there. There was nothing stopping him from doing so now. She was recreating the quilt, and his fortune would be saved.

He moved closer to her but stopped suddenly. His predicament hadn't changed. He was still close to ruin. How could he be sure that Mary Dunston hadn't been out to make sport of his grandfather? And if there was a map, suppose someone had discovered the treasure long ago?

No, he couldn't shirk his responsibility just to satisfy his lust for Baines. Although he knew she desired him as much as he did her, someone had to use common sense. Neither could he confess his love to her—not until he was certain that he had fulfilled his obligation to his father and had saved their wealth.

Besides, how would Baines fare in the urban sophistication of London? Some women there had the same narrow-minded predilection as Belinda Myers.

Recalling how Baines had set Belinda in her place at his party, Gray smiled. All doubts were erased. Baines could survive in London, or anywhere else she desired to go.

"I've never seen a body enjoy chicken like you appear to, Gray," Baines remarked, biting into a succulent strawberry. "Why, you're grinnin' from ear to ear."

Gray shook his head. Was he turning into a complete idiot? In her presence or not, Baines invaded his thoughts, rivaling his obsession with Mary's Fortune.

Now, however, he could blame everything on the atmosphere. The lazy afternoon created a sense of wonderment for him. He'd imagined sitting under this very tree with Baines and thought it would be a unique experience. The reality of it enraptured him.

Well, he would bloody well get control of the situation. Firmly he reminded himself again that his situation was a bit too tenuous.

He looked at Baines. "I understand the people of this part of your country named this chicken after them."

Her lips stained with strawberry juice, Baines frowned. "We did?"

"Aye. This is called Southern fried chicken."

"Oh." Baines laughed. "It's the best kind."

A flock of passenger pigeons flew overhead, momentarily darkening the skies with their huge numbers as they headed toward the woodlands. A steamboat whistle blew.

The boat approached the bend cautiously, slowing down for its landing at the docks a short way up.

Yet the glory of the afternoon and the presence of Baines couldn't entirely alleviate the fear that was settling into Gray. Would Baines duplicate the quilt correctly?

As he helped her clear away their leavings, he decided to take a cue from Baines. He didn't want to be poor, but for the time being he would make the best of his unusual circumstances and bask in the company of the bewitching enchantress who held his future in her hands.

30

"DARLIN', IT WOULDN'T BE Christian of me to expect a full day's work from you, knowin' what you have facin' you."

Baines applied a stopper's knot to the inside of the bodice she'd just attached to its skirt. Placing the garment on the counter, she responded to Miz Annabelle. "I can't let you do that, Miz Annabelle. There's no reason your business should suffer on my account. I only have one more week to work at the Horse and Mule before Luther expects Sally to return. I can manage until then."

"Yes, and by then you'll be tired enough to take to your bed, child, where you'll do a body no good a'tall."

"But Miz Annabelle—"

"No *buts*," the widow interrupted as Baines retrieved the gown and put it on a dress form. "You said Gray didn't cotton to you going to Luther's anymore. Even if you had gone to the tavern last night, I don't think Luther would have expected you. He didn't even know you were back home."

Baines ruffled the sleeves to make the gingham dress as attractive as possible. "What are you gettin' at, Miz Annabelle?"

"Just that you have to know what's important, darlin'. You told me your Englishman is desperate to get his quilt back or one just like it. If *you* make the quilt, Baines, you'll need the time to do it. Somethin' you won't have if you work full days here and half the night at the Horse and Mule. When will you have time to rest if you go home from Luther's to stitch on your quilt?''

"Miz Annabelle, haven't you heard a word I said? I'll only be workin' another week at Luther's. I can manage until then.''

Shaking her head, the widow went to the back of the shop. When she returned a few minutes later, she carried a tray with two glasses of lemonade and a plate of day-old cookies on top.

"I won't have it." She placed the tray on a table in front of a small sofa, then beckoned Baines to join her. "Baines Marshall, I know how independent you are, but you are *not* made of iron. You're a fast and efficient worker. You can get near as much done in half a day as you can a full one. So don't argue with me.''

"No, ma'am,'' Baines said in resignation. As determined as she was, Miz Annabelle seemed a mite more so. Feeling her friend's gaze on her, Baines nibbled at a cookie, then sipped some cool, tart lemonade from her glass. She guessed Miz Annabelle wanted to know why Gray needed the quilt so bad and why she was so hell-fired to recreate it for him. It took quite an effort to ignore the hurt look in Miz Annabelle's eyes. Usually they shared everything. Since meeting Gray, however, Baines hesitated to reveal anything.

Yet how could she tell her this? It had been so hard for Gray to confess his predicament to her. She couldn't betray that confidence, not even to the woman she loved like a mother.

"Miz Annabelle,'' she said softly, "I want you to trust me. There is a reason why Gray must have Mary's Fortune within six months, but I can't reveal it without betrayin' him. Please forgive me for not being able to tell you.''

Patting Baines on the cheek with affection, Miz Annabelle smiled. "Never mind about forgivin', darlin'. I'm mighty proud of you. I know you wouldn't do anything without good reason. Just know when you need to unburden yourself with what you *can* tell me, I'm always ready to listen.

"Now, when you finish your lemonade, stitch a hem on the gown you put on the form, then trim it with rickrack to complete it. After that, I want you to start out for home. Give yourself a chance to work on that dang quilt with the lovely name."

"Yes, ma'am." Baines looked at Miz Annabelle with tenderness. What would she do without her? After setting her glass down, she went to complete her tasks.

∞

GLOWERING, GRAY SAT AT a table in a darkened corner of the Horse and Mule. He'd gone there to escort Baines home when her chores were done. In spite of Lincoln Marshall's warning, Gray knew there were men out there who were willing to harm her.

He was more than able to see to the task of protecting her alone, but his bloody cousin insisted on accompanying him. Gray's scowl deepened as Roc called out to Baines.

"Baines! Please bring us two glasses. Two *clean* glasses, so give them a little extra dip in the water."

A burly patron rose unsteadily to his feet. "Iffen one dip is good 'nuff fer us, one dip order be good 'nuff fer a coupla fancy nabobs," he proclaimed.

"And so it is, my friend," Gray quickly announced. "Bloody ass," he hissed for Roc's ears alone. The urge to bloody kick his cousin possessed him. If he must fight tonight, he wanted to do it on Baines's behalf, not because his cousin lacked diplomacy. "They're every bit good enough for you. To prove it, this gentleman will allow you and every man here to refill your glasses with whatever you're drinking. Twice. His generosity knows no bounds. So fill up and drink up."

No less then ten huge, hairy giants rushed from their seats. Glasses shook and tables rattled as a minor stampede to the long, wooden bar commenced.

"Now, that was a cheeky thing to do, Grayling," Roc admonished with a frown. "Why would I want to buy those rodents a drink?"

Gray smiled tightly. "I figured it was better than leaving with your head in your hand, Rochester. That chap didn't like your insinuation that *they* drank out of dirty glasses and we couldn't."

Roc patted his chest where he had his pistol. "I think my friend here would have dispelled any hostile advancement," he bragged.

"A cannon couldn't stop those furry weasels, cousin. Just be grateful they accepted your offer—"

"*My* offer?"

"*My* offer, *your* money," Gray corrected. "The purpose in coming here is to keep Baines safe. How safe would she be if a brawl ensued? Or us for that matter?"

Shoving his hand through his hair, Roc sighed. "You're right, Gray. What was I thinking? The cheek of me for wanting a clean glass!" He grinned at Gray and took a bottle of expensive scotch from the pocket of his topcoat. After opening the top, he tipped the bottle to Gray in salute, before taking a long swig. "To your health," he gulped.

Baines banged the glasses down on the table, her eyes flashing green fire. "To both your lives," she snorted. "Those boatmen are meaner than cornered alligators hankerin' for a cause to fight. I advise you to pay Luther for the drinks you bought them, Roc, and leave while they're occupied imbibin'. There's an army of them and just two of you!"

"Three," a male voice corrected from two tables away.

The familiarity of the tone snapped Gray's attention to where the sound came from. He stiffened. The man was blond, with pale eyes and a clean-shaven face. Though not as well dressed as Gray and Roc, he was better dressed then anyone else in there. He stood and walked over to Gray's table.

"Hello, Grayling. It's been a long time. I see you haven't changed. Doxies still seem to appeal to you. Or do they go by a different name in this part of the world?"

Gray's disbelieving stare turned into a menacing scowl. He stood from his chair. "You have a choice, Jamie," he snarled, low and threatening. "You can apologize to the lady now or *after* I tear every limb from your body. That decision wouldn't be too complicated for a sane man. Or do you lack as much wits as you do integrity?"

Jamie McKay remained quiet for a moment. Shifting his glance to Roc and Baines, then back to Gray, he smiled crookedly. "My mistake, milord. My integrity may be in question, but no one can accuse me of lacking wits." Turning to Baines, he bowed low. "Please accept my deepest apology, mistress. I meant no offense."

Baines nodded with a slight movement of her head. Glaring at Gray, she stalked back to her duties. She recognized the stranger from the shop, who'd been in New Orleans as well, but didn't deem him worthy enough of a response. Besides, Gray had assured her that he knew the man in question, and he seemed well in control of the matter.

"What do you suppose is wrong with her, Gray?" Roc asked. He didn't get a response.

Gray stood glowering at Jamie. With only the table between them, he was ready to throttle him. "I never thought I'd ever see you again, James. Better than that, I never *wanted* to see you again."

"Your anger is justified, Gray," Jamie said quietly. "Another apology is due. This time to you."

Barely able to restrain himself from the urge to leap across the table and pound Jamie into the floor, his former friend's announcement took him by surprise. "What?"

"I was forced to lie that night, Gray."

Gray opened his mouth to reply, but he didn't get a chance to utter a sound. Jamie rushed on with his explanation.

"Your father was the one with the power and respect. When he was nominated for the board of regents, my father was loathe to accept that. Becoming a member of that prestigious board was a goal he'd prepared for for many years. It was bandied about that His Lordship, Pierce Dunston, would emerge victorious. My father couldn't abide that. So he forced me to aid him in creating a scandal that would force Pierce to decline the position.''

Laughing without mirth, Gray shook his head incredulously. "My father's interests were wide, Jamie, but they never included governing on the board of regents at Eton.''

"For *my* father's ambitions, I lost my best friend,'' Jamie continued. "I never thought I'd ever get the chance to say this to you, Gray, but I was a young fool who admired his father. I regret the loss of your friendship. I apologize for the harm I caused you.'' Uncertainty in his features, he stood. "I'm first mate on the *Venerable* docked in New Orleans.'' With that he strolled from the place.

"Who was that, and what was that all about?'' Roc demanded, watching Jamie's retreat.

"I don't want to talk about it, Roc,'' Gray answered. He was still reeling from his encounter with Jamie McKay, and unsure how to feel. For years he'd told himself that he would never consider anything Jamie had to say in his defense. He remembered what a tyrant Jamie's father was and felt a moment's pity for the predicament his former friend must have faced. Yet he wouldn't allow that reasoning to pierce the anger he still felt at Jamie's betrayal. He doubted anything ever could and decided to push this encounter out of his mind. "We'd best take possession of Baines and get free of this blasted place.''

"Anything you say, Grayling,'' Roc said. "You are certainly a man of intrigue.'' He looked around the room and found no sign of Baines. "Where is the light of your life, whom you refuse to acknowledge as such?''

"What?''

"Baines, Gray. She doesn't seem to be anywhere in here.''

"She's probably somewhere in the back chamber.'' Gray strode to the bar. Most of the patrons remained there, still drinking the ale Roc had yet to pay for.

"You come to pay yore bill, Mr. Dunston?'' Luther asked to neither Dunston in particular, since they both stood at the bar.

"Pay up, Rochester,'' Gray commanded.

Roc dug into his coat pocket. "Bossy sort, aren't you, Grayling?"

Gray ignored him. "Luther, I think it would be prudent for me to accompany Baines to her home at this time. I'm sure you can manage the remainder of the evening without her. Please fetch her from the back."

"It'd be my pleasure, mister, if she was back there. Baines up and went while you was talkin' to the nabob who left," Luther informed them.

Once again astonishment nearly rendered Gray speechless. "Bloody hell," he managed, and stalked to the opened door. A confused Roc followed close behind.

31

FURIOUS AT THE BASENESS of men, even highborn ones, and Gray in particular, Baines asked Luther to allow her to leave early this evening. Wanting to avoid a possible brawl, Luther readily agreed.

"I'll let Jessie see you home safe, Baines," Luther admonished. "And if you can't keep them crazy nabobs outta here, I'll have to git 'long wit'out you. Don't want my place tore up from a slingin' match. They's givin' my place a bad name anyway. They's too uppity, 'specially that English cuss."

The hint of censure she detected in Luther's tone annoyed her. Hoping to cover her feelings, she lowered her eyelids. She didn't want to offend Luther. He was her friend and he'd helped her out of a lot of tight spots. But neither did she care for him talking about Gray like that.

"Luther, I'll talk to him," she said, not entirely able to hide her vexation.

"Sally ain't done mournin' over her pa yet, but she'll be comin' back the day after tomorrow, Baines. I appreciate yo' willingness to help me, but you've been gone almos' as long as Sally—"

Baines laughed at Luther's exaggeration. "I've only been gone a week, Luther."

Luther snorted. "I knows that, Baines. My point is, I

done got 'long fine wit'out you or Sally in that week. Go along, honey. I can manage good," he assured her.

Patting Luther on his hairy arm, Baines smiled at him. "Thanks."

She paused briefly at the entrance. Small bits of the conversation Gray was having with Jamie reached her. The men's discussion made no sense to her, and Gray's anger prevented him from noticing her departure.

She glowered in his direction. If Gray was there to see that no harm befell her, he sure was doing a fine job! She could have been dragged from the place by her hair, and he wouldn't have noticed. As for Roc, he stood with his mouth gaping open, looking dumber than a carp in a fishing boat.

Barely refraining from throwing a glass in their direction, Baines rushed out of the open doorway. With Jessie serving as bodyguard, she arrived home in less than ten minutes.

"Baines, I ain't never seen you walk so fast b'fore," Jessie panted. "Somethin' got you riled?"

"I got things to do, Jessie," Baines gritted. "I'm beholden to you for seein' me home."

Jessie walked up to the porch. "I could keep comp'ny wit' you for a while if you like."

"Good night, Jessie." Baines unlatched her door. "Thanks again." After stepping inside, she closed it behind her.

Ten minutes later she was at her worktable, another yard of cloth spread over it. She picked up her shears to begin cutting. She'd barely measured and cut three blocks when she heard *his* footsteps on the porch. Instinct told her it was Gray even before the knock.

"Baines Marshall!" His angry voice blared through the door. "You little idiot! Are you in there?"

After putting down her scissors, Baines walked to the door but didn't open it. "Yes," she called back.

A moment of silence ensued.

"Well?"

"Well what?"

"Are you going to let me in?"

"Well, dang! You never said you wanted to come in, Gray."

"I'd like to if I may," Gray scoffed.

Baines opened the door. A black frown on his face, Gray stood there, handsome and muscular in his fine clothes and polished boots. In contrast, Roc stood beside him, grinning like a Cheshire cat, dressed expensively but casual.

She moved away from the door in silent invitation, and they stepped inside. "Welcome to my home, Roc. If you care to sit a spell—"

"No, he *doesn't* care to sit a spell, Baines," Gray snapped. "I don't even know why he's here."

"We only have one horse and buggy between us, Grayling, and you were doing the driving." Roc's grin split wider. "Does that give you a hint?"

Ignoring Roc, Gray turned to Baines. "Why in bloody hell didn't you let me bring you home?" he demanded. His blue eyes blazed down into hers. "That's what I'd gone there for."

"It seems every time you go to the Horse and Mule, you come close to startin' a brawl, Gray," Baines declared. "Which could be cause for your demise."

"She's right, you know, Gray," Roc cut in. "Those river whales would have obliterated us, including the brave man who offered to join in on our side. A friend of yours, cousin?"

"Roc, I'll be a few minutes. Wait for me in the buggy. And for whatever reason that grin is fixed upon your face, try to remedy it. Or *I* will."

Roc laughed. "I don't know how you got him to stay, Baines. Belinda Myers is put out with the power you appear to have over him; DeEdria is delighted. Me? I'm curious to know what's going on." He strode to the door. "See you outside, Gray."

Alone again, Gray faced Baines. He searched her face. "Know this, Baines. As long as you're working at that . . . that place, I'll be there to see you home safely."

Unwelcome excitement surged through her. She dared not believe he was there for her, but his words, the sound of his voice affected her deeply. Her anger melted. She smiled tenderly at him, the warm night made hotter with his nearness. "Is it my safety that concerns you, Gray, or the quilt?" she asked without rancor.

Uncertain, Gray stared at her. "What do *you* believe? Never mind, Baines. I'm not sure I care to hear the answer. You've obviously formed a conclusion in your mind." He made for the door. "Roc's waiting for me. I'll let you get back to whatever you were doing. I'll see you tomorrow." Placing his hand on the doorknob, he paused. "Just for the record, little mouse, your safety means much to me. The quilt has nothing to do with it. Good night, my dear," he added softly and left her there alone.

Gray had been angry because he feared for her safety. True, he also seemed angry with Jamie in the tavern, but Gray had come seeking her out to bluster and bully her. Well, she couldn't let him bully her, but she would ease his concern by telling him Sally would be returning in a day, and Luther had decided he could fare just as well without her.

Thinking that Jamie definitely was handsome without that dang beard, Baines returned to her cutting, contented.

Once again, Gray had worried about *her*!

And once again, hope filled her heart with joy.

32

WORKING PAST MIDNIGHT, BAINES completed her cutting.

She divided the lining into blocks also, deciding to sew it onto each block. It would be easier for her to handle that way, and she wouldn't have to stuff the quilt or shake it to distribute the stuffing evenly after she finished it. Since she wasn't involved in a quilting bee, and as large as she projected Mary's Fortune Two to be, it would have been a task to fit the lining inside properly.

Setting her shears on the table, she stood and stretched her muscles. She had been sitting since Gray left over three hours ago.

A warm feeling spread through her middle, and she smiled. Maybe he was her knight in shining armor after all.

With that happy thought, she completed her preparations for bed, then lay on her cot. She fell asleep with the image of Gray dancing in her head.

∞

RISING EARLY THE NEXT morning, Baines cleared the table of her quilting notions, then put on a pot of coffee to boil. It was warm and cloudy today, but she hoped the rain would remain at bay.

When the coffee was done, she poured herself a cup and sat at the table. Today was Sunday, but she decided to skip church services again, giving her the entire day to work on Mary's Fortune. *Baines's Inspiration,* she corrected herself and smiled.

Her smile faded. As soon as she completed the quilt, Gray would leave. The thought of slowing her progress crossed her mind. Then she would have Gray with her longer, or at least until he confessed his love for her. If only she had the chance to spend time with him, she felt sure he would realize his feelings for her. She could think of nothing that would stop him.

Then she remembered his grief and sorrow over his predicament. If the quilt didn't indeed lead to a treasure, Gray would be penniless. Baines doubted he would ever be honest about his feelings under those circumstances. Deep in thought, she blew into her cup, then took a sip of the steaming coffee. Didn't he realize by now that money didn't mean everything to her? She had lived without it all her life. She could continue to do so.

Realization struck like a bolt of lightning. Since she had met him, the only thing she'd ever discussed fervently was her desire to get away from Under-the-Hill. She'd even tried to blackmail him in an attempt to have the money she wanted, to speed up her and Uncle Linc's move.

Now the thought to deceive Gray once more had crossed her mind. How could she? She wouldn't have him thinking she had tricked him again. She would continue at her fast pace. It didn't matter how quickly or slowly she worked. She couldn't deceive Gray again.

Putting her cup down on the table, she moved to the padded bench where she'd laid some of her blocks, needles, and threads. Taking up a needle, she threaded it. Afterward, she placed a square of lining to a block, then began stitching them together. Careful to use tiny, even stitches, she left enough of a seam on all sides in order to attach it to the next block.

For the time being she didn't need a quilting frame.

There wasn't enough material sewn together in Mary's Fortune to hang over a drinking glass.

In the next three hours Baines stitched together twenty lined squares. Very pleased with the progress, she surveyed her work. Inspecting her handiwork, she saw that she was on the right track and delighted in her headway.

The cool river breezes blew through the open door and window, and Baines walked out on the porch.

Her heart lurched, and she swallowed a squeal of delight.

Hands beneath his dark head, Gray was lying on a blanket spread out under the chinaberry tree. The picture of sleek grace and potent virility, he reminded her of a big cat. His topcoat and waistcoat lay beside him, but instead of his usual trousers, he wore form-fitting breeches, accentuating his long limbs and hard muscles.

Scurrying down the steps, Baines joined him and dropped down on the blanket, crossing her legs. A smile softened his features, and his eyes brimmed with tenderness and passion.

She stared with longing at him, not caring if he noticed her desire. He had taken the initiative to see her, and that meant a lot.

Tethered to the tree, his palomino stood sedately, his tail swishing at some unknown insect. The river traffic was busy as always and barely noticeable. For a moment they stared at each other. The horse nickered, breaking the moment, and Baines laughed nervously.

"Hello, Gray," she murmured. "I didn't know you were here."

He drew his knees up. "I acted quite the dolt last night, Baines. I wouldn't want you angry at me for disturbing you while you work."

Baines scooted closer to him. "I need detainin' for a spell." She fanned her fingers out. "My fingers are sore from all the stitchin' and needle-threadin'."

Taking her hands into his, Gray gently massaged them. She hadn't realized how big his hands were compared to hers. Neither had she realized how long his eyelashes were.

They were almost too long for a man, yet that didn't detract from his masculinity.

His tender ministrations continued, his palms warm against her skin, stirring her blood, inciting her passion. Sensations rushed along her nerve endings, and heat flamed within her, causing her to grow weak.

Slowly and gracefully, she reclaimed her hands and ended the torture. Until she was sure of his feelings, she couldn't succumb to his lovemaking again—as badly as she wanted to.

Gray looked at her.

"All I need do is give them a rest, Gray," she said quietly. "Of course, the massagin' helped."

He laughed and stretched out once again on the thick, soft blanket. "Of course." An awkward silence followed before he spoke again. "I want to know?"

"What?"

"If you truly believe I want you safe merely for you to finish the quilt."

Baines smiled down at him. She shook her head. "I misspoke last night from anger, Gray. I didn't mean it."

Reaching up, Gray pulled her down on his chest. "Baines. Little mouse. You're all I ever think of, all I could ever want. I would die to keep you safe."

His fingers rippled through her hair as he coaxed her head down and brought her lips to his mouth. He held her to his body like a vise, firmly but delicately, as though she were a precious flower.

His lips claimed hers with demanding mastery and tantalizing persuasion. She actually believed the words he'd spoken to her and reveled in them. Rapturous yearning seized her, and she clung to him, squirming against his hard body, feeling the evidence of his arousal.

Gray never wanted to stop kissing Baines; he never wanted to stop holding her and feeling her softness next to his body. Her breathless encouragement nearly drove him witless.

But his responsibility intruded. He had duties to see to; duties to his father, his heritage, and Baines.

He wanted her to share his life for the rest of hers. Yet even with that confession to himself, he couldn't continue with this madness. Not in a rush under a tree near a levee, and not while his future was so uncertain.

Even if the quilt she was making didn't reveal a map that led to a treasure, he wanted her with him. But he would have to think of a way to make a living for the both of them. He certainly wouldn't have her working in taverns and shops.

Raising up, he brought her with him. He swallowed, looking at her flushed skin and dreamy eyes. "Baines, my sweet," he croaked.

She splayed her hands against his chest and nuzzled his neck, her breath warm against his neck. "Gray," she implored.

He knew what she was feeling because he was feeling the same thing. His arousal hurt, and he wanted to give them both succor. But he had enough restraint and self-discipline to alleviate the situation by walking away. Perhaps he would go no farther than the porch, but it would give them both time to compose themselves.

Standing, he took Baines's hand and helped her to her feet. Gray brought his hand to her cheek and caressed it, and for a few seconds Baines held his hand in place with her own.

Finally he stepped away from her.

Baines sighed. "Would you like to see the beginnings of Mary's Fortune?"

"Aye, Baines," he said softly. "I would like to glimpse Mary's Fortune Two's origins."

Walking with him into her house, Baines proudly showed off her work. Gray seemed impressed, and Baines explained to him what else needed to be done.

"It appears quite a job for one person."

"I'm the only person who knows how to assemble this particular quilt, Gray. It must be exactly like the original. So *I* must do it alone."

"Why are you so eager to help me, little mouse?"

Baines wanted to shout *because I love you* at the top of

her lungs, but she didn't dare. Not while he held himself back. She smiled sedately. "If there's a chance the quilt can save your heritage, Gray, I want to help."

"Is there anything you need?"

"Not at the moment." She walked to the stove. She needed to get her bearings. "Would you like a cup of coffee?"

"Aye. A cup of coffee would be nice."

Baines poured out two cups and set them on the table. Gray pulled out a chair for her, then seated himself.

"Who was that man in the Horse and Mule last night, Gray?"

Leaning back in his chair, he steepled his fingers beneath his chin. He contemplated her. "Someone from my past," he said finally and straightened himself. He reached for his cup and took a sip of coffee.

"I see. And you don't care to reveal your connection to him or how he came to be in this country?"

"No, I don't."

Gray had a right to his privacy, but still she felt hurt that he wouldn't confide in her.

"But I will." Without allowing her to respond, he continued. "James McKay was my boyhood friend. I haven't seen him since I was sixteen."

"Why would you not see your friend for . . . how old are you?"

"Baines," Gray snapped in annoyance, "if you are to hear my story, I advise you to cease your queries."

"Very well," she huffed, biting back an acerbic response to his bossiness. It was difficult enough for him to open up. Still, she couldn't resist a bit of sarcasm. "Please do go on, my lord."

Gray delighted in her pique. He chuckled and said, "Thank you. Anyway, to shorten a long story, little mouse, as schoolboys, Jamie and I decided one night to carouse."

"Carouse?"

"Aye, Baines . . . uh, philander," he clarified, seeing her questioning look. "We rendezvoused with a lady of the evening."

Baines gasped. "You mean you . . . ? At sixteen!?"

"Silence, Baines!"

"Sorry!"

"When we returned to Eton, I found the headmaster in my chamber. I had been accused of stealing a very valuable watch. It was in fact found in my chamber, put there by none other than Jamie himself. He swore he hadn't seen me the entire day. His betrayal nearly got me kicked out of Eton. Fortunately the woman we spent the day with came forward with testimony to corroborate my story, thus clearing my name."

"What happened to Jamie when the truth came out?"

"His plan backfired, and *he* was dismissed."

"But why would someone do that to a friend?"

"I only learned the reason last night, Baines. He claims he did it for his father. His father had the misconception that *my* father was about to be elected to the board of regents at Eton, a position that Jamie's father coveted. He had no way of knowing that my father had no interest in the job."

"Did he get the position?"

"No. I didn't realize it at the time, but the scandal he attempted to create for me cost Jamie his place at Eton and his father a place on the board.

"For three months I sat disgraced, branded a thief. During that entire time, my only friend was my father. From that time until I met you, I never trusted anyone but my father again."

"Oh, Gray." Baines reached out to him and opened her mouth to speak, to apologize again for almost ruining his newfound trust. But he moved out of her grasp and stood.

"I don't want your pity, Baines. That happened a long time ago. It's over." He smiled sadly at her, as if he still felt the sting of his friend's betrayal.

Now she understood why he'd been so angry and hurt with her. Yet she couldn't believe Gray was so unforgiving. She cleared her throat and met his gaze.

"Gray, don't you think it's time you forgave Jamie?" His expression closed, but she rushed on. "He was only being a dutiful son when he followed his pa's dang, dumb orders—"

"I'd best go now and leave you to your stitching." Jaw clenched and giving no indication he intended to take her advice, he started for the door. "Perhaps I'll stop in tomorrow."

"You're always welcome, Gray," she said as she walked to the door with him.

"Don't work too hard, little mouse."

Without looking back, he went down the steps and hurried to his horse. He untethered the palomino and flung himself in the saddle while Baines watched him ride away.

Going back inside, she decided to get as much stitching done today as possible since she was due at Miz Annabelle's tomorrow. Picking up her needle, she sighed.

She wondered what the coming weeks would bring. Gray had opened up to her, but his old fears and uncertainties made him retreat once again.

33

SIX ARDUOUS WEEKS WENT by before Baines saw her labor emerge as a quilt. Yet doubt stamped out the satisfaction she should have felt. Though it looked beautiful, even half finished, she didn't believe it was a replica of Mary's Fortune. In her haste to complete the quilt, it seemed as if she had left out some crucial part.

Not wanting to unduly alarm Gray, she hesitated to tell him of her uncertainty. In an attempt to discover what was niggling her about the quilt, she threw it over Uncle Linc's quilt on the frame. She found it perfectly even, but nothing else came to mind.

After sewing twenty six-by-six squares together into one block, Baines stitched twenty of those blocks together, creating one half of the quilt. She still had to stitch the other side, attach the back, and sew on the binding. Working at Miz Annabelle's, she would never meet her deadline with Gray.

Baines studied the unfinished quilt further. The designs she recalled had all been put in their proper place. She was certain of that. But how could she tell Gray that there didn't appear to be a map?

Feeling dejected, she sat down on the padded bench to await Gray's arrival. He came every afternoon after she left the sewing shop.

The past weeks had been the happiest time of her life. Gray wasn't at all stuffy. He jested with her constantly. At times they laughed at silly nonsense until they were both breathless.

Gray had even attempted to sew a stitch or two in a block. Baines smiled to herself at the recollection. She had allowed the loose stitch, twice the size of hers, to remain. That way he could always remember their time together.

Since the day under the chinaberry tree, he hadn't even tried to kiss her again. Though she missed his scalding kisses and couldn't get their one passionate encounter out of her mind, their developing friendship was just as important. If he returned to England without her, she didn't know if she would ever recover.

"Knock, knock, darlin'."

"Miz Annabelle." Baines smiled, too tired to rise from her seat. She needn't have bothered anyway. Her arms filled with wrapped parcels, Miz Annabelle had already floated through the open doorway. Curiosity filled her. She hadn't long left the shop. "What brings you here?"

"I just left the market, Baines darlin', and I couldn't resist pickin' up a few items for you." Miz Annabelle dropped the packages on the table with a loud thud.

Baines walked over to the table and opened the bundles. She found leafy mustard greens, sweet and white potatoes, flour, and pork chops. She snorted in aggravation. "Miz Annabelle! You shouldn't have," she exclaimed in irritation.

Miz Annabelle *really* shouldn't have. The one thing Baines didn't feel like doing was cooking, and she had no other way of preserving the pork chops and greens. With her uncle away and fatigue wearing her down she had been quite satisfied eating her biscuits and preserved food from jars.

"Nonsense, child. I bought myself a mess of greens and pork chops. I invited Mr. Foxe to dinner tonight. Wouldn't have time to bring some already prepared to you. So I reckoned you could fix your own."

Baines made ready to reply but closed her mouth. A

shadow darkened the room, and she glanced up. Gray's huge body filled the entire space in the doorway.

"Come in, Gray." Baines walked to him and, taking his hand, led him to the table where Miz Annabelle stood. "In all the time you've been here you've never met my friend. This is Annabelle Shepard."

A smile lit Gray's features. "How do you do, madam? It's a distinct pleasure to finally meet you. Baines has spoken highly of you. I'm Grayling Dunston." Bowing, he brought her hand to his lips.

Baines laughed with delight at his actions. "Ain't he a caution, Miz Annabelle?"

"He sure is, child." Miz Annabelle chuckled and sat down. Spreading her magenta skirts primly, she eyed Gray up and down, then cleared her throat. "Grayling, is it?"

He nodded.

The widow narrowed her eyes. "Well, Grayling. What's your intentions toward my Baines?"

He stiffened and glanced at her in shock. "I beg your pardon?"

"Miz Annabelle!" Heat rushed into Baines cheeks. She wished her floor could have opened up and swallowed her then and there.

"Don't mean to go over the line," Miz Annabelle said, responding to their outraged indignation and patting her hair. "But when a hound dog gets an itch, the scratchin' is automatic."

An inky brow slashed up, but amusement crinkled his mouth. "Am I to understand that I'm being compared to a dog, madam?"

"Miz Annabelle, please," Baines implored, too mortified to do anything else.

"It's all right, little mouse. I'm not offended."

Gray strolled to the table and seated himself. Although he wasn't dressed as informally as Roc had been the day she'd gone to Dunland, Baines realized just then that Gray was wearing buckskin breeches, a white lawn shirt, and black riding boots.

"Mrs. Shepard is to be commended for her interest in

your well being." Cradling his hands behind his head, he leaned back in the chair, his manner as relaxed as if it was his home. "You needn't concern yourself, madam. I have the utmost regard for Baines and wouldn't use her ill."

Approval and satisfaction in her features, Miz Annabelle smiled. "I'm pleased to hear that, Grayling." She stood abruptly and picked up her remaining packages. "Well," she announced breathlessly. "I'd best be goin' on so you can do your callin' and leave soon so's Baines can get back to her quiltin'. She sure is doin' a right smart job. Good day." With that, Miz Annabelle breezed out the door.

Shaking his head, Gray laughed good-naturedly and stood. He cast a glance at Baines as she sat on the bench, her usual bubbliness missing today. He frowned. "What's wrong, little mouse?"

Leaning her head back on the wall, Baines closed her eyes. "Oh, Gray," she said with a sigh. "I'm so tired, and Miz Annabelle was kind enough to bring some food over. But it has to be cooked today or it'll spoil."

"Oh, is that all?" he asked nonchalantly. "Just instruct me in how it's done, and I'll do it."

Baines raised her eyebrows, a smile playing upon her lips. "You?"

Gray planted his hands on his hips and glared at her. "Point me to the stove, woman!" he shouted in feigned indignation. "I can cook as well as . . . as . . . any *cook*."

Squealing with laughter, Baines got up and showed Gray where the necessary utensils were situated. Afterward, he insisted she sit back and relax.

Loosening the top button of his lawn shirt, Gray rolled up his sleeves and went to work. She didn't miss his initial trepidation. For a moment he stared at the raw meat and uncooked vegetables and frowned.

"Gray—"

His scowl silenced her.

Her heart tripping, Baines smiled. To think this English lord would happily stoop to doing menial chores—for her— just as he had pointedly neglected to mention his title to Miz Annabelle.

When the time came, how could she let him go? If only she could find the map, their future would be sealed. She felt certain that Gray loved her as much as she did him. But if she told him she would put undue pressure on him. She hoped her support was a comfort to him.

From her place on the bench, she told him what to do to make candied yams, how to boil the greens, and make pork chops and gravy. Finally she told him how to make biscuits.

Two hours later he bade Baines come to the table. He set a plate before her and one at his own place. "And now, my lady, I will dish out a culinary masterpiece."

Baines sniffed the steam rising from the dishes and closed her eyes in pleasure. "Gray, it smells wonderful."

"Of course it does," he bragged and served Baines a healthy offering of greens. "Would you like it all at once, little mouse, or as a three-course meal?"

"I like to see you work." Baines giggled. "Make it a three-course meal."

Gray narrowed his eyes at her in mock anger. "If you tell anyone I did this, I'll deny it." Sitting down, he picked up his fork and tasted the greens. He nodded in satisfaction. "Not bad."

Baines agreed, but she couldn't say so after that. The candied yams were raw and crunchy. Gray could barely extract the pork chops from the gravy, so thick were they. And the biscuits were so hard, they could have been used as cannonballs.

Pushing her plate aside and doubling over in amusement, Baines released peals of laughter. Gray frowned darkly at her hilarity over his valiant efforts.

"I'm thinking I may have to kill you to keep this from going further than this house, Baines Marshall." He rose from his seat and took a few menacing steps toward her. Reaching her side, he pulled her into his embrace. "You little witch! Your gratitude for my kindness leaves much to be desired." He gave her a chaste kiss, then released her. In truth, he wanted to ravish her with kisses. But he kept his passion under control since the day he'd nearly succumbed to his desire under the chinaberry tree. Although he felt compelled to see her every day, he kept his visits short.

Gray knew how hard Baines had been working on his behalf. She needed a respite, and he would soon take her for a ride along the Trace. Roc told him how beautiful it was and that it was well traveled during the day. The extreme danger came at night or in winter, when traveling was at a minimum. He wouldn't subject Baines to danger, however, without some form of protection. On the day he took her to the Trace, he would bring his pistol along. But for now he would see to getting her a decent meal.

"Baines, do you still feel the need to eat?"

"I couldn't eat another bite," Baines said, laughter still in her voice. "Why?"

"Well, I would take you to Jackson's Inn for some delicious food. Besides, I think you need to get away from Mary's Fortune Two for a spell."

For a spell? Baines smiled. Not only was Gray loosening up a bit, but he was also picking up on her language. "Oh, well, in that case, I would be delighted," she responded. Her heart pounding, she stood. "Please step outside while I change into something presentable for Jackson's Inn."

Laughing, Gray shook his head and stepped out onto the porch. Baines gently closed the door behind him, then she went to the seaman's trunk and lifted the lid.

34

TWO WEEKS LATER AND with three new completed blocks sewn into the second half of the quilt, Baines walked through the double doors of the little church she attended when she wasn't working and into the afternoon sunlight. Dressed in her Sunday best, she smiled up at Gray. He had attended morning services with her and looked reflective during the preacher's sermon on how it was easier for a camel to go through the eye of a needle than for a rich man to enter the gates of heaven.

She wondered what had gone through his mind, but decided not to ask, not wanting to pry. Instead, she smiled at how pretty she felt.

She wore a wide-brim straw-and-feathered hat, one Gray had gifted her with yesterday. The golden yellow bow tied under her chin matched the color of her day dress. It had a long flowing skirt and form-fitting bodice, with puffed sleeves trimmed in lace.

"Are you ready for our jaunt on the Trace, Baines?"

Walking to where their horse and buggy waited in the shade of a magnolia tree, Baines nodded enthusiastically. "Yes, Gray, I am. But before we begin our journey, let's go to the bluff."

"Of course, little mouse." After handing Baines up and

climbing in beside her, Gray commanded the horse to move. "But why there first?"

"It's a surprise."

Gray laughed, the sound husky and endearing. "For me?"

"You wish," Baines responded, joining him in laughter.

Following Baines's directions, Gray maneuvered the buggy through the Sunday traffic. On the way to their destination, Baines pointed out the Widow Shepard's house and sewing shop. A few blocks away stood neat little white-washed cottages.

"Stop here, Gray."

Reining in the horse, Gray stopped in front of a house that appeared to be empty. Like the others it was a gleaming white clapboard. A dainty, white picket fence surrounded it, and lots of yard space with trees and flowers filled the grounds.

"I saw it Friday on my way from the shop," she whispered with awe. "Isn't it beautiful? Come on, Gray, let's look inside," she urged, tugging on his sleeve.

He cleared his throat. "Should we? There's no one around, and the door may be locked." He noted the yearning on Baines's face, and his heart beat faster. "Why are we here?"

"To see my dream house, silly. This is where I'll be living inside of a year."

"You're that sure, are you?"

"Danged sure, Gray," Baines asserted. "I aim to work hard to see my dream come true."

How could he have forgotten her dreams—dreams that didn't include him? She'd picked out the house she wanted to live in, without thought to the future they might have had. But then, how much consideration had he given their future since Baines had begun recreating Mary's Fortune? He'd only spent an inordinate amount of time with her, but had said nothing.

"Let's take a look a your house, Baines." Feeling oddly annoyed, Gray helped her from the buggy. It should have pleased him that she was so determined to move from

Under-the-Hill. Her determination was part of her charm. But not when he felt so threatened by it, as he sometimes did. Like now.

Silently they walked to the gate and opened it. Bursting with energy, Baines nearly ran to the porch. He watched as she tried the door and found it unlocked. She laughed in delight and hurried inside.

Except for a table with a note on it instructing any perspective buyer on whom to contact, the first room was empty and quite large. Sunlight gleamed through the three big windows in the parlor, highlighting the wooden floors, clean walls, and the fireplace. Exploring the rest of the house, they found three additional rooms—a kitchen with a pantry and two bedrooms. While the kitchen had one window, the two bedrooms each had two and their own separate fireplace.

"Oh, so many windows," Baines blurted. "I will have to make curtains for every one of them."

Her enthusiasm amused Gray. "Indeed you will." In spite of himself, he liked the cozy little place because Baines seemed so enamored with it.

"I'll be placing my sofa in front of the fireplace."

"No other place will do," Gray agreed. "That way you'll get direct heat on cold nights."

Baines looked at him. "Do you like it, Gray?"

He wondered at the expectation in her voice. Not commenting on it, he said, "Nothing suits you better, Baines. I think it's wonderful."

"Thank you." Baines wasn't sure why, but his approval gladdened her. She stood gazing at him a few moments, then giggled nervously. "I guess we'd better go now. There ain't no guarantee this house will stand empty for a whole year, but I know there'll be others like it."

"Of course there will, Baines." Gray held the door opened for her as she gazed one last time around the place. After helping her onto the buggy seat, he then climbed aboard.

As the horse pulled away, Baines looked back at her dream house. They drove toward the Trace in silence.

∞

"DID I REMEMBER TO tell you how stunning you look, little mouse?" Gray asked as the horse ambled along at a sedate pace two hours later.

"Only every second." Baines breathed in the air, her senses alive with Gray's nearness. Summer was waning, but it was hardly noticeable in the woodlands. Pine and magnolia trees mixed in the scenery along fields of tobacco, cotton, cane, and soybean that dotted the Trace.

"DeEdria and Roc invited you over for an evening repast, Baines. I told them yes for you."

"But I need to work on the quilt, Gray," Baines half-heartedly protested.

"Which is why I answered for you. The only way I know to keep you from working today is to keep you away from the quilt. So I'll have no objections from you. Do I make myself clear?"

Baines smiled at him. "Yes, my lord, quite clear." She wished he would clear up the matter of whether or not he loved her. "Will Belinda Myers be there?"

Gray shrugged. "Belinda's visits have been infrequent lately."

"Oh? Why?"

"Quite frankly, her visits shortened after *your* last visit at Dunland to see me. Could she possibly be angry at someone?" He glanced slyly at her.

"Hmm. I wonder who?" Baines asked innocently. "*You* obviously disappointed her when you showed no interest in her."

"And you obviously angered her when you locked yourself in Roc's study with me."

"Gray!" Baines gasped. "Oh, how you make it sound! Anyway, the door wasn't locked, and the study was your idea, you river rat."

Gray laughed so hard he barely kept the horse on the trail. "It matters not, little mouse, who Mistress Myers is piqued at," he said, his voice quaking. "Her absence at

Dunland makes life so much easier to bear.''

''So much easier,'' Baines echoed and sidled a glance at him.

Wonder softened his face as he held his mirth in check to take in the Trace's raw scenery. ''Baines, your America is quite beautiful.''

Farther along the trail, oak and hickory trees joined large pines to stand like sentries, turning parts of the Trace into dense forest. The path continued through to the woodlands again.

Baines laughed at a squirrel leaping through the leaves and branches of the trees and dropping acorns to the ground. Its head furiously vibrating, an ivory-billed wood-pecker, among several kind abundant along the Trace, hammered its beak against a sturdy oak. Nuthatches, owls, orioles, and mockingbirds joined in the racket. A white-tail deer scooted across the path. In the distance she heard the unmistakable sound of an alligator bellowing. Suddenly the forest sang with the sounds of their music, transporting Baines with pleasure.

''I never want to leave this place,'' she said with a sigh.

''It is something to see, my dear, but it's prudent that we begin our journey back. I don't wish to press our luck.''

''There's been no one on the trail to bother us, Gray.''

''Precisely. There's been no one except us on this trail for the last hour and a half. Besides, it'll be evening when we reach Dunland. Just in time for dinner.''

Barely fifteen minutes into the ride back home, the horse reared. Pawing the air in terror, the palomino nearly toppled the buggy.

A shot rang out. Baines's scream reverberated through the forest.

35

"BAINES?" GRAY'S SOOTHING VOICE reached her, and his protective arms around her calmed her fears. She breathed in deeply and rubbed her hand across his back, checking for wounds. When she found none, she frowned. She'd distinctly heard a pistol shot.

Leaning away from Gray, she checked herself. Another moment passed before she realized they hadn't been shot.

"It's all right, little mouse."

"Wh-what happened, Gray? Who shot at us?"

"I discharged the gun, Baines," Gray explained gently. "A large snake crossed our path and spooked the horse. I killed the snake."

Baines swallowed, her heart still racing wildly. "What kind was it?"

"I don't know. I'm not that familiar with snakes."

A bird swooped in front of them, and Baines jumped. "Gray, get me off this road. I would even be willing to trade an evening with Belinda Myers just to get back home safely."

"No sooner said than done." Gray urged the horse into a gallop. He wouldn't admit to Baines how startled he'd been by the horse's actions, thinking the danger came from some backward thief out to rob them. He cursed himself for placing Baines in such jeopardy. She was still visibly shaken, and he couldn't get out of there soon enough.

"I trust you won't find it necessary to tell Roc about the dinner I so generously prepared for you?" he asked casually. He wanted to put her at ease for the rest of the journey back.

Baines chuckled. "I'd forgotten all about that," she admitted. "I guess Roc would tease you about it."

"The rotter would bloody never let me live it down."

"Then I won't tell him."

"You have my gratitude."

Baines seemed to be relaxing again. Not wanting to tire the horse, Gray slowed his pace. The late-afternoon sun cast shadows through the trees.

It was the perfect place to confess his love to Baines. If only it was the perfect time. Gray ached solely for Baines. He wanted to fill his arms with her and never let her go.

"Gray?"

Her voice was soft, sweet, awakening primitive desire within him. Desire that could be sated only by taking her into his arms again. Which he couldn't do. "Aye?"

"What happens if the quilt doesn't reveal a map?"

He gingerly guided the horse over the stone bridge. Water ran in the stream below at a brisk pace, as quickly as the blood rushed through his veins at her question.

"Are you having doubts?" he asked more sharply than he intended. The question brought his worst fears to the fore, however, fears he'd tried to keep at bay.

Baines sighed. "The quilt's nearly completed, and not even a trace of the map has appeared."

Foreboding welled deep within him. "By all the gods, Baines!" he snapped. "Are you sure your recollections have been accurate?"

"Yes!" Baines said, stiffening her shoulders. "Are you sure that letter wasn't a hoax?"

Except for the movement of his hands to guide the horse, Gray went motionless. He hadn't fully believed the letter to begin with, but because of Baines's enthusiasm he'd harbored a crazy mixture of fear and hope.

Now she was telling him she couldn't see a map. He

should have been furious with her. He should have been ranting and raving and looking to get on the first ship back to London.

His resignation, however, surprised him.

"No," Gray answered. "I'm not sure if it's a hoax or not."

Baines touched his arm. "Gray," she said softly. "Just because I can't see it doesn't mean it isn't there."

Gray gave her a penetrating look.

"What?" she asked.

"You just spoke a perfect sentence, little mouse. I'm very proud of you."

"Thank you," she said shyly. "I try."

"Baines, finish the quilt. We can only be sure about it then. I'm sure it'll be accurate. And I know you're doing your best."

Holding back her tears, Baines smiled at Gray. She wanted him to have his dream as much as he wanted her to have hers. Although she still had her dreams, her priorities had shifted. She wanted Gray foremost and above all.

It surprised her when Gray finally turned off the Trace and onto Plantation Lane, toward Dunland. The last mile to the manor house melted quickly, and Baines readied herself for her evening with Gray and his family.

∞

"I DON'T KNOW WHAT possessed Roc to persuade Gray to take you on the Trace!" DeEdria cried angrily ten minutes later. She and Baines sat in her bedchamber, a pink frilly room with delicate furnishings and fresh flowers in crystal vases. She carefully studied her appearance in the cheval mirror. "It's too dangerous."

"I know, but it's beautiful. I enjoyed the ride until the snake incident."

Turning around in a swish of skirts, DeEdria stared at Baines with widened eyes, her hand on her chest. "My word! What snake incident?"

Baines related the story to her. "That's when Gray decided it was time to go home," she finished.

"Oh, you poor thing." DeEdria hugged Baines. "I'll have Millie bring up some water so you can freshen up from that hot, miserable ride."

Filled with mirth at DeEdria's obvious disapproval and horror, Baines burst out laughing. "I take it you don't like the Trace?"

DeEdria chuckled. "How can you tell?" Her voice dropped almost to a whisper. "Baines, how did you get Gray to stay in Natchez? Should we be preparing you for a wedding?"

Baines looked at her in amazement. "You mean you would give me a wedding party here?"

"Why, of course, my dear," DeEdria expressed with a bright smile. "You would be family."

"Oh, DeEdria, I really don't know what to say. I do appreciate the offer. Unfortunately, Gray hasn't proposed. And as to why he's still here, it's a question you should ask him. I'm not at liberty to say."

"I understand, although I'm a little disappointed." She seated herself next to Baines on the settee. "Can I trust you with a secret?"

Baines widened her eyes at DeEdria's conspiratorial tone, but a thrill of pleasure surged through her. She liked the mistress of Dunland, and judging from the anticipation gleaming in DeEdria's brown eyes, Baines felt the feeling was mutual. She nodded, DeEdria's excitement contagious.

"I believe I may be expecting," DeEdria announced happily.

Baines squealed in delight, ignoring the twinge of envy she felt. "Congratulations!" She hugged DeEdria. "I'm plumb happy for you."

"I haven't told anyone else yet, especially Roc. We've been so disappointed time and again. I've already lost three babies, but I just can't give up my dream of one day cradling Roc's child in my arms."

Dreams. Everyone had them, but Baines was beginning to realize that all of *her* desires and hopes that she thought would make her happy weren't necessarily the case. She didn't need a lot of money or her own shop to make her happy. She derived as much or more pleasure by simply making Gray's quilt to help him as she would have for pay.

She knew her true happiness came from within, but Gray's love would strengthen it.

She hugged DeEdria again. "If there's anything I can do for you, you just holler. And don't fret. I know everything is going to work out for you."

"Oh, Baines, my dear, I'm so glad to have met you." She stared at her. "And whatever happens between you and Gray, you're always welcome here." She stood up gracefully. "Now, perhaps I'd better join the men. I'll send Millie up straightaway and see you downstairs as soon as you're put to rights."

∞

BAINES ALMOST WENT INTO apoplexy at the dinner table. The menu consisted of pork chops and gravy, candied yams, turnip greens, and fluffy biscuits. Blackberry dumpling and cream completed the meal.

She and Gray could hardly look at each other without chuckling.

"Is there something in the food that's ticklish?" Roc asked when the chuckling appeared in danger of erupting into full-blown laughter.

"It's nothing, Roc," Gray said. "Just a little incident neither of us seem capable of forgetting."

"Well, let us in on it," DeEdria urged.

"There's really nothing to tell, DeEdria," Baines imparted. "It's just that recently we had practically the same kind of food that was served here tonight."

Gray narrowed his eyes at Baines. He hoped she saw the warning in his gaze. "That's right."

"I see nothing funny about that." Roc frowned in concentration. "About two weeks ago you two were seen at Jackson's Inn, dining."

"What are you getting at, Rochester? What has that to do with this?"

"I don't rightly know, Grayling."

"Well, I think Baines probably burned the dinner to force Gray to show her off," DeEdria speculated with a laugh.

"What's funny about that?" Roc persisted. He shrugged. "So Baines burned a meal. Now I'll tell you what would be funny. If *Gray* had burned the meal . . ."

Gray's complexion turned scarlet.

Roc slapped his thigh. "By God, that's it! That's it!" He guffawed. "I have this image of you in an apron, Mistress Grayling—"

"Stop it, Roc!" DeEdria chastised. She turned to Gray. "Is that how it is?" she asked him. Her voice trembled with controlled laughter, but Roc's contagious howls made it very difficult.

Abandoning all pretense of control, Baines walked away from the table, holding her sides with laughter.

"Traitor!" Gray accused. Watching Roc, Gray thought about pounding the laughter right out of his cousin.

"Gray, I didn't tell them," Baines gasped. "They figured it out."

"Roc, you bloody fool. Get up off the blasted floor, and I'll tell you what happened," Gray said. Realizing it really was quite funny, he let himself relax.

This was his family, with whom he had formed a bond. No matter that most of the time Roc was a blasted idiot, Gray had become quite fond of him.

Tonight no shadows of guilt or worry hounded him. There was only an intense pleasure. He could never remember feeling so carefree or loving anyone as deeply as he did Baines.

It was a new experience and a heady feeling. Laughter bubbled inside him.

Getting up and dusting himself off, Roc went back to his place at the table. "Well, tell me, Gray. Exactly how did you burn Baines's supper?"

Gray related the story, only to see Roc go into spasms

again. "You're a hard man to like, Rochester." He cut into his pork chop and found it succulent and tender. "Baines, see if you can manage to rejoin us, now that I've been thoroughly humiliated."

"I'm sorry, milord," Baines chuckled. "Your effort may have failed, but I will always cherish the reason behind it."

"She calls you 'milord'?" Roc asked with mockery.

"Roc!" DeEdria said. "That's enough! You've thoroughly embarrassed Gray. I won't have you start in on Baines."

"You're right, DeEdria, love. I have enough fodder on His Lordship to keep him in line. No need to make Baines suffer." Roc winked at Baines. "Call for the dessert, dear."

36

MUCH LATER THAT EVENING Baines stood on her porch, saying good night to Gray. The moon shone full and bright against a starless sky, its midnight color magical. A slight breeze blew from the river, making the branches of the chinaberry tree sway and ruffling Gray's dark hair.

Baines ached to kiss him, to touch him, but she was afraid that he would reject her, afraid that he would guess her true feelings.

"I'll never forget this evening, Gray. It was wonderful."

"Neither will I." His brilliant blue eyes burned with some unknown emotion. "One thing in particular stands out in my mind about it."

"Really?" He watched her intently, and a tingling began in the pit of Baines's stomach. She shifted her weight. "And what's that?"

"The fact that you'll cherish the reason I attempted to cook for you." Gray stepped closer to her. His smile was seductive, provocative. "What do you think that reason is, Baines?"

Her pulse hammered at his intimate tone. "I-I don't know," she whispered, unable to speak the truth.

"Don't you?" Gray asked in a husky voice. "Haven't you come to realize how much I love you?"

He pulled her into his embrace and kissed her with aching tenderness, sealing his declaration with sweet deliberation. When the kiss ended, Baines clung to him.

"Oh, Gray, how I've yearned to hear those words from you. I love you so much!"

Gray held her close, drinking in her nearness, delighting in the feel of her soft, supple body. But he dared not kiss her again. Not if he wanted to hold to his resolve and not make love to her again until he saw in which direction his life would lead him.

He wanted to lay the world at her feet. He'd lived in wealth all his life, but he'd seen poverty put into perspective.

Gray slid his hands up and down her back. Holding her flushed face between his hands, he kissed her forehead. "I love you, little mouse. But I must leave now. You and the night hold too many temptations. Go in and light your candles, so I can know that you are safely inside."

While he watched from the doorway, she did as he had bade her. Then she went up to him and kissed his lips.

Holding himself rigid, Gray groaned. He knew if he touched her, his willpower would desert him. "Good night, little mouse," he said, firmly stepping away from her. "I'll see you tomorrow."

Baines went inside and bolted the door. Contentment filling her, she leaned against the door and closed her eyes. Gray loved her! He'd finally admitted what she wished for for so long.

She felt like dancing around in joy. She felt like rushing over to Miz Annabelle to tell her. But most likely Miz Annabelle would be keeping company with Mr. Foxe.

In all honesty, Baines didn't exactly know how to feel. Questions abounded in her mind, demanding answers that she didn't have, answers she might not like.

Where would she and Gray go from here? He'd merely confessed his love to her, not a desire to spend the rest of his life with her. She would never sleep tonight, not with her emotions churning as they were. Unless she slept in Gray's arms, she would probably never sleep again.

She had to do something! Her gaze fell on the quilt.

That's it! She would use her newfound energy to work on it. Walking forward with purpose, she picked up the cloth and her needles and settled back on the bench.

෨

THE NEXT FOUR WEEKS took wings and flew. The days went by so fast, they left Baines breathless. It was late summer, and the days were becoming cooler as the atmosphere slowly readied for the dawning of fall.

Gray's daily afternoon visits were sheer magic. Their differences appeared to have been accepted for the time being as he gently taught her correct English.

Baines thought she knew why he so readily overlooked all that stood between them, but refused to let such thoughts mar her peace. Her love for Gray grew stronger each day.

Though he limited his time with her to no more than an hour and a half, that time was nothing short of enchantment for Baines. Today, however, was different. She had completed Mary's Fortune Two and knew Gray's departure would come soon.

"You're very talented, little mouse," Gray said as he helped her spread the quilt out on the floor. "It's a beautiful piece of work. Like a fine painting. You've done an exemplary job."

"Thank you," Baines said in a low, composed voice. She tried to keep the anxiety she felt out of her tone but didn't quite succeed. The only thought that ran through her head was that Gray was going to leave her.

But he didn't comment. He only had eyes for the quilt. He rubbed his hands together. "Well," he said with unmistakable expectation, "let's see what we'll find."

Sitting on the floor opposite each other, Baines studied one side while Gray studied the other. It was a beautiful creation, one that Baines was proud to have been involved with. Swirls and loops were stitched into certain blocks, and sapphire markings sat atop the mulberry corners, just as Baines remembered.

She and Gray studied every square, every stitch, every

pattern, and found nothing that could remotely be called a map.

Tears welled in Baines's eyes and spilled down her cheeks. "I'm so very sorry, Gray," she sobbed. "Maybe I did something wrong."

Gray's features paled. She saw his grief and disappointment. He grabbed her hand and kissed it, then rubbed it against his colorless cheek. For endless seconds, Gray remained silent, anguish marring his handsome face. Finally he cleared his throat.

"No, little mouse, don't be sorry," he said quietly. "Since I've never seen my great-grandmother's quilt, I wouldn't know if you did something wrong, Baines. *Your* quilt appears perfect, however. I believe you made it the way you recalled the original Mary's Fortune to be. But I was a fool to believe that letter was anything more than a bloody cruel jest."

Baines blinked in an effort to stop her flow of tears his sorrowful plight caused her. "What happens now, Gray?"

He stood, once again the remote lord he had been upon his arrival in Natchez. "I must leave, Baines, to settle my estate."

She rushed to him and threw her arms around his waist. "Let me come with you."

His jaw clenching, Gray shook his head. Without touching her, he moved out of her embrace. "I must go alone. I don't know what I have to face, or even if I'll have a roof over my head."

A suffocating sensation shuddered though her. The hope and contentment she'd felt these last weeks deserted her, and desolation swept through her. She worked the muscles in her throat in an effort to speak, to voice her grief and protests. Instead, she merely asked, "W-when will you leave?"

"As soon as possible. I haven't much time left. I must retrieve my family heirlooms before the foreclosure and subsequent auction. I booked passage on the *Venerable* due to leave New Orleans on Wednesday."

She had known all along this would happen. Still, his

admission stunned her. On leaden legs she walked to her table and slowly ran her hand along the edge. "I see. When did you arrange this?"

"Last week. When you told me the quilt would be completed today."

"Then you'll be leaving immediately?"

"Not immediately. But, aye, I will be leaving today. The *Natchez Belle* put into port today and should be leaving in about an hour. Roc told me not to worry about booking passage, since he knows Cordair."

He spoke matter-of-factly, as if his departure from her meant no more to him than the killing of a pesky insect. Certainly he didn't sound like a man who'd shared a great passion. He'd made plans before he knew how the quilt would turn out, and she hadn't fit into any of them, despite his confession of love.

Baines stared, unseeing, at the quilt, her back to Gray. "Will I ever see you again?"

Without answering, she heard Gray's footsteps pounding toward the door. Baines thought to call out to him, to plead for him to stay, but she couldn't. He knew she was there for him if he needed and wanted her. She didn't know what else to say to convince him that she loved him, whether he was rich or poor, noble or common.

She waited for the door to close and announce his exit. She couldn't bear to watch his departure without crumpling to the ground in misery. Instead, she felt him behind her, felt his warm breath on her neck.

"I love you, Baines," he whispered in a tormented voice. "If only you knew how much, little mouse. I thought I had everything settled in my mind, that I had it all worked out. I had planned to ask you to wait for me until I could acquire some money. But I can't. It wouldn't be fair to you—"

"Gray, I'll come with you—"

"For what bloody purpose?" He turned her around to face him, his features an effigy of bleak determination.

Their gazes met and melded for an endless time. Volumes of unspoken promises reflected in them.

"Dammit, Baines! I don't want you with me. I'll only fail you as I've failed my father and my heritage."

He pulled her into his embrace. Stopping her flow of words, he kissed her with all the passion, love, and regret in him. He kissed her eyes, tasting the salt of her tears; he kissed her hair, never wanting to forget its silky texture; he kissed her beautiful, pale face that would haunt him for as long as he lived.

He held her until she quieted, until she resigned herself to their destiny. Then he released her. A lightless future faced him, one without Baines, without her friendship and laughter.

She had altered his outlook on life. Because of her, he realized that in wealth or in poverty, what you are is more important than who you are. And what he was was a man trapped by guilt. In all the months he had been here, he might have harbored some doubt, but he never thought he'd fail. Yet he had. He had lost everything that was dear to his father. When he could have been in London devising another plan, he'd been here falling in love with Baines and believing the antiquated ranting of his great-grandmother.

"I can't give you the answer you desire, little mouse. So I won't say anything else except farewell." He turned from her then. Without looking back, he strolled through the door.

"I love you, Gray," she sniffled to the silence that surrounded her. Her heart shattering, she stood in the center of the room until the sound of his retreating footsteps faded.

Walking on leaden legs to the bench, she sat and regarded the quilt again. Tears blurred her vision. What would she ever do without Gray? She had her dreams, and she would see them through, but her life would never be the same again. For the rest of her life, she would wonder what could have been between her and Gray.

If only fate had been kinder.

She could always bring the original quilt back to Gray when Uncle Lincoln returned, but she didn't really see the point. By then, it would be too late. Gray would have already lost his fortune. He would have already been humiliated before the world in which he lived.

Baines cried until her throat ached, until there were no
tears left in her. Evening was approaching, stealing the
waning light. She surmised Gray had already left Natchez,
since he had a two-day journey to New Orleans in order to
board the *Venerable* there. Just then, the whistle of a paddlewheeler sounded, and she said a last goodbye to Gray.

Picking up the quilt, she began folding the ends together.

She halted, her hand in midair. Her pulse beating a rapid
tattoo, she stared with widened eyes at her discovery. The
ends were forming a map! *The map that Gray had come
all this distance to get.*

Hands trembling, she pulled the ends together. A shout
of joy escaped her lips.

There it was as plain as day! The map they had searched
for, with arrows and everything on it.

Tears of happiness fell down her cheeks. Then realization
struck. Gray! Pray that he wasn't on the boat she heard.
The boat landing wasn't far, so she hoped to reach him
before the ship broke anchor.

Maybe, just maybe, however, he was still at Dunland.

Throwing the quilt over her arm, she hurriedly darted out
her door, barely remembering to close it behind her. Rushing down the street, she clutched the large covering like a
protective armor. It was awkward to do so, and it slowed
her down, but she went as fast as she could. Just as she
reached the docks, the gangplank on the *Natchez Belle* was
being lifted.

"No! Wait!" she called in desperation to a uniformed
man she thought she recognized standing on deck. "Captain Cordair!"

"I am the first mate, Mr. Roberts, madam!" the man
called back. "The captain is engaged at this time. I can
give him your message."

The vessel moved slightly.

"Oh, no!" Baines cried. "I must get this quilt to Grayling Dunston. He's on your boat."

"I'm sorry, madam," Mr. Roberts said. "Everything's been set in motion. We can't stop it."

"Please!"

"Step back, madam!" the first mate yelled.

Baines did, and a grappling hook landed near her feet.

"Quickly, ma'am," Mr. Roberts instructed. "Secure the quilt onto the three prongs, and I'll reel it in."

Working rapidly, she did as she was told. She cupped her hands to her mouth. "Tell Gray the secret's in the quilt's ends. Fold them together. He'll know what I mean."

Standing in the shadows, Jamie McKay watched the puzzling drama unfold. Immediately he recognized the beautiful Baines. It came to him to call out to her and inform her that Gray wasn't on the boat, but it was no use. His voice would be swallowed by the river breeze.

Still she stood there, her worry and fear obvious. He wondered what his former friend's interest was in a quilt. As the first mate studied it, Jamie saw that it was a rather unique-looking article.

Maybe the girl had made it for Gray, and he'd forgotten to take it. But take it where? Obviously Gray must be leaving Natchez, since Baines thought he was on the *Natchez Belle*.

Perhaps he was returning to England?

Jamie strolled up to the first mate and tapped him on the shoulder, an idea hitting him. "I don't believe it!" he exclaimed in feigned relief. "My good man, that's the quilt I have been in my cabin searching for and realized I had forgotten. How did you come by it, my friend?"

"Why, you must be Grayling Dunston," the first mate said. "A young woman brought it. She said to fold the ends together. You'll know what she means." He handed the quilt to Jamie.

"Aye." Wondering about the cryptic instructions, Jamie smiled. "Thank you, my good man."

Quilt in hand, he retired to his cabin, where he laid the huge covering on the bed and fixed himself a drink.

The brandy swirled warmly in his middle, and he sat on the sofa, brooding in the direction of the beautiful quilt. He thought about Gray and his own problems, most of which were his own doing.

He thought of Tate, with her cool aquamarine eyes and fiery red hair. She was spoiled and unbiddable, but she was also his wife. One day he would have to return home and face her wrath. But he reminded himself he hadn't wanted to wed her.

Throwing the remainder of his drink down his throat, he stood and went to the bed. Curiosity overtaking him, he followed Baines's instructions.

For a moment he stood there, shocked. Then he smiled very, very slowly.

37

"GRAY, I'M SO SORRY things didn't work out as you planned," DeEdria said as she sat with him in the parlor at Dunland. She was four months into her pregnancy and blooming. "I'm sure Baines will send you the quilt as soon as Lincoln returns with it from his voyage. We all know how sentimental you are about it."

"Baines already assured me that she will return it, DeEdria." The sadness and defeat he felt contradicted the short laugh he expelled. It crossed his mind to tell DeEdria the real reason why he so desperately wanted Mary's Fortune, but he couldn't. "I know I can rely on her."

DeEdria wrung her hands and smiled with uncertainty at him. "Er . . . um . . . I think Baines is a lovely girl, Gray." She searched his face. "I thought maybe there was something between you two. Oh, I would have been delighted to plan and host your wedding—"

Gray laughed genuinely. "And here I thought your matrimonial plans for me included Belinda Myers."

Had he been in a position to ask for Baines's hand in marriage, he knew Roc and DeEdria would have approved. After all, these American Dunstons were the only family he had left. And had he retained his fortune, he wouldn't have kept his distance. He would have visited Dunland at least every two years.

"Those matrimonial plans were Linny's plans for you," DeEdria said with a giggle. "But when you showed no interest, she turned her attention elsewhere."

Gray shifted in his seat and glanced at the timepiece on the mantel. "Wise woman," he said. "DeEdria, I hate to sound impatient, but I do have a ship to catch. Where is that bloody husband of yours?"

"Right here," Roc answered, materializing in the doorway like an apparition. "Sorry about the delay, Gray, but all the cabins on the *Natchez Belle* have been taken, including Cordair's daughter's stateroom. I got you a cabin on the *Mississippi Lady*, the same boat you boarded in New Orleans for your return trip back here. It's not as elaborate as the *Belle,* but—"

"It'll serve my purpose of getting me to New Orleans to catch a ship to London," Gray interrupted. He thought of Baines. "When will we depart?"

"In an hour's time, Gray," Roc explained. "We'll have your belongings loaded on the carriage and get you there in plenty of time."

The two men stared at each other. Then Roc held out his hand. "I'll miss you, cousin."

Gray stood and readily accepted the proffered hand. "As will I."

"Maybe DeEdria and I will make the journey across the ocean after the baby is born." Roc looked at DeEdria tenderly, and she blushed.

Suddenly wishing Baines had conceived from their encounter, Gray cleared his throat. "A sterling idea, Roc," he said. The image of Baines grew stronger. He had time to spare. He couldn't leave without seeing her one last time. "I have need of your beautiful palomino one last time. I must tell Baines farewell."

"Of course you must," DeEdria said briskly, rising from her seat. A gleam of satisfaction and expectation lit her eyes. "Roc, hurry. See that Sultana is saddled. Gray may wish to spend a few extra minutes with Baines."

"Your wish, my dear, is also mine," Roc teased. "Come on, Gray, we'll get you there and back in no time."

Gray hugged DeEdria affectionately. "After my visit with Baines I'll go straight to the boat, DeEdria. I won't be coming back here, so I'll say farewell now."

"Goodbye, Gray," DeEdria said in a quavering voice. "It's been so wonderful having you here with us. Please come again."

"I may very well do that one day," Gray responded. "Take care, DeEdria. It has been wonderful being here. Goodbye, my dear." He walked to where Roc awaited him, just outside the parlor door. "When it's time, bring my belongings to the boat. I'll meet you there, and you can take Sultana with you." He smiled reverently. "You know, I never knew that horse's bloody name until a few moments ago."

Roc laughed, that ever-present twinkle in his blue eyes sparkling. They started for the entrance door through the beautiful foyer. He grinned devilishly at Gray. "Would you mind telling me why you have to go back to tell Baines goodbye a second time? I thought you did that when you left her."

"That's none of your bloody business, Rochester," Gray grumbled and followed Roc out into the evening sunset.

∽

REACHING BAINES'S HOUSE A short time later, Gray dismounted Sultana. He bounded up the rickety steps. After walking across the small porch, he knocked on the door. No one answered. Testing the knob, the door swung open.

"Baines?"

Getting no response to his call, he looked around, but found nothing out of the ordinary. She must have left in a hurry to have neglected to lock her door.

He felt disappointed that he'd missed her. Wondering just why the bloody hell he had come, he allowed his gaze to roam the little place again, taking in every small detail.

Roc had been right. He and Baines had already said their goodbyes, and if she'd been here, it would have only deepened wounds already too deep to heal.

Seeing everything in its place, Gray realized he wanted
to tell her there was no need to repay him the money she'd
borrowed. He wanted her to accept that as payment for all
the trouble he'd put her through.

He considered waiting for her. Yet not knowing when
she would return put him at risk of missing his boat. He
surmised she'd gone to the Horse and Mule. Maybe Luther
had asked her to work one more night.

She needed a good tongue lashing for her carelessness
at leaving her door unbolted, however.

Pacing the length of the shack, he came to a decision.
He didn't want her to live here another day longer. He had
all the money he possessed in the world with him, twenty-
five thousand dollars in bank notes.

Quickly counting out five thousand dollars and knowing
he would have to invest the remainder wisely to rebuild his
wealth, he placed the money in the same pouch he'd given
Baines in New Orleans. Then he hurriedly scribbled a note
to her. He knew her pride wouldn't let her accept the
money outright, so he told her it was for services rendered
and that he still expected her to pay him the three hundred
dollars whenever she could afford to.

He still didn't want the money back, but if he expected
her to accept the five thousand without protest, then he
wanted to convince her that her aid was worth the money.

Completing the note, he looked around for a place to put
it, along with the money. He loathed to leave it in an un-
secured house, but he had no choice. He hoped Lincoln
Marshall's threats would keep away any would-be thief.

After some thought, Gray decided to leave it in plain
sight where Baines would notice it almost immediately. If
he hid it from thieves, he would also be hiding it from
Baines, and she would never find it.

Looking around one last time to etch every little detail
of the house into his memory, he went to the door. He
slammed it tightly shut, descended the stairs, and mounted
Sultana, who was grazing contently under the chinaberry
tree.

Halfway to the docks, Gray realized he hadn't seen the
quilt.

38

TWENTY MINUTES LATER BAINES returned home.

Feeling ambiguous, she walked around the room. She thought to light the potbellied stove to ward off the coolness, but decided against it.

Her gaze fell on a familiar brown money pouch on the table, with a note attached. Immediately knowing who it came from but wondering when he left it, she removed the missive from the pouch and sat at the table to read it.

Gray was precise and to the point.

My dear Baines,

Your efforts in trying to help me recover Mary's Fortune were much appreciated. Unfortunately the results proved disappointing. Nevertheless, I am compelled to reward you for those efforts. Inside the pouch you'll find five thousand dollars in one-hundred-dollar bank notes. The money is for you to purchase the house on the bluff that you showed me. This, however, doesn't free you of your debt to me. I'll still expect you to keep our bargain and repay the three hundred dollars. I don't know where you are at the moment, little mouse, but you neglected to bolt your door. Until you move to a safer area, I implore you to be more diligent.

Good luck in your endeavors, little mouse. I bid you
farewell.

                                        Gray

Baines thought her heart would shatter. He'd said he was
penniless and he'd possibly given her all the money he
possessed. His letter seemed cold and indifferent in contrast
to his unselfish deed. In his own way, he was trying to
make her dream a reality.

Bitter tears streaked her cheeks, and she brushed them
angrily away. She had said often enough what she wanted
for herself that Gray thought she would prefer his money
rather than his name.

Maybe he would write to her when he got to London.
She had promised to repay the three hundred dollars she'd
borrowed from him while they were in New Orleans.
Surely he would acknowledge *that* when she did.

Baines fingered the pouch. *Her efforts*, he'd written. It
had been *their* efforts. And though it wasn't the quilt he
came seeking, the one she'd made proved just as valuable.

Mary's Fortune had become Baines's fortune and, she
prayed, Gray's redemption.

Picking up the pouch and the note, she placed it inside
the seaman's trunk.

Realization hit, and a fit of panic seized her.

Gray was here? He'd been *here* while she was at the
docks? Then who . . . ? Heavenly Father! To whom did she
give the quilt?

No! Impossible! Maybe Gray had left the money this
morning when he'd been there with her, and she just hadn't
noticed it.

Wishful thinking, Baines Marshall.

Her anxiety threatened to steal her breath. In the note
Gray had warned her to bolt the door. How would he know
it wasn't locked unless he had been there?

She had sealed Gray's fate and would never forgive herself. But she wouldn't weep.

Somewhere deep inside herself, she'd already decided to

go to England as soon as Uncle Lincoln returned. She wanted to bring Gray the original Mary's Fortune. Now the present circumstance made that decision all the more urgent. She would seek him out and hope he would still be able to find the treasure the map revealed.

Settling down on her cot, she went over in her mind how she would proceed tomorrow. Tomorrow, without Gray for the first time in three months. Surely she would have enough to do to keep her occupied. She still had Uncle Linc's quilt to complete. Seeing to the purchase of her new house would also absorb some of her time. When she was able, she would work in the sewing shop.

A feeling of anticipation descended on her, replacing her acute heartache. Suddenly she knew everything would be fine. It didn't matter that Gray had left her. Nor did it matter that she'd lost his quilt—twice, the original and the duplicate.

Somehow everything *would* be fine.

39

GRAY WALKED OUT ON deck of the *Venerable*.

The first star of the evening shone with promising brilliance in the clear autumn sky, a direct contrast to his bleak, uncertain future.

He'd been lonely before, but never in his life had he felt so alone, so without an anchor. Three days had passed, and he missed Baines terribly. He missed her unpretentiousness. Her rustic charm. Her beauty. Her embrace. *Everything* about her.

He'd so wanted to make her his wife. He loved her. Although he wasn't quite sure when it had happened, it had. He loved her with all that was in him, but he could never, would never, make her his.

He walked the length of the ship and back again, thinking, hurting, weary.

How could he bear to part with his heritage? Two hundred and thirty-five years of family heirlooms and treasures. Where would the repossession begin? With his mother's jewels? The ones *his* father had given to her or the ones *her* father had given to her?

Gray had always pictured himself presenting those jewels to the woman he married. It was what his parents had expected. He had been weaned on those expectations.

But he'd never pictured himself being married until he

met Baines. His lovable Baines. She deserved every precious bauble. Instead, Pierce's creditors would take them and place them on the auction block.

Gray could hardly restrain himself from weeping.

Yet he'd long ago concluded that he might have to live as a poor man. That wasn't what bothered him. Not being able to clear his father's debts was what tore at him. Even the wealth of his precious heirlooms wasn't enough to do so.

The sky had become inky with the night. Stars twinkled above like fireflies. The moon, full and bright, luminated the ship with its light as the huge vessel plowed its way toward the Atlantic from the Gulf of Mexico on calm seas.

Not so with Gray. His thoughts were anything but calm. He was certain that he would rise above all his woes. Somehow. Just as he was certain he'd left his heart in Natchez and would never get over his love for Baines.

He turned his predicament over and over in his mind and knew there was no other way but to face it head-on. Which is what he intended to do.

Then why was he so agitated? Baines. Suppose she were to commit herself to marriage to some chap who happened along and convinced her he was the answer to a woman's prayer?

Gray's blood pounded at the thought, yet he refused to dwell on it. He couldn't see Baines in the arms of anyone else but himself. Yet he couldn't claim her. He wouldn't marry her just to keep her in poverty.

Weary, he lost count of how many times he walked around the deck. The moon had shifted, and he knew it was getting late. Suddenly he got the uneasy impression of being watched again. Glancing cautiously around, he decided it was time for him to retire, then made his way to his cabin.

∽

TWICE JAMIE THOUGHT TO approach Gray as he watched him pace around the deck, but retreated with each attempt. Gray's air of isolation made Jamie reconsider. Yet he wondered at the anguish on Gray's features.

Could it be the quilt? Jamie might have been mistaken at what he saw in the quilt's end, but he had a good recollection of Briarwood. Because Jamie couldn't stand being around his despotic father and Gray's parents were rather more unpretentious, he and Gray used to play all over Briarwood as lads.

What would Baines be doing with a map of Gray's house? Or had she made the quilt from Gray's instructions?

His cabin walls wouldn't answer his questions, and standing in the shadows on deck wouldn't get him answers, either. He was off duty, so he'd best bring Gray his quilt and settle that matter at least.

Before Jamie doubted facing Gray again, he went swiftly to Gray's cabin and knocked on the door.

"It's unbolted," Gray called. "Come in."

Jamie did as he was bade and stopped.

For a moment, the drone of the ship's engine was the only sound to be heard. Sitting beside a small table with a bottle of brandy, Gray looked at him, his mouth opened in shock.

"H-hello, Gray," Jamie said, uncertain. The censure in Gray's eyes almost made him leave.

Gray stood slowly from his chair. "Are you bloody following me?" he bellowed. "What the deuce are you doing here?"

"You used to listen when spoken to, Grayling." Jamie didn't move from the doorway. Every muscle in his body tensed. It had been years since he and Gray had shared any camaraderie, but still he missed him. At one time he and Gray had been closer than some brothers. If he couldn't reach out to his wife, at least he could try with his friend. "When I saw you at that tavern that night, I told you I was first mate on the ship *Venerable*. If you didn't hear that, I guess you didn't hear the rest of what I said, either."

Frowning, Gray threaded his fingers through his hair. He hadn't made the connection when he'd boarded this ship yesterday in New Orleans. Neither had he given much thought to Jamie or his explanation, not even when Baines had implored him to forgive Jamie's transgression against him. Jamie had only tried to be a dutiful son.

"Well?"

"Well, what, Jamie?"

"Do you recall any of our last conversation?"

Silently he contemplated a moment, then drew in a long breath. "All of it," Gray finally said.

Jamie bowed his head.

"And I do accept your apology, Jamie. Had those orders come from my father, I would have gladly done his bidding."

"Thank you, Gray."

"I was about to pour myself some brandy." He smiled, miserable and sad. "Would you care to join me?"

"Aye," Jamie said, stepping fully into the cabin and closing the door behind him. "I would."

Gray poured out two glasses of brandy and handed one to his old friend.

"It's been a long time, Jamie," Gray said quietly. "I've missed our camaraderie."

Jamie nodded his blond head. "Aye. If I'd had the courage, I would have come to you a long time ago, Gray. But I was afraid of my father and couldn't bear to see the scorn in your eyes."

"I'm not sure I would have listened to you, Jamie. But my stay in Natchez has changed me. What made you finally decide to come forward?"

"I saw you in New Orleans at Tremoulet House. While I debated whether or not to approach you, the most beautiful woman in the city glided down the stairs and straight into your arms." Merriment lit his pale eyes. "I couldn't very well interrupt such a moment."

"That was over two months ago. Had you been there all that time?"

"Aye. Well, between here and Natchez. The ship needed repairs, and it took a while to round up another reliable crew. Luckily about half the men signed on again."

"It was luck that you retained your old crew."

"Aye, 'twas," Jamie agreed easily, downing his brandy,

then poured himself another. "I shadowed you almost all the time you were in Natchez. Then I saw you in the Horse and Mule and didn't know if you would need my assistance or not. You were about to tangle with the scum of the river."

Gray laughed and swallowed half his drink. "And of course you would have saved my bloody hide?"

"I would certainly have given it a try." Jamie chuckled. "You never did know when to quit." He fell silent, and his mood turned serious. "Allow me to apologize once again for the remarks I made about Baines. She's very beautiful but still just a tavern wench."

Gray bristled. Jamie did, too, but not from an instinctive reaction. It was because of that bloody Tate. A tavern wench might have been preferable to his wife, the spoiled daughter of the duke and duchess of Camden, who had been involved in one of the most spectacular heists ever. Jamie thought he was saving her life. Instead, he'd walked right into her lair.

He wondered if she had disposed of the stolen art. Those paintings, and she, had become the bane of Jamie's existence. Even now, he felt like throttling her. Just what in bloody hell would he do when he returned to England?

"Baines is no tavern wench, Jamie. She's the same girl you saw with me at Tremoulet House. She's a seamstress and quiltmaker by trade," Gray explained heatedly. "She was at the Horse and Mule to give a friend a hand, until his regular help returned. Make this the last time you refer to her in a derogatory manner!"

Jamie eyed Gray, astonished at his vehemence. Obviously he was in love with Baines. Jamie had seen her no less than three times and hadn't made the connection to the girl at Tremoulet House. Whatever she was, a tavern wench or a house frau, if Gray loved her and it didn't matter to him, then it didn't matter to Jamie, either. He wouldn't do anything, ever again, to jeopardize their friendship.

"I had no idea. I'll never again disparage Baines."

"Then let's drop the subject, my friend," Gray said

grouchily. "I have two-thirds of this brandy left, and we have a lot of catching up to do."

"That we do, Gray." Jamie smiled. "But hold that thought a moment. I have something that belongs to you. I'll just hop to my cabin and get it."

Jamie darted out the door, leaving Gray staring after him. Back before he was missed, he rushed in carrying the quilt.

Gray gasped. "What . . . ?"

"Your Baines sent it to you, Gray. She thought you were on the *Natchez Belle,* and cajoled the first mate to give it to you even as the boat started to move. The chap caught it with a grappling hook."

Gray's heart pumped fast and furious. He stared at the quilt, his mind racing.

"Baines sent instructions to fold the four corners together," Jamie explained softly. He watched Gray closely. "There's a map that leads to the third-floor parlor of Briarwood, Gray. What does all this mean?"

"What does it all mean?" Gray shouted joyously. "What does it all mean?" He grabbed Jamie in a bear hug, then let his laughter float upward. "It means she loves me, Jamie! It means she's wonderful!"

"Well." Words almost failed Jamie at Gray's unusual emotional display. The years had certainly changed him. "This most assuredly calls for a drink. Maybe you can tell me what this is all about."

"Nothing to tell, my friend," Gray said, unable to contain his happiness. "Baines made me a quilt to my specifications, and I forgot it."

Jamie frowned skeptically. "But what about the map?"

Gray waved a hand in dismissal. "Only a game. I described the house and told her to weave a room into the quilt. She chose the third-floor parlor and dared me to find it."

"It was quite cleverly hidden," Jamie said. "I never would have found it. Even *with* a clue."

Gray laughed at his friend's lame joke. "Drink up, my friend," he said, raising his glass in salute, "for this is a night of new beginnings!"

40

"BAINES, DARLIN', THIS IS about the finest cottage on the bluff." Miz Annabelle sat at the new wooden table in Baines's kitchen. "Excusin' mine, of course."

Laughing, Baines leaned over and put her arms around Miz Annabelle's slender neck. She hugged her warmly. "You're wonderful. Thanks for all your help these past two weeks. I couldn't have made this move without you."

Miz Annabelle patted her hand. "You would have if you had to." She stood. "You did a real good job makin' those curtains, too, young lady. Eight pairs in two weeks..." She shook her head. "I swear I don't understand why you're workin' yourself into such a frenzy."

"There are eight windows all told in this house, Miz Annabelle. They all need coverings."

Miz Annabelle went to the new wood-burning stove where a pot of coffee sat heating. After getting two cups from the cupboard, she set them on the table then filled them with the brew. "Sit down, darlin'," she gently commanded, reseating herself.

Baines took a seat opposite her.

"That new stove of yours do a pretty good job of heatin' this kitchen, Baines."

"Yes, it does." Baines took a sip of her coffee.

With her five thousand dollars she was able to purchase

the house, add new pieces of furniture to what she'd already had, purchase material for curtains—and squirrel away the price of passage to England. She felt Miz Annabelle's gaze on her. "May I get you more coffee?" she asked absent-mindedly.

"I ain't finished with what I have, Baines," the widow snapped impatiently. She regarded her young friend with kind eyes. "Baines, darlin', you know I don't like to guess at anything. Invariably I discover the truth anyway. You told me Gray paid you five thousand dollars for making that quilt, then left with no hint of when or if he'll return. Is that the right of it?"

"Yes. Pretty much."

"Child, if I wrote a book with that kind of endin', my writin' future would be in dire jeopardy. What ain't you tellin' me, Baines, honey?"

Baines took a long swallow from her cup. Why shouldn't she confide in Miz Annabelle? She had no one else to talk to. Miz Annabelle had replaced the mother she'd lost. Baines certainly would have confided in her own mother.

"You've changed, Baines. You seem more mature, more quiet. What's worryin' you?"

"Miz Annabelle," Baines said and sighed. "Gray told me what he did in confidence. I need your promise not to repeat anything I tell you."

"I promise," Miz Annabelle quickly answered. "Normally I wouldn't pry, darlin', but I feel you need to share whatever's troublin' you. You may feel better."

Miz Annabelle not pry? Baines smiled inwardly. "Very well," she agreed. "The quilt Gray was seeking has a map woven within its pattern—"

"A map? How come?"

"Yes, Miz Annabelle, a map. It supposedly will lead to a treasure. A treasure that will free Gray of the debts his father made and was unable to repay before he died. If Gray can't save his family's fortune, he'll be penniless."

"Well, that explains his desperation to recover the quilt and why he waited around for you to make a copy of it.

That copy has probably made him a very happy man by now.''

Baines merely nodded, declining to go into detail about why Gray didn't have the quilt, after all.

''Yes, you *have* changed. A body can plainly see you's pinin' after that Englishman.''

''Am I that obvious, Miz Annabelle?''

''Yes, child. I'm thinkin' you feel you'll never see him again, just 'cause he left you with no nevermind. Your dreams ain't finished comin' true, darlin'. Take heart. Gray Dunston appears an honorable man. I strongly feel you ain't seen the last of him. He didn't do all he did for you just for pity's sake. It was for *his* sake. And you talkin' now as good as any fancy nabob. That was done for both of you. He won't forget that *or* you so easily.''

With her heart shattered over Gray's absence, Baines had worried about what Gray's present plight was. Yet with her plan to go to England, she had no doubt that she would see him again.

The problem was, exactly how would he receive her?

''Miz Annabelle, you're such a comfort to me. I'm glad I told you about Gray. You always make me feel better. One other thing. The Dunland Dunstons don't know about Gray's predicament.''

Miz Annabelle waved a dismissing hand. ''Don't worry, darlin','' she said airily. ''I gave you my word. I live by my honor. What you spoke today will never escape my lips.'' She rose from her seat and began clearing away their coffee cups.

Baines smiled. Miz Annabelle always felt it necessary to tidy up after them. But she wanted the widow to relax. ''I'll do that, Miz Annabelle. You're my guest, remember? Sit down and tell me what's going on with you and Mr. Foxe.''

''Baines Marshall!'' Miz Annabelle said and gasped. ''Never think of me as a guest,'' she said with hurt inflected tones. ''I'm your friend and old enough to be your mama. I'm proud of the change in you, child. Just don't go get too fancy-like.''

''Don't fear, Miz Annabelle,'' Baines said. She rose and

put her arms around her friend's waist. "The only thing that's changed about me is my speech. I will never become a fancy nabob."

Miz Annabelle patted her affectionately on her arm. "That's my Baines," she said, smiling. "As for that old coot, Nathaniel Foxe, he's plumb fine. Speakin' of him, darlin', we're gonna go and see a play that the Theatrical Association is hosting. I'll see you at the shop tomorrow, honey."

Standing on her porch, Baines watched Miz Annabelle walk sedately down the lane toward her house. Evening was descending, and the night jasmine in her garden was blooming. She breathed in deeply, thinking of the first time she'd gone to Dunland.

With a wistful smile, she went inside to ponder her new and safe surroundings. Yet she couldn't help but wonder what Gray was doing at that particular moment, and if she was anywhere in his thoughts.

41

TIME SEEMED TO HAVE stopped.

The seasons were changing as late summer bloomed into early autumn, setting the landscape alive with the reds and golds of fall and bringing in crisp, cool days.

Baines stared morosely out of Miz Annabelle's shop window as she sat at the drafting table, the splendid beauty of the afternoon unable to liven her spirits.

With a rueful smile she thought about her little shack situated so perfectly by the river. As always, her thoughts turned to Gray and all the time they'd shared in her former home.

Barely comprehending the emptiness engulfing her without him, Baines sighed, close to tears. Had it really only been four weeks since his departure?

It felt like a lifetime ago, and she didn't know how much longer she could be without him before she went to London. Each day she waited for Uncle Lincoln to return. Logically, however, she knew she had about six more weeks before he was due to come home.

"How you doin', darlin'?"

Miz Annabelle spoke from behind her. The widow had been in the other room completing an evening gown for one of her clients.

"Fine, I guess," Baines mumbled without turning around.

"Do you like the gown, Baines, honey?"

Baines stared straight ahead. "I suppose so." She swallowed back a sob as a well-dressed gentleman on a palomino rode passed the shop. For a moment she thought it was Gray on his golden horse. But just as quickly her hopes were dashed.

"Baines Marshall!"

Her throat aching with her effort not to cry in disappointment, Baines slowly turned. Hurt and dejected, she met Miz Annabelle's annoyed gaze. A tear slipped down Baines's cheek, and she swiped it angrily away.

"Oh, my word, child." Setting the gown on the counter, Miz Annabelle rushed to Baines. She hugged her tightly. "Go home, darlin'."

Home? Baines squeezed her eyes shut at the thought. Home to a lonely house, one that she had pined for but one that was empty and lonesome.

"I couldn't, Miz Annabelle," Baines whispered. She stood and walked to the counter. "I have four more hours until quitting time and I refuse to leave." She held up the gown. The velvet bodice had tiny pearls and delicate beadwork stitched into it. "This is lovely and—"

"I insist you leave," Miz Annabelle interrupted. "You could be coming down with somethin' and you need to go home to take care of yourself. Your work will still be here in the mornin' if you feel like comin' in."

Baines nodded. She didn't have it in her to argue with Miz Annabelle. "I'll make it up to you next week."

She got her coat off the rack and headed for the door.

"If there's anythin' I can do for you, Baines honey, let me know."

"Thanks, Miz Annabelle."

As Baines started the short walk to her house, she thought the widow had been partially right. Baines had *already* come down with something—a real bad case of lovesickness.

But she didn't know how to feel any different. All she

ever did was think about Gray; the joy she had felt when she was with him; and their days together in her little house while she made Mary's Fortune.

The more she thought of Gray, however, the worse she felt.

Heavy with despair, she unlatched the gate to her beautiful new home. She did love this house, truly so. But her anguish made it impossible to enjoy.

Opening her door, she let herself inside and lit several candles. A chill hung in the air, so she also threw some logs into her fireplace. Soon a small blaze warmed her.

Sitting on the sofa by the window, she leaned back and raised her feet off the floor, then closed her eyes.

Images of the raw passion on Gray's face as he made love to her danced through her mind. She recalled the feel of his hands skimming the length of her body, his fingertips burning a trail of desire wherever he touched. His warm tongue caressing her breasts and his mouth against her femininity had driven her senseless.

But coupled with his unashamed eroticism was the sense of humor she'd discovered beneath his veneer of stoicism. His generosity and chivalry made him the type of man many women longed for. Only now did Baines understand the honor that had kept him from making love to her again—

A light tap sounded on the door and Baines sat up. She looked out the window but couldn't see who the caller was. Going to the door and opening it, she gasped in surprise.

"DeEdria!"

A warm smile curved DeEdria's mouth. "Hello, Baines. I hope you forgive me for intruding, my dear."

For a moment Baines remained speechless. She stared at the glowing DeEdria Dunston, who held a bouquet of fresh flowers in her hands. The swell of her belly attested to her advanced state of pregnancy, and Baines glimpsed beyond her. A gray phaeton guided by a team of grays sat outside the fence.

Baines could scarcely credit that DeEdria had defied protocol, to come to the bluff to see her. Yet the thought was fleeting. Knowing how genuine DeEdria was and remembering the lady's wish that they remain friends, Baines's surprise didn't last long.

"Oh, DeEdria, of course you're not intruding." Baines stepped aside. "Please come in."

"Thank you, Baines." DeEdria walked inside and handed the flowers to Baines. "For your new home."

"Thank you." Accepting the sweetly scented bouquet, Baines showed her to the sofa. "Please sit down."

DeEdria's gaze roamed around the parlor, then focused on Baines. "Oh, my dear, it's lovely. I'm so happy for you." She sat down and laid her hands atop her belly. "I really *didn't* mean to intrude, Baines, but since you haven't accepted my open invitation to visit Dunland, I thought I would visit you."

"I'm proud to have you, but you shouldn't have. Not in your condition, DeEdria." And not when Baines couldn't look at DeEdria without recalling her first time at Dunland with Gray.

"Don't take on so, Baines." DeEdria smiled, her brown eyes searching. "I really shouldn't have, but I'll be all right."

Baines hoped DeEdria wouldn't mention Gray, for she didn't think she could stand to even hear his name mentioned without dissolving into tears. She busied herself with placing the flowers in a vase and arranging them as she spoke. Later she would fill the container with water.

"I'm surprised Roc allowed you to come."

"He wouldn't have if he were here." DeEdria laughed. "He's away on business in Jackson. I expect him home tomorrow. The baby and I are doing wonderful, so I decided to 'borrow' my phaeton and take a short ride." Sighing deeply, she brought her hand to her chest. "Roc's been horrible! Insisting I stay in bed for days at a time. I understand his worry, but Doc Kent says I'm out of danger and can proceed with normal living. Still, it's so lonely at home without Roc there to order me around."

Baines took control of her emotions. Where were her manners? DeEdria was extending a hand of friendship, and she was all but ignoring it. True, she missed Gray, but she liked DeEdria. Baines smiled. "Will you stay awhile?"

DeEdria looked relieved. "If you'll have me."

"I have sweet dough that's been rising since this morning and I can set a pot of coffee to boiling—"

"Say no more, Baines! My appetite is scandalous. Just get those biscuits baked."

With a laugh Baines started for the kitchen. "If you don't mind, we can sit at the table in my kitchen while the biscuits bake."

DeEdria rose, still graceful, and followed behind Baines. Nearly an hour later the two women sat at the table, eating the hot biscuits and sipping coffee.

"You do look wonderful, DeEdria. Are you sure you're well?"

"Not always, but that's to be expected. It's nothing serious." DeEdria took a delicate bite of biscuit. "And you, my dear? How are you? How's the quilting?"

Leaning back in the chair, Baines sighed. "I'm afraid my quilting's been suffering, what with moving and all. But I've been sewing a good amount at Miz Annabelle's."

Tasting her coffee, DeEdria placed her cup on the table and smiled at Baines. "I went to the shop to see you, but Mrs. Shepard told me you seemed to be ailing. Are you sure you're all right?"

"Of course, DeEdria. I'm just fine." Baines laughed nervously. She didn't want DeEdria to question her about Gray, and she had a sinking feeling the conversation was steering in that direction. "I'm just feeling guilty for taking so long to finish my uncle's quilt," she lied. "But I promised myself to finish it before he comes home." At least that part was true, but until a few moments ago she had scarcely thought of Uncle Linc's birthday quilt in weeks.

"You'll get it done, Baines," DeEdria said with encouragement. "I know you will. Mrs. Shepard showed me some of your work, and I can see you're very talented."

Baines smiled, pleased at the compliment and Miz Annabelle's pride in her. "Thank you, DeEdria."

A moment of awkward silence ensued. The shadow of Gray hung between both women. Baines didn't want to mention him, and DeEdria seemed near to bursting with her need to do so.

"Well, how's *Linny*?" Shocked at her sarcasm in the company of the woman's best friend, heat rushed into Baines's cheeks. "I-I mean . . . Miz . . . um . . . Belinda."

DeEdria laughed so hard, her eyes watered. "Oh, Baines, you're priceless. Please don't be embarrassed. Belinda Myers is my friend, but she's a consummate snob. And to answer your question, she's fine. She's set her sights on a planter from Louisiana. Her hopes of marrying Gray shattered when he went back home."

Grief and desolation swept through Baines, but she was determined to ignore DeEdria's reference to Gray. Yet how could she have asked about Belinda Myers without realizing Gray would undoubtedly be mentioned? She shifted in her seat.

"I kind of feel sorry for Miz Myers, DeEdria, so desperate to get married and all."

"She means well, Baines. It's just that she's already twenty-eight and feels opportunity is swiftly passing her by." DeEdria gently patted her belly. "You *are* a good cook, and I enjoyed the biscuits very much." Her velvety brown gaze fell on Baines's face. "Do you miss him?"

Caught off guard, Baines stood and began stacking the dishes in the dishpan. She pretended ignorance to get control of her emotions. "Why, whoever do you mean?"

"I don't mean your uncle, Baines," DeEdria chided gently.

Baines left the dishes and sat back down, all pretense gone. "Yes, I miss Gray," she whispered. Her lower lip trembled. "I love him," she admitted hoarsely.

DeEdria reached across the table and grabbed Baines's hand. "Oh, my dear, please don't despair. I know you'll hear from Gray again. I don't believe he came all this way just for an old quilt. Well, maybe he did, but then he found you. And his honor won't allow him to stay away. He'll be back, so take courage."

Baines opened her mouth to protest, to tell DeEdria that her courage was failing her mightily at the moment.

"I don't want to hear it, Baines," DeEdria ordered. "Gray is a Dunston through and through, and the Dunston men are a gallant, passionate lot. I know this from personal experience." She leaned in closer. "Listen to me. I was sixteen when I met Roc and seventeen when my daddy forced him down the aisle with a shotgun aimed at him." She giggled at the memories. "It's easy for me to laugh now," she said at the surprise in Baines's features, "but I was horrified at my shotgun wedding, and Roc was furious. I didn't think he'd ever forgive me, and I was sick in love with him, which is why we had to get married." A blush stained her pretty features, and she dropped her voice lower. "We became intimate, and my daddy found out when I became pregnant, which is why he forced us down the aisle."

"How did you two ever get through that? Anyone can see how much you two love each other."

"Roc eventually came to his senses and said he was being a stubborn ass—his words, mind you. But his honor made him realize that his false pride was destroying what was between us."

"And the baby?" Baines asked softly, although she already knew the answer.

"I lost it in the fourth month and nearly died along with it."

Baines patted DeEdria's arm. "Thank you for sharing that," she whispered. "I do feel better."

DeEdria stood. "I'm glad," she said. "Come to Dunland Sunday after church for a repast. We'll talk again then. Right now I'd best be going. I wouldn't put it past my husband to return home early. But it's been a wonderful afternoon, and I hope this is the beginning of a long friendship, my dear."

"I'm glad you enjoyed it, DeEdria. Thank you for coming and thank you for the bouquet. The flowers are beautiful."

At the door DeEdria gave Baines an affectionate hug.
"I'll see you Sunday?"

Baines nodded. "Goodbye, DeEdria. Until Sunday."

Standing in the doorway, she watched as DeEdria
climbed aboard her phaeton. Baines leaned against the door,
contemplating her choices.

She could continue to feel miserable, or she could add
some swatches to Uncle Lincoln's quilt. She wouldn't exactly forget about Gray, but at least her mind would be on
something else.

DeEdria waved one last time and rode away. Baines went
inside and closed the door, then went to her sewing sack
to get her swatches.

42

NEARLY TWO AND A half months had gone by since Gray's departure, and Baines settled back into her regular routine. She completed Uncle Linc's quilt and spread it across his bed in his small bedchamber, then began work on another likeness of Mary's Fortune.

Well, it wasn't going to be an exact likeness. She'd decided to use the same pattern, but darker material, and she would eliminate the treasure map altogether. Although without actively searching for it, it was unlikely that anyone ever would have found it. Still, to Baines it was personal and sacred, of no value to anyone but Gray.

Gray.

She sighed and gritted her teeth, determined not to cry. Yet she still missed him deeply, and each day that went by only increased her loneliness.

With a huff of frustration she sat on the sofa she had placed in front of the double windows that looked out onto the porch. A supply of dark patches lay beside her, stacked in neat rows. Her sewing basket at her feet held a goodly amount of various needles, thimbles, threads of every color, rickrack, buttons, and fasteners.

All her needs at her fingertips, she began stitching patches of blue, brown, black, purple, and green together. Upon completing the two large blocks consisting of ten small squares each, she put her quilting aside.

Baines's heart just wasn't in quilting today. It hadn't been for . . . two and a half months.

Sighing miserably, she looked out of the window. It was late October, and the outside was wrought in fall colors, yet it was a chilly, gloomy day to match her mood.

She was sick with longing for Gray and couldn't keep her mind on anything she attempted to do. Even the house and the ease in which she now lived didn't alleviate her melancholy, proof that attaining one's desires didn't necessarily lead to lifelong happiness.

It was a shocking discovery, but one she had began to realize right before Gray departed. Yet it was only through her disappointment and heartache that she fully understood the importance of that fact.

After years of plotting and pining, now that she'd realized most of her dreams, she couldn't have cared less. Baines shook her head. Life was funny that way.

Since DeEdria's visit three and a half weeks ago, they had kept in touch. Baines had indeed gone to Dunland that Sunday and was well received by Roc as well as DeEdria. Now the two women saw each other twice a week. Every Sunday Baines went to Dunland, and on Wednesdays Roc allowed DeEdria a two-hour visit at Baines's house. This past Wednesday DeEdria had mentioned that Gray would soon arrive in London, if he already hadn't. Sometimes ships pulled into port early, and Gray had been gone for almost eleven weeks.

Tomorrow was Sunday, and DeEdria had gracefully extended an invitation for Miz Annabelle to join Baines at Dunland for their weekly visit.

Still Baines was so miserable she felt like weeping. So lonely she could hardly bear it. Often she remembered the one night she spent in Gray's arms and she would become hot and flustered.

Did he remember as well? Or had he already forgotten that encounter and had now turned his attention elsewhere? What about Mary's Fortune? *Had* he received it?

Her mind wouldn't allow her to think that he hadn't, for

when she'd gone to the *Natchez Belle* to investigate, the firstmate assured her that one Grayling Dunston did in fact receive her quilt.

Knowing Miz Annabelle was always there for her and wondering how much longer it would be before Uncle Linc returned, Baines sighed. She missed him as well, and hoped he would be home in time to spend Christmas with her. She didn't relish spending her favorite holiday without Gray *and* Uncle Lincoln.

Trying to cheer herself at how Uncle Lincoln would react to her accomplishments, she forced a smile. She *really* wished he would come home. The sooner he came home, the sooner she would be able to set sail for England and Gray. She had to see him again, if only for finality.

Getting up at the disparaging thought, Baines threw another log into the fireplace, then went into the kitchen and pumped out water for coffee.

Going back into the parlor, she decided to put her sewing away for the day. With that in mind, she began gathering up her swatches, glancing absently out the double windows.

She frowned, her heartbeat speeding up.

A large, barrel-chested man was coming through the gate. His weathered complexion highlighted the gray sprinkled throughout his black hair and thick beard.

Baines stood to her full height, her chore of tidying up forgotten.

Uncle Lincoln?

Carrying a large traveling bag, he swaggered proudly up the walk. In a second there was a loud banging on the door.

Releasing a glad cry, Baines rushed to open the door, and Uncle Lincoln nearly fell inside. He scooped her up in a bear hug and swung her around.

"I done heard, Baines, honey! I knowed you had talent 'nough to make a quilt worth a lot o' money. I'm right proud o' you!"

"Uncle Lincoln!" Baines squealed happily. She laughed helplessly as he swung her around again. "Put me down!"

Uncle Lincoln set her on her feet.

Hands on hips, her heart banging against her chest in

delight, Baines faced him. "What in the world are you doing here at this time? I thought you said you would be gone six months?"

"Them's the words I done tole Albert to write, Baines. An' I aimed to stay six months, so's I could give you a start wit' yo' sewin' shop. But Eli upped an' got sick wit' a fever. We was in the Caribbean when it happened. So I done ketch a ship comin' this-a-way wit' Eli. The whole time we was a-comin' he feared he would die before we reached land an' get dumped in the sea for fish bait."

"Oh, Uncle Lincoln!" Baines put her hand on her breast in worry. "Poor Eli." Despite the fact that the man had stolen from her and turned her life upside-down, she still felt sympathy for him. She still considered him family. If not for Eli, Gray wouldn't have stayed in Natchez as long as he had. She cleared her throat, not wanting to think of Gray for the moment. "Did you get Eli home in time?"

"In time for what?"

"His burial, of course!"

Uncle Lincoln shrugged. "I don't reckon Eli will allow hisself to git buried, Baines, seein' as he ain't daid yet."

Baines chuckled. "I thought you said . . . Oh, never mind!" She threw her arms around his waist. "Oh, I'm so glad you're back. I've missed you so."

Uncle Lincoln kissed her forehead. "I've missed you, too, honey." Stepping away from her, he glanced around the room. "This sure is a pretty place." He looked at her, then bowed his grizzly head. "You done accomplished all this by yo'se'f in six months what I been promisin' to do fo' ten years." His watery gaze met hers. "I am plumb proud, Baines. It's a fine house."

Baines took his big hand. "Come, Uncle Lincoln, let me show you around."

∽

TWO HOURS LATER WITH Lincoln's tour over, he had freshened up. Now he sat at the kitchen table, drinking coffee with Baines. He stared at her, his look fatherly and all-knowing. He took a sip of his coffee. "I done brought yo' quilt back, honey."

Baines smiled enigmatically. "That's wonderful, Uncle Linc," she said, squirming under his intense gaze. Trepidation filled her. Soon she would be on her way to see if she and Gray had a future together, but first she had to tell her uncle. "I've been waiting for it. Why would Eli steal it?"

"'Cause he's a danged thief, Baines. It weren't even cold when he done stole it," Uncle Lincoln said angrily. "But I don't reckon he'll steal from us again. Not unless he wants his head broke."

"Where is he?"

"Down at the Horse an' Mule, o' course. He was too scairt to face you, honey. He tole me to tell you he's powerful sorry fo' takin' yo' quilt."

Baines nodded. "Well, then, he's no longer ailing?"

"The fever done left him a week ago." Silence fell between them as Uncle Lincoln tasted his coffee again, then he turned a level look to Baines. "Now tell me, honey, how we come to own this here fine house."

"You must promise me that you will keep an open mind, Uncle Lincoln," Baines implored, leaning forward and placing her hand atop his.

Uncle Lincoln frowned but said, "I promise," and smiled. "You sure talk nice, Baines. I like the sound o' yo' words."

Baines returned his smile. "Thank you, Uncle Linc."

She related the story of the quilt to him, omitting Gray's true reason for wanting it. She noted that he listened intently, with no trace of judgment on his features. When she finished, he hugged her.

"So you's stuck on this nabob, huh, honey?"

"I love him, Uncle Lincoln," Baines said miserably. "But I don't really know how he feels about me."

"Seems to me there ain't but one way to find that out, honey. Go there and ask him."

Baines blinked in surprise. She hadn't expected that from Uncle Lincoln. She'd loathed to tell him she wanted to go to Gray, fearing he would say it wouldn't be proper for her to go under such circumstances.

"Are you saying you wouldn't object to my going to England?"

"I want to see you happy, Baines. If England's where he's at, then that's where you needs to go," Uncle Lincoln declared. "I've got a pocket full o' money, honey. I'll pay yo' passage there an' back."

"Oh, Uncle Lincoln!" Baines jumped from her seat and hugged her uncle. "I think you're wonderful."

"'Course I am," Uncle Lincoln teased. "How soon do you wants to leave?"

"Yesterday!" Baines laughed.

"Awright, honey. We'll make arrangements the first thang tomorry. In the meantime, I jus' wants to git acquainted wit' our new house."

Baines had a good supply of food in the house and prepared pork chops, greens, and corn bread. Thinking of her meal with Gray, she was seized with giggles. Uncle Lincoln thought she had lost her dang wits.

Finished with tidying up the supper dishes, Baines bade Uncle Lincoln good night. She knew he wanted to get the feel of his new bedchamber and thought she saw a tear when she presented him with his birthday quilt as a belated present. His heartfelt emotions over her simple gift warmed her.

Now, alone in her own spacious bedchamber, she took the original Mary's Fortune in with her. Looking at it with apprehension, she slowly brought the four ends together. She didn't know whether to laugh or cry at her discovery, since she wasn't sure if Gray had taken possession of the quilt she took to the boat.

Holding the ends of Mary's Fortune together, Baines found that *her* copy was a perfect replica!

Still, if Gray had indeed gotten the quilt, would it actually lead to the treasure he so desperately needed?

43

A COOL BREEZE ROLLED off the Thames, and familiar fog hung in London as the *Venerable* pulled into port in late October.

Gray should have been happy to be returning home. His attention should have been focused on his debts and an alternate last-ditch solution if the quilt led to nothing.

But all he could think of was Baines and the untamed beauty of the Trace during their afternoon ride together. He wondered how DeEdria fared and what bloody mischief Roc was getting into.

Disembarking from the ship, it surprised Gray to find Denholm, his dour butler, waiting at the pier. He went to where the man stood next to Gray's horse and carriage, emblazoned with the Montegut coat-of-arms. Two dragons were situated on each side of a raised sword. Fire spurted from their nostrils and curled upward. The words *toute pour honour* sat beneath.

"Denholm, old boy," Gray greeted cheerily. "What are you doing here?"

"Good day, my lord." Denholm bowed, his features remaining stoic. "I have been coming every day for a fortnight. I knew you were due to arrive within that time, sir, from your missive." He noticed the quilt Gray had draped over his arm. His mouth curved into a wide grin.

Gray laughed at the old man's reaction. "It seems to do strange things to people, my friend. Like start them laughing for no reason. Believe me, it has the same effect on me."

Denholm was chief steward at Briarwood and also Gray's friend. He had been in the family's employ for twenty years, since Gray was ten. Despite the mistrust Gray had harbored for almost everyone, he had confided in Denholm. Since he would also have ended up in the streets, Gray gave him the option of seeking other employment before he'd departed for Natchez.

Yet the old man had been Pierce's friend, and now his. Denholm promised to stay to the bitter end.

Gray threw the quilt inside the coach and slapped Denholm on the back. "I only have one travel case, Denholm," he said. "Load her up and let's go home."

"Gray!" Jamie called, rushing through the bustling crowd. "I'm off to visit my father. Perhaps we can get together again sometime."

"You know where I live, Jamie," Gray said. "The door is always open to you."

"Thank you, my friend." Jamie extended his hand.

"Those words sound wonderful, Jamie." Gray shook his hand. "I'll see you soon."

After Jamie departed, Gray climbed into the carriage, grinning at Denholm's perplexed expression. "It's a long story, Denholm," he said. "Aye, that was Jamie McKay you just saw. I'll explain later."

"Very good, my lord," Denholm said, and closed the door.

⟳

REACHING BRIARWOOD, GRAY DISEMBARKED from the carriage and strode quickly into the foyer, amid greetings from his myriad servants.

Carrying the quilt, he nodded politely and continued on to the wide, sweeping mahogany staircase. He ascended them two at a time, up to the third floor.

His heart thundering wildly, he rushed down the brightly lit hallway to the parlor that the map described. He stopped before the fireplace and gazed at the mantel.

Though this was the servants' floor, it was kept in order and dust free, leaving nothing to hinder his inspection for . . . what?

The map indicated a treasure in this spot. But the fireplace stood here. Undoubtedly the bounty was behind it. There could be no other explanation, but how was he to gain access to it? Nothing was visible to show how to remove the mantelpiece. Bloody hell! Was he supposed to tear away the entire damn wall?

With a frustrated sigh, he folded the four ends of the quilt together again, trying to detect a clue to his dilemma.

There it was. The arrows. Four of them. Two pointing to the underside of the mantel, and two appearing to point to a stone on each side of it.

Gray stooped down and peeked into the fireplace, but saw nothing, not even soot. Straightening himself, he studied the bricks. He laughed.

Hardly noticeable, unless closely inspected were two stones on each side of the mantel that were different from the rest. He walked to one and pressed down on it. Nothing happened. With a curse, he did the same on the other side.

Still, nothing changed.

Finally he twisted the stone. A creak sounded. His breath came rapidly as he repeated the same motion with the other stone. Another creak, and the entire fireplace and mantel shifted six inches from the wall, then stopped.

"Bloody hell," Gray muttered and stooped again to look under the mantel.

A small portion of the back end had recessed itself. Gray pressed the middle with considerable force, and the fireplace and mantel swung open.

For a moment he stared into the gloomy darkness of a secret chamber. His eyes adjusted, and he detected a gleam.

Pulsating with anticipation, he took a candleholder off the mantel and lit the candle resting in it. Crawling inside the tiny cubicle, he found he could barely stand.

Illuminated by the glow of the candlelight, he saw at least ten sacks stacked against the wall. Spiderwebs clung to the corners, and a rat scampered across the floor into a hole in the wall. A lone coin lay on the floor, the source of the initial gleam.

Sweat beaded Gray's brow. Swallowing the saliva gathering in his mouth, he picked up the nearest bag and carefully undid its cord wrapped around the top.

His eyes widened in disbelief, and he gasped, loud in the silence of the room. A fortune in gold nuggets winked at him.

He tore open sack after sack and found the same. Each one was filled to capacity with the nuggets, leaving just enough room to secure the tops.

Good God. Where had it all come from?

Holding the candle aloft, he glanced around the musty room. On the floor in the corner a flat, dusty, leather money carrier lay, folded over like a book.

Gray picked it up and opened it. On paper yellow with age were the words *Pirate, bags of gold. Hide from authorities*. He couldn't make out the date, but surmised his ancestors had roamed the high seas, preying on wealthy merchant ships.

His laughter echoed around him. This much gold represented *years* of pirating.

What would his proud and noble father think of that? And he, Gray, had maligned Lincoln Marshall for being a thief. Marshall was only a petty thief compared to his illustrious ancestors. They had stolen a fortune to last several lifetimes.

Whatever other mysteries lay behind the cache of gold, Gray would never know. It would remain just that, a mystery. But his quest had ended beyond his wildest imaginings. It was time now to settle his debts.

Dusting himself off, he departed the chamber. The words on his coat-of-arms came to mind. He smiled.

All for honor, indeed.

44

DRIFTS OF SNOW FLOATED past the mullioned windows. Trees stood outside in stark contrast against the whitewashed land, barren sentinels to usher in the new year. A crisp fire blazed in the marble fireplace of Gray's drawing room, warding off the afternoon chill.

Sitting on the sofa, Gray held a brandy snifter in his hand, contemplating the quilt on the floor before him. Mary's Fortune Two. It was a beautiful creation, and Baines had done an absolutely splendid job.

If that wasn't enough, his little mouse had attempted to get it to him on the *Natchez Belle*. If Jamie hadn't rescued it, Gray had no doubt that Captain Cordair would have gotten the quilt to him once Gray reached New Orleans.

He'd paid off his debt nearly three months ago, and now in the first week of 1822 he still wasn't completely settled. He had duties in the House of Lords to return to, but for him that didn't take precedence at the moment. Baines did. He pondered whether to send for her or make the trip back to America and personally fetch her.

He tasted his brandy and frowned. Would she receive him? He'd left her with no vow to return. But how could he? He hadn't known if he would have a place to live, let alone have shelter for *her*.

He missed her terribly, and his arms ached to hold her.

Good God. That settled it. It would take a missive as long to reach her as it would for him to get there. He would travel back to America and bloody get her himself.

The quilt and his fortune meant nothing to him without his quaint, lovable Baines, whose innocent kisses and passionate lovemaking set his blood afire.

Gray thought about Pierce and how important the social codes were to him. But surely he'd repaid his obligation to his father and his family heritage. Surely what he felt for Baines was more important than what others thought of him, even his beloved father.

Pierce would want Gray happy. Of that, he had no doubt. And he finally realized that with his fortune or without, *Baines* made him happy.

A light knock on the door interrupted his thoughts, so soft he could have imagined it.

Although Denholm was somewhere about, he'd given everyone the entire day off, and Jamie had only called upon him once. Rumors circulating around his club said that Jamie was married. Knowing there was a story there, Gray vowed to call upon his friend.

The knock sounded again.

Finishing off his drink, Gray looked up from his seat. "Come in."

Slowly the door opened.

She stood there, wearing a wine-colored, long-sleeved, scooped-neck gown. Her green eyes shone with brilliant fire, and her ebony tresses hung past her waist. She was a breathtaking vision.

Or was she an apparition?

Gray bounded from his seat, aching to touch her and discover the truth. "Baines?"

"Yes, Gray. I-I—"

He had a bad habit of kissing her without warning, and he did so now, hungrily and wildly.

"Baines, my love," he murmured. He kissed her eyes, her nose, her cheeks. "I have longed for this moment. What are you doing here?" he asked, guiding her to the sofa.

Walking around the quilt on the floor, Baines sat down.

"I-I brought you the original Mary's Fortune," she said, her gaze searching, tender. "I discovered I brought the other quilt to the wrong boat and worried that you didn't get it, although I was informed otherwise. How did you get it, Gray?"

He leaned over and thoroughly kissed her again. "Jamie took possession of it on the *Natchez Belle*," he explained between kisses. "Thank you, little mouse. Your selflessness saved Briarwood." Mind-numbing desire was flaring within him, hot and bright. "How I've missed you, my sweet love."

Thunderous sensation raced along Baines's nerve endings. "G-Gray," she whispered. She couldn't let this happen, not without being assured that he wouldn't send her away. "I-I have to talk to you."

His blue eyes burning with passion, Gray pushed a little apart from her. "Of course you do, my darling," he said in a husky voice. "Forgive my eagerness." He kissed her again. "It's just that I am overjoyed to see you."

Baines regarded him through misty eyes, her heart beating rapidly. What if he turned her away? He still hadn't mentioned that he wanted to spend his life with her. Or that he still loved her. She swallowed. "I-I want to thank you for my new house, Gray," she said in a rush. "A-and I brought the money I owe you."

"What money?"

"The three hundred dollars."

Gray smiled. "Here it's pounds, little mouse. How did you come by the money?"

She shifted in her seat to put distance between them. She *had* to keep her head about herself. "Well, I saved part of the five thousand dollars, and Uncle Lincoln helped with the rest."

"He had no objection to your coming here?" Gray asked, surprised.

Baines shook her head. "He offered to pay my passage."

"I think it's time I met your uncle. After all, he's going to become my uncle, too."

A lurch of excitement spun through her at his oh-so-casual announcement. She threw her arms around him. "Gray!"

"Baines, my angel, my little mouse, I love you so. I want you to become my wife, the Countess of Montegut. I was a fool to leave without you and I need you with me. Without you, I am disconnected. Will you marry me, sweetheart?"

"Gray! Oh, my love! Yes! Yes, I'll marry you. I do love you so."

Slanting his firm lips over hers, he kissed her with all the love he possessed. She'd freed him of his prejudices and his fears. Never had he thought himself capable of loving so completely.

Baines felt Gray's hands caressing her body, and all reason deserted her. When he bared her breasts, her skin burned, and heat threatened to consume her. Greedily he suckled them, making her senseless with need.

"I love you," he declared once again. "I can never stop saying that."

Striding to the door, he picked up the quilt she'd dropped, then closed the door. He let it fall on top of the duplicate.

"Let me make love to you, Baines," he whispered in an unsteady voice.

Her answer was simple. She began unbuttoning his lawn shirt with trembling fingers. When they both stood naked, she swayed in his arms, and he sank down on the quilts, bringing her down with him and kissing her passionately.

There upon the softness of Mary's Fortune One and Two, they consummated their love with rapturous hunger and soul-searing tenderness.

Gray's easy rhythm left her bereft of all reason, and she clawed at his back, hardly able to fathom the achingly sweet torture he inflicted upon her.

The pleasure of his beloved Baines was almost too much for Gray to bear. His blood ignited like a wild fire, and her center scalded him. He spiraled into a vortex of unbridled passion. It rippled along his veins, searing him with its heat as he drove himself deep within her.

Her moans grew louder, and she shook her head from side to side. Holding her hands above her head, he watched the ecstacy written on her beautiful face. With a deep, guttural groan, he gave one final thrust and released his seed inside her.

Laying beneath him, Baines quivered. He clung to her, holding her tight against him. When she quieted, he gently released her, then withdrew from her. He brushed damp strands of hair from her flushed face.

"Are you all right, my love?" Gray asked huskily.

Smiling at him, Baines nodded.

"Would you prefer to be married here or in America? I'm sure you'd want your uncle here and Annabelle Shepard."

"Yes, I do," Baines said excitedly. "But I'm afraid they may not have the price of passage."

"Never fear, darling, I do." He looked at her. "Going to America would be much quicker than sending a missive and waiting for them to arrive, little mouse."

Baines nodded. "Oh, yes, Gray, you're right."

"The trip across the ocean is a long one, Baines," Gray said in a serious tone. "I want us to marry as soon as possible."

"I don't understand, Gray."

"Darling, I want you to become my wife here. I don't want to wait the time it takes to get to Natchez to marry you—"

"Dang, Gray! You just said—"

"I know what I said, little mouse. You can have your formal wedding in America. Having met and gotten acquainted with DeEdria, she'll be delighted to host it—although I suspect by now she's delivered her baby. But I would prefer that the woman with whom I make love for the next three months aboard a ship to be legally mine. I'll have no objections from you, Lady Baines."

Baines laughed. "You sure are a caution, my lord." She patted the quilts. "Mary's Fortune is a true treasure, Gray. It brought us together. I think Mary Dunston had the right idea, don't you?"

Gray's lips touched her throat. "Indeed."

She closed her eyes as heat spiraled through her. "I think we should do something as wild for a future generation." She gasped when his tongue found her ear. "Use Mary's Fortune for our heirs to find wealth and possibly love."

"Aye, my lady," Gray whispered, caressing her breasts. "Now let's see if Mary's Fortune will give us that heir."

Without Mary's Fortune, Gray wouldn't have been able to save his family's wealth, Baines never would have been able to get Uncle Lincoln out of the life he was leading, and she and Gray never would have found each other.

In comparison, Gray's request seemed simple.

"Of that I have no doubt," she said throatily.

As she yielded to Gray's demanding kiss, she had every confidence that Mary's Fortune would continue to work its magic.

Mary's Fortune was a treasure indeed.

Turn the page for a preview of

JILL MARIE LANDIS'S

latest novel

Blue Moon

Coming in July from Jove Books

Prologue

SHE WOULD BE NINETEEN tomorrow. If she lived.

In the center of a faint deer trail on a ribbon of dry land running through a dense swamp, a young woman crouched like a cornered animal. The weak, gray light from a dull, overcast sky barely penetrated the bald-cypress forest as she wrapped her arms around herself and shivered, trying to catch her breath. She wore nothing to protect her from the elements but a tattered rough, homespun dress and an ill-fitting pair of leather shoes that had worn blisters on her heels.

The primeval path was nearly obliterated by lichen and fern that grew over deep drifts of dried twigs and leaves. Here and there the ground was littered with the larger rotting fallen limbs of trees. The fecund scent of decay clung to the air, pressed down on her, stoked her fear, and gave it life.

Breathe. Breathe.

The young woman's breath came fast and hard. She squinted through her tangled black hair, shoved it back, her fingers streaked with mud. Her hands shook. Terror born of being lost was heightened by the knowledge that night was going to fall before she found her way out of the swamp.

Not only did the encroaching darkness frighten her, but so did the murky silent water along both sides of the trail. She would soon be surrounded by both night and water. Behind her, from somewhere deep amid the cypress trees wrapped in rust colored bark, came the sound of a splash as some unseen creature dropped into the watery ooze.

She rose, spun around, and scanned the surface of the swamp. Frogs and fish, venomous copperheads and turtles, big as frying pans, thrived beneath the lacy emerald carpet of duckweed that floated upon the water. As she knelt there wondering whether she should continue on in the same direction or turn back, she watched a small knot of fur float toward her over the surface of the water.

A soaking wet muskrat lost its grace as soon as it made land and lumbered up the bank in her direction. Amused, yet wary, she scrambled back a few inches. The creature froze and stared with dark beady eyes before it turned tail, hit the water, and disappeared.

Getting to her feet, the girl kept her eyes trained on the narrow footpath, gingerly stepping through piles of damp, decayed leaves. Again she paused, lifted her head, listened for the sound of a human voice and the pounding footsteps which meant someone was in pursuit of her along the trail.

When all she heard was the distant knock of a woodpecker, she let out a sigh of relief. Determined to keep moving, she trudged on, ever vigilant, hoping that the edge of the swamp lay just ahead.

Suddenly, the sharp, shrill scream of a bobcat set her heart pounding. A strangled cry escaped her lips. With a fist pressed against her mouth, she squeezed her eyes closed and froze, afraid to move, afraid to even breathe. The cat screamed again and the cry echoed across the haunting silence of the swamp until it seemed to stir the very air around her.

She glanced up at dishwater-gray patches of weak afternoon light nearly obliterated by the cypress trees that grew so close together in some places that not even a small child could pass between them. The thought that a wildcat might be looming somewhere above her in the tangled limbs, crouched and ready to pounce, sent her running down the narrow, winding trail.

She had not gone a hundred steps when the toe of her shoe caught beneath an exposed tree root. Thrown forward, she began to fall and cried out.

As the forest floor rushed up to meet her, she put out her hands to break the fall. A shock of pain shot through her wrist an instant before her head hit a log.

And then her world went black.

1

Heron Pond, Illinois

NOAH LECROIX WALKED TO the edge of the wide wooden porch surrounding the one-room cabin he had built high in the sheltering arms of an ancient bald cypress tree and looked out over the swamp. Twilight gathered, thickening the shadows that shrouded the trees. The moon had already risen, a bright silver crescent riding atop a faded blue sphere. He loved the magic of the night, loved watching the moon and stars appear in the sky almost as much as he loved the swamp. The wetlands pulsed with life all night long. The darkness coupled with the still, watery landscape settled a protective blanket of solitude around him. In the dense, liquid world beneath him and the forest around his home, all manner of life coexisted in a delicate balance. He likened the swamp's dance of life and death to the way good and evil existed together in the world of men beyond its boundaries.

This shadowy place was his universe, his sanctuary. He savored its peace, was used to it after having grown up in almost complete isolation with his mother, a reclusive Cherokee woman who had left her people behind when she chose to settle in far-off Kentucky with his father, a French Canadian fur trapper named Gerard LeCroix.

Living alone served Noah's purpose now more than ever.
He had no desire to dwell among "civilized men," especially now that so many white settlers were moving in
droves across the Ohio into the new state of Illinois.

Noah turned away from the smooth log railing that bor-
dered the wide, covered porch cantilevered out over the
swamp. He was about to step into the cabin where a single
oil lamp cast its circle of light when he heard a bobcat
scream. He would not have given the sound a second
thought if not for the fact that a few seconds later the sound
was followed by a high-pitched shriek, one that sounded
human enough to stop him in his tracks. He paused on the
threshold and listened intently. A chill ran down his spine.

It had been so long since he had heard the sound of
another human voice that he could not really be certain, but
he thought he had just heard a woman's cry.

Noah shook off the ridiculous, unsettling notion and
walked into the cabin. The walls were covered with the
tanned hides of mink, bobcat, otter, beaver, fox, white-
tailed deer and bear. His few other possessions—a bone-
handled hunting knife with a distinctive wolf's head carved
on it, various traps, some odd pieces of clothing, a few pots
and a skillet, four wooden trenchers and mugs, and a rifle—
were all neatly stored there as well. They were all he owned
and needed in the world, save the dugout canoe secured
outside near the base of the tree.

Sparse but comfortable, even the sight of the familiar
surroundings could not help him shake the feeling that
something unsettling was about to happen, that all was not
right in his world.

Pulling a crock off a high shelf, Noah poured a splash
of whiskey in a cup and drank it down, his concentration
intent on the deepening gloaming and the sounds of the
swamp. An unnatural stillness lingered in the air after the
puzzling scream, almost as if, like him, the wild inhabitants
of Heron Pond were collectively waiting for something to
happen. Unable to deny his curiosity any longer, Noah
sighed in resignation and walked back to the door.

He lingered there for a moment, staring out at the growing shadows. Something was wrong. *Someone* was out there. He reached for the primed and loaded Hawken rifle that stood just inside the door and stepped out into the gathering dusk.

He climbed down the crude ladder of wooden strips nailed to the trunk of one of the four prehistoric cypress that supported his home, stepped into the dugout *pirogue* tied to a cypress knee that poked out of the water. Noah paddled the shallow wooden craft toward a spot where the land met the deep dark water with its camouflage net of duckweed, a natural boundary all but invisible to anyone unfamiliar with the swamp.

He reached a rise of land which supported a trail, carefully stepped out of the *pirogue* and secured it to a low-hanging tree branch. Walking through thickening shadows, Noah breathed in his surroundings, aware of every subtle nuance of change, every depression on the path that might really be a footprint on the trail, every tree and stand of switchcane.

The sound he thought he'd heard had come from the southeast. Noah headed in that direction, head down, staring at the trail although it was almost too dark to pick up any sign. A few hundred yards from where he left the *pirogue,* he paused, raised his head, sniffed the air, and listened to the silence.

Instinctively, he swung his gaze in the direction of a thicket of slender cane stalks and found himself staring across ten yards of low undergrowth into the eyes of a female bobcat on the prowl. Slowly he raised his rifle to his shoulder and waited to see what the big cat would do. The animal stared back at him, its eyes intense in the gathering gloaming. Finally, she blinked and with muscles bunching beneath her fine, shiny coat, the cat turned and padded away.

Noah lowered the rifle and shook his head. He decided the sound he heard earlier must have been the bobcat's cry and nothing more. But just as he stepped back in the direction of the *pirogue,* he caught a glimpse of ivory on the trail ahead that stood out against the dark tableau. His

leather moccasins did not make even a whisper of sound
on the soft earth. He closed the distance and quickly realized what he was seeing was a body lying across the path.

His heart was pounding as hard as Chickasaw drums
when he knelt beside the young woman stretched out upon
the ground. Laying his rifle aside he stared at the unconscious female, then looked up and glanced around in every
direction. The nearest white settlement was beyond the
swamp to the northeast. There was no sign of a companion
or fellow traveler nearby, something he found more than
curious.

Noah took a deep breath, let go a ragged sigh and looked
at the girl again. She lay on her side, as peacefully as if
she were napping. She was so very still that the only evidence that she was alive was the slow, steady rise and fall
of her breasts. Although there was no visible sign of injury,
she lay on the forest floor with her head beside a fallen log.
One of her arms was outstretched, the other tucked beneath
her. What he could see of her face was filthy. So were her
hands; they were beautifully shaped, her fingers long and
tapered. Her dress, nothing but a rag with sleeves, was
hiked up to her thighs. Her shapely legs showed stark ivory
against the decayed leaves and brush beneath her.

He tentatively reached out to touch her, noticed his hand
shook, and balled it into a fist. He clenched it tight, then
opened his hand and gently touched the tangled, black hair
that hid the side of her face. She did not stir when he moved
the silken skein, nor when he brushed it back and looped
it over her ear.

Her face was streaked with mud. Her lashes were long
and dark, her full lips tinged pink. The sight of her beauty
took his breath away. Noah leaned forward and gently
reached beneath her. Rolling her onto her back, he straightened her arms and noted her injuries. Her wrist appeared
to be swollen. She had an angry lump on her forehead near
her hairline. She moaned as he lightly probed her injured
wrist; he realized he was holding his breath. Noah expected
her eyelids to flutter open, but they did not.

He scanned the forest once again. With night fast closing

in, he saw no alternative except to take her home with him. If he was going to get her back to the tree-house before dark, he would have to hurry. He cradled her gently in his arms, reached for his rifle, and then straightened. Even then the girl did not awaken, although she did whimper and turn her face against his buckskin jacket, burrowing against him. It felt strange carrying a woman in his arms, but he had no time to dwell on that as he quickly carried her back to the *pirogue*, set her inside, and untied the craft. He climbed in behind her, holding her upright, then gently drew her back until she leaned against his chest.

As the paddle cut silently through water black as pitch, he tried to concentrate on guiding the dugout canoe home, but was distracted by the way the girl felt pressed against him, the way she warmed him. As his body responded to a need he had long tried to deny, he felt ashamed at his lack of control. What kind of a man was he, to become aroused by a helpless, unconscious female?

Overhead, the sky was tinted deep violet, an early canvas for the night's first stars. During the last few yards of the journey, the swamp grew so dark that he had only the yellow glow of lamplight shining from his home high above the water to guide him.

∞

RUN. KEEP RUNNING.

The dream was so real that Olivia Bond could feel the leaf-littered ground beneath her feet and the faded chill of winter that lingered on the damp April air. She suffered, haunted by memories of the past year, some still so vivid they turned her dreams into nightmares. Even now, as she lay tossing in her sleep, she could feel the faint sway of the flatboat as it moved downriver long ago. In her sleep, the fear welled up inside her.

Her dreaming mind began to taunt her with palpable memories of new sights and scents and dangers.

Run. Run. Run, Olivia. You're almost home.

Her legs thrashed, startling her awake. She sat straight

up, felt a searing pain in her right wrist and a pounding in her head that forced her to quickly lie back down. She kept her eyes closed until the stars stopped dancing behind them, then slowly opened them and looked around.

The red glow of embers burning in a fireplace illuminated the ceiling above her. She lay staring up at even log beams that ran across a wide planked ceiling, trying to ignore the pounding in her head, fighting to stay calm and let her memory come rushing back. Slowly she realized she was no longer lost on the forest trail. She had not become a bobcat's dinner, but was indoors, in a cabin, on a bed.

She spread her fingers and pressed her hands palms down against a rough, woven sheet drawn over her. The mattress was filled with something soft that gave off a tangy scent. A pillow cradled her head.

Slowly Olivia turned her aching head, afraid of who or what she might find beside her, but when she discovered she was in bed alone, she thanked God for small favors.

Refusing to panic, she thought back to her last lucid memory: a wildcat's scream. She recalled tearing through the cypress swamp, trying to make out the trail in the dim light before she tripped. She lifted her hand to her forehead and felt swelling. After testing it gingerly, she was thankful that she had not gashed her head open and bled to death.

She tried to lift her head again but intense pain forced her to lie still. Olivia closed her eyes and sighed. A moment later, an unsettling feeling came over her. She knew by the way her skin tingled, the way her nerve ends danced, that someone was nearby. Someone was watching her. An instinctive, intuitive sensation warned her that the *someone* was a man.

At first she peered through her lashes, but all she could make out was a tall, shadowy figure standing in the open doorway across the room. Her heart began to pound so hard she was certain the sound would give her consciousness away.

The man walked into the room and she bit her lips together to hold back a cry. She watched him move about purposefully. Instead of coming directly to the bed, he

walked over to a small square table. She heard him strike
a piece of flint, smelled lamp oil as it flared to life.

His back was to her as he stood at the table; Olivia
opened her eyes wider and watched. He was tall, taller than
most men, strongly built, dressed in buckskin pants topped
by a buff shirt with billowing sleeves. Despite the coolness
of the evening, he wore no coat, no jacket. Indian moccasins, not shoes, covered his feet. His hair was a deep black,
cut straight and worn long enough to hang just over his
collar. She watched his bronzed, well tapered hands turn
up the lamp wick and set the glass chimney in place.

Olivia sensed he was about to turn and look at her. She
wanted to close her eyes and pretend to be unconscious,
thinking that might be safer than letting him catch her staring at him, but as he slowly turned toward the bed, she
knew she had to see him. She had to know what she was
up against.

Her gaze swept his body, taking in his great height, the
length of his arms, the width and breadth of his shoulders
before she dared even look at his face.

When she did, she gasped.

∽

NOAH STOOD FROZEN BESIDE the table, shame and anger welling up from deep inside. He was unable to move,
unable to breathe as the telling sound of the girl's shock
upon seeing his face died on the air. He watched her flinch
and scoot back into the corner, press close to the wall. He
knew her head pained her, but obviously not enough to
keep her from showing her revulsion or from trying to
scramble as far away as she could.

He had the urge to walk out, to turn around and leave.
Instead, he stared back and let her look all she wanted. It
had been three years since he had lost an eye to a flatboat
accident on the Mississippi. Three years since another
woman had laughed in his face. Three years since he moved
to southern Illinois to put the past behind him.

When her breathing slowed and she calmed, he held his

hands up to show her that they were empty, hoping to put her a little more at ease.

"I'm sorry," he said as gently as he could. "I don't mean you any harm."

She stared up at him as if she did not understand a blessed word.

Louder this time, he spoke slowly. "Do-you-speak-English?"

The girl clutched the sheet against the filthy bodice of her dress and nodded. She licked her lips, cleared her throat. Her mouth opened and closed like a fish out of water, but no sound came out.

"Yes," she finally croaked. "Yes, I do." And then, "Who are you?"

"My name is Noah. Noah LeCroix. This is my home. Who are you?"

The lamplight gilded her skin. She looked to be all eyes, soft green eyes, long black hair, and fear. She favored her injured wrist, held it cradled against her midriff. From the way she carefully moved her head, he knew she was fighting one hell of a headache, too.

Ignoring his question, she asked one of her own. "How did I get here?" Her tone was wary. Her gaze kept flitting over to the door and then back to him.

"I heard a scream. Went out and found you in the swamp. Brought you here—"

"The wildcat?"

"Wasn't very hungry." Noah tried to put her at ease, then he shrugged, stared down at his moccasins. Could she tell how nervous he was? Could she see his awkwardness, know how strange it was for him to be alone with a woman? He had no idea what to say or do. When he looked over at her again, she was staring at the ruined side of his face.

"How long have I been asleep?" Her voice was so low that he had to strain to hear her. She looked like she expected him to leap on her and attack her any moment, as if he might be coveting her scalp.

"Around two hours. You must have hit your head really hard."

She reached up, felt the bump on her head. "I guess I did."

He decided not to get any closer, not with her acting like she was going to jump out of her skin. He backed up, pulled a stool out from under the table, and sat down.

"You going to tell me your name?" he asked.

The girl hesitated, glanced toward the door, then looked back at him. "Where am I?"

"Heron Pond."

Her attention shifted to the door once again; recollection dawned. She whispered, "The swamp." Her eyes widened as if she expected a bobcat or a cottonmouth to come slithering in.

"You're fairly safe here. I built this cabin over the water."

"Fairly?" She looked as if she was going to try to stand up again. "Did you say—"

"Built on cypress trunks. About fifteen feet above the water."

"How do I get down?"

"There are wooden plank nailed to a trunk."

"Am I anywhere near Illinois?"

"You're in it."

She appeared a bit relieved. Obviously she wasn't going to tell him her name until she was good and ready, so he did not bother to ask again. Instead he tried, "Are you hungry? I figure anybody with as little meat on her bones as you ought to be hungry."

What happened next surprised the hell out of him. It was a little thing, one that another man might not have even noticed, but he had lived alone so long he was used to concentrating on the very smallest of details: the way an iridescent dragonfly looked with its wings backlit by the sun, the sound of cypress needles whispering on the wind.

Someone else might have missed the smile that hovered at the corner of her lips when he had said she had little meat on her bones, but he did not. How could he, when that slight, almost-smile had him holding his breath.

"I got some jerked venison and some potatoes around here someplace." He started to smile back until he felt the pull of the scar at the left corner of his mouth and stopped. He stood up, turned his back on the girl, and headed for the long wide plank tacked to the far wall where he stored his larder.

He kept his back to her while he found what he was looking for, dug some strips of dried meat from a hide bag, unwrapped a checkered rag with four potatoes inside, and set one on the plank where he did all his stand-up work. Then he took a trencher and a wooden mug off a smaller shelf high on the wall, and turned it over to knock any unwanted creatures out. He was headed for the door, intent on filling the cook pot with water from a small barrel he kept out on the porch when the sound of her voice stopped him cold.

"Perhaps an eye patch," she whispered.

"What?"

"I'm sorry. I was thinking out loud."

She looked so terrified he wanted to put her at ease.

"It's all right. What were you thinking?"

Instead of looking at him when she spoke, she looked down at her hands. "I was just thinking . . ."

Noah had to strain to hear her.

"With some kind of an eye patch, you wouldn't look half bad."

His feet rooted themselves to the threshold. He stared at her for a heartbeat before he closed his good eye and shook his head. He had no idea what in the hell he looked like anymore. He had no reason to care.

He turned his back on her and stepped out onto the porch, welcoming the darkness.

Presenting all-new romances—featuring ghostly
heroes and heroines and the passions they inspire.

♥ *Haunting Hearts* ♥

__*A SPIRITED SEDUCTION*
    by Casey Claybourne   0-515-12066-9/$5.99

__*STARDUST OF YESTERDAY*
    by Lynn Kurland   0-515-11839-7/$5.99

__*A GHOST OF A CHANCE*
    by Casey Claybourne   0-515-11857-5/$5.99

__*ETERNAL VOWS*
    by Alice Alfonsi   0-515-12002-2/$5.99

__*ETERNAL LOVE*
    by Alice Alfonsi   0-515-12207-6/$5.99

__*ARRANGED IN HEAVEN*
    by Sara Jarrod   0-515-12275-0/$5.99

Prices slightly higher in Canada

Our Town

...where love is always right around the corner!

__*Cedar Creek* by Willa Hix — 0-515-11958-X/$5.99

__*Sugar and Spice* by DeWanna Pace — 0-515-11970-9/$5.99

__*Cross Roads* by Carol Card Otten — 0-515-11985-7/$5.99

__*Blue Ribbon* by Jessie Gray — 0-515-12003-0/$5.99

__*The Lighthouse* by Linda Eberhardt — 0-515-12020-0/$5.99

__*The Hat Box* by Deborah Lawrence — 0-515-12033-2/$5.99

__*Country Comforts* by Virginia Lee — 0-515-12064-2/$5.99

__*Grand River* by Kathryn Kent — 0-515-12067-7/$5.99

__*Beckoning Shore* by DeWanna Pace — 0-515-12101-0/$5.99

__*Whistle Stop* by Lisa Higdon — 0-515-12085-5/$5.99

__*Still Sweet* by Debra Marshall — 0-515-12130-4/$5.99

__*Dream Weaver* by Carol Card Otten — 0-515-12141-X/$5.99

__*Raspberry Island* by Willa Hix — 0-515-12160-6/$5.99

__*Pratt's Landing* by Martha Kirkland — 0-515-12180-0/$5.99

__*Wine Country* by Kathryn Kent — 0-515-12272-6/$5.99

__*Mending Fences* by Livia Reasoner — 0-515-12211-4/$5.99

Prices slightly higher in Canada